LIKE DOVES SUMMONED BY DESIRE:

Dante's New Life in 20th Century Literature and Cinema

Essays in memory of Amilcare Iannucci

Edited by Massimo Ciavolella and Gianluca Rizzo

ISBN: 978-0-9816330-4-6

Book design: Danilo Montanari

AGINCOURT PRESS
P.O. Box 1039
Cooper Station
New York, NY 10003
www.agincourtpress.org

Table of Contents

Introduction

> *That corpse you planted last year in your garden,*
> *Has it begun to sprout? Will it bloom this year?*
> T.S. Eliot – *The Waste Land*

The scene opens on a banner, deep red in color, waving across the screen, one end weighted down by a metal ornament in the shape of a cross. The cloth soon reveals a title, *Dante's Inferno*, set against a backdrop filled with a dark, viscous fluid that could be blood, or weak ink, or thick pea soup. And then, announced by the grim quote "Let us descend into the blind world –Canto V," the main event begins. A pseudo-Gregorian chant picks up, and through a rapid montage we are shown a very blonde Beatrice weeping at one end of a table; a sad horseman, with a gigantic blade hanging from his back, traversing a lush and somewhat disquieting rendering of the Tuscan countryside. We hear the voice of Virgil, recounting his conversation with Beatrice. We witness what appears to be a home invasion, and then the killing of the blonde heroin. The horseman has arrived too late. By now we know he must be Dante, strangely sporting the garb of a crusader. He kneels over Beatrice's body, whose soul has just abandoned her lips and is abruptly dragged away by a fumarolic demon. The chant halts, interrupted by sudden screams and sinister noises. Drums start beating a steady march, as we are taken through a gate engulfed in flames. We are shown a close up of a demon's horse-like mouth, and then we follow the coriaceous back of yet another demon through a landscape scorched by fire. The drumbeat accelerates; more quotations fly by, while a remarkably athletic Dante jumps left and right, wielding his gigantic blade, vanquishing infernal creatures of all shapes and sizes. The drums reach a parossistic rhythm, as we witness the Poet slashing, slicing and hacking away at legions of damned souls. Finally everything stops. In the ensuing silence Lucifer himself, screaming and exuding molten lava, rolls his head about, like the lion of the MGM. The pea-soup background returns; a sudden gush of dark blood floods the screen, revealing the game's catch phrase: "Dante's Inferno," pause for dramatic effect, "Go to Hell."

This is one of the latest (and not necessarily the most outrageous) adaptation of Dante's masterpiece: a video game released in 2010 by Electronic Arts, and very well received by critics and gamers alike. Needless to say, a sequel to this first installment, probably titled *Dante's Purgatory*, seems to be in the works. In fact, this new incarnation of the *Comedy* has been so popular that typing "Dante's Inferno" into a search engine will produce hits dealing mostly with the video game. In order to read about Dante's epic one must scroll down to the bottom of the page.

Some *dantisti* (among the few who were aware of the existence of this video game) showed a bit of discomfort in seeing their favorite author flying around dispatching demons, and yet, over the centuries, the *Divine Comedy* has seen many unusual transformations: it has been translated into dozens of different languages, borrowed and appropriated by generations of writers, artists, illustrators, and musicians, inspiring movies, plays, and even comic books (or should we say graphic novels?). To say nothing about the myriad of unorthodox readings and interpretations it has elicited. In fact, a delightful book edited by Pozzato, *L'idea deforme: Interpretazioni esoteriche di Dante* (Milano: Bompiani, 1989), collects and analyses the production of some of the worst offenders (Rossetti, Aroux, Valli, Benini, Pascoli, and Guénon). At the same time, the volume offers a reflection on the limits of interpretation and on the qualities a decent, acceptable or 'correct' interpretation should possess. In his introduction, Eco comments on how "sacred" texts of different kinds, across different cultures, seem to attract an excess of attention, which often results in excessive interpretations.

> As soon as a text becomes 'sacred' within a given culture, it elicits paranoid readings and thus excessive interpretations. It has already happened to classical allegories, to Homeric texts, to the Sacred Scriptures at the time of the Church Fathers, and to the Talmudic interpretations within Jewish culture. [...] This approach to sacred texts (sacred, in the literal sense) was later transferred (in a secularized manner) to those texts that had become sacred in a metaphorical sense, because of their critical success (but also, one should hope, for their poetic polysemy). [...] This being the case, Dante's works were no exception. (p. 27-9.)

In fact, the *Divine Comedy* possesses qualities that attract all sorts of people, refined and uncouth alike, as much today as in the past. In 1373, for instance, a group of semi-literate citizens of Florence (they called themselves *non grammatici*) petitioned local authorities to institute a venue for the public declamation and explanation of the *Divine Comedy*. This was the beginning of the *Lectura Dantis*, with Giovanni Boccaccio as its first resident commentator. Thus a popular response to the *Commedia* has been there from the very beginning, and so have its readers, commentators and imitators.

> But how does one explain Dante's enduring popularity, and that of his harsh eschatological masterpiece in particular? The answer, I believe, lies in the poem's distinctive textual characteristics. The *Comedy is* neither an open nor a closed text (Eco, *The Role of the Reader*); it is neither writerly nor readerly (Barthes, *S/Z*). Rather it is more like what Fiske in *Television Culture* calls a 'producerly' text. A producerly text is polysemous and combines the easy accessibility of the readerly with the complex discursive strategies of the writerly. These peculiar textual qualities allow the poem to produce meaning and pleasure in audiences which run the gamut from the uneducated to the most sophisticated and discerning.
> The *Comedy*'s uncanny ability to generate meaning derives not so much from its formal, hierarchical allegory as from the allusive density of its literal narrative. [...] In saying this, I do not mean to imply that the *Commedia*'s polysemy is boundless and structure-less: the poem defines the terrain within which meaning may be made. (p. iv)

This is how Amilcare Iannucci describes the *Commedia*'s appeal in his "Foreward" to *Dante Today*, a special issue of *Quaderni di Italianistica* dedicated to the Poet. We share his fascination with the *Comedy*'s ability to be constantly reborn, to always captivate new audiences and to adapt to ever-changing means of communication. In fact, this volume owes its existence to a conference first envisioned by Iannucci himself, one aimed at exploring how the 20th century revisited Dante's legacy. It was called "Dante's New Life" (playing on the title of Alighieri's collection of poems) and was hosted by the UCLA Center for Medieval and Renaissance Studies and the Department of Italian in 2006. In addition to the articles presented there, this volume includes contributions from a number of diverse scholars, resulting in a multifaceted, colorful, and surprising definition of Dante's new lives (in the plural). Regarding the criteria used for selection, we followed the same ecumenical approach outlined by Iannucci in his foreword:

> In keeping with [our] editorial policy, no critical approach or ideology has been favored. On the contrary, as the editor of this special volume I have

included as many perspectives as possible. Methodologically, the various papers range from traditional philological and historical research to deconstruction and beyond. (p. vii)

Looking at all the different essays, one finds a few common threads that run through them. A first group investigates the translations of the *Commedia* into different languages and media. Sona Haroutyunian explores Dante's fortune in Armenia, within a culture that values translation as a sacred art, and its practitioners as venerable and holy men. The presence of an Armenian enclave in Venice, in San Lazzaro degli Armeni to be precise, has insured over the centuries a constant exchange between these two cultures. Dante has naturally become one of the most recognizable and appreciated ambassadors of Italian culture in Armenia.

A rather different fate has befallen Alighieri in Poland, where he became, at least during the 20th century, the center of a heated national debate. In his contribution, Piotr Salwa outlines the long and passionate relationship Polish readers have established with Dante's works, often appropriated for political reasons. He was so beloved that, in the absence of a complete Polish translation, many authored private ones, for their own use as well as that of their friends.

James Miller, instead, focuses on a different type of translation: the intersemiotic one that took the *poema sacro* from the written page onto the silver screen and into the art galleries. He writes about the queer appropriations that filmmaker Derek Jarman, and visual artist Robert Rauschenberg made of the *Commedia* in their works. In particular, Miller looks at Jarman's *Edward II* and his early Super-8 films, and at Rauschenberg's illustrations of the *Inferno*. These artists used Dante as a means to reflect on their struggle to assert their own aesthetic in a hypocritical and homophobic society.

Raffaele Pinto is also interested in the cinematic appropriations of the *Divine Comedy*, and writes more specifically about *Sherlock Jr.*, a very peculiar movie by Buster Keaton. This 1924 film quotes one of the most famous episodes of *Inferno*, that of Paolo and Francesca. The critic starts from this curious discovery to unravel a fascinating reflection on how the work of art (literature, but also film) can be used as a symbolic mediator of desire according to the theories of René Girard.

The *Commedia* is also used to speak of certain difficult, traumatic or even ineffable historical events. The contributions of Mary Alexandra Watt, Karla Mallette, and Rossend Arqués deal precisely with this issue. The first scholar explains the role Dante played in shaping the narrative that surrounded Columbus' discovery of the New World. According to this perspective, the Genoese sailor was a new Paul, the man who would fulfill the prophecies formulated in the Middle Ages. He journeyed to an "other world," that could very well have contained mount Purgatory, with its earthly paradise at the top.

Mallette, instead, focuses on how Dante has come to embody the intellectual who resists oppressive regimes and is consequently exiled from his beloved homeland. She traces the history of this particular *topos* through the writings of two scholars, Auerbach and Said, and four writers, Djebar and Pamuk for the struggle of intellectuals in the Islamic world, and Heany and Mcdonagh for those living and working in Ireland.

Arqués shows how Dante's text is often used in Holocaust literature as an aid to express the unspeakable. Whenever there is an extremely traumatic event that needs to be recorded and passed down to future generations, his poetry becomes a blueprint for the narration, as well as a source of images and quotations. In fact, his *Inferno* is often crucial in illustrating the process of de-humanization that took place in the extermination camps.

Roberto Fedi and Carolynn Lund-Mead are interested in a very different aspect of the new life Dante's works enjoy: the inter-textual connections that render the *Commedia* a powerful catalyst in the history of literature. Fedi engages in a close reading of Sonnet 36 of Petrarch's *Rerum Vulgarium Fragmenta*, which leads to the surprising discovery of dantean references.

Lund-Mead, instead, brings to fruition one of Iannucci's last projects, which involved the study and the cataloguing of biblical references within the *Commedia*, in connection to the different commentators that identified them over the centuries. The result of this exercise is an unprecedented perspective on how Dante's readership changed over the years.

Natascia Tonelli chooses a very different topic, investigating how the death of the woman has become a recurring motivation for many poets throughout Italian literature. Beginning with Dante and his *Vita Nuova*, this theme has experienced countless new lives in the poems of Landolfi, Giudici, Caproni, Gozzano, and even Valduga.

Luigi Ballerini confronts one of the best-known *terzine* of the entire *Inferno*: "*amor che a nullo amato amar perdona.*" He begins by reviewing the many difficulties commentators have found in interpreting this line. He, then, proposes his own solution to the conundrum by bringing into the picture Guido Cavalcanti (the friend/rival of Dante's youth) and his very peculiar brand of *stilnovista* love.

Finally, Di Pede explores the main hermeneutical approaches that have dominated Dante criticism, from the medieval period to today, in an attempt to explain the diverse and often incompatible interpretations of the *Commedia*. His essay redefines its relevance in terms of its ability to offer specific insights into particular situations. In his opinion, texts mean different things to different people because of their prior induction in language, history, culture and tradition. Hence, the many "new lives" enjoyed by Dante's masterpiece.

In sending this volume to press, the editors would like to thank the Center for Medieval and Renaissance Studies and the Department of Italian at UCLA for their financial and logistical support, for having hosted the conference that originated this book, and for periodically gathering the leading scholars in the field, which allows the exchange of knowledge to take place.

The editors would also like to thank Dominic Siracusa for his help in translating and proofreading some of the essays here collected.

This volume is dedicated to the memory of Amilcare Iannucci.

Rossend Arqués (UAB)

Dante in the modern "Inferno": literature after Auschwitz

1. **Dante's *Inferno* in modern literature**

The process of rediscovering Dante, especially the first cantica of the *Divine Comedy*, through the works of the Romantics, has turned Dante's *Inferno* into a paradigm for describing any wretched reality, both worldly and other-worldly. Lamartine claimed that Dante was the "poet in whom our age sees its own image", and it is no coincidence that Balzac would title his work *Comédie humaine*. "Dante," writes Sozzi, "è per tutti il poeta dell'umanità dolor-ante, del male del mondo, dell'indicibile pena, più che il poeta dell'ebbrezza, dell'ineffabile allegrezza, del riso dell'universo".[1] In addition to mentioning him in the poem *La vision de Dante* within the *Légende des Siècles*, Victor Hugo also used its structure and forms in *Les Misérables*, because he inter-prets Dante's inferno in realistic terms, that is, as an objective transcription of human life as it really is: "L'Enfer c'est la vie," wrote Hugo in the poem opening *Voix intérieurs*. Gogol, in turn, wrote *Les ànimes mortes* as if it were the first part of his own peculiar Slavic *Divine Comedy* that he would never complete. What is more, in 20th century literature, there is a surfeit of writers who measure themselves by Dante's *Inferno*, ranging from the Baudelairean Eliot of *Unreal City* in *The Waste Land*, to many works by Beckett, which clearly reference and echo the inferno and purgatory. Nor should we fail to mention the extremely rich vein in the novels dubbed 'splatterpunk', which have made explicit, albeit superficial and melodramatic, use of the first part of Dante's epic, and have been the inspiration for a hugely popular series of films.[2]

Post-World War II Italian literature has also featured the stylistic, for-mal and thematic modules of both the *Inferno* and the *Divine Comedy* in general. Among many of them, I could mention those in which this tribute is the most obvious, namely Pavese's *La luna e i falò*, which he himself re-garded as his own *Divine Comedy*; Vittorini's *Conversazioni in Sicilia*, the narration of a journey through Sicily and the author's personal childhood, in the company of a type of Virgilian guide, represented by his mother, Concezione, in which several characters (and not just the Great Lombard) find their counterparts in other characters from the first of the three parts in the *Divine Comedy*. I could also mention Curzio Malaparte's *La pelle*, a novel that begins with an implicit reference to the *Inferno* III 22 ff., when "una terribile folla... squallida, sporca, affamata, vestita di stracci" exists alongside soldiers who "urtavano e ingiuravano in tutte le lingue e in tutti i dialetti del mondo".[3] To this incomplete list, I would like to add the brief text by Dino Buzzati entitled "Viaggio agli inferi del secolo" (1966) and the dense dialogue with which Manganelli uses a Dantesque vision to establish many of his works, especially his novel *Dall'inferno*, in which Hades has ceased to be an otherworldly place and has come to occupy everything that we tend to call life or reality.

Contemporary to these texts, which are more or less realistic (although they are all broadly symbolic), are the main characters of the great dramas that convulsed Europe and the world in the 20th century. Valerio Marucci claims that "la memoria *strutturale* della *Commedia* presiede e sottende le opere *epiche* che cercano di rappresentare la tragedia bellica del secolo e in essa la ricerca della salvezza, individuale e/o colettiva (in Italia ne é un esempio il libro di Primo Levi *Se questo è un uomo*): basti citare *Una giornata di Ivan Denisovic* (1962), di Aleksandr Solcenicyn; *Der Untergang der Titanic*, di Hans Magnus Enzensberger, come pure il dramma di Peter Weiss, *Die Ermitlung* ("L'indagine"), tragico confronto tra le vittime dei lager e i loro aguzzini, ispirato alla *Commedia* per dichiarazione dello stesso autore." Dante, wrote Eugenio Montale, "non può essere ripetuto (...). Poeta concentrico, Dante non può fornire modelli a un mondo che si allontana progressivamente dal centro e si dichiara in perenne espansione. Perciò la *Commedia* resterà l'ultimo miracolo della poesia mondiale"[4]. However, this does not prevent it from still being a text that one must confront, even for those who regard it as superseded or even deny that is has any value today.

2. Dante in post-Auschwitz literature

The literature from the Nazi death camps[5] has posed and continues to pose a variety of critical problems, primarily related to the fact that they are texts that speak about extremely painful, harrowing experiences. The enormity of this human tragedy has led many of the written testimonies to not even consider that there might be a *how* to say things. What mainly mattered was *what* to say and *who* was saying it. Thus, to them, the only possible style consisted of solely focusing on *what* they had experienced and the urgency and need to communicate it in all its tragic, inhumane reality.[6] However, they did not take into account that their, shall we say, ingenuous narration would meet two stumbling blocks: the impossibility of communicating the experience in the guise of a realistic narrative, and the thesis, used solely by those wishing to negate the facts, that whomever was saved cannot truly be a witness. Thus, the issue was and remains much more complex. In recent years, there has indeed been a heated debate, which has often led to personal discreditment, not only on the *how* of communicating (and its ethical value and truth), but also on *what* to communicate and *who* was communicating it. The question of *how* has led negationists to question whether those who wrote fiction about the camps could be witnesses. Regarded as works of art, those narrations lost, according to those biased interpretations, their denotative and denunciatory strength in order to become narrations that were the fruit of their authors' imagination. "Il ne peut avoir échappé," wrote Paul Rassinier, founder of modern negationism, "à l'opinion que l'imagination du romancier, les excés de lyrisme du poète, la partialité intéressée du politicien ou les relents de haine de la victime, servent tour à tour ou de concert, de toile de fond aux récits jusqu'ici publiés". This is one of the paradoxes we shall address in this article: if they seek realism, the texts do not affect readers' moods, yet in contrast if they are 'fictionalised' accounts, they are not believed because they are invented. In a text from Delbo's book, we can read:

> Vous ne croyez pas ce que nous disons
> parce que
> si c'etait vrai
> ce que nous disons
> nous ne serions pas là pour le dire
> il faudrait expliquer
> l'inexplicable
> expliquer
> pourquoi viva qui etait si forte
> est-elle morte
> et non pas moi
> (...)

> Pourquoi
> Pourquoi
> Parce que tout ici est inexplicable.

Can we convey the *true* experience of the camps through words? And if so, what are the possible *ways* of communicating these true experiences and the pitfalls each entails? We aim to analyse the mechanisms and textual strategies that certain writers/witnesses have adopted to convey their experiences, while simultaneously stressing the paradoxes deriving from the use of literary tradition, and in particular Dante's otherworld, in striving to convey the horror of the camps. We are aware of the controversy spurred by interpreting the journey to the death camps through Dante's descent into the inferno, based mainly on Steiner's claim: "the bibliography of the concentration camps is quite extensive, but nothing in it equals the fullness of Dante's observations".[7] In attempting to find some possible responses to the role of aesthetics in the narrations of the concentration camp experience, we have questioned the works of a handful of authors: Robert Antelme, Gradowski, Imre Kertész. Primo Levi, David Rousset and Elie Wiesel, although we have also considered works by other narrators such as Jorge Semprún, Georges Perec, Xalamov, etc.[8]

2.1. *The unutterability of experience*

Dante also poses the question as to the unutterability of experience in terms of comprehending/representing his otherworldly experience. The *Paradise* is full of examples in which the poet bemoans the impossibility of properly describing what he has seen so that the reader can reconstruct it in his or her mind. Let us cite one example:

> Perch'io lo'ngegno e l'arte e l'uso chiami,
> sì no'l direi che mai s'imaginasse;
> ma creder puossi e di veder si brami. (*Pd*, X, 43-5)[9]

However, it is important to bear in mind that the entire *Divine Comedy* is not a 'fantastical' voyage – that is "a journey taken with the imagination, and with the help of an exceptional vision and an extraordinary visual capacity"[10] – thanks to which Dante has gained access to the invisible world and has been able to convey it to us. This would truly be difficult for the modern reader to understand, as we are solely accustomed to visible things. And to us the invisible is a merely decorative element. The earliest commentators on Dante's journey, however, took these images very seriously because they did not regard them as strange, for the invisible was part of their image of the world, of their mindset. Thus, it is worth considering the 'reality' of Dante's vision which attempts to make tangible to the reader the journey of the human spirit through the various circles, until it finally reaches the divine light, described through words and figures. Dante experiences with his senses what he later explains to us, and he is able to narrate it because these things have affected him directly. In contrast, when his senses no longer allow him to decipher the experience either physically or mentally, the narration is interrupted, that is, the linguistic transcription of the otherworldly experience ceases:

> **Oh quanto è corto il dire e come fioco**
> **al mio concetto! e questo, a quel ch'i' vidi,**
> **e tanto, che non basta a dicer "poco".** (...)
> Qual è'l geomètra che tutto s'affige
> per misurar lo cerchio, e non ritrova,
> pensando, quel principio ond'elli indige,
> tal era io a quella visione nova:
> veder voleva come si convenne
> l'immago del cerchio e come vi s'indova;
> **ma non eran da ciò le proprie penne:**
> se non che la mia mente fu percossa
> da un fulgore in che sua voglia venne.
> **A l'alta fantasia qui mancò possa;**
> ma già volgeva il mio disio e'l velle
> si come rota ch'igualmente è mossa,
> l'amor che move il sole e l'altre stelle.
> (*Pd*, XXXIII, 121-3 and 133-45)

Only at that time Dante's mind – which is human – is overwhelmed by deeds, that is, when human virtue – which is also human experience – reaches its limit. Man can imagine the unimaginable because the images, though belonging to the invisible (*phantasmata*), do not exceed the capacity of human understanding, even though their true understanding and thus their translation into words often requires an incommensurate strength. Only the utter absence of images leads to the total inability to understand and at the same time to verbalize.

Different yet in a sense similar, is the question that the narrators/witnesses of the death camp pose early on regarding the possibility of *imagining* and *explaining* that atrocious experience.[11] "A nous-mêmes," writes Antelme (p. 9), "ce que nous avions à dire commençait alors à nous paraître *inimaginable*." It had to be explained, but to the very characters themselves it seems implausible, inconceivable and thus, impossible to narrate. David Rousset, another political prisoner in the communist area, also stresses the impossibility of fully conveying the horrors of the camps: "Les hommes normaux ne savent pas que tout est possible. (...) Les concentrationnaires savent. (...) La mort habitait parmi les concentrationnaires toutes les heures de leur existence. Elle leur a montré tous ses visages. Ils ont touché tous ses dépouillements. Ils ont vécu l'inquiétude comme une obsession partou présente. (...) Ils on cheminé des années durant dans le fantastique décor de toutes les dignités ruinées. Ils sont séparés des autres par une expérience impossible à transmettre." (pp. 181-82).[12] Especially because the recipients of these messages do not have the parameters needed to properly interpret a similar experience.

However, that does not mean that the camps themselves are incomprehensible in that they are the horrifying spawn of irrational forces and that there is no explanation for Auschwitz, as some claim. In his novel *Kaddish for a Child Not Born*, Kertész is not very clear on this issue, and he explicitly says so in a sentence that brings to mind the rational distribution of evil in Dante's *Inferno*:

> Evil always has a rational explanation. Perhaps Satan himself is irrational, as Iago is too, but their children are rational, all their acts can be deduced like a mathematical formula; one can deduce a type of interest, a desire for lucre, laziness, a desire for power and pleasure, cowardice, satisfaction of this or that instinct, or otherwise, a type of madness, paranoia, manic-depression, pyromania, sadism, of sexual murder, masochism, demiurugic megalomania (...), because what truly has no explanation is not evil but its opposite: good.

"The terrible, the unutterable, the unthinkable banality of evil," to say it with another overused phrase by Hannah Arendt, is explainable and utterable through the images of blind yet not gratuitous violence, even if it seems incomprehensible. Dante uses these figures to represent, for example, the struggle between the men on the streets of Florence and so many other corrupt cities and nations, and not just the terrible violence with which divine justice strikes the guilty, whether they be tyrants, murderers or selfish people. Rastier's rejection of the patheticness of the "horrifying infernal visions" and the consequent literary complacency that predominates some interpretations of extermination literature (especially that of Steiner) is understandable. Yet this does not mean that we should ignore the parallels between the specific description of humanity immersed in the pain of concentration camp literature and the dramatic and equally concrete expressiveness that populates that first cantica in the *Divine Comedy*: "genti dolorose" (*If*, III, 17), "sospiri, pianti e altri guai / risuonavan per l'aere senza stelle" (*If*, III, 22-3), "Diverse lingue, orribil favelle / parole di dolore, accenti d'ira (*If*, III, 25-8).

Agamben underscored the impossibility that the survivors could fully give testimony to the reality of the camps, turning into absolute, universal statement Levi's observation about the 'partiality' of the point of view of those who have been able to return home, when compared to the total truth of the 'Muslim'[13]. Whoever has survived, as Wiesel and Levi paradoxically write, "has not hit rock bottom", which is tantamount to saying that 'they have enjoyed some sort of privilege'. Thus, in Agamben's mind, at the heart of all testimony there is an 'unwitnessable' nucleus. The negationist literature has started precisely from this point in order to demolish the testimony of the 'saved', so that their 'half-truths' cannot approach the absolute truth of the *sommersi*, the only ones who know the whole truth. The 'Muslim' has become a mute icon of the horror, which has only served to make the testimony and real experience of the survivors relative and banal, rather than mythical or mythologized by the most imposing machine of dehumanisation and extermination.

Believing and affirming that the experience of the camps is 'unutterable' has also paved the way for the concept of divine punishment for human sins. This is not a case in which the terms that Jewish historians use are 'holocaust' (derived from *olah*, the biblical sacrifice) and *shoa*, which means 'devastation, catastrophe' and which in the Bible is also related to the very idea of divine punishment.[14]

The purported unutterability of this extreme experience, to which the 'Muslims' – that is the *sommersi* – were the only true witnesses, is refuted by the narrations of the survivors, who at some point in their lives in the camps were the true 'Muslims', even though they were able to come back to tell about it later. This is the case, for example, of Gyurka, the young character in the story in which Kertész summarises the experience of the universe of the Lagers:

> And then he asked me whether I wanted to strike a deal there, if I wanted to return home, and I do not know what answer he must have read in my face, but in his I saw a kind of stupefaction, a kind of alarm, that same expression that one generally sees on the faces of the most unfortunate, of the condemned or, we might say, of the plague-stricken. Then I recalled what he had said about the Muslims.

However, unutterability is particularly discussed in the narrations by those few members of the so-called *Sonderkommando*, who, even though they did not survive, did manage to convey their heart-rending testimonies. Testimonies not so much of their own death, as that of the thousands of victims of the gas chambers and crematoria, including the host of people who just arrived at the camp and were already fated to die because they were too young or too old, former prisoners or 'Muslims' who were no longer useful, and thus had been placed on the list of the 'chosen ones'. They witnessed to the death of others precisely because they helped them to die, and then cleaned up their remains. There is nothing more shameful. Though it is true that they never actually talk about death itself, it is clear that they have been, like Dante, privileged witnesses to the horror. And although it is conceivable that the horror is unimaginable, that does not mean that it cannot be represented, as I hope I managed to explain. Unlike the character Dante, who arouses stupor amongst the dead people he finds because he crosses Hades alive and well, the *Sonderkommando* character/narrator tries to describe the inferno on earth, portraying himself as if he were dead: "Can a dead person," Gradowski wonders, "cry for the dead?"

2.2. *Is it possible to represent the horror of the camps? Problems of aesthetics*

If the utterability of the camps is possible because they are a real fact, the other major obstacle that the survivors have had to overcome is the *way* in which they communicate the horror of that experience, sometimes even because of their legal involvement, as we have seen. The war, the camps and the resistance to Nazism and Fascism left a huge body of testimony. Post-war literature – which tends to fall within the label of 'Neo-Realism' – embraces: a) memories without major literary pretensions written by people who belonged to the resistance, and b) novels or literary texts whose characters are men and women fully involved in the folly of the war, or main characters of stories set in the resistance and/or in the death camps. Authors falling into the latter category include Fenoglio, Calvino, Bassani and P. Levi. For these authors, the 'Neo-Realism' label is too constrictive. Nevertheless, Calvino was the one who implicitly condemned the dangers entailed in the attempted live recording of the reality that the militant critics of the age theorised. Years later, in *Lezioni americane*, he would resolve this perplexity in the myth of Perseus, the hero who had to face Medusa. It is well known that to slay that monster, Perseus had to avoid looking her in the eyes in order to not be turned into stone. The stratagem for beating Medusa is looking at her indirectly via Perseus' shield-mirror. In this trick, Calvino grasps the same reality that exists between the writer and reality: literature can convey the reality of life as long as it does so indirectly by creating a distance between the subject of the utterance and the object of the utterance, which is equivalent to a type of allegory or simile. The reader who manages to grasp the meaning also manages to penetrate the marrow of reality, yet with the freer perspective of someone who looks at it from enough distance to control its negative effects.

This is also the road that some of the best writers/witnesses invoked in an attempt to overcome the great paradox that is the voice narrating the literature of extermination, of all extermination: if it tells the truth of the deeds it is not believed, yet if, on the other hand, it creates literary and aesthetic universes in order to be more effective, more credible, and somehow more realistic, it is accused of being fictitious. However, the latter seems to be the best path. Narrating the horror is a necessity, an inescapable priority, but not something natural and spontaneous. Narrating that drama means accepting a contradiction without solution, but one that must be confronted. In *I sommersi e i salvati* Levi records the warning the SS addressed to deported people: "Regardless of how this war ends, we have won the war against you. (…) And even if no proof remains, and one of you survives, people will say that the deeds you describe are too monstrous to be believed… We ourselves shall dictate the history of the *Lagers*" (p. 3).

In another passage from the same work, Levi speaks about the Gorgon to refer to the *sommersi*, that is, to the 'Muslims', who have seen the face of the ultimate, horrifying reality of the camps and who, for this very same reason, have not returned and have not spoken about it. Thus, the duty of the *salvati* is to talk about it with all the wariness necessary to not be devoured by the black hole (*Arschloch der Welt*) of the terrible vision of the 'Muslims.' Their enterprise requires a vast effort at stylisation, formalisation and construction, because otherwise there is always the danger, as Kertész provocatively wrote, that the description of the camps might be read "only as a literary text, not as a reality"[15], not so much because readers often ignore the truth, or more accurately they almost always prefer to be deceived, but because all texts have literary and, even worse, fictional connotations.

These texts, in which Wiesel saw the birth of a new literary genre, that of "testimonial", should extricate themselves, if possible, from the concept of literary fiction, as is the case of Primo Levi's *Se questo è un uomo*. Contrary to the option chosen by Antelme, Wiesel and Kertész himself, who have declared that they write 'novels', only an ideally neutral literature, set in a type of ground zero from the standpoint of literary genre and thus not contaminated by fiction, could bear witness to the difference separating these texts from other literary works, whose characters do not exist outside the text itself (Madame Bovary, Sherlock Holmes, Bloom...). However, we should ask ourselves if it is possible that not only the literary witness but also primarily the recipient of this testimonial can read it without linking it to other authors and other works that use language in its poetic-evocative function, and thus to the history of literature? This is a rhetorical question which can only be answered in the negative: it is not possible to read this type of text without linking it to other literary texts. Once written, as non-fictitious as the author may want a text to be, it becomes part of the literary universe and, whether desired or not, it has literary and fictional connotations. The reader, according to his or her culture, cannot but relate a text to the aesthetic-literary tradition, seen – and this should be strongly emphasised – as a group of previously established rhetorical-stylistic instruments for communicating a specific message. A good example would be the 'strategies of reluctance' that Dante uses in the *Divine Comedy* to express the inexpressible, which have also been used in some works about the concentration camps precisely to overcome the problem of realism and bring the reader inside the suffering and the horror through the eyes of the characters.

3. Is the *Divine Comedy* a guide book?

In his book *In Bluebeard's Castle*, George Steiner claims that of the many works that have been written about the death camps, none surpasses the acuteness of Dante's observations:

> But whoever can grasp, in canto XXXIII of the *Inferno*, the full meaning of "the very weeping there forbids to weep" –
>
> > Lo pianto stesso li pianger non lascia,
> > e'l duol che truova in sugli occhi rintoppo,
> > si volge in entro a far crescer l'ambascia –
>
> will, I believe, have grasped the ontological form of the camp world. The concentration and death camps of the twentieth century, wherever they exist, under whatever regime, are *Hell made immanent*. They are the transference of Hell from below the earth to its surface. They are the deliberate enactment of a long, precise imagining. Because it imagined more fully than any other text, because it argued the centrality of Hell in the Western order, the *Commedia* remains our literal guide-book – to the flames, to the ice-fields, to the meat-hooks. In the camps the millenary pornography of fear and vengeance cultivated in the Western mind by Christian doctrines of damnation, was realized.[16]

In Chapter 10 of *Ulysses à Auschwitz. Pietro Levi, le survivant*,[17] entitled "Lire après", François Rastier criticised what he called the 'aestheticising' point of view that predominates Steiner's criticism, and asked whether Dante's *Inferno* can serve as a guide for understanding Auschwitz. The question posed by the French linguist is more than legitimate. And regardless of how much death camp literature mentions the *Inferno*, especially canto III in which Dante sketches out his overall vision of the netherworld, we believe that it is necessary to question what purpose this vision of a world of eternal damnation serves in the works recalling the extermination. Regardless of the answer – model of reference, contrast or negation – it is difficult for the *Inferno* to cease to be paradigmatic.[18] We should also add that the reception of a work – especially a work like the *Divine Comedy* – does not happen in a global sense – as a whole – rather partially, through some of its small lexical, figurative, thematic or rhythmic cells.[19] In this sense, we should recall that the attempts to emulate the *Divine Comedy* as a whole have been tallied,[20] and they have all failed, including Hugo, Lamartine and Gogol. The majority of the texts mentioned in the first section of this article have only taken into consideration some of the elements of the poem, regardless of how essential they are (the journey, the descent into the inferno, etc.), or some of the images (the dreadful multitude, the fire, etc.) or some of the most famous characters (Ulysses, Ugolino della Gherardesca, Francesca da Rimini, Caronte, Dante and Virgil, Beatrice, etc.), but none have taken the entire work into account. Not even Primo Levi, the author who for obvious biographical reasons has the strongest ties to Dante, never considers a relationship with the entire poem, nor even with the first cantica. Rather he culls a selection of figures, syntagmas and moments from the first two canticas. Dante is not a model, that much is clear.[21] He serves as a grammar of the infernal narration, the figurative repository of mythical images and artistic expressions that are incomparably concise in their violence. Thus, it does not make much sense to negate its reception by the simple fact that Dante's poem, organised around the distribution of sins and the desire for divine grace, narrates the quest for meaning, while the death camps have no meaning, as has been claimed.[22] It is an obvious, valid objection that is true for all literature that has used the Dantesque world, ranging from 18th century realistic literature to Romanticism. One thing is to warn about the obvious differences between the Italian poet's Gothic cathedral and the modern works that concern us, another very different thing is to deny the influence that Dante's *Inferno* – not just the *Inferno*, given the widespread modern acceptance of the *Purgatorio*[23] – has had and continues to have in world literature. Furthermore, there is an entire lexical and figurative mediation that has shifted presumably from Dante to many of the authors we are examining. I am obviously thinking about Levi, but also about Antelme, Rousset and Wiesel.

At this point, however, we must make a distinction between the more or less intentional presence of the Dantesque world in the author's imagination and that of the reader's, for the reader is required to decode those texts without any references other than the *Inferno* constructed by Dante upon the foundations of Christianity. Perhaps the epithet – "il nostro Caronte" – with which Levi (1958: 20) refers to the German soldier who, with monstrous friendliness, invites prisoners to give up all their possessions is enough for any minimally cultured reader's mind to think immediately of *Inferno III*. And it is impossible that in the brutal contrast between the coarseness of one ("Guai a voi, anime prave! // Non isperate di veder lo cielo: / io vegno per menarvi a l'altra riva / ne le tenebre eterne, in caldo e'n gelo", vv. 84-87) and the friendly cynicism of the other, the German does not stand out dramatically before our eyes, as a new raftsman of death. Aside from the ideological and mental distinctions, and the different functions of the characters and images, the Lager is an engineered world, which is reached after a lengthy journey, passing through other Lagers, other non-places – "invisible" especially to the people living beside them – and does not appear to fall under any human logic, despite the fact that it pullulates with infinite, varied humanity from which only a reduced number of witnesses has emerged (and who are gradually extinguishing and vanishing). This is a structure that – as we have mentioned – no one before Kafka, Jarry or Celine, had established as effectively, in our Western imaginations, as Dante.

It is fairly clear that, unlike Dante's inferno, the camps do not follow the logic of the sin-punishment relationship, wherein the violence suffered by the damned finds a logical explanation in the quality and quantity of errors committed while living. The concentration camp universe is not only a place of general terror, it is also the site where different levels of power are exerted, connected to each other, in a destructive mechanism, although it can also exceptionally serve as a saving mechanism for those who manage to survive it. From this standpoint, it is possible that the image of Dante's *Inferno*, as *the* site of evil, functioned more as an obstacle in capturing the different 'social' components that formed the mass of the deported people, and the different types of treatment.[24] Assuming Auschwitz as the model for all other death camps led Agamben to construct a synthetic and paradigmatic structure that can cast its shadow over political modernity.

The inferno, the "tristo buco" to use Dante's words (*If.* XXXII 2), the *Arsloch der Welt*, to use the expression employed by the SS, is nevertheless a metaphor that can be found in all the narrations dealing with death camps. Perhaps the author who uses it the most is Gradowski, at the very beginning of his narration of the *Sonderkommando*. Such a device is utterly logical for he saw nothing but the living dead, who in a single instant became smoke and ashes. "Welcome reader. You will find in these lines the narration of the suffering and torments that we, the most wretched people on this earth, have undergone in the time of our 'life' on this *inferno on earth* [emphasis added] that is called Auschwitz-Birkenau". In addition, he resorts to the same metaphor when speaking of the gas chambers and the crematoria:[25] that place where the wails of the deported people blended with the cries of the executioners, described as malevolent beasts. 'Down there' is a generic direction, virtually a euphemism, used to refer to the crematorium, the heart of the inferno where tongues of fire ceaselessly devoured infinite victims[26]. Gradowski – whose work, surprisingly, does not lack a certain concern for stylistics and aesthetics – like Dante in many episodes of the *Divine Comedy*, stops to introduce us to some of the inmates, providing a brief glimpse into their past serene lives, their different family settings, and their home countries. For example, we meet a daughter and a mother, who still has the courage to insult a member of the SS[27] – a young married women –, only to conclude with these words:

> The doors have been flung wide open, the inferno is about to welcome its victims. (…) I am on one side and I observe both groups. The bandits, the great assassins – and my sisters, the unfortunate victims. The march, the death march has begun. (…) I have the impression that worlds, entire worlds, have been stripped and have arrived here, along this diabolical path. (p. 114)

The camps are an inferno for Robert Antelme as well: "L'Enfer, ça doit être ça, le lieu où tout ce qui se dit, tout ce qui s'exprime est vomi à l'égalité comme dans un dégueuli d'ivrogne." (p. 141). Rousset, in chapter 7, entitled "Les Ubuesques", insists upon this image as he describes common prisoners: "Je ne sais rien qui puisse rendre, avec une égale intensité, plastiquement, la vie intime des concentrationnaires, que la Porte de l'Enfer et les personnages qui en sont issus" (pp. 70-71). In these words we can also find a possible allusion to August Rodin's "Porte de l'Enfer", which was installed in the garden of the Rodin Museum in Paris in 1937, and from which the figures of Paolo and Francesca, Ugolino and other "ombres" emerge.[28]

The description of this work included by Levi at the beginning of his book mixes Dantesque suggestions with Kafkan or even Becketian atmospheres.[29] Despite his narrative essentialism, Wiesel manages to avoid this comparison when evoking the spectre of selection: "It mattered little if the work was hard. The important thing was that we were far from the blok, far from death, far from the centre of the inferno (*La nuit*, p. 75). And in *Fateless* by Imre Kertész, the young main character replies to everyone who speaks to him about the camps as a veritable inferno with these words: "The inferno does not exist; Auschwitz exists". For this Hungarian writer, Dante's inferno is an abstract world that bears little resemblance to the reality of the Lagers. Neus Català, a Catalan woman deported to Ravensbrück, begins her testimony in the documentary "Ravensbrück: The Inferno of Women" with the following words: "Dante described the inferno, but he never knew Ravensbrück".

Infernal literature, including Dante's *Inferno*, represents a bridge between the narrator – and his or her brutal experiences – and the reader, for whom it would be impossible to comprehend the death camps without the help of the literary figures of hell, despite the aesthetic deviations that literature might lead to.[30] Luba Jurgenson argues that the use of a literary framework is simultaneous to the experience itself, to the way it is read and understood, which, in turn, is constructed in and with literature: the unavoidable misery and power of literature.

3.1. *The dehumanisation of Ulysses' shadow*

Dehumanisation, the complete loss of any human characteristic, is the major concern of all the narrators who do nothing other than record the process of degradation into the animal condition, or even worse, into an inanimate object, prior to being transformed into a pure skeleton.[31] "One day," Wiesel recalls (p. 112), "I managed to get up, after having summoned all my forces. I wanted to look at myself in the mirror that was hanging on the wall across the way, I hadn't seen myself since the ghetto. From the depths of the mirror, a cadaver looked at me. I have never forgotten his look in my eyes." However, this transformation had already taken place immediately after entering the camps, as the majority of witnesses claim. Let us read what Levi wrote in *Se questo è un uomo*:

> Eccoci trasformati nei fantasmi intravisti ieri sera. Allora per la prima volta ci siamo accorti che la nostra lingua manca di parole per esprimere questa offesa, la demolizione di un uomo. In un attimo, con intuizione quasi profetica, la realtà ci si è rivelata: siamo arrivati in fondo. Più giù di così non si può andare: condizione umana più misera non c'è, e non è pensabile. (...) Ci toglieranno anche il nome: e se vorremmo conservarlo, dovremmo trovare in noi la forza di farlo, di fare sí che dietro al nome, qualcosa ancora di noi, di noi quali eravamo, rimanga. (p. 23)

The degradation is also psychological, not only physical, and includes also those who were part of the *Sonderkommando* and thus obligated to muffle their feelings, to become cold like Branca Doria:[32] "One has to become an automaton, not see anything, not feel anything, not understanding anything." (Gradowski, p. 142) Any fraternal bond is lost. The weakness of human was depicted in all its tragic weight. Nothing was left but the survival instinct, which proved to be lethal, because it took control of everyone, suffocating any type of modesty or fear. This biological transformation is similar to what happens with the jailers, described as "cruel and savage beasts" or "murderous beasts" (Gradowski), and compared to the very same ferocious beasts – lonza, lion, she-wolf, Cerberus, Geryon, harpies, dogs, pigs, snakes… - which torment the damned in Dante's inferno.

However, to reach this level of dehumanisation a great deal of ingenuity and much deception was needed, as Gradowski saw with merciless clairvoyance in his diaries, where he recorded all the states through which the victims passed to reach the total atrophy of their feelings, the absolute indifference to the fate of others, regardless of whether they were friends, mothers, children or siblings.[33] The 'selection', with its horrifying ambiguity, was performed by the SS, the Kapos or blok leaders who, as modern versions of the mythical Minos, decided the fate of the inmates, both upon their arrival to the camps (let us recall the macabre scenes of selections taking place at the stations inside the camps after a horrible journey that might have lasted for days and days) and during imprisonment. The king of Crete, Minos, is placed by Dante at the beginning of the *Inferno* (*If.* V 4-12), recreates Virgil's homonymous character (*Aen* VI 432-433), and is in charge of situating the damned based on their sins:

> Stavvi Minòs orribilmente, e ringhia:
> esamina le colpe ne l'intrata;
> giudica e manda secondo ch'avvinghia.
> Dico che quando l'anima mal nata
> li vien dinanzi, tutta si confessa;
> e quel conoscitor de le peccata
> vede qual loco d'inferno è da essa;
> cignesi con la coda tante volte
> quantumque gradi vuol che giù sia messa.

A similar procedure is followed in the camps. "In meno di dieci minuti," Levi narrates (*Se questo…*, p. 20), "tutti noi uomini validi fummo radunati in un gruppo. Quello che accadde degli altri, delle donne, dei bambini, dei vecchi, noi non potemmo stabilire allora né dopo: la notte li inghiottì, puramente e semplicemente. Oggi però sappiamo che in quella scelta rapida e sommaria, di ognuno di noi era stato giudicato se potesse o no lavorare utilmente per il Reich; sappiamo che nei campi rispettivamente di Buna-Monowitz e Birkenau, non entrarono, del nostro convoglio, che novantasei uomini e ventinove donne, e che di tutti gli altri, in numero di più di cinquecento, non uno era vivo due giorni più tardi."[34] Yet the selection could also take place at any other time during life in the camps, as almost all the witnesses have recounted (Wiesel, Rousset, etc.).

Let us recall the famous verses from the *Inferno* XVI 116-118: "Considerate la vostra semenza / fatti non foste a viver come bruti, / ma per seguir vertute e canoscenza". This is the final part of the speech Ulysses delivers to his companions, and these words ring in Levi's ear "come uno squillo di tromba, come la voce di Dio", awakening another Ulysses in him, the one who would not only have to use rationality to understand that world, but who would also have to follow the appropriate moral code whose responsibility he felt invested of. The sentence that closes the chapter "Il canto di Ulisse" is quite enigmatic: "qualcosa di gigantesco che io stesso ho visto ora soltanto, forse il perché del nostro destino, del nostro essere oggi qui...". It leaves the reader flabbergasted, because it is the only incomplete sentence in the book. It is as if the narrator had a grandiose, apocalyptic illumination. In an interview conducted years later, the author explained this vision in part, saying that he felt guilty, although he did not say about what. We can assume that this sense of guilt is related to the twofold fate of the Greek hero, who while reminding his companions of the lofty, noble fate characterised by "virtù e canoscenza" that brings them together, is also capable of employing all means, including deception, to reach his personal goal. If Dante saw in Ulysses reason without divine grace, it is quite likely that Levi saw in him an immoral reason, and that he perceived in this duplicity parallels with himself and his times. Man not only operates according to reason, in order to counter his predominant irrationality, but also according to a moral code, which is in opposition to the immorality of the Greek sailor, for whom any means are valid to achieve his goal. Dante's Ulysses does not go back; he is not the hero of *nostos*. He gets shipwrecked in front of the mountain of earthly paradise. Ulysses-Levi, instead, is shipwrecked not in his attempt to narrate submerged humanity, but in the desire to free himself from the guilt of having contributed to constructing such a savage universe without any apparent meaning. His journey does not have Du Bellay's serene conclusion for Ulysses, as Antelme mentions:

> Hereux qui, comme Ulysse, a fait un bon voyage,
> ou comme cestuy-là qui conquit la toison,
> Et puis est retourné, plein d'usage et raison,
> Vivre entre ses parents le reste de son âge! [35]

While in the concentration camps, the inmates did nothing but dream about their return to the same home they had left, and they did not know that Auschwitz had stolen away the "sweet world" of the past. It is certain that they will not come back from Auschwitz, for the world to which they were to return has disappeared. The Ulysses returning from the camps no longer finds his home nor his wife and family. Rather, he finds a house occupied by others, relatives who neither understand nor are willing to understand anything the victim says. Antelme constructs his entire book, aptly entitled *La espèce humaine*, around the prisoner's progressive distancing from his human condition. He goes so far as to state that man has been reduced to another species, beast or plant, "to that which only makes an effort to eat and dies if he doesn't eat", who has been obligated to "live in conditions that no one – I repeat no one – could ever imagine" (p. 229). And yet despite this, Antelme is convinced that no one can stop man from belonging to the human species. "C'est parce que nous sommes des hommes comme ceux que les SS seront en définitive impuissants devant nous. (...) nous ne pouvons devenir ni la bête ni l'arbre. Nous ne pouvons pas et les SS ne peuvent pas nous y faire aboutir. (...) Il peut tuer un homme, mais il ne peut pas le changer en autre chose" (pp. 229-230). This attitude is similar to that of some of the more noble characters in the *Divine Comedy*, such as Piccarda and Costanza di Altavilla, who could not be deprived of their spiritual freedom by any physical violence (*Pd.* III).

3.2. *Narrator and character*

Perhaps it would be a good idea at this juncture to reflect on the differences between the "I" narrator (the one who is talking) and the "I" character (the one being spoken about) in the *Divine Comedy*, for they can provide us with some useful information for interpreting the modern texts we have been examining. The *auctor* of the *Comedy* is "libero, dritto e sano" (*Pg.* XXVII:

140), and he has no need for a guide because he has already been freed from the slavery of passions and because he 'knows' the way divine justice works. The miseries and weaknesses of humanity in Dante's time, however, can be found in the *agens* that is put in the danger. In need of a guide, he identifies with many of the characters he meets upon the way, because he relates to their state of confusion and loss.

In contrast, the *agens* in the modern texts has lived and suffered, without any type of guide whatsoever, an experience whose dimensions and size he cannot grasp, and he finds himself undecided between the desire to survive and the indifference towards his own fate, constantly tempted to abandon it and become one of the thousands of 'Muslims' who – to use Levi's words – "si esita a chiamare vivi: si esita a chiamare morte la loro morte, davanti a cui non tremano perché sono troppo stanchi per comprenderla" (p. 113). Despite this, this *agens* has embarked on the road to salvation. Indeed, the ones to be saved were not only those who had the enormous luck others were unable to enjoy, but also those who were capable of orienting themselves in the concentration camp universe and exploiting their own resources and skills, based on, for example, a knowledge of the German language. The Dante-character does not manage to repress a gesture of sympathy for the damned (such as Paolo and Francesca). The prisoners, on the other hand, even though they may have become narrators later, after distancing themselves from the events and the *sommersi*, tend to have a highly dormant sensibility that does not allow them to suffer excessively when faced with the vision of that degraded humanity. Indeed, at that time their only concern was finding something to eat ("Nous sommes au point de ressembler à tout ce qui ne se bat que pour manger et meurt de ne pas manger, au point de nous niveler sur une autre espèce," Antelme writes, in his defence of the impossibility of reducing man to an inhuman species) and save their skin however they could. More precisely, contact with and even the very presence of the so-called 'Muslims' had to be avoided because they represented the point of no return for those who had not yet reached that stage of dehumanisation, after which there is nothing but the gas chambers and the crematoria.

Unlike the *agens*, is it more difficult to categorise the *auctor* of these many narrations from the death camps. For example, there is the autobiographical, analytical narrator in the works by Levi, Rousset, Wiesel and Antelme, the 'fictional' narrator in Kertész of *Fuga sense destí*, the diary-writer in Salmen Gradowski, for whom the distance between deed and writing is minimum compared to that found in the other texts, along with many other kinds.[36] In every instance, the voice is that of a narrator whom the spine-chilling experience has left marked for life, and who cannot stop searching for the meaning of those deeds, without ever finding it. An experience that, rather than bringing him closer to God, has made him lose all hope in the God that has let such an inferno exist on earth.[37] After being stripped of their families, houses and things, and finding themselves in foetid cargo trains without really understanding how or especially why, the narrator of these texts – unlike the narrator of the *Divine Comedy* – although he does not believe he was chosen to be cast in the abyss of human degradation, now, upon returning to the 'sweet world' feels, just like Dante, the responsibility of explaining exactly what he experienced, in order to ensure that posterity knows the scope of the crime against humanity perpetrated by the Nazis, and extract the necessary lesson.

They feel the insatiable need to communicate the truth in order to save at least the memory of the *sommersi* from the anonymity of death. Their job resembles that of Dante *auctor*. However, unlike Dante, the survivor is pervaded by a vast sense of guilt (see Primo Levi, Jean Amery, et al.) and even shame at having emerged from that horrifying experience.[38] Obviously he cannot be a man who is "libero, dritto e sano," like the *auctor* in the *Divine Comedy*, for he is forever trapped in the memory of the camps. He is a *survivor*, a living corpse. One who has never come back from Auschwitz. There is no coming back from Auschwitz. One remains a living dead forever. Like Branca Doria (*If.* XXXIII: 141)[39] and Coleridge's Ancient Mariner – who Levi mentions in his poem *Il superstite* – the survivor never feels truely alive, nor is he completely dead. It is a feeling similar to what Dante experiences when seeing Lucifer:

> Io non mori' e non rimasi vivo;
> pensa oggimai per te, s'hai fior d'ingegno,
> qual io divenni, d'uno e d'altro privo. (*If.* XXXIV: 25-7)

The tears and pain have been forever etched on the face of the survivor, who lives in constant pain, and the memory of the pain of the *sommersi*, to whom he wants to give a voice, makes it even more unbearable.

Il y a deux ans, durant les premiers jors qui ont suivi notre retour, nous avons été, tous je pense, en proie à un véritable délire. Nous voulions parler, être entendus enfin. On nous dit que notre apparence physique était assez éloquente à elle seule. Mais nous revenions juste, nous ramenions avec nous notre mémoire, notre esperiénce toute vivante et nous éprouvions un désir frénétique de la dire telle q'elle. Et dès les premiers jours cependant, il nous paraissait impossible de combler la distance que nous decouvrions entre le langage dont nous disposions et cette experiènce que, pour la pluipart, nous étions encore en train de poursuivre dans notre corps. (Antelme, 1957, p. 9)

Memory is one of the fundamental issues of the literature we have been examining. There are essentially two types of memory: the memory **in** the camps, and the memory **of** the camps. They both share the breathtaking pain caused by evoking the past. Memory is differentiated by the degree of difficulty in the re-evocation: the memory of the past in the camps is possible, though it is not very wise, for it decreases the chances of survival, making it hard to adapt to the harsh conditions of the camps; the memory of the camps is virtually impossible, at least initially. In fact, a period of almost complete amnesia is very common among former prisoners. Only later, for better or worse, the memories come back.[40] And there are even survivors who needed decades to break their silence and speak about their experience in the terror camps. It is as if they had to wrench the memories from the deepest fibre of their being, where the trauma experienced has been indelibly recorded, branded with fire.[41] Over time, however, for the vast majority of the survivors, remembering becomes one with conveying those memories, regardless of how painful they may be: "Written," says Gradowski, "with the intention that at least part of the truth becomes known to the world, and that you may reap vengeance, World, vengeance for all of this!" Along the same lines, Levi writes: "I ricordi della prigionia sono molto vividi e dettagliati rispetto a qualsiasi altra cosa che è accaduta prima e dopo", "direi," he adds, "quasi una preparazione inconscia a testimoniare".[42]

An appropriate epigraph for this first type of memory could be the words with which Francesca da Rimini addresses to Dante in canto V (vv.121-3) of the *Inferno*, quoting Boeci:[43]

Nessun maggior dolore
Che ricordarsi del tempo felice
ne la miseria; e ciò sa il tuo dottore.

These verses constitute the backbone around which all the references to the memory of the past are arrayed in the narration of the surviving prisoners: the memory of the *dolce mondo*, as Levi called it in his poem entitled *Buna* ("Se ancora ci trovassimo davanti / Lassù nel dolce mondo sotto il sole / Con quale viso ci staremo in fronte?"),[44] uses the same syntagma as Farinata.[45] In most cases, the memories of civil, free life act as a spring of renewed suffering, as does the awareness that the concentration camp experience makes any return to their past identity impossible. Antelme wrote (p. 114): "Ils étaient, dans la nuit de Noël [...] Alors, ils ont essayé de racconter des histoires. Ils ont parlé de leurs femmes et de leurs gosses.[...] *L'enfer de la mémoire* fonctionnait en pleine." Language is a spell that takes one's breath away, that causes the body to shrivel.[46] Thus, one was forced to distance oneself from those words that reminded them of the "dolce mondo". They reserved these evocations for later, when nothing more could be extracted from either the body or the will. When they would know for sure they would never again see the sea. But as long as a future was still possible, they had to remain mute.[47] Therefore, Dante's Ulysses, with his non-return, can also serve as a literary representation of the condition of narrator-prisoner in the death camps.

However, the other type of memory, that of the 'saved,' resembles the question that Farinata poses to Dante (*If.* X), modelled after the one Aeneas asked Dido in the *Aeneid* II:[48]

> E se tu mai nel dolce mondo regge,
> dimmi: perché quel popolo è sì empio
> incontr'a' miei in ciascuna sua legge?". (*If.* X 81-84)

Just like Farinata, they wonder about the reason behind so much bestiality and violence. The most common kind of memory is the one summarized by the epigraph to the verse "ricordati di me, che son la Pia" (*Pg.* V: 134). Throughout his journey, Dante meets souls that ask the living beings to remember them for a series of reasons. In this case, Pia dei Tolomei does so in order to shorten or speed up her penitence in Purgatory. The narrators of the concentration camp texts, however, evoke many figures of people who did not survive, many *sommersi* who are often mentioned using nicknames (Il Greco in Levi's *La tregua*), while others appear with their own names (Hurbinek, et al.). All of them, just like the throngs of Dante's souls, are real representations of the horror. Nevertheless, the most excruciating memories are those of the *Sonderkommando*. The narrator is aware that those shadows, the *sommersi*, live only because of their words. Speaking about a three year old child named Hurbinek, Levi writes "Nulla resta di lui: egli testimonia attraverso queste mie parole" (*La tregua*, p. 167). Furthermore, "tutti i musulmani, che vanno in gas hanno la storia, o, per meglio dire, non hanno storia. [...] La loro vita è breve ma il loro numero è sterminato; sono loro, i Muselmänner, i sommersi, il nerbo del campo; [...] Essi popolano la mia memoria della loro presenza senza volto."

4. Conclusions

A more exhaustive study would have stressed the presence of other infernos in modern literature (Kafka, *Ubu Roi*, Céline, Beckett, etc.) and not limit itself to just one. However, I hope to have sufficiently proven that literary mediation is fundamental to both the mental and textual construction of the Lager, and to the mediation of its narrative representation. More precisely, these are two different sides of the same coin, they derive from the same collective imagination. Within this literary mediation, I am certain that the stylistic, rhetorical and narrative modules of the *Divine Comedy* have a fundamental importance for the interpretation of the experience by both the narrator and the reader. No one can deny the role that Levi's *Se questo è un uomo* has played in the hermeneutics of the concentration camps. By placing himself in Ulysses' shadow[49] – somewhat confusing himself with Ulysses – he made the *Divine Comedy* the interpretative key to viewing/reading the concentration camp universe, not only because it was one of the first to be published (in 1947, the same year that Antelme released *L'espèce humaine*, one year after David Rousset's *L'univers concentracionaire* and much earlier than Elie Wiesel's *La nuit*, which was published in 1958), but especially because of the worldwide success it enjoyed, due to its extraordinary literary qualities.

This article aimed to be a modest attempt at examining the continuity of the reception of Dante's poem in our age, and, in particular, within the searing literary realms that, as I have attempted to demonstrate, are faced with numerous difficulties from the very beginning. Difficulties and obstacles remain present in testimonies whenever there is a genocide, regardless of how small, numerically speaking, when compared to the scope of the

Nazi-Fascist genocide. They demonstrate the need to explain the meeting with Medusa and her petrifying stare. We don't know whether such a tragedy will take place again in the future of human kind. In any event, it is likely that the parallels with Dante's voyage to the netherworld will continue to provide some of the interpretative and expressive keys to representing the horror that human eyes can witness. Dante's sensitivity and acuteness serve as one of the most profound reflections on the fate of humanity.

> *L'enfer n'est pas le lieu de la douleur. Il est* le lieu où l'on fait souffrir.
> E. Jabès, *L'Enfer de Dante* (1991).

Notes

[1] Lionello Sozzi, "La letteratura francese e l'Italia," in *Storia della letteratura italiana*, ed.by Enrico Malato, vol. XII. *La letteratura italiana fuori d'Italia*, pp. 643-46.

[2] I am referring to filmmakers such as Clive Barker (*Books of Blood*), Thomas Harris (whose novel, *The Silence of the Innocents* inspired the film *The Silence of the Lambs* directed by Jonathan Demme) and David Fincher's film *Seven*.

[3] There are many parallels between Malaparte and Dante: *If.* V: 35: "quivi le strida, il compianto, il lamento", which associates 'strida' with a cry of compassion (com-pianto), is virtually identical to the paragraph in which Malaparte says: "uno stridor di denti, un pianto soffocato" or *If.* XII: 102: "dove i bolliti facieno alte strida", in which the word 'strida' is associated with a prosperous situation that Malaparte describes in the scene of the tyrants immersed in a boiling river of blood ("Or ci movemmo con la scorta fida / lungo la proda del bollor vermiglio,dove i bolliti faceano alte strida. Io vidi gente sotto infino al ciglio..."). Or the 'orribili teste' that emerge from the water 'mozze dalla mannaia' and seem to have a life of their own ("Per tutto il giorno quelle teste parlaron tra loro") and which recall Dante's images: Geryon appearing in the middle of the darkness (*If.* XVII: 8: "sen venne, e arrivò la testa e 'l busto") or the mutilated bodies of the 'seminatori di discordie' and the representation of the poet Bertran de Born who holds up his own head (*If.* XXVIII: 129: "levò il braccio alto con tutta la testa/ per appressarne le parole sue").

[4] E. Montale, "Esposizione su Dante" (1965).

[5] And the other horrors related to the Gulag, the genocide of the Armenians, the Chinese purges perpetrated by Mao, the war in Rwanda, the extermination of the Kulaks and many others. For an overview of exterminations in the modern world with its blood-curdling figures, see the following website: http://www.liceolevi.it/GENOCIDI/home.htm.

[6] We should remember that according to historians, the victims of Nazi genocide are as follows: 5.6-6.1 million Jews, 3.5-6 million Slavic prisoners; 2.5-4 million prisoners of war; 1-1.5 million political prisoners; 500,000-800,000 gypsies (both Romas and Sintis); 200,000-300,000 handicapped persons; 10,000-250,000 homosexuals.

[7] Steiner 1971 and the critique by Mesnard 2005, pp. 98-101.

[8] See the extremely fascinating book by Mesnard and Kahan 2001 and Mesnard 2005, pp. 67-108. Also see Wardi 1986.

[9] Also *Pd.* I: 4-6 and 70-1, XIV: 103-5, XXIV: 22-7.

[10] Horia-Roman, p. 12. Bettetini 2004.

[11] See, among others, Jurgenson 2003 and Wardi 1986.

[12] Agamben 2002, p. 10, writes: "Così esattamente –scrive Lewental nel suo semplice jiddish – come gli avvenimenti si verificano non può essere immaginato da nessun essere umano e infatti è inimmaginabile che si possa riportare così esattamente come accaddero le nostre esperienze".

[13] 'Muslim' was the name in Auschwitz slang given to the prisoners who hunger, abuse, illness and suffering had virtually consumed, until they were lead to the terminal stage in their tragic stint at the camp.

[14] Agamben 2002, pp. 26-9 and Sullam Calimani 2001.

[15] Kertész 2000 in Mesnard 2000.

[16] Steiner 1971, pp. 47-8.

[17] Rastier 2004.

[18] Here, we follow Blumenberg's reflections in his *Arbeit am Mythos*, where, by tracing the myth of Prometheus in contemporary literature (especially in Kafka), he shows it

still at work despite being the object of satire or denigration: "One of the extreme transformations of the myth is [...] its omission. Even in the negation of all its elements, it is
always presented as a diagram of an orientation".

[19] This is yet further proof of the accuracy of Dolezel's reasoning about the importance of the relations between different worlds of fiction and their intertextual links; he
claims that "Le opere letterarie sono collegate non solo a livello della *texture*, ma anche,
in modo non meno importante, a livello di mondi finzionali. [Questi] Passano da un
creatore di *fiction* all'altro, da un periodo all'altro, da una cultura all'altra come entità
estensionali, quando ormai la *texture*, lo stile, i modi della narrazione e di autenticazione
originari sono stati dimenticati. Un mondo finzionale è più memorabile della *texture* che
lo ha fatto accedere all'esistenza. [...] Ciò spiega perché l'intertestualità intensionale [...]
è soprattutto implicita, mentre la succesione dei mondi finzionali è quasi sempre esplici-
ta, e assai spesso in modo molto accentuato." L. Dolezel, *Heterocosmica. Fiction e mondi
possibili*, (Milano: Bompiani, 1999), p. 203.

[20] Pollman 1973.

[21] Rastier 2005, p. 61.

[22] See the criticism on the meaninglessness of the camps contained in Kértesz's work
Kaddish for a Child Not Born: "And now stop saying, I should say, that there is no explanation for Auschwitz, that Auschwitz is the result of irrational forces that are inconceivable by reason, because Satan himself is irrational, just as Iago is too, but their children
are rational, all their acts can be deduced like a mathematical formula" (p. 52).

[23] Examples that come to mind include Becket's *Waiting for Godot* and some of
Kafka's short stories.

[24] Mesnard 2001, pp. 54-5.

[25] "Men, young boys and old men, fathers and sons, were taken to this inferno, or
down there, in the other inferno, and brutally shoved towards death" (p. 98).

[26] "Not much time will be needed for these five thousand human beings, these five
thousand worlds to be consumed in the flames" (pp. 144-5).

[27] "Then, addressing herself to the wife [of the SS]: 'You have come too, cruel beast,
murderer of women, to savour our ruin. But remember that you too have a child, a family, but you'll never enjoy them! They will kill you, and your son, like mine, will not
live much longer [...] You will pay for this, the entire world will punish you.' [...] This
woman, over the tomb, has pulled the mask off them and has predicted the future, close
at hand, that awaits them." (p. 116).

[28] See Aida Audeh, "Rodin's *Gates of Hell*. Sculptural illustration of Dante's *Di-
vine Comedy*", in *Rodin: a magnificent obsession* (2001), pp. 92-125; Liana De Girolami
Cheney, "Rodin's *Gates of Hell*: an interpretation of Dante's *poema sacro*", in "Italian
Culture", XI (1993), pp. 103-26.

[29] "Questo è l'inferno. Oggi, ai nostri giorni, l'inferno deve essere così, una camera
grande e vuota, e noi stanchi di stare in piedi, e c'è un rubinetto che gocciola e l'acqua
non si può bere, e noi aspettiamo qualcosa di certamente terribile e non succede niente e
continua a non succedere niente" (p. 19).

[30] "Les homme normaux," writes Rousset, "ne savent pas que tout est possible. Même
si les témoignages forcent leurs intelligence à admetre, leurs muscles ne croient pas. Les
concentrationnaires savent" (p. 181).

[31] "Peut de concentrationnaires sont revenus, et moins encore sains. Combien sont
des cadavres vivants qui ne peuvent plus que le repos et le sommeil!", recalls Rousset,
p. 182.

[32] Branca d'Oria *If.* XXXXIII: 140-1: "ché Branca Doria non morì unquanche / e mangia e bee e dorme e veste panni." Dante speaks on seeing Lucifer: "Io non mori' e non rimase vivo; / pensa oggimai per te, s'hai fior d'ingegno, /qual io divenni, d'uno e d'altro privo" (*If.* XXXIV: 25-7).

[33] In contrast, in the second part of his diary, Gradowski analyses the effect of the division and the selection processes on the members of the so-called *Sonderkommando*.

[34] "Sappiamo anche – Levi continues - che non sempre questo pur tenue principio di discriminazione in abili e inabili fu seguito, e che successivamente fu adottato spesso il sistema più semplice di aprire entrambe le portiere dei vagoni, senza avvertimenti né istruzioni ai nuovi arrivati. Entravano in campo quelli che il caso faceva scendere da un lato del convoglio; andavano in gas gli altri." Wiesel also creates a narrative that is similar to *La nuit*.

[35] Happy the man who, like Ulysses, has made a fine voyage, or has won the Golden Fleece, and then returns, experienced and knowledgeable, to spend the rest of his life among his family.

[36] "The doors have been swung wide open, the inferno is ready to welcome its victims. [...] I'm in a corner and I observe two groups" (p. 114).

[37] "I wasn't the only one," writes Wiesel, "who had lost faith in those days of selections. I met a rabbi from a small Polish town [...] who one day told me, 'It's over. God is no longer with us. [...] Where is God? How can I believe in a merciful God?'"

[38] Agamben 2002, p. 82 ff.

[39] "ché Branca Doria non morì unquanche / e mangia e bee e dorme e veste panni" says Dante to Fra Alberigo (*If.* XXXIII: 140-1).

[40] Rousset.

[41] Jurgenson claims: "Je crois que c'est par le corps que le texte s'écrit. [...] Le corps est le principal acteur de l'œuvre sur le camp. Dans la logique concentrationnaire, il est toujours en trop, et c'est de cela qu'il porte témoignage. Dans tout procès réel ou virtuel, le corps est l'ultime pièce à conviction, il est en soi un témoin. Il est ce lieu où se réalise l'état extrême de l'individu. Car le corps concentrationnaire est déjà un texte, marqué par le camp comme pourrait l'être un livre".

[42] Levi, *Se questo..*, p. 225, 220.

[43] "nei momenti di avversità l'essere stati felici costituisce la forma più straziante di dolore" (*Convivio* III: 4.2).

[44] See Rastier 2005, p. 63.

[45] *If.* X: 81, verses that we refer to below.

[46] Antelme: "Le langage était une sorcellerie. La *mer*, l'*eau*, le *soleil*, quand les corps pourrissait, vous faisaient suffoquer. C'était avec ces mots-là comme avec le nom de M.... qu'on risquait de ne plus vouloir faire un pas ni se lever. [...] Il fallait garder ça. Pouvoir être son propre sorcier plus tard encore, quand on ne porrait plus rien attendre du corps ni de la volonté, quand on serait sûr qu'on ne reverrait jamais la mer. Mais tant que l'avenir était possible il fallait se taire" (p. 169).

[47] Gradowski: "Quando esco dalla mia tomba in questa terra maledetta e dannata, e vedo con quanta insolenza la luna rischiara un lembo del mio mondo di tenebre, nel quale sono così profondamente immerso e di cui sono impregnato – faccio ritorno di corsa nella mia tomba oscura. Non riesco più a fissare il suo chiarore. (...) Solleva una tormenta che sconvolge il mio spirito, fa zampillare in me una quantità di ricordi che mi lasciano privo di forze, mi spezzano il cuore. Sono trascinato da quest'onda schiumeggiante in un oceano di sofferenza. Mi ricorda il tempo passato, l'incanto di allora, e mi svela tutto

l'orrore di questo tragico presente. (...) La notte scura è la mia compagna, i pianti e le urla sono i miei canti, il fuoco che bruccia le vittime è la mia luce, l'atmosfera di morte è il mio incenso, l'inferno è la mia dimora" (p.59). "Non devono più vedere la tua luce [luna] gli uomini che si sono trasformati in bestie selvagge e sanguinarie" (p. 63). "e guarda come si danno da fare, come pazzi furiosi, i servitri del diavolo, i barbari di questo mondo, e come cercano, frugano le strade e le case, forse riusciranno ancora a catturare una vittima [...] Guardali, mentre settacciano o campi [...] per trovare altre vittime [...] tante ne ha divorate in questi anni [il loro dio] – ed è sempre affamato, furioso e folle, e attende fremendo nuove vittime [...] senti la confusione e le grida?" (p. 65). "Piangono, si tormentano, scossi da spasmi. Pensare alla propria vita, fare il bilancio degli anni li sconvolge, li scuote nel profondo [...] Si ricordano del tempo passato, quando la loro vita era bella, quando era felice! Rivedono il film dei tempi passati, ormai finiti per sempre, e allora si mostra in tutto il suo orrore la cruda realtà, che sta davanti ai loro occhi. Si sentono travolti e disperati nell'attesa della fine. Sono tutti oppressi e tormentati dalla pena, dall'attesa che arrivi l'attroce e orribile morte" (p. 81).

[48] "Infandum, regina, iubes renouare dolorem [...] Sed si tantus amor casus cognoscere nostros / Et breviter Troiae supremum audire laborem, / Quanquam animus meminisse horret luctuque refugit, / Incipiam" (vv. 3, 10-13).

[49] As indicated by the title of Rastier's book, *Ulysse à Auschwitz. Primo Levi, le survivant*.

Bibliography

Agamben, G., *Quello che resta di Auschwitz*, Turin, Einaudi,

Arendt, Hanna, *Essays in Understanding*, edited by Jerome Kohn. Harcourt Brace, 1994.

Bauman, Z., *Modernity and Holocaust*, Madrid, Sequitur, 1997.

Bertoni, A., "L'Olocausto e l'identità letteraria", in G. Anselmi (a cura di), *Mappe della letteratura europea e mediterranea. III Da Gogol' al Posmoderno*, Bruno Mondadori, Milan, 2001, pp. 198-252.

Didi-Huberman, Georges, *Images malgré tout*, Paris, Ed. Minuit, 2003.

Grass, G., *Escribir después de Auschwitz*, Barcelona, Paidos, 1999.

Jurgenson, Luba, *L'expérience concentrationnaire est-elle indicible?*, Editions du Rocher, 2003.

Kremer, S.L., *Women's Holocaust Writing. Memory and Imagination*, University of Nebraska Press, Lincoln-London, 1999.

Marucci, Valerio, Il "mercato globale", in in *Storia della letteratura italiana*, Enrico Malato, *vol. XII. La letteratura italiana fuori d'Italia*, pp. 867-870.

Mengaldo, Pier Vincenzo, "Lingua e scrittura in P. Levi", in *Primo Levi: un'antologia della critica*, Einaudi, 1997, pp. 169-242.

Mengaldo, Pier Vincenzo, *La vendetta è il racconto. Testimonianze e riflessioni sulla Shoah*, Turin, Bollati Boringhieri, 2007.

Mesnard, P.-Kahan, C., *Giorgio Agamben à l'épreuve d'Auschwitzk*, Paris, Kimé, 2001.

Horia-Roman, Patapievici, *Gli occhi di Beatrice. Com'era davvero il mondo di Dante?*, Milan, Bruno Mondadori, 2006.

Parrau, Alain, *Écrire les camps*, Belin, 1995.

Pollak, Michael, L'expérience concentrationnaire, Ed. Metailié, 1990.

Rastier, F., *Ulises en Auschwitz. Primo Levi el sobreviviente*, Translation by Ana Nuño. Barcelona, Reverso, 2005.

Reiter, A., *Narrating the Holocaust* [1995], Continuum, London-New-York, 2000.

Rin, Michael, *Les récits du génocide. Semiotique de l'indicible*, Delachaux et Niestlé, Paris, 1998.

Sozzi, Lionello, *La letteratura francese e l'Italia*, in *Storia della letteratura italiana*, Enrico Malato, vol. XII. La letteratura italiana fuori d'Italia, pp. 643-646.

Sullam Calimani, Anna-Vera, *I nomi dello sterminio*, Einaudi, Turin, 2001.

Traverso, Enzo, *Le passé, modes d'émploi. Histoire, mémoire, politique*, La Fabrique, 2006.

Vidal Naquet, Pierre, *Reflexions sur le génocide. Les juifs, la mémoire et le présent III*, La Decouverte, Paris, 1995.

Wardi, C., *Le génocide dans la fiction romanesque*, Puf, Paris, 1986.

Wieviorka A., *L'ère du témoin*, Parigi, Plon, 1998.

«*Au coeur de l'enfer*» by Zalman Gradowski, Paris, Ed. Kimé, 2001. (Italian translation Gradowski, Salmen, *Sonderkommando. Diario da un crematorio di Auschwitz, 1944*, a cura di PH. Mesnard and C. Saletti, Venice, Marseilles, 2002).

"*Des voix sous la cendre; manuscrits des Sonderkommandos*», Ed. Calmann-Lévy, Paris, LGF, 2006.

Antelme, Robert, *L'espèce humaine*, Paris, Gallimard, 1957.

Bruck, Edith, *Signora Auschwitz. Il dono della parola*, Marseilles, Venice, 1999.

Delbo, Charlotte, *Auschwitz et après:* (volume 1): «Aucun de nous ne reviendra»; (volume 2): «Une connaissance inutile»; (volume 3): «Mesure de nos jours», Paris, Minuit, 1970.

Jabès, Edmond, *L'Enfer de Dante*, Fata Morgana, 1991.

Kertesz, Imre, *Kaddish for a Child Not Born* / translated by Christopher C. Wilson and Katharina M. Wilson. – Evanston, Ill. : Hydra Books, 1997. – Uniform title: Kaddis a meg nem született gyermekért.

Kertesz, Imre, *Liquidation* / translated from the original Hungarian by Tim Wilkinson. – New York : Knopf, cop. 2004. – Uniform Title: Felszámolás.

Kertesz, Imre, *Fatelessness: A Novel* / translated from the Hungarian by Tim Wilkinson. - New York : Vintage International, 2004. – Uniform title: Sorstalanság.

Kogon, Eugen, *L'Etat SS* [1950], Paris, Seuil, 1993.

Levi, Primo, *Informe sobre Auschwitz*, a cura di Leonardo Debenedetti, Castelló, La trossa, 2005.

Levi, Primo, *Se questo è un uomo*, in *Opere*, vol. I a cura di C. Cases, Torino, Einaudi, 1988.

Levi, Primo, *La tregua*, in *Opere*, vol. I a cura di C. Cases, Torino, Einaudi, 1988.

Levi, Primo, *Sommersi e salvati*, in *Opere*, vol. I a cura di C. Cases, Torino, Einaudi, 1988.

Perec, George, *W ou le souvenir d'enfance*, Paris, Denöel, 1975.

Rousset, David, *L'Univers concentrationnaire* 1965, Paris, Editions de Minuit, 1965.

Semprun (Jorge), *La Mort qu'il faut,* Paris, Gallimard, 2001.

Semprun, Jorge, *Le grand Voyage,* Paris, Gallimard, 1972.

Semprun, Jorge, *L'Écriture ou la vie,* Paris, Gallimard, 1996.

Spiegelman (Art), *Maus: un survivant raconte,* Paris, Flammarion, 1998.

Steiner, G, *In Bluebeard's Castle. Some Notes Towards the Re-definitions of Culture*, Londo, Faber & Faber, 1971.

Wiesel, Elie, *La nuit* , Paris, 1958.

Luigi Ballerini (UCLA)

Paolo and Francesca: A Cruel and Unforgiving Love

Hoc habeo quodcumque dedi
Lucio Anneo Seneca, *De Beneficiis*

I have what I have given
Gabriele D'Annunzio, *The Dead City*

Verses that have achieved undisputed notoriety over the centuries are too numerous to list. For those who are familiar with the authors of these lines and their intentions (and for those who cannot even imagine nourishing an interest in such questions), they constitute a sort of common patrimony, from which anyone can generously barrow without ever depleting it.

Fewer are the verses that – when read or listened to closely – have instilled peace and serenity in the minds of those who attempted the arduous task of interpreting them according to precise methods of philological investigation; or those who were so bold as to challenge the interpretations of others.

And then there are verses in a sort of a limbo or state of apparent calm – like a break in a storm; like a fire, dormant under its ashes, that might nonetheless flare up instantly; or (in the parlance of our times) like a brain coming down from a drug high.

Among this last group of 'calming' verses (which are consequently, anything but calm), whose meanings mix together to simultaneously vex and delight both cerebellum and precordium, there are some that truly stand apart, even when they come from a veritable goldmine of proverbial expressions such as Dante's *Commedia*.

"Amor che a nullo amato amar perdona" is the most sublime and the most repeated of them all. It is a verse that has puzzled less than it should have and that is because many have simply glossed it over throughout the centuries. Even some of the finest commentators have stuffed it into a hermeneutic box that often reflected their own desire to see a particular truth inscribed within it, rather than identifying the values that needed to be assigned to the words so as not to stray too far from the meaning Dante (in all probability) intended. However, all of them based their readings on several common inter-textual observations — thus legitimizing their overt appropriation of the words on the page.

It is a palpitating line, worthy of the notes of Puccini's "Nessun dorma" sung by Pavarotti. It has palpitated ever since Love dictated it to Dante, who in turn placed it at the center of his most renowned anaphora. Rivers (or oceans!) of ink have transformed it into one of the most singular opportunities to exercise that epistemological perversion known as *reciprocity* (an immaterial smirk of the mind, just like *symmetry* or that Hegelian ghost of *synthesis*).

In the prevailing opinion, the famous verse means nothing more than this: those who are loved cannot help but love the person who loves them in return. This would explain, even if only apodictically, the fatalism and inevitability of the relationship between Paolo Malatesta and Francesca da Rimini (or da Polenta). Restricted by this reductive interpretation, the verse has circled the globe. For example, in his praise-worthy translation of the *Commedia* into English, Henry Wadsworth Longfellow renders this verse as: "Love that exempts no one beloved from loving,"[1] according to which exemption is not an option, a dead end. If someone loves you, then you are obliged to love back. It is debatable, however, whether this was the meaning Dante had in mind.

Let's ignore the fact that such an obligation runs counter to bourgeois values and that it is not entirely contemptible for it does have its advantages. In particular, it allows us to establish a tragic or classical paradigm (one in which there are no extenuating circumstances) that renders the two lovers' damnation, and the *contrappasso* of their punishment, absurdly appropriate. Yet if they couldn't do things differently, the logical person – who is not satisfied with the *quia* – will ask: why place them in hell, with a whole range of vulgar fornicators? Although Paolo and Francesca surrender reason to desire,[2] they do so only because, according to Francesca, they were forced by a kind of love that closely resembles the virtuous one Virgil praises in *Purgatorio* XXII: 10-12: "...*Amore, / acceso di virtù, sempre altro accese, / pur che la fiamma sua paresse fuore.*"[3]

Here we get a sense of the distance Dante places between himself and his characters, as well as of the discomfort he feels in talking about them. Paolo and Francesca's sin is *analogical*. The two lovers hide behind a truth principle that only works for virtuous love, and not for their carnal love. Buti, among others, gently comments: "Carnal [love] does not always kindle, for it only kindles the carnal lovers; but virtuous love always kindles the virtuous." I said "gently" but not without "difetto di saver" [lack of knowledge] —Buti's reasoning slips into a pernicious and inconclusive duality that hardly reveals the carnal lovers' destiny.

It is easy to distinguish "always" from "not always," but if we add "only the carnal lovers" to the equation, the reader is left to wonder if there is any difference at all between the two. As a result, it is not clear whether human beings are equipped to resist this sort of solicitation or whether to resist it is to fight human nature. After all, Buti had said unequivocally that Love *always* strikes carnal lovers reciprocally when commenting on the verse that causes us such perplexity:

> [Dante] continues: *Amor che a nullo amato amar perdona*. That is: love, which always forces him who is loved to love and does not exempt the beloved from loving. It is impossible that the beloved does not love back whoever loves him, provided he is aware of it.

Yes, the lover must also be privy to it. Therefore, Paolo—who does not say a single word in *Inferno* V[4]—must have spoken at some point. However, the fact that they were reading about Lancelot could suggest a simultaneity of loving feelings.

Buti is neither the first nor the last to try and avoid the logical quicksand of the medieval casuistry. Boccaccio (whose commentary stops at Canto XVII of the first canticle) had previously raised the problem in his own explanation of the episode involving Paolo and Francesca, and he sought, somehow, to keep his distance from Dante. Boccaccio had also turned to the verses cited above from *Purgatorio* XXII (as Buti would do later, though less lucidly): "This characteristic, with due respect to the author, does not actually come about from such a love. Instead, it is caused by honest love, just as the author himself says in the twenty-second book of the following canticle...[5]" Even Boccaccio finds it hard to contradict his author. In fact he continues by writing:

> One could say, nevertheless, that this does sometimes [not always!] happen but seldom does a man tightly bind himself in love to something that is not, wholly or in large part, in conformity with his nature. In the event that such a thing did occur, what the author says here could in fact take place, even though each thing naturally desires what is similar to it. Consequently, when the woman who is desired learns that the demeanor and the habits of her lover are in conformity with her own, she will yield straightaway to love for him just as he loves her. Thus, Love will not excuse one who is loved; that is to say, Love will not excuse in him anything that would not cause the one he loves to love him in return.[6]

Here, "always" has become "sometimes," and the circumstances are clearly specified. Love's reciprocity happens only when the beloved feels the "the demeanor and habits of her lover are in conformity with her own." Yet even this statement is debatable, since there are many cases—right before our eyes—in which love ignites between individuals of opposing habits and manners. For now, however, the differences between Boccaccio and Buti will suffice.

Moving to an older commentator, we find that Dante's contemporary, Ottimo, felt the statement was a bit risky and could be misread and, in the very least, should be taken with a grain of salt. Ottimo proposes an argument based on the difference between *effetto* and *affetto*— one that, though subtle, does not seem particularly suited to the case of Paolo and Francesca who, beyond *affetto* [affection], did not disdain the *effetto* [effect] of their repeated encounters. In spite of this, they do not seem to fit under the rubric of "some base lovers." In fact, there is no trace of this to be found in or outside the text, neither in Dante nor among his commentators. But let's read the exact words of Ottimo's reasoning:

> …love has such qualities that no one who is loved is spared from being struck in the chest by its arrow. Many subscribe to this point, and they take their proof from the *effect*, rather than the *affection*. Therefore, against those in favor of such a belief, we argue that […] the true benefactor loves the person who receives benefit because he placed his trust in him and not because he [the benefactor] expects the same in return. The one who receives the benefit loves his benefactor not only for the benefit received (for which he is in debt) but also for the affection toward him that he found in the benefactor. The person who is truly beloved behaves in the same way. He loves the lover not for the effect toward which base lovers aim, but for the affection that the lover shows in being faithful, obedient, and in service to the beloved. Unless

he was born from two stones, he still loves the lover, seeing her own image in him, like a reflection in a mirror. Thus, the heart of the lover is completely filled with the image of the beloved.

Solving such a conundrum is not easy, and perhaps not even necessary. Ottimo writes like someone who is caught between two conflicting desires. On the one hand, he wants to agree with Dante. On the other, he realizes that as far as the effect is concerned, Paolo and Francesca certainly did not hold back. However, it must be noted that Ottimo brings three important terms – *faith*, *obedience*, and *service* – to the discussion on love, reminding the reader of the *Stil novo*.

Thus, even Ottimo can be listed among the overwhelming majority of commentators who see verse 103 of *Inferno* V as an example of the mechanical reciprocity between lover and beloved, even if only among those who have a noble heart. These are the people Dante addresses when he writes: "Amore e 'l cor gentil sono una cosa, / sì come il saggio in suo dittare pone / e così esser l'un sanza l'altro osa / com'alma razional sanza ragione."[7]

Yet they are a few commentators who remain skeptic, take for instance Benvenuto da Imola, who closely read not only Dante but also Ottimo's commentary. On the issue of love's reciprocity— which he does not believe — Benvenuto reasons in an original way, shifting responsibility for the statement from the author to his character. The distinction between character and author, allows the reader to understand the choices Francesca makes in framing her speech. Dante is not arguing in favor of this fatal reciprocity, but rather Francesca. This is an exegetic move of great finesse that is worth savoring in detail:

Amor. Hic Francisca narrat quomodo et quare ipsa redamaverit ipsum; et volens se excusare dicit breviter, quod amor est tantae virtutis et potentiae quod semper cogit personam amatam redamare amantem, et e converso; et ideo non potuit facere quod non redderet vicem suam tali amatori. Dicit ergo: *Amor ch'a nullo amato amar perdona*, idest, amor quie non remittit alicui amato amare amantem, *mi prese del piacer costui si forte*, idest ita me strinxit ad complacendum isti de mea pulcra persona [...] Sed hic nota, lector, quod sententia praemissa est saepe falsa. Certum est enim quod sepe quis amat unam et non redamatur ab ea, et e converso.

Yes, dear reader, the *sententia praemissa* is false. Furthermore, the arguments that try to justify such a statement in order to protect Dante's reputation are misguided, for the words belong to Francesca and not to the poet (see, for instance Ottimo, Boccaccio, and Buti). Benvenuto continues:

> ...dicunt quod magis debet considerari affectus quam effectus. Unde dicunt quod nisi sit natus ex saxo amatus amat amantem; sed hoc est penitus falsum; nam de rei veritate multae fuerunt et sunt acerbissime odientes amantes, imo aliquae prociderunt eis nasum a facie cum dentibus, imo aliquae occiderunt se ipsas, sicut scribit Augustinus primo de Civitate Dei, et Paulo supra hoc narravi de Didone quae potius elegit sibi mortem quam amorem nuptialem regis Jarbe. Et posito quod esset verum nihil faceret ad propositum quia isti devenerunt ad effectum, et omnes de quibus auto rest supra locutus.

Finally, there are those who, in order to prove the truth of *istam sententiam*, quote what Dante wrote in *Purgatorio* XII, where he said more or less the same thing. Against these, Benvenuto argues that our author "loquitur ibi de amore virtutis quae fundatur super honesto," and thus that *sententia* is undoubtedly true. But here, (and we can almost feel Benvenuto's frustration with these third-rate commentators) we are speaking of "de amore voluptatis qui fundatur supra delectabili" (and therefore not "super honesto") and thus we must reiterate that "hic sententia est falsa." In fact, there are countless people who "quorum aspectum horriblem omnes fugiunt, qui amant reginas et nobiles dominas formosas et virtuosas!" without being loved in return by them... "nimis est hoc absurdum inconveniens."

In conclusion Benevenuto calmly delivers his final blow, of which we spoke before:

> Considera subtiliter lector quod autor non ponit istam sententiam tanquam veram, sed fingit istam mulierem luxuriosam hoc dicere ad excusationem sui, sicut sepe loquitur mulier amorata quando loquitur de suo fallo et delicto patenti, quod negare non potest. [...] Ergo bene dixit autor in persona istius meretricis.

That said, and setting aside the shameless epithet used for our heroine (there must be *some* difference between adulteress and whore), it would be wise to repeat the "structuralist" invitation that Benvenuto addresses to his colleagues: "Et sic nota quod multa talia dita autorum sepe male intelliguntur, quia non consideratur quomodo, et quare et quando dixerint."

Although Benvenuto attributed the statement to Francesca rather than Dante, he still interprets the verb *perdonare* in the same 'reciprocal' way the majority of commentators did. There's no two ways about it: once the god of love orders, his injunction turns into an "unforgiving" malady.

But since certainties are boring – typically leading to sterile faith, and thus hindering thought, which must remain unexpected in order to function properly – let's re-examine the entire issue, beginning with a close analysis of the verb *perdonare*. We are inspired here by Antonio Pagliaro's commentary, made in 1952, on the verb *offendere*, another verb that appears in *Inferno* V, at the end of the tercet immediately preceding our "amor che a nullo amato amar perdona":

> Amore che'al cor gentil ratto s'apprende,
> prese costui della bella persona
> che mi tolta; e il modo ancor m'offende.[8]

Pagliaro was not convinced that this verb referred to the indignation Francesca felt for the brutal way in which she had been killed by her husband, who caught her and his brother in *delicto flagrante*. In fact, this is how nearly all commentators interpret the line, understanding the offense as being directed toward the *bella persona*, which, having been taken suddenly, did not have the chance to repent. Building on some of the ancient commentators (Buti and Landino, in particular), Pagliaro convincingly demonstrates that *offendere* must be linked to the main clause. Thus the offense perpetrated against Francesca is caused by the "intensity of Paolo's love, which deprived her of any defense while alive and still keeps her under its spell in hell." But let's read the reasons that brought Pagliaro to this conclusion:

> The linguistic foundation of this interpretation lies in the irrefutable fact that in Dante, the verb *offendere* is also used with the meaning [...] "to maim"— a secondary meaning that was already present in Latin, different from the primary meaning of "to offend, to insult." In fact, we find the verb used as such to indicate, in particular, the harmful consequences of the heart's affections: in *Inf.* VII : 71 ("O creature sciocche, quanta ignoranza è quella che v'offende")[9] and in *Inf.* II : 45 ("L'anima tua è da viltate *offesa*").[10] Obviously, Paolo's passion for his sister-in-law was so strong that her defenses, her feminine modesty, her faithfulness to her husband, were overwhelmed—and this is still true, for the passion that consumed her still commands her. In other words, Paolo's love for her is as alive in hell as it was on earth.[11]

Since we also seek a meaning that is more satisfying (or less stigmatized) than the one suggested by tradition, we will do with *perdonare* what Pagliaro did with *offendere*. Hopefully, we will not stray too far from our target in attempting to identify the object to which that verb refers, be it person, thing, or fact.

First, we must state that the verb comes from the late Latin *perdonare*, used in ecclesiastical texts since the tenth century, in place of the classic *condonare*, which is still very much alive, as in the Italian expression "to condone [i.e., to forgive or forfeit] a debt." *Perdonare* functions on two semantic levels. According to the Battaglia dictionary, *perdonare* came to mean, on the one hand, "to disregard a blow, offense, or damage caused by others (in particular, against oneself), to generously renounce any revenge, and to repress any resentment toward the offender." On the other hand, it meant "to save someone from an unpleasant experience, humiliation, suffering, or even a burdensome obligation, a difficulty"—in other words, to allow someone to evade their responsibilities.

With this distinction in mind, we have searched the *Commedia* for instances where Dante uses this verb (or the noun *perdono*). We found that all the examples belong to the first of the two meanings. In addition, we came to the conclusion that when examined closely, the second meaning is but a sub-category of the first. They are listed here for the benefit of the reader who wishes to inspect them personally. The trusting reader, of course, is free to skip them:

> E qui Calliopè alquanto surga
> seguitando il mio canto con quel sono
> di cui le Piche misere sentiro
> lo colpo tal che disperar *perdono*
> (Invocation of the muse in *Purg.* I:9-12)[12]

> Poscia ch'io ebbi rotta la persona
> di due punte mortali, io mi rendei,
> piangendo, a quei che volentier *perdona.*
> (Manfred speaking in *Purg.* III:118-120)[13]

> Che potea io ridir, se non "Io vegno"?
> Dissilo alquanto del color consperso
> che fa l'uom di *perdon* talvolta degno
> (Dante, reproached by Virgil, responds in *Purg.* V:19-21)[14]

Noi fummo tutti già per forza morti
e peccatori infino all'ultima ora:
quivi lume del ciel ne fece accorto,
sí che, pentendo e *perdonando*, fora
di vita uscimmo, a Dio pacificati
che del disio di sé veder n'accora
> (Those late to repent explain to Dante the favor they have
> received—"light from heaven"—in *Purg.* V:52-57)[15]

E come noi lo mal ch'avem sofferto
perdoniamo a ciascuno, e tu *perdona*
benigno, e non guardar lo nostro metro
> (Paraphrase of the *Our Father* in the canto of the Proud: forgive
> our debts, as we forgive our debtors... in *Purg.* XI:16-18)[16]

Lo fren vuol essere del contrario sòno:
credo che l'udirai per mio avviso,
prima che giunghi al passo del *perdono*
> (Before the erasure of the sin of envy, in *Purg.* XIII: 40-42)[17]

Così li ciechi a cui la roba falla
stanno a' *perdoni* a chieder lor bisogna,
e l'uno il capo sovra l'altro avvalla,
perché 'n altrui pietà tosto si pogna
> (Dates of religious holidays and places
> [sanctuaries, etc.] where one obtains pardons...and where
> one pays for earns indulgences, in *Purg.* XIII: 61-64)[18]

E lui vedea chinarsi, per la morte
che l'aggravava già, inver la terra,
ma degli occhi facea sempre al ciel porte,
orando all'alto sire, in tanta guerra,
che *perdonasse* a' suoi persecutori
con quello aspetto che pieta dissera
> (St. Steven, visions of meekness in *Purg.* XV: 109-114)[19]

Noi siamo di voglia a muoverci si pieni
che restare non potem, però *perdona*
se villania nostra giustizia tieni,
> (Those who were slothful in life cannot wait
> to be blessed, in *Purg.* XVIII: 115-117)[20]

> Ma dimmi e come amico mi *perdona*
> se troppa sicurtà m'allarga il freno,
> e come amico ormai meco ragiona:
> come pote trovar dentro al tuo seno
> loco avarizia, tra cotanto senno
> di quanto per tua cura fosse pieno?
> > (Virgil presumes that Statius may be stingy and
> > asks him why, in *Purg.* XXII: 19-24)[21]

After such a string of situations in which *perdonare* is used "normally," we wonder if it would be more productive to interpret this line in the same way as well. Thus, in Francesca's line, "amar" serves as a direct object, "perdonare" as the main verb and "a nullo amato" as the indirect object, to whom the interdiction is addressed. Paradoxically, such a straight-forward and unbiased reading of the text leads to the following statement: Love itself *disapproves* of—and therefore does not condone/pardon—the feeling of reciprocal affection that the beloved could feel for the lover.

This is not *a* possible meaning of Dante's line; it is *the* only meaning from which it is best not to stray—even if it is the exact opposite of the traditional explanation. Naturally, we will have to provide a plausible justification for the impossibility of a reciprocal relationship between lover and beloved, especially since it is voiced by a character who seems to embody the fact that the contrary is true. For now, however, we must emphasize that this meaning is closer to the letter of the text, and that whatever message one might draw from it must begin with this interpretation.

In fact, it would seem that we have traded one paradox for another: if we abandoned the idea that an inevitable passion bound Paolo and Francesca together for all eternity, we must accept that Love, in order to survive, cannot allow (condone) the beloved's loving back (that is, to become a lover him/herself). It is important to emphasize that this prohibition does not concern the lover, who is very free to love. The beloved, however, by Love's express mandate, commits a sin by loving back. We believe that, in Dante's world, this statement might make more sense than those that have been generally proposed until now. While we assume full responsibility for our statements, we are not inclined to fight those who might dispute its validity: everyone is free to live "diablement dans les idées recues," as Ezra Pound wrote, even with respect to Dante, in his essay on Cavalcanti, published in *Make it New* in 1934.

We will leave for another time an in-depth examination of the difference between Erastes and Eromenos, proposed by Plato in his *Symposium* (which Dante could not have read). However, we can suggest that, after the *Vita Nuova*—and throughout the *Commedia*—Love does not play the part of the *Heauton Timorumenos*[22]—that is, the self-punisher who condemns the effects of those causes that constitute its very *raison d'être*. Rather, Love is the engine, the driving force, the inspiration of illuminations. It is always present, it keeps stretching, and never relaxes. From a theological standpoint, this is what happens when Beatrice is transformed from a beloved creature (who does not love back) into a blessed soul and "bearer of *soprasenso*," that is transcendent meaning, (as Contini writes in his essay, "Cavalcanti in Dante" from which we will draw shortly[23]). In fact, at the summit of mount Purgatory, Beatrice scolds the poet for having fallen prey to false (and therefore reciprocal) loves and having stooped to such a lowly state that, as soon as his beloved "di carne a spirto era salita / e bellezza e virtù cresciuta m'era," she became "men cara e men gradita."[24] Thus, the unrepentant Alighieri "volse i passi suoi per via non vera, imagini di ben seguendo false, [...]. Tanto giù cadde, che tutti argomenti / alla salute sua eran già corti, / fuor che mostrarli le perdute genti,"[25] among whom we find the reciprocal lovers, Paolo and Francesca.

However we will not pursue this line of investigation any further, for we are urged to follow another that raises questions of poetics and literary influences. It is based, once again, on an analysis of the verb *perdonare*, isolating the component of *dono* (gift) and *donare* (to gift). One of the many implications of this rich signifier points to Calvalcanti. That is, it dates back to the poet whose "shadow" and "thought" (as Contini writes) accompanied Dante "until the end of a career, so different from its beginnings, in which he had to settle the score with the patron of his poetic youth (I say 'to settle' because, given the author's peremptory tone, he seems to insist on settling it once and for all)."[26]

Contini advances two considerations of particular interest to highlight the presence of Dante's *primo amico* in his poetic writings. First, "in order to enact the process of transfiguration marking his detachment from Cavalcanti, Dante utilizes fantastic-linguistic elements typical of Cavalcanti's style."[27] Second, "Dante's homage to Cavalcanti is more vivid outside of an obvious *Stilnovo* context, in the exhaustively 'comic' realm of the *Commedia*."[28]

Contini also closely examines two episodes from Dante's epic. First, his meditation on the speech of Oderisi da Agobbio (*Purg.* XI: 94-99— we are on the ledge of the proud, who must prove their humility). Here he speaks of the glory of language: he starts by describing Guido Cavalcanti's victory over Guido Guinizzelli and then he suggests (with barely dissimulated pride) that *perhaps* (which is nothing but a feeble form of courtesy) he will be replaced by the up-and-coming Dante Alighieri. The distinguished critic then contemplates *Inferno X* in which, through the pilgrim's conversation with Cavalcante (and Farinata), "the contemplator of metaphorical death, the pessimistic and saturnine poet of love [Guido Cavalcanti], is semi-alive in an interval or suspended limbo in that great report on the afterlife [i.e. *The Divine Comedy*]; an interval predicated on the fact that he still resides among the living."

If this were not enough one could find more elements in *Il fiore* (whose "attribution to Dante has been widely documented through many stylistic observations"). Furthermore, we can turn to those clues ("traces that are unintentional, and therefore more reliable") that Contini (*homo venator*, and even *viator*) considers as evidence of a Cavalcantian presence. Like a sublime magician, he uses them to re-open a controversy on authorship. In 1939, Contini introduces the sonnet "Io sento pianger l'anima nel core" by writing: "traditionally, commentators have been unsure whether to attribution it to Cino or Dante [...] Perhaps the first is more likely; in fact, it is sometimes taken as a typical example of Cino's style from his sorrowful phase."[29] Later, however, he writes "...In one 'incipit' in particular, that of 'Io sento pianger l'anima nel core,' two Cavalcantian quotations are joined together: 'I' sento pianger fra li miei sospiri' (from *Gli occhi di quella*); and 'ch'i' sento lo sospir tremar nel core' (ibid), or better yet, 'l'anima sento per lo cor tremare' (from *Io non pensava*). Such an observation would probably be of some use in determining to whom the sonnet should be attributed."[30]

To such varied and extremely well-documented Cavalcantian findings, it is time to add another in the hope that, through it, we may find more reasons to support the necessity of a non-reciprocal love in the poems of these two authors. As far as Guido Cavalcanti is concerned, non-reciprocity is something like the preliminary condition for immersion in the enjoyment of knowledge. Naturally, the kinds of knowledge Dante and Guido pursue are radically different: the one is after an eschatologically predetermined knowledge; the other relishes in the very act of speculation. In closing these observations, we can now re-read the entire tercet of Francesca's peremptory affirmation:

> Amor che a nullo amato amar per*dona,*
> Mi prese di costui *piacer sì forte,*
> che, come vedi, ancor non m'*abbandona.*[31]

Within this tercet we have a lexicon and an atmosphere that, in many ways, closely mirror one of Cavalcanti's isolated stanzas, which is conventionally numbered XIV:

> Se m'ha del tutto oblïato *Merzede,*
> già però Fede – il cor non *abandona,*
> anzi ragiona – di *servire a grato*
> al dispietato – core.
> E, qual sì sente simil me, ciò crede;
> ma chi tal vede – (certo non persona),
> ch'Amor mi *dona-* un spirito 'n su' stato
> che, figurato, - more?
> Ché, quando lo *piacer mi stringe tanto*
> che lo sospir si mova,
> par che nel cor mi piova
> un *dolce amor sì bono*
> ch'eo dico: "*Donna,* tutto vostro sono."[32]

In Cavalcanti, we find a will to love (*servire*) a merciless (*dispietato*) heart without any prospect of immediate gratification. Rather, pleasure is drawn from not being loved back, for love is –and must be— unrequited (*a grato*). All other pleasures fade before this one, which "so wrings" Guido and "seize[s]…so strongly" Dante. It is born of a kind of disproportion, an asymmetry. Thus we find a disquieting Cavalcantian presence in an episode that is normally interpreted according to the strict rules of courtly love.[33]

Furthermore, we are faced with an unlikely poetic ancestor (or maybe an older brother, if we want to consider the other Guido [Guinizzelli] as the founding father), whose influence on Dante is felt even when denied or discarded. These elements should encourage the reader to be extra cautious when interpreting the verse at hand and to refrain from projecting their own agenda on its structure. If such caution leaves us *speechless* (*senza parole,* as is the case with Paolo, who speaketh not at all), this means we are approaching the heart of the conundrum. Other pages, yet to be written, await the reader committed to exploring the mental and physical immodesty of the Francesca da Rimini myth. Dante framed it without making any concessions to his "well-meaning" readers. Most of them, on their part, did everything they could to ignore his healthy, explicit, and perhaps counter-intuitive statement. On the one hand, he attempts to go beyond human love by transforming it into a metaphysical and redemptive experience (an attempt to which he dedicates his energies as a religious and civic poet). On the other, he displays a Cavalcantian libido predicated on restraint: he seems to stop just shy of every exit or way out, relishing in the experience of the threshold and taking advantage of the energy caused by the inexhaustible proximity to death. In this verse Dante seems to be focused on the "here-before" rather than the "here-after"; a "here-before" where truth is necessarily precarious and is not to be found in rigidly plausible premises, but rather in their constant revision based on ever-changing circumstances.

Between the absurdity of an impossible demonstration and the happiness that springs from connecting a few luminous points within the chaotic pinball game we inhabit, the glimmer of a perhaps unconscious quotation demands to be fully acknowledged.

[Translated by Gianpiero W. Doebler]

Notes

¹ *Inf.* V: 103. The English translations throughout this essay are drawn from Longfellow's classic translation. Verse citations to the original are provided for those who may wish to consult other editions.

² See *Inf.* V: 39.

³ "The love / Kindled by virtue aye another kindles, / Provided outwardly its flame appear."

⁴ In one of his rare *lapsus calami*, Dante writes: "These words *they* spoke to us." We can explain this, however, by speculating that Paolo must have accompanied Francesca's words with gestures.

⁵ *Boccaccio's Expositions on Dante's* Comedy, Michael Papio, trans. (Toronto: University of Toronto Press, 2009), p. 283.

⁶ Ibid.

⁷ *Vita Nuova*, XX. "Love and a gentle heart are but one thing, / as the philosopher in his sentence wrote; / so they without each other live dare not / as rational spirit without reasoning." *Dante's Lyric Poems*, Joseph Tusiani, trans. (Brooklyn: Legas), second edition, 1999.

⁸ *Inf.* V: 100-102: "Love, that on gentle heart doth swiftly seize, / Seized this man for the person beautiful / That was ta'en from me, and still the mode offends me."

⁹ "O creatures imbecile, / What ignorance is this which doth beset you?"

¹⁰ "Thy soul attainted is with cowardice."

¹¹ "Canto V of *Inferno*," *Nova lectura Dantis* (Roma: Angelo Signorelli Editore, 1951), p. 17. Pagliaro writes in more detail on this same issue, commenting on the modern reader's of Dante with whom he disagrees (Parodi, Ricci, etc.), in the eleventh chapter of his *Saggi di critica semantica* (Mesina-Firenze: Casa Editrice G. D'Anna, 1953). See, in particular, pp. 342-346 and 350-353.

¹² And here Calliope somewhat ascend, / My song accompanying with that sound, / Of which the miserable magpies felt / The blow so great, that they despaired of pardon.

¹³ After I had my body lacerated / By these two mortal stabs, I gave myself / Weeping to Him, who willingly doth pardon.

¹⁴ What could I say in answer but "I come"? / I said it somewhat with that color tinged / Which makes a man of pardon sometimes worthy.

¹⁵ Long since we all were slain by violence, / And sinners even to the latest hour; / Then did a light from heaven admonish us, / So that, both penitent and pardoning, forth / From life we issued reconciled to God, / Who with desire to see Him stirs our hearts."

¹⁶ And even as we the trespass we have suffered / Pardon in one another, pardon thou / Benignly, and regard not our desert.

¹⁷ The bridle of another sound shall be; / I think that thou wilt hear it, as I judge, / Before thou comest to the Pass of Pardon.

¹⁸ Thus do the blind, in want of livelihood, / Stand at the doors of churches asking alms, / And one upon another leans his head, / So that in others pity soon may rise,

¹⁹ And him I saw bow down, because of death / That weighed already on him, to the earth, / But of his eyes made ever gates to heaven, / Imploring the high Lord, in so great strife, / That he would pardon those his persecutors, / With such an aspect as unlocks compassion.

[20] So full of longing are we to move onward, / That stay we cannot; therefore pardon us, / If thou for churlishness our justice take.

[21] But tell me, and forgive me as a friend, / If too great confidence let loose the rein, / And as a friend now hold discourse with me; / How was it possible within thy breast / For avarice to find place, 'mid so much wisdom / As thou wast filled with by thy diligence? (To please the most obsessive of our readers, we must also add *perdonanza*, found in *Par* XXIX : 120).

[22] From the title of a lost comedy by Menander that was re-written in Latin by Terence.

[23] From the edition of the *Rime di Giudo Cavalcanti* (Verona: Editiones Officinae Bodoni, 1968). Now in *Varianti e altra linguistica* (Torino: Einaudi, 1970), pp. 433-445.

[24] *Purg.* XXX: 127-129: When from the flesh to spirit I ascended, / And beauty and virtue were in me increased, / I was to him less dear and less delightful.

[25] *Purg.* XXX: 130-1, 136-8: And into ways untrue he turned his steps, / Pursuing the false images of good, [...] So low he fell, that all appliances / For his salvation were already short, / Save showing him the people of perdition.

[26] Contini, *Rime*, p. 433. Literature is made of texts that, when closely examined, will reveal things that one didn't know could be found and even things one didn't know they were looking for. It allows for unexpected openings and rhizome-like connections that renew (or restore) the meaning of quotations and echoes, whether deliberate or not.

[27] Ibid, p. 440.

[28] Ibid, p. 442.

[29] From Dante Alighieri, *Rime*, edited by G. Contini (Torino: Einaudi, 1995), p. 249.

[30] G. Contini, *Varianti...*, p. 444. Contini, however, certainly remembers that Cino felt compelled to defend himself from accusations of plagiarism raised by Cavalcanti himself. See his "Qua' son le cose vostre ch'io vi tolgo, / Guido, che fate di me sì vil ladro? / ..."

[31] *Inf.* V: 103-105: Love, that exempts no one beloved from loving, Seized me with pleasure of this man so strongly, / That, as thou seest, it doth not yet desert me; (Obviously, its other merits notwithstanding, Longfellow's translation follows the traditional reading of verse 103.)

[32] If Favor has forgotten me entirely, / Not for that does [my] heart forsake Loyalty, / But rather intends to serve without reward / [Her] pitiless heart. / And he who thus feels like me believes this; / But who sees (surely no one) / That Love grants me a sprit of his own dignity / Which, once it is figured forth, dies? / For when pleasure so wrings me / That sighing begins, / It seems as if into my heart rains / So fine a sweet love / That I say: "Lady, I am all yours." *The Poetry of Guido Cavalcanti*, Lowrey Nelson, Jr., trans. (New York, Garland) 1986, p. 21.

[33] Principally, Rule XXVI, in the third book of Andrea Cappellano's *De arte honeste amandi*: "Amor nil posset amori denegari."

Robert Di Pede (The University of Edinburgh)

Dante's New Life and Reparative Reasoning

> Understood hermeneutically, in terms of a dialogue be-
> tween past and present, the question of the truth of the
> *Commedia* does not concern merely a textual artifact; it
> interrogates the questioner and places modernity *en face*
> of a claim out of its past.[1] (William Franke)

Introduction

Dante may well be, as John Scott once described him, one of the few poets belonging to all peoples of all times in all places.[2] And yet there was a time after Boccaccio and before modernity when Dante's verse had fallen by the wayside: his audience numbering no more than a few nineteenth-century Italian philologists, Anglo-American literati, and Italian school children practiced in the art of memorization.

The twentieth century, in contrast, saw a resurgence of interest in Dante. Many attempts were made to translate, explicate, and adapt his works for an increasingly wider, more popular public. One need only consult the work of Amilcare Iannucci – author of *Dante, Cinema, and Television* (2004), *Dante: Contemporary Perspectives* (1997), and *Dante today* (1989) – for an idea of how widespread and incredibly diverse were the efforts and means used to bring Dante's message to as wide an audience as possible.

The resurgence of interest in Dante is a striking and curious event at various levels. No one can fail to notice, for instance, that Dante's rep-resentation in modern literature and cinema bridges, in a manner worthy of commentary, the medieval-modern divide. At another level, while remaining medieval in appearance, Dante is substantially transformed into a new man with a new life bestowed on him by a new generation of readers. And on still closer examination it begins to seem that to speak of Dante's new life is mis-leading when there are in fact new *lives* of which to speak. There are today as many ways of reading the medieval poet as there are kinds of audience to whom his works can be represented: from theatre goers and art connoisseurs to college students and blue collar workers.[3]

The attempt to mediate between Dante's age and our own has at once been the attempt to mediate between the discipline of literary studies and ordinary life. Texts such as the *Divine Comedy* and the *Vita Nuova* have been adapted to new audiences in several distinct ways. Two of the most traditional kinds of adaption are historical and ahistorical. Historical interpretations regard the text as an answer to questions that arise. Meaning, therefore, must be sought in the historical and contextual particularity of the text's origins. Historical approaches emphasize difference and are weary of attempts which require equivalency to be assumed between periods. Non-historical approaches are less reluctant to assume equivalency because they are firm contenders of universal questions to which literature is always a response. What counts here is the reader's response to the texts contemporary significance.

The dialectic between these two poles is a commonplace in the history of literary criticism. Each pole has vied for supremacy over the other in an *agon* of mutually exclusive illuminations. Historically-minded critics accuse non-historically-minded critics of lacking interpretive restraint and compromising the seriousness of literary studies. Non-historically minded critics accuse historically-minded critics of spoiling the imaginative enterprise of "creative thinking" and reducing the text to a museum piece. A third option opens up with the resolution of binaries: fiction and non-fiction are posited as one. Success for the interpreter lies in casting light on principles from the author's work which are universally significant; meanwhile, peculiarities are investigated in the way an ethnographer or anthropologist investigates foreign cultures.

Now each of these attempts to mediate between Dante's age and our own are unsatisfactory for different reasons. If the first two fail for not doing justice to the complexity of a narrative such as the *Commedia* which is both historical and fictional, universal at the level of truth claims and yet filled with all kinds of particularities, the third fails because it renders the narrative redundant: if all that might be said about a text can be said without it, why should anyone seek to give it new life?

I want to explore a fourth option: binaries are not the same yet they are inseparable and related in complex ways and are still able to be distinguished. In other words, I want to suggest that new life for a text is itself a valid principle, that such a principle can be successfully applied to Dante's texts as to any ancient text according to this fourth option, and that this requires a certain condition to be met: that the text be considered in its capacity as *for me* and *for you*. In other words, using the categories of history and non history I want to explore what it would mean for an historical text to become relevant again at the level of particularity when the questions arising for new readers are substantially different from the questions which the text had been written to answer.

The remainder of this essay falls into three parts. The first part rehearses the hermeneutic of the middle course, on which recent critics and readers have based a text's longevity, testing the viability of this hermeneutic to mediate between past and present. The test finds problems with middle course hermeneutics, which are presented at the conclusion of the first part. The second part offers a contrast between middle course hermeneutics and the medieval tradition of interpretation, drawing attention to Dante's own interpretive practices. The third section attempts to repair middle course hermeneutics and offers some general commentary on interpretive implications for critics of Dante's new life.

Throughout the essay I will use the analytical language and categories of Nicholas Adams, who following Peter Ochs explores, similar problems of authorial authority and interpretation in the context of scriptural reasoning.[4] I will also draw on Charles Taylor's framing of Romantic expressivism and the modern identity crisis to help highlight some important distinctions in how Dante's new life is interpreted.[5]

Questions ever ancient ever new: reconciling *difference*

In the introduction to her book *Holy Feast and Holy Fast*, Caroline Walker Bynum writes: "If readers leave this book simply condemning the past as peculiar, I shall have failed. But I shall have failed just as profoundly if readers draw direct answers to modern problems from the lives I chronicle."[6] Having set this two pronged criterion against which to benchmark her study of medieval literature, Bynum navigates a hermeneutical approach between yesterday and today, between writer and reader, where the moment of encounter is pregnant with existential possibility. Bynum's way of imagining how a medieval text might resonate with the modern reader is analogous to Paul Ricoeur's claim that the "world of the text" is completed by the "life of the reader."[7]

For Bynum, the implied possibility of reconciling the medieval past to the modern present in a way that is existentially valid should be of interest to any medievalist, above all to those for whom the text commands – or ought to command – contemporary attention. Inasmuch as the medieval text continues to be read in terms of its otherness (i.e., by which the past is discarded as peculiar), Bynum worries that its status in modernity may always be a little precarious – even if its mythical mystique elicits the kind of fascination at the level of cultural studies.

So how does someone usher Dante into the mainstream today without caricaturizing the poet or the age in which he lived? The ability of the text to engage and elicit a response from the reader means having to bridge an incontrovertible historical chasm. For Catherine Brown, the stringency in literary studies demanded by positivism – the emphasis on being factual which would reiterate the vastness of the chasm between 'him' and 'us' – cannot but treat the reader with suspicion. The attitude of having "to get the text objectively right," of having "to treat it as a sole and ultimate authority," of having "to legitimate our reading solely by the text," [...] "remains a potent assumption in scholarly debate despite its having been called into question several times in the last century."[8] According to another critic, Kathleen Biddick, positivism has wounded the medieval discipline. In *The Shock of Medievalism* she contends that the gap separating medieval cultures and ideologies from modern ones can be bridged only by tempering positivist proclivities in order that the traditional separation of past from present, of history from theory, of medieval studies from medievalism be deemphasized.[9] For Biddick, the drive for pure objectivity which is integral to the respectability of the discipline should not ban a reader's imaginative interaction with the text.

Just when the recession of the positivist tide seems to hold promise of new life for medieval texts, Singleton's refrain – that the truth of Dante's fiction is that it is not fiction – returns to confound interpreters.[10]

That Dante should have anything to offer today's reader cannot be taken for granted. Such a claim, as William Franke points out, has to be placed *en face* of a claim out of its past, and this is no small task. If we accept at this early stage that questions of meaning are among the most searching moral concerns of our time – they are the locus of the most important evaluations of our lives – then the query of *how* Dante remains important today is really one of how he helps moderns broach new concerns. These concerns, Charles Taylor points out, turn on questions of meaning and identity:

> There are questions about how I am going to live my life which touch on the issue of what kind of life is worth living, or what kind of life would fulfill the promise implicit in my particular talents, or the demands incumbent on someone with my endowment, or of what constitutes a rich, meaningful life – as against one concerned with secondary matters or trivia. These are issues of strong evaluation, because the people who ask these questions have no doubt that one can, following one's immediate wishes or desires, take a wrong turn and hence fail to lead a full life.[11]

On the importance we accord to questions of identity, Taylor's remarks are significant because they show that Dante (not unlike Augustine[12]) is well positioned to strike the modern reader's sensibilities owing to certain features of his narrative which are analogous to our questions of identity. The theme of pilgrimage in the *Commedia* is a preeminent example. As Angela Weisl has shown in *The Persistence of Medievalism,* the theme of pilgrimage is still familiar in contemporary culture through the variety of ways it conceives of modern *loca sancta* or by the ways it refers to life as a journey.[13] Many of Dante's readers today would not have it within their repertory to walk to Compostella or Canterbury from a distant village in order to seek a papal indulgence, and yet the peregrinal metaphor endures in modernity, though variously transformed. The dark wood, the path abandoned, the journey from hell through purgatory and into heaven, the struggle against lust and the desire to love continue to be available as metaphors for the self-reflexive modern subject. They are familiar at least in North Atlantic Western world, which is the world of Dante's inheritance as well as of Dante's sources, including Plato and Augustine in this connection, from whom the posture of self-reflection was learned.

The many points of intersection between Dante's age and our own were drawn out by Iannucci in *Already and Not Yet: Dante's Eschatological Anxiety.* Dante's resonance in modern times, according to Iannucci, cannot be isolated from his experience of exile, from his stance against history and the chaos of the world, and from the clairvoyance with which he redresses the moral void in the *civitas* during the eclipse of the two lights, Empire and Church.[14] Each of these Dantean moments has a modern analogue: in place of exile, modernity has the dislocation of the Self; world chaos translates into social injustice, fear of terrorism, economic crisis; and the eclipse of the two suns is a metaphor for institutional failure. Moreover, all of *Inferno* 1.1-16 has been read in contemporary criticism as a parallel to the image of modern man or woman in the grips of an appalling spiritual crisis, wherein "the world loses altogether its spiritual contour, nothing is worth doing, the fear of a terrifying emptiness, a kind of vertigo, or even a fracturing of our world and body-space."[15] Dante speaks to these problems, according to Iannucci's article, even though his spiritual crisis was different from the modern one. Iannucci is deliberate in his choice of words when he writes concerning Dante's *eschatological* anxiety and not Dante's *existential* anxiety. The careful use of terms owes to much more than a perspicacious sense of historical difference. What distinction is being marked here?

The modern identity-crisis would not have been comprehensible to Dante.[16] His spiritual crisis was the prospect of irretrievable exile and divine condemnation; the meaning of the universe was never in question for him. One leaves the *Commedia* with the sense that Dante's quest was undertaken to restore his sense of personal integrity and to challenge his contemporaries to undertake the same task. Of course, Dante framed this quest differently: his was a journey to truth on which he was drawn by Divine Love (rather than by a personal sense of mission); his was the experience of being reoriented in order that he might love (rather than lust); his journey was at the service of a fuller expression of human life through communion (rather than a quest to transcend the hurly burly). Can any of these particularities of Dante's tale be discounted as sources of repair today? Iannucci does not seem to think so. At the dawn of the new millennium he looks to Dante's *Commedia* as a deep source of repair for today. The life of the reader is completed by the life of the text. And yet the precise way a text can be said to complete the life of its readers needs spelling out a little. I shall attempt to clarify this notion below.

But first there is another point of view which needs to be distinguished from Iannucci's; that which grounds the text's renewed capacity for meaning in its correspondence with universal truth claims, i.e., claims which can be known outside the text. On this account, while it would be impossible to foreclose on the foreignness that lies between Dante's age and our own, his decision to make spiritual crisis the topic of his poetry – his *own* crisis – is not, to borrow from Paul Ricoeur's definition of myth, "a logical operator between any propositions whatsoever, but involves propositions which point towards limit situations, towards the origin and the end, towards death, suffering and sexuality."[17] On the Ricoeurean account, the text's longevity drives less from getting the literal meaning right than exploring how it speaks to universal concerns. New life, it follows, refers to representations of the text. But in what sense can a text said to be "living" if it comes down to its readers as a representation? Whereas historical approaches pick out the text over the reader, and non historical approaches privilege the reader over the text, the Ricoeurean hermeneutic posits equivalency between reader and text on the basis of a common ground of universals.

It is not clear how such equivalency might be established. At any rate, Dante posits an alternative hermeneutic: reader and text are not the same but inseparable and related in complex ways, and are still able to be distinguished. The longevity of the text has to do with matters turning on why and how it is used by a community of interpreters who privilege it as a matter of correspondence with a tradition. This idea recurs to Iannuicci's investigations into modern adaptations of Dante's works.

Analogy and the *accessūs* commentary tradition

According to scholastic theologians such as Thomas Aquinas, actual existence could be known either from experience or inferred from another actuality. So while God could not be known to humans in their terrestrial condition (i.e., since the essence of God is unknown to the human mind), his existence could be inferred on the proposition that he exists, which is by considering God's effects. The possibility of making such inferences relies on the possibility of analogy: the bringing of distinct terms into relation with each other for the purpose of clarification without assuming equivalency.

The most striking feature of any knowledge grasped analogically is its reliance on interpretation. All analogies are he product of interpretation. The use of one term to grasp another relies on the genius of a poet, which is both a matter of intellectual ability and certain habits of thought which enable kinds of reasoning to take place. In order for an analogy to work the terms must be distinguishable, yet inseparable and related in complex ways. To some extent, analogical inferences are the basis of the *accessūs* commentary tradition of the late-medieval period. According to the *accessūs* tradition, scriptural exegetes shift their focus from the divine author to human agency to elucidate the meaning of the text. As Alasdair Minnis explains: "Although technically subservient to the literal sense of Scripture, these writers were supposed to have acted personally and with a measure of independence...."[18]

Dante himself practices an interpretive programme which is in line with the *accessūs* tradition. Thus, in *Inferno* IX, Dante addresses the following comments to his reader:

> O voi ch'avete li'ntelletti sani
> mirate la dottrina che s'asconde
> sotto il velame de li versi strani.[19]

> (O you of sound mind,
> consider the teaching that is hidden
> behind the veil of these strange verses.) [20]
> (*Inf.*, IX, 61-63)

Similarly, in *Purgatorio* VIII, Dante invites the reader to peer beneath the subtle veil of the text to see the truth:

> Aguzza qui, lettor, ben li occhi al vero,
> che 'l velo è ora ben tanto sottile,
> certo che 'l trapassar dentro è leggiero.

> (Here, reader, set your gaze upon the truth,
> for now the veil is drawn so thin
> that piercing it is surely easy.)[21]
> (*Purg.*, VIII, 19-21)

Dante's texts were written as analogies for certain truth claims. And yet he invites his reader to be the interpreter of the hidden meaning in his verse.[22] The interpreter's task, then, is to explicate the truth. The process may sound circular, but in reality what it describes is continuous. Each successive attempt at interpretation renews the text's original capacity for meaning. It is significant, moreover, that the reader of sound mind who peers beneath the subtle veil to reach the bedrock of truth acts with care. In *Vita Nuova* 29.4, when Dante concludes his excursus on the number nine, he enjoins the reader with the following task: *Forse ancora per più sottile persona ci vederebbe in ciò più sottile ragione; ma questa è quella ch'io ne veggio, e che più mi piace.* ("Perhaps someone more subtle than I could find a still more subtle explanation, but this is the one which I see and which pleases me the most").[23] The solicitation of a subtler reader capable of giving a more subtle *ragione* is unsettling for readers who seek to break away from the text's particularity. But even Dante who invites other points of view has as his principal goal the elucidation of a truth of which he is not the author. Of what then is Dante the author? Of the analogies by which the truth is grasped.

But the term "subtler" as it applies to the creation of analogies is still vague and cries out for further determination. Is Dante gesturing at certain precise limits by which to circumscribe the interpretive exercise he inaugurates? If so, where are these limits prescribed? To answer these questions I have found it helpful to consult Dante's more technical descriptions of interpretation.

The determination of "subtle reading" can be calibrated by grasping the interpretive patterns used by Dante which give content to his interpretive terminology. Albert Ascoli has ventured to analyze Dante's interpretive vocabulary and has drawn some conclusions about modern interpretation.[24] The terms which fall under Ascoli's etymological scrutiny are: 1) *agens,* from the *Epistle to Cangrande*; 2) *autore,* from the *Convivio*; and 3) *avientes* and *actor*, respectively, from *De vulgari eloquentia (DVE)*.

First, concerning *agens*: In the *Epistle to Cangrande* when Dante is called an *agens* and not an *auctor,* or an "efficient cause," the writer prevents Dante from being confounded with the authority of the classical *auctores*, or the human authors of the Bible – and this despite the fact that Dante's participation in the *accessūs* tradition could suggest otherwise.

Second, concerning *autore*: In the *Convivio* Dante's reference to *autore* can be linked to the prestige etymology of *autentin*, i.e., "one worthy of *fede e obbedienza.*"[25] Dante, however, does not attach his authorial authority even to this sense, but rather to another sense derived from *aveio* – a marginal etymology underscoring a poetic sensibility in the artist's capacity "to bind words in verse."

Third, concerning *avientes* and *actor*: In *De vulgare eloquentia* Dante sees himself, the poet, not only as a "binder of words" (*avientes* in *DVE*, II, i, I), but also as an *actor* (*DVE* II, viii), deriving from *agere*, which Ascoli translates as "the human agent who is the *maker* of artifacts, a fabricator, rather than a timeless guarantor of faith-compelling truth or impersonal channel of power that must be obeyed."[26]

Ascoli shows that Dante's authorial authority progresses ever more assertively from the literal conveyor of truth claims to the authority of the poet-artist as fabricating poet. Following Minnis he writes, "[Dante] is most autonomous and god-like, most proleptic of the Renaissance author-God to come."[27]

Ascoli's description of the Dantean *actor* will strike some readers as consonant with Taylor's description of the Romantic expressivist: "the human agent who is the maker of artifacts, a fabricator, rather than a timeless guarantor of faith-compelling truth or impersonal channel of power that must be obeyed."[28] For Taylor, the man to whom we are yoked through a definition of art that is "no longer defined mainly by imitation, by *mimēsis* of reality, but understood more in terms of creation" is ostensibly of Romantic provenance.[29] According to Ascoli, by adopting the authority of the creator, Dante acts as an agent of a "much larger transformation of culture and of the place of individual persons within culture, one which surely gives rise to Petrarch, 'the first modern man,' but to many others, less famous, as well."[30]

The formulation of Dante's poetic practice, particularly in the terms of the poet-artist or creator genius, is proleptic not only of the Renaissance author-God to come, but of the Romantic expressivist to come; and of Johann Gottfried von Herder, in particular, from whom expressivism received one of its earliest articulations: "to heroize the artist, to see in his or her life the essence of the human condition, and to venerate him or her as a seer, the creator of cultural values."[31] Herder's expressivism, elaborated by other poets and writers, comes down to moderns as artistic self-creation: "If we become ourselves by expressing what we're about, and if what we become is by hypothesis original, not based on the pre-existing, then what we express is not an imitation or the pre-existing either, but a new creation."[32]

Mindful both of the requirements of late-medieval exegetical practice and the danger of reading Dante anachronistically, Ascoli makes sure to balance his Romantic-sounding conclusions with the recognition of Dante as *scriba Dei*: a designation which required the poet to acknowledge his human fallibility and his ultimate reliance on divine inspiration for his artistic creation. Thus, in *Purgatorio* XXIV, 52-54, Dante writes: "quando / amor mi spira, noto, e a quel modo / ch'e' ditta dentro vo significando." (I am one who, when Love inspires me, takes note and, as he dictates deep within me, so I set it forth.) The medieval recurrence to Divine Assistance does put into question the temptation to read Romantic expressivism into Dante's text. On the historical reading, the sources of Dante's inspiration are too easily put aside on account of their particularity; once acknowledged, they seem to go no further in interrogating the interpreter's Romantic proclivities. Ascoli is not representative of the Romantic interpreter, but the invocation he finds in Dante to act as an *actor*, where *actor* is understood as creator, is far from any positivist deferral to pre-existing meaning.

Reframing the problem

Perhaps it is very much on account of this Romantic approximation that Dante resonates with his modern readers. The expressivist connection registers with the Pre-Raphaelites and Dante Gabriel Rossetti, for example, and with the modernists, such as Ezra Pound, Evelyn Waugh, T.S. Eliot, and Samuel Beckett, as well as with more recent popularists such as Seamus Heaney, Rolando Perez, and Daniel Halpern. In each instance a reading is possible according to Iannucci above: the life of the reader is completed by the life of the text. Does that mean, in light of the accessus tradition, that we may be content with saying that Dante's hermeneutic offers a very modern program of interpretation through which subjective projections are not without warrant, and truth is unveiled in layers through his uses of allegory? I think so, but not without clarifying the role interpreter, because at this juncture the danger is to carry the narrative through the negation of all horizons of meaning. As Franke notes, when contermporary readers explore pragamatic applications of Dante's text, it is tempting "to embrace hermeneutics as the good news of a radical and irreparable breaking away from any transcendental standpoint beyond historical consciousness."[33] What we really need is to learn from Dante: "We stand to understand our own interpretive reality," Franke writes, "by heeding the phenomenon of interpretation revealed with a certain primordial wholeness in Dante's poem. His belief in eternal truth lies beyond, not shy of, the 'revelation' of historical contingency, and specifically of the historicity of the truth, which has had so great an impact on the present age that no recovery from this insight – blinding like all insight – seems yet to be in sight."[34]

What phenomenon of interpretation does Dante reveal with a certain primordial wholeness? Franke retrieves Dante's interpretive programme from the story of Paolo and Francesca in *Inferno* 5. According to Franke, Francesca's recitation of her personal narrative stirs her lustful desire for Paolo, because it anticipates by its self-referential goal the solipsism which is behind all sinful acts. Carrying this analogy further, Franke argues that unrestrained literary interpretations, because they are similarly self-referential (i.e., disengaged from author and history) are tantamount to Francesa's solipsism; they are turned inwardly and, therefore, are a variation on the theme of self-love against which Dante polemicises.[35] If I am reading Franke correctly – both literally and in the pattern of his interpretation of *Inferno* V – I take the matter of interpretation to presuppose two movements: the need to go beyond the plain meaning of the text and, in so doing, not evacuating the text of its particularities. I take the matter similarly with Minnis when he states that in the *accessūs* tradition the medieval exegete was "expected to act with a measure of independence." In other words, "independence," as Minnis uses it here, has a meaning other than "a radical and irreparable breaking away from any transcendental standpoint beyond historical consciousness." But how is "independence" or "going beyond the plain meaning of the text without evacuating it of its particulars" not a vague statement? If subjective projections are not without warrant, how are they to be framed so as to allow the truth of Dante's text to be unveiled in layers through his uses of allegory?

Reframing the answer

This question is not a paper doubt. For starters, it interrogates the interpretive practices which are at work right across the humanities. Secondly, more pertinent to the present discussion, it draws attention to a text's renewability in terms of its use by an interpretive community, as opposed to its *a priori* superiority over others. A text's capacity for renewal, on this account, concerns a method of reading that is formally, when not materially, analogous to scriptural interpretation. This method is one way to answer the question above. There are others as well.

Merely "representational" versions of an ancient text, while they may be interesting, as a foreign language is interesting, are not enough to warrant the designation "new life." A "living text," in contrast to the "represented text," is one that is used to answer real questions, irritations, even sufferings arising with real people; it concerns, to quote Adams, "how an actual body of texts functions as a deep source of repair for actual bodies of people." There are those who have adapted Dante's texts for twentieth century literature and cinema to probe some of the most searching moral questions of our time. The uses of his text for this purpose – whether the manifestation is philosophical, poetic, cinematic, artistic, or otherwise – is indeed generative of "new life" and not merely representation.

Now the interpretive dilemma raised by Franke, which recurs to the modern status of the *accessūs* tradition, concerns the question of how to mediate the tension between the interpreter's subjective projections, on the one hand, and the authority of authorship, on the other. There are some who have tried to separate interpreter and text, as we saw above, in the case of non-historical and historical interpretations. There are others who have merged the interpreter and the text into an amorphous whole, as we also saw above, in the attempt to deemphasize difference. And yet none of these ways of reading Dante has offered a satisfactory account of how to go beyond the plain meaning of the text while not evacuating it of its particularities, as Iannucci and Franke maintain.

I want to suggest, following Peter Ochs, that the crux of such an interpretive dilemma concerns how to identify the *for me* and *for you* qualification of interpretive propositions.[36] To spell this out a little, I will refer to the discussion of Ochs's *Pierce, Pragmatism, and the Logic of Scripture* in Nicholas Adams's seminal article "Reparative Reasoning" (450-51), leaving interested readers to probe Ochs's text on their own.

The main issue concerns "intuitions." Adams frames the matter as follows: "Intuitions are solutions to problems that flash into the inquirer's mind with the force of inevitability. [...] They are the indispensable moment of spontaneity – uncaused and unbound by rules – that brings a train of thought to a temporary close. Intuitions are well and good." But the intuitions we have concerning a problem can be different, not to mention incommensurable, with another person's intuitions about the same problem. A logical approach to such a dilemma calls attention to "the relation between being satisfied with one's own thinking and a noticeable uncertainty regarding how others think."[37] What happens, Adams wonders, in the case of rival intuitions?

There are those who are profoundly skeptical of the reliability of intuitions to determine a correct course of action. They turn to supposedly harder facts for certainty about how they should act. There are others who seek to confirm their intuitions by consulting authoritative figures in a tradition.

According to Adams, Ochs' understanding of intuitions follows a quite different pattern. Intuitions are intermediary solutions to problems that arise, not the terminus of investigation concerning how to resolve the problem. "Moreover, your intuitions are not my intuitions. Your axioms are not my axioms. Your hypotheses are not my hypotheses." The corollary is as follows:

An intuition is a response to a problem. If you do not have that problem then my intuition, which is a response to that problem, has limited significance for you. A problem is a sign that a system of axioms is in crisis. What I expected to see, I did not see. At least one of the practices I take as axiomatic may need to be questioned. In a tradition some axioms are inviolate; others are debatable. If a system of axioms is in crisis, then it is one of the debatable axioms that needs to be converted into an hypothesis and then tested. What is inviolate in my tradition may not be inviolate in your tradition. The axioms we are prepared to convert into hypotheses may be different. In sum: What is axiomatic for me may be hypothetical for you. What is hypothetical for me may be axiomatic for you.

Let me apply this account of intuitions to the question of Dante's new life and at the same time draw this paper to a close with an explication of its methodological implications for criticism. In doing so, it will become evident that "new life" refers to the *for me* and *for you* qualifications of textual propositions.

Dante's "new life" in the twentieth century arises from a problem; namely, that the metaphysical axioms on which Dante's poem is constructed are today in crisis. These axioms range from propositions about sin and salvation to love and the Great Chain of Being. Unless you share some concern in how these propositions are articulated, how a commentator or film producer or painter interprets them will be of limited interest to you. Some axioms of Dante's works are inviolate, others are debatable. For instance, one could argue that Dante's stance concerning ecclesiastical corruption is inviolate, while Dante's stance on human sexuality is debatable. It is the latter type of axiom, the one which is debatable, that interpreters convert into hypotheses and test. The axioms that we are prepared to convert into hypotheses differ for different readers. What is hypothetical for Theodolinda Barolini may be axiomatic for Michele Barbi; what is hypothetical for Michele Barbi might be axiomatic for Theodolinda Barolini. Several factors come into play with the interaction of multiple traditions, including the differences in intuitions, axioms, and hypotheses. The cluster of these factors are the *for me* and *for you* qualifications of interpretative propositions.

The implications for interpretive methodology are twofold. In the case of the critic, something of ethnographical attentiveness is called for; namely, investigating interpretations at the level of questions asked and answers given, rather than attending only to the varieties of interpretation given. In the case of the interpreters themselves, what renews a text is not its original power of disclosure, as Ricoeur maintains, implying the need of privileged access to meaning, but the actual practices of interpretation performed by a community. As a result, a text like the *Commedia* acquires new life not as a generic answer to every problem conceivable, but as a response to a particular problem that arises in an actual body of people; and the answer given is not a positivist application of the text to a new problem, but is reflective of a pattern of repair learned from the *Commedia* itself. The *Commedia* is itself the logic of repair. Each expression of Dante's new life, then, attempts to bring out the pattern of repair in a manner suited to the problem, irritation, or suffering it seeks to address.

Conclusion

Nicholas Adams concludes his article, "Reparative Reasoning," with a quotation from Peter Ochs regarding scriptural pragmatism, which could preface any consideration of what it means for a community to treat an ancient text as new. At the risk of relying too heavily on Adams (as I have already done), I would like to conclude with the same quotation, which reminds Adams of the Preface of the Saint John's Gospel.

> The world of experience is served by a finite set of common-sense beliefs, and there are terrible occasions when this world breaks down and common sense is confounded. There is more than *this* world, however: for scriptural pragmatists there are resources *out* of this world for correcting the inadequacies of this world. The source of correction is of this world in the sense that it is written in the language of this world, but it is not only from this world. It is written in texts whose plain sense belongs to everyday language and respects the rules of common sense but which, to the attentive reader, also displays certain errors and vaguenesses that cannot be resolved within the rules of common sense and the terms of everyday language. Discomforted by what appear to be the text's burdens, the attentive reader is stimulated into a process of corrective reading … [yet] as the process of reading continues, the very text that gives rise to the discomfort also gives rise to an unexpected sense that, while as yet inapparent, a solution is already available.[38]

Notes

[1] William Franke, "Reader's Application and the Moment of Truth" in *Dante: Contemporary Perspectives*, ed. Amilcare A. Iannucci (Toronto: University of Toronto Press, 1997) 259-80 (see 259).

[2] John A. Scott, *Dante's Political Purgatory* (Philadelphia: University of Pennsylvania Press, 1996).

[3] See Rolando Perez, *The Electric Comedy* (New York: Cool Grave Press, 2000).

[4] See especially Nicholas Adams, "Reparative Reasoning" in *Modern Theology*, 24:3 (July 2008). See Peter Ochs, *Peirce, Pragmatism, and the Logic of Scripture* (Cambridge: Cambridge UP, 1998).

[5] See especially Charles Taylor, *The Malaise of Modernity* (1991; Toronto: House of Anansi Press, 2003), and *Sources of the Self: The Making of Modern Identity* (Cambridge, MA: Harvard UP, 1989). See *A Secular Age* (Cambridge, MA: Harvard UP, 2007).

[6] Caroline Walker Bynum, *Holy Feast and Holy Fast: The Religious Significance of Food to Medieval Women* (Berkeley: University of California Press, 1987): 9.

[7] "History and Fiction Together," Karl Simms, *Routledge Critical Thinkers: Paul Ricoeur*, (London: Routledge, 2003): 94-8.

[8] Catherine Brown, "In the Middle," *Journal of Medieval and Early Modern Studies*, 30.3 (2000): 558. See Mary Carruthers, *The Book of Memory: A Study of Memory in Medieval Culture* (Cambridge: Cambridge University Press, 1990): 164.

[9] Cathleen Biddick, *The Shock of Medievalism* (Durham: Duke University Press, 1998): 3.

[10] Charles Singleton, "The Irreducible Dove" in *Comparative Literature* 9 (1957): 124-35 (see 129).

[11] Charles Taylor, *Sources of the Self*, 14.

[12] I am gesturing broadly at a connection to be drawn between Dante's use of the confessional genre and Augustine's *Confessions*, as also between Augustine's *Confessions* and Descartes turn to the self, and, it follows, between Dante's confessional genre and his connection to modern sensibilities on questions of selfhood and identity.

[13] Angela Jane Weisl, *The Persistence of Medievalism: Narrative Adventures in Contemporary Culture* (New York: Palgrave Macmillan, 2003).

[14] Amilcare A. Iannucci, "Already and Not Yet: Dante's Eschatological Anxiety" in *Dante for the New Millennium*, ed. Teodolinda Barolini and H. Wayne Storey (New York: Fordham University Press, 2003): 334-48 (see esp. 334).

[15] Charles Taylor, *Sources of the Self*, 18.

[16] See Charles Taylor, *Sources of the Self*, 16: "One of the most important ways in which our age stands out from earlier ones concerns [...] A set of questions [...] which turn around the meaning of life and which would not have been fully understandable in earlier epochs. Moderns can anxiously doubt whether life has meaning, or wonder what its meaning is. However philosophers may be inclined to attach these formulations as vague or confused, the fact remains that we all have an immediate sense of what kind of worry is being articulated in these words."

[17] Paul Ricoeur, "What is a text?," 161.

[18] Alasdair J. Minnis, *Medieval Literary Theory and Criticism, c. 1100-c. 1375: The Commentary-Tradition*, (Oxford: The Clarendon Press, 1991): 3-4: "Twelfth-century exegetes were interested in the author mainly as a source of authority. But in the thirte-

enth century, a new type of exegesis emerged, in which the focus had shifted from divine author to human author of Scripture… Once the suggestion had been made that theology might be basically affective and in some deep sense 'poetic,' no theologian could avoid considering those aspects of poetics and rhetoric which Alexander of Hales and his successors had deemed appropriate to the subject. Here, then, is the late medieval version of 'the Bible as literature.'"

[19] Georgio Petrocchi, ed. *La Divina Commedia* 2nd ed. rev., vols 1-4 (1966-67; Florence: Le Lettere, 1994). All subsequent quotations of the *Commedia* are from this edition.

[20] English: Robert Hollander and Jean Hollander, *Inferno* (New York: Doubleday, 2000).

[21] English: Robert Hollander and Jean Hollander, *Purgatorio* (New York : Doubleday, 2003).

[22] See L. Jenaro MacLennan, "Autocomentario en Dante y comentarismo latino" in *Vox Romana* 19 (1960): 82-123.

[23] Michele Barbi, ed. *La Vita Nuova* (Firenze: Bemporad, 1932). English translation by Mark Musa, *Vita Nuova* (Oxford: Oxford University Press, 1992).

[24] Albert Russell Ascoli, "Access to Authority: Dante in the Epistle to Cangrande" in *Seminario Dantesco Internazionale / International Dante Seminar*, vol. 1, ed. Zygmunt Barański (Florence: Le Lettere, 1997), 309-52.

[25] See Albert Russell Ascoli, "The Vowels of Authority (Dante's *Convivio* IV.vi.3-4)," *Discourses of Authority in Medieval and Renaissance Literature*, eds. Kevin Brownlee and Walter Stephens (Hanover, N.H.: University Press of New England, 1989), 23-46.

[26] Albert Russell Ascoli, "Access to Authority: Dante in the Epistle to Cangrande," 337-338. Italics are Ascoli's.

[27] Albert Russell Ascoli, "Access to Authority: Dante in the Epistle to Cangrande," 338.

[28] Albert Russell Ascoli, "Access to Authority: Dante in the Epistle to Cangrande," 338.

[29] Charles Taylor, *The Malaise of Modernity*, 62.

[30] Albert Russell Ascoli, "Access to Authority: Dante in the Epistle to Cangrande," 338.

[31] I borrow the definition from Charles Taylor, *The Malaise of Modernity,* 62. I am drawing on Taylor at this point to formulate an account of the historical shift in the nineteenth century which characterizes the Romantic movement, and which underpins modern conceptions of the self and the idea of authenticity as an act of artistic self-creation. Cf. *The Malaise of Modernity*, 62: "Let's look a bit closer at this case, which has become a paradigm for us, where I discover myself through my work as an artist, through what I create. My self-discovery passes through a creation, the making of something original and new. I forge a new artistic language – new way of painting, new metre or form of poetry, new way of writing a novel – and through this and this alone I become what I have it in me to be. Self-discovery requires *poiēsis*, making."

[32] Charles Taylor, *The Malaise of Modernity,* 62.

[33] William Franke, "The Reader's Application and the Moment of Truth," 276. See Donald Marshall, "Truth, Tradition, and Understanding," *diacritics* 7 (1977): 70-77.

[34] William Franke, "Reader's Application and the Moment of Truth," 276-277.

[35] William Franke, "Reader's Application and the Moment of Truth," 276.

[36] I am following closely the discussion on Ochs' concept of intuitions in Nicholas Adams, "Reparative Reasoning," 450-51.

[37] Adams, 447.

[38] Peter Ochs, *Peirce, Pragmatism, and the Logic of Scripture* (Cambridge: Cambridge University Press, 1988): 319; quoted in Nicholas Adams, "Reparative Reasoning," 457.

Roberto Fedi (Università per Stranieri di Perugia)

Dante in Petrarch: Some reflections on Rerum Vulgarium Fragmenta, 36

1. Throughout the history of literary criticism, Sonnet 36 of the *Rerum vulgarium* has been interpreted in a variety of ways: ranging from the biographical – or even clinical – approach to a more reasonable metaphorical one[1]. Let us begin with the poem itself:

> S'io credesse per morte essere scarco
> del pensiero amoroso che m'atterra,
> colle mie mani avrei già posto in terra
> queste membra noiose, et quello incarco;
> ma perch'io temo che sarrebbe un varco
> di pianto in pianto, et d'una in altra guerra,
> di qua dal passo anchor che mi si serra
> mezzo rimango, lasso, et mezzo il varco.
> Tempo ben fôra omai d'avere spinto
> l'ultimo stral la dispietata corda
> ne l'altrui sangue già bagnato et tinto;
> et io ne prego Amore, et quella sorda
> che mi lassò de' suoi color' depinto,
> et di chiamarmi a sé non le ricorda.

> [If I thought that by death I would be lightened
> of this amorous care that weighs me down,
> by now, by my own hand I would have buried
> these loathsome limbs of mine and that weight too;
> but since I fear that it would be a passage
> from grief to grief, from one war to another,
> on this side of the pass still closed to me
> I half remain (oh grief) and half cross over.
> And it is high time that the merciless cord
> release now from its bow the final arrow,
> already wet and stained with others' blood;
> and I beg Love for this and that deaf one
> who left me painted shades of her own color
> and who forgets to call me to herself.]

As we can see this is a rather typical text. This same metric pattern (ABBA, ABBA, CDC, DCD) can be found in the *Canzoniere*. In regard to the quartets, the pattern appears in 313 of the 317 sonnets; in regards to the tercets, the pattern appears in 113 sonnets. Together with the ABBA, ABBA, CDE, CDE of the sonnet that precedes it (35), it is the most frequent pattern found in the book. More complicated is the system of rhymes, and even more so, that of assonances: if the *aequivocatio* of 5:8 is almost self evident, more subtle and almost undetectable is the unraveling of assonances in A, B and D (*-arco:-erra:-orda*). And in addition, it must be noted that A and D have the same vowels, although they are inverted. Furthermore, *scarco: incarco* (1,4) and *atterra: terra* (2,3) are "*rime derivate*"; *spinto: depinto* (9, 13) and *corda: ricorda* (10,14) are "*rime ricche.*"

After all, it is not much different from the usual refined Petrarchan metric repertoire, with a few intra-textual references that may or may not be intentional (the pair *atterra: terra* was already present in 26, 1:4, but inverted and disguised as a sort of *aequivocatio*: "a terra":"s'atterra," which is based on a clear phonosyntactic reduplication). According to Santagata[2], this sonnet forms a diptych with the one preceding it, *Solo et pensoso*. The second verse of this poem serves as the link between the two sonnets (*pensiero*) for it echoes the *incipit* of *Solo et pensoso*, and "illustrates two of the most pernicious effects of love's passion." According to Bettarini[3], the sonnet "addresses the subject of 'voluntary death' understood as the ultimate projection of the polarized system in which the suffering lover lives." In his notes on the sonnet, Carducci succinctly states: "If he thought death to be the end of all suffering, he would have killed himself. Or else passion and sickness would have killed him! [4]" And then in a later addition: "Forn[aciari], acute observer that he was, did not consider this to be one of those typical pointless issues, but instead thought it touched on something meaningful. In his commentary on the 11th verse, he seems to believe it was composed after the Laura's death. However, considering the structure of the *Canzoniere*, it would rather appear to have been written after the recovery from the sickness mentioned in the previous sonnets[5]." It should be noted that the text certainly could not have been composed after September 1336, as Wilkins[6] has tried to show. Naturally, Carducci could not have known and much less Luigi Fornaciari. And thus, given the "structure" of rhymes in the book, Carducci's observation appears all the more noteworthy for it correctly and shrewdly rejects the hypothetical dating of "post 1348".

It is unproductive to focus on the flimsy hypotheses concerning Laura's illness – and here even Carducci agrees – for not only is it hard to link the *Canzoniere* to Petrarch's biography (except of course for the references to Laura's death or to his correspondence), but also because the text itself is of more interest than its historical context. In other words, for example, it would be more productive to inquire into the meaning of Leopardi's *Infinito* than it would to dwell upon the dates or specific occasions in which the young poet went for a walk on the Tabor Hill (*l'ermo colle*). It will suffice to say that Santagata[7] believes that the (presumed) sickness of Laura is related to the epidemic of the summer of 1334 (an "indemonstrable hypothesis," as the commentator himself notes), while Bettarini – rightfully so – maintains that: "the chronological reference to the epidemic of 1334 – which, according to the letter *Sen.* IX 2, was nothing more than a collective rash due to the Avignon heat – has been downgraded to an imaginary anecdote by Zingarelli, falling into the same category as the legend of Laura's 'illness' (as most recently argued by Santagata and Tonelli)[8]."

2. Even on the first reading, one can detect the separation that clearly divides, quite dramatically, verses 1-8 from 9-14, or in other words the quartets from the tercets. "The quartets," Bettarini notes, "carry the weight of obsession, with rhymes almost entirely derivative … or improper…, as an external manifestation of a thought that builds upon itself through variations," while the tercets "push the Petrarchan (and subsequently Leopardian) poetics of attenuation to the limit, as if the cryptic message of verse 7 were not enough to indicate death[9]." The two nuclei (quartet + quartet and tercet + tercet) also represent two conceptual moments that are distinct but follow each other in a logical sequence. Basically, as Antonio Marsand stated in a brief comment, the character-poet "knows that death cannot cure him from his suffering, and in spite of this he invokes it, tired of suffering[10]." Therefore, it is clear the text can be divided into two distinct parts, which from now on I will refer to as A and B.

The first thing to note is the strong *incipit* of both: *S'io credesse…* (A) and *Tempo ben fôra…* (B). If we venture to discover inter-textual elements, we will see that the first *incipit* refers, so to speak, to the past, while the second looks to the future (although here Petrarch functions only as a passive point of reference). Let us clarify this last point. The stylistic device, at once strong and memorable, becomes the *incipit* of a sonnet by Giovanni Della

Casa. In number XVI of his *Rime* we find "– Tempo ben fôra omai, stolto mio core[11]," a dialogue between the Poet and his Heart that is entirely carried out in the dramatic debate between what one should to do and what one wants to do, at the risk of appearing stupid. It is, in other words, a Petrarchan (and only Petrarchan) stylistic device utilized in a sonnet with strong existential tones and destined to endure in Petrarchan circles and even beyond the Petrarchan school. We will return to this point later.

More noteworthy, for our purposes, is the first *incipit*, together with the entire first part. Here the commentators[12] have noticed a clear Dantean influence from *Inferno*, XXVII, 61-65, the episode of Guido I of Montefeltro:

S'io credesse che mia risposta fosse
a persona che mai tornasse al mondo,
questa fiamma staria sanza più scosse;

ma però che già mai di questo fondo
non tornò vivo alcun, s'i' odo il vero,
sanza tema d'infamia ti rispondo […].

["If I thought my reply were meant for one
who ever could return into the world,
this flame would stir no more; and yet, since none –

if what I hear is true – ever returned
alive from this abyss, then without fear
of facing imfamy, I answer you.] [13]

This is the eighth circle, eighth *bolgia* in which the fraudulent counselors are held. Here Guido says: 'If I believed that my response was directed at a person that sooner or later were to return to the world of the living, this flame, in which I am hidden, would be still and silent; but since no one living returns from this abyss, as far as I know, I will talk to you without fear of being dishonored because of my damnation.'

Here Dante treats the damned with malice, as he sometimes does throughout the *Inferno*. For things in reality are exactly the opposite of what Guido believes; Dante will return to the world of the living, and the story of the Ghibelline count's sin will be told – that is, the fact that, after joining the Franciscans, he was a fraudulent counselor to Pope Boniface VIII ("il gran prete, a cui mal prenda!", v. 70; "Lo principe d'i novi Farisei", v. 85) (*cordigliero*, v. 67).

The entire passage is predicated on a hypothetical sentence that is true from Guido's point of view, while it is false from Dante's (and the reader's). In fact, while the premise ("S'io credesse che mia risposta fosse / a persona che mai tornasse al mondo", vv. 61-62) is real for Guido, for he believes he is speaking with a dead soul, it is actually false, given that the essence of Dante's journey lies in his return to the living, in order to recount his divine voyage through the three realms of the afterlife. It is therefore a dual truth, or better yet, a truth that contradicts appearances and thus fitting for a "fraudulent counselor," skilled in modifying reality and making it seem different from its essence. And not surprisingly, in the canto that precedes it, Ulysses was paying for his deception with the wooden horse, which also served a "duplicitous" function: seen by the Trojans as a gift to the gods, but in reality was a mechanism of death. Guido is punished in the same bolgia for having been duped by Boniface VIII, who had promised him preventative absolution for his fraudulent advice (vv. 100-111). The fraudulent counselor was, in turn, misled. Upon his death, although his soul was claimed by Saint Francis, a devil, one of the "black cherubs" (v. 113), drags him to hell as a fraudulent counselor (v. 116), uttering this famous tercet:

> ch'assolver non si può chi non si pente,
> né pentere e voler insieme puossi
> per la contradizion che nol consente»
> (vv. 118-120)

> [one can't absolve a man who's not repented,
> and no one can repent and will at once;
> the law of contradiction won't allow it]

Since we are in the canto dealing with fraud and dual truths – what one man believes to be true is not necessarily the only way of understanding reality. Moreover, it is impossible – given the elementary Aristotelian principle of non-contradiction – for anyone to desire something and its opposite at the same time (in this case to repent and the desire to sin). For this reason, the episode assumes a certain flavor of "sarcastic tragedy." It slips towards an "almost grotesque" ending, with the contrast between the Saint of Assisi and the so-called black cherub. The episode is "painted in the colors and techniques of the folkloric mystery" in which the devil has the last word, being a "logician and theologian," and is victorious in the face of an astonished Saint Francis. Here, evil has triumphed over good in a context in which truth is syntactically and rhetorically upturned.[14]

3. Let us now return to sonnet 36, which is strewn with Dantean references, in addition to the one we just discussed. The *war* of v. 6 (nearly synonymous with the preceding *cry)* recalls Dante's *Rime* 7, 62 and 43, 62 (it should be noted that the word also appears in *Inferno* XXVII three times: 38 and 86, and in 28 in rhyme position; the adjective of the *dispietata corda* (merciless string) hints at the "dispietata lima" (merciless file) of Love mentioned in the poem *Così nel mio parlar* from the *Rime petrose* (46, 22; but also in *Rime* 7, 1 and 45, 36), and the topical image of the bow of Love "seems to contain Dantean connotations,"[15] such as those of *Inferno* VIII 13 ("Corda non pinse mai da sé saetta") ["Bowstring has not thrust from itself an arrow"], and the *arrow* that is cast is *tinged* with blood like the infernal furies of *Inferno* IX 38 ("tre furïe infernal di sangue tinte") ["three infernal Furies flecked with blood"]; the final invocation of death recalls Dante's invocation of the *Donna Pietosa*, vv. 77-78 ("Vedi che si desideroso vegno / d'esser de' tuoi, ch'io ti somiglio in fede") ["See how I approach with such a desire / to be one of yours, for in faith we resemble one another].[16]

Dante's poetry is not only employed as a stylistic device, but is also the key to interpreting this sonnet. And it is not by chance that a *sui generis* Petrarchan such as Della Casa, who is not unaware of Dante, would adopt one of his key verses (v. 9) as the *incipit* of the dialogical sonnet we mentioned before, therefore exploiting its dramatic tones. The deception into which false counselor Guido falls is, once again, that of believing his premise to be true. But just the opposite is the case. Therefore his whole speech is predicated on a dramatic misrepresentation of reality: if I believed that you were alive, Guido basically says, I would not say anything; but since that is impossible, I will speak. The key to the text lies in the discrepancy between what the subject *believes* to be true and what in reality it actually *is*.

Thus let us now reread the sonnet—or at least the quartets (part A as we called it above). "If I believed," says the poetic *subject*, "that death was going to deliver me from the oppressive weight of this love, I would have already killed myself with my own hands, so that this weight would have been lifted from me"[17]; "but since I'm afraid that it would be only a matter of moving from one cry and torment to another,"[18] given that I am on this side of death and crossing to the other side is forbidden by divine law, I am suspended "between life and death."[19] The hypothetical sentence is technically irreproachable. It expresses the desire for death that the poet could achieve "by his own hands" (v. 3), that is to say, through suicide.[20]

It is a theme that is not infrequent in the *Rerum vulgarium*. It appeared three times prior to this and it will return in three more. Let us examine them in detail.

In sonnet 21 (*Mille fiate, o dolce mia guerriera*), the poet outlined the topic:

> Or s'io lo scaccio, et e' non trova in voi
> ne l'exilio infelice alcun soccorso,
> né sa star sol, né gire ov'altri il chiama,
> porria smarrire il suo natural corso [...]
> (vv. 9-12)

> [Now if I banish it, and it cannot
> find help from you in its unhappy exile,
> or live alone, or answer other callings.]

In other words, the poet is saying: if I do not banish my heart (which wants to come to you but you do not want it), and if you do not help it during its unhappy exile, since it cannot stand alone, nor go where other women call it, then it may sway from its natural course, which means to die or to voluntarily go astray, given that the verb "to sway" implies a sense of derangement from the natural course of things.

In canzone 23 (*Nel dolce tempo de la prima etade*), the *topos* returns, clearer and more dramatic:

> Morte mi s'era intorno al cor avolta,
> né tacendo potea di sua man trarlo,
> o dar soccorso a le vertudi afflitte;
> le vive voci m'erano interditte;
> ond'io gridai con carta e con incostro:

Non son mio, no. S'io moro, il danno è vostro. [...]
(vv. 95-100)

[Death had now wrapped itself around my heart,
and silence could not take it from her hands,
or give assistance to my hurting powers.
To use my spoken voice had been denied me
And so I shouted out with pen and paper;
"I'm not mine, no! If I die, it's your fault."]

In the great canzone of metamorphosis, the poet is transformed first
into a *stone* then into a *spring*, and cries his pain "with pen and paper," ac-
cusing the woman: "I'm no longer my own, but yours: therefore if I die, it's
your loss," as Leopardi explained.[21] Thus if the poet kills himself, the moral
loss will be the woman's, since by now he is completely and entirely hers.

It would seem to be a suicide by proxy, with Laura as the executioner.
Even more explicit in this escalation is the direct reference to death by his
own hand, found in the *coblas unissonans* canzone 29, where the obsessive
repetition of the rhymes underscores the desperation and almost inevitability
of the decisive choice:

Da me son fatti i miei pensier' diversi:
tal già, qual io mi stancho,
l'amata spada in se stessa contorse;
né quella prego che però mi scioglia,
ché men son dritte al ciel tutt'altre strade,
et non s'aspira al glorioso regno
certo in più salda nave. [...]
(vv. 36-42)

[My thoughts are now like strangers in my mind:
one driven like me once
had plunged the loving sword into herself;
but I do not beg her to set me free,
for other roads to heaven are less straight,
and one cannot hope for the realm of glory
in any ship that's stronger.]

It is as if the poet were saying: 'my thoughts are contradictory (in the
sense that they seem to contradict and clash with what I feel and want). It

already happened in the past that a woman, like me, overwhelmed by love's labors, killed herself; however, I don't ask that (because of this suffering) she (Laura) delivers me (from the bounds of love's passion), given that this passion is the safest road to gain salvation,' "and certainly, one cannot sail in search of paradise on a safer ship, in other words, a more robust and solid ship than that offered by this love."[22]

The real core of the issue is a lethal contradiction: on the one hand, the poet would like to follow the example of Virgil's Dido – who killed herself out of unrequited love. On the other hand, he feels compelled to love Laura even more.[23] It is a dilemma similar to that presented in the episode of *Inferno* XXVII where the black cherub dragged Guido to hell. In fact, one can at the same time wish for eternal salvation and suicide, but the alternative – that is, obtaining eternal salvation through *love's passion* – is difficult or impossible.

4. And this is how we arrive at sonnet 36, where the theme of suicide unfolds in a similar manner as that in the episode in Dante's *Inferno* XXVII. And here the allusion to Guido's speech becomes apparent; so evident, in fact, that one could call it a quotation rather than an allusion. That which Guido holds to be true, as we mentioned, is actually false, because his logical premises are false. If we apply the same reasoning to part A (the quartets) of sonnet 36 – and the connector "*s'io credessi… ma*" functions as a veritable indicator – we easily arrive at a new discovery. The hypothetical sentence should be read in the negative; the premise should be considered false. "If I were to believe that killing myself would cure my torment, I would do it; but since I'm afraid that it would only mean falling into a different torment, I chose not to act." In light of Guido's episode, this should be understood to mean: 'perhaps the premise is false and therefore death would truly be the end of all torments, the peace after such a long war.' And therefore, 'if I were to believe the premise, I would be wrong.'

Thus this sonnet exposes Petrarca's intentions of suicide, still very early in the *Canzoniere*, which has usually been characterized as "the book of a life" and a book of confessions. Furthermore, if we look at part B (the tercets) it is "superbly" clear (and here we quote the adverb from Bettarini)[24] how the poet insists on a funereal theme (the *arrow*, the *merciless string*),[25] on the theme of *blood* and that of a merciless death (*quella sorda*).

5. The theme of suicide is reiterated in three other texts, which are scattered across the collection according to a typically Petrarchan procedure. In these texts the suicidal thoughts are pushed even further. Let us consider canzone 71, *Perché la vita è breve* (vv. 42-45):

> Ma se maggior paura
> non m'affrenasse, via corta et spedita
> trarrebbe a fin questa aspra pena et dura;
> et la colpa è di tal che non à cura.

> [But if a greater fear
> did not stop me, a short and quicker way
> would end this suffering, bitter and hard –
> it is the fault of one who does not care.]

And again in the canzone 268, written after Laura's death (vv. 64-65):

> quel ch'Amor meco parla
> sol mi ritien ch'io non recida il nodo.

> [it is what Love tells me
> alone that will not let me cut the knot.]

And finally in sonnet 272 (vv. 7-8) the theme acquires a new dimension in which self-pity overcomes the fear of the afterlife:

> se non ch'i' ò di me stesso pietate,
> i' sarei già di questi pensier' fora.

> [if I did not take pity on myself,
> I would, by now, be free of all such thoughts.]

These verses refer back to the *incipit* of the section "in morte," vv. 1-2 of canzone 264, "I' vo pensando, et nel penser m'assale / una pietà sì forte di me stesso."

In this truly Petrarchan series (seven *loci*: certainly not a random number) sonnet 36 is the centerpiece, the hinge between the first and the last three poems. It is a fundamental text for the development of this theme, which we were able to interpret as it unfolded thanks to the Dante reference we analyzed. I would like to conclude with a final intuition of a numerological nature: if we add the two digits of 36 (3+6) we have 9; that is the same number we obtain if we add the two digits of canto 27 (2+7). If everything "holds together" in the *Canzoniere*, perhaps this is not the product of chance.

Notes

[1] I am thinking principally of the comments by M. Santagata, *Canzoniere* (Milan: Mondadori, 1996 and 2006), vol. I and R. Bettarini, *Canzoniere* (Turin: Einaudi, 2005), vol. I. In particular, Bettarini suggests (p. 193) that it is a "sonnet that the old commentators tie to the woman's in the book (pointing to XXXI-XXXIII) or to an illness the poet avoided (mentioned in verse 13). On the question of Laura's illness (though not with specific reference to this sonnet) see N. Tonelli, *"Linee di cultura medica per la lettura di Petrarca Rvf 47, 48, 49,"* *Per Leggere*, III, 2002, pp. 5-23. Drawing on A. Noferi's *L'esperienza poetica del Petrarca* (Florence: Le Monnier, 1962), p. 240, Santagata associates the sonnet and the one that precedes it (35: *Solo et pensoso*) to a passage of the *Secretum* in which Augustine admonishes Francesco about the devastating effects of love's passion: "Cogita nunc ex quo mentem tuam pestis illa corrupuit; quam repente [...] eo miseriam pervenisti [...] cum rerum omnium contemptus viteque odium et desiderium mortis; tristis er amor solitudinis atque hominum fuga"; F. Petrarca, *Secretum*, ed. E. Fenzi (Milan: Mursia, 1992), Book III, pp. 224-26. According to Santagata, sonnets 35 and 36 are articulated in reverse order from the passages of the *Secretum* cited above. The text of the *Canzoniere* cited in this essay is the version edited by Santagata (hereafter cited as Santagata). The same text is found in Bettarini's edition, however the notes are different (hereafter cited as Bettarini). English translations of Petrarch are drawn from Francesco Petrarch, *The Canzoniere, or Rerum vulgarium fragmenta*, trans. M. Musa (Bloomington: Indiana University Press, 1996).

[2] See Santagata.

[3] See Bettarini.

[4] F. Petrarca, *Le Rime di su gli originali*, with commentary by G. Carducci e S. Ferrari (Florence: Sansoni, 1899), new anastatic reprint with a preface by di G. Contini (Florence: Sansoni, 1960), p. 54 (henceforth this text will be cited as Carducci).

[5] Ibid.

[6] E.H. Wilkins, *The Making of the 'Canzoniere' and Other Petrarchan Studies* (Rome: Edizioni di Storia e Letteratura), 1951, pp. 89, 147-48.

[7] See Santagata's comment on sonnet 31.

[8] See Bettarini's comment on sonnet 31. The reference to N. Tonelli is "Petrarca, Properzio e la struttura del 'Canzoniere'," in *Rinascimento*, s. II, XXXVIII 1998, pp. 249-315: 287-89.

[9] See Bettarini for both citations.

[10] *Rime* del Petrarca secondo la lezione del Professor Antonio Marsand, vol. I (Padua: Minerva, 1829), p. 22. Marsand, of course, counted the poems in a different manner; for him, this is sonnet XXIII.

[11] G. Della Casa, *Le Rime*, ed. R. Fedi (Rome: Salerno Ed., 1978), tome I, p. 18. See also the commentary by G. Tanturli in his edition of the *Rime* (Parma: Fondazione P. Bembo/Ugo Guanda Editore, 2001), pp. 40941; see also S. Carrai in his edition of the *Rime* (Turin: Einaudi, 2003), pp. 46-48, esp. p. 46 for a brief reference to similar instances of this *incipit* in the sixteenth century.

[12] Santagata, *ad loc.*; Bettarini, *ad loc.* Oddly, Carducci overlooks this citation and mentions a different passage from Dante (*Inferno*, V 141), but only in regard to the verb ending in –*e* ("io venni men così com'io morisse"), and to other older instances regarding the question of Latin endings (Enzo and *Novellino*).

¹³ Dante Alighieri, *Commedia. Inferno*, ed. E. Pasquini and A. Quaglio (Milan: Garzanti, 1982), p. 333; see also the edition edited by A.M. Chiavacci Leonardi (Milano: Mondadori 'Meridiani', 1991), pp. 812-13. The English translations are by Allen Mandelbaum, *The Divine Comedy of Dante Alighieri: Inferno*. (New York: Bantam Books, 1980). For Dante's *Rime*, which will be referred to below, I have used the edition edited by G. Contini (Turin: Einaudi, 1965). The English versions of the *Rime* have been provided by the translators of this essay.

¹⁴ See A.Quaglio's comments on canto XXVII, p. 342. See also A.M. Chiavacci Leonardi, p. 822, notes at vv. 118-20.

¹⁵ See Santagata.

¹⁶ For the Dantean references, see also Santagata and Bettarini.

¹⁷ This is Leopardi's paraphrase, cited in Santagata.

¹⁸ This is Santagata's paraphrase.

¹⁹ This is the expression that Petrarch uses in 23, 89 ("mezzo tutto quel dì tra vivo et morto"). Drawing upon Fornaciari, Carducci notes: "it expresses everything that colloquially we call being half dead out of fear, out of pain, etc., and that Dante (*Inf.* XXXIV, 25) describes as, "I did not die, and I was not alive".

²⁰ As Santagata notes, the expression "colle mie man" recalls Guittone, *Lasso pensando quando*: "…ciò m'è guerra, – onde morria / de mie man" (vv. 9-10), and Davanzati, *La mia vita, poi ch'è*: "de le mie man' saronne micidiale" (v. 64).

²¹ Cited in Santagata.

²² See Santagata; the final paraphrase is Leopardi's.

²³ This too recalls Dante. See verses 36-38 of the Petrosa *Così nel mio parlar*: "con quella spada ond'elli ancise Dido, / Amore, a cui io grido / merzé chiamando, e umilmente il priego», which also have an echo in Petrarch's «né quella prego», v. 39.

²⁴ See Bettarini.

²⁵ In this regard, Carducci correctly explains: "I wish that the *merciless string* of death's bow would *push against me* the murderous *arrow*" (p. 54). Therefore love and death own the same bow, and "exchange one another's attributes". (Bettarini, comment *ad loc.*).

Sona Haroutyunian (Venice, Ca' Foscari University)

"The Homer of Modern Times": the Reception and Translation of Dante in the Armenian World

One of the masterpieces of world literature, the *Divine Comedy* has played such a role in the history of culture and civilization that it requires no introduction. We will therefore immediately begin by looking into how this rich heritage was received in Armenian culture, paying particular attention to its role and significance. We will then provide an overview of references to Dante and his works, focusing especially on the contributions of the Mekhitarist Fathers, and finally a third section will discuss Armenian translations of the *Commedia*.

I. The art of translation in the Armenian world

For Armenians, the art of translation is as ancient as literature itself and is considered highly prestigious. The "blessed" or holy translator—as he was called from the time the craft first began—is the bearer of a divine gift and grace which, thanks to assiduous, continuous work, culminates over time into experience and erudition. The Armenian Church is probably the only one in the world to have canonized its translators and dedicated a feast day to them. Called, appropriately enough, the "Eve of the Holy Translators,"[1] it offers a clear indication of how highly the art of translation is considered in this culture.

The 5th century was a crucial period in establishing this tradition. The principal events of this time are the invention of the Armenian alphabet, the revision of the liturgy, and the creation of an ecclesiastical and national literature. Three men are prominently associated with these innovations: *vardapet*[2] Mesrop Maštots[3], *Catholicos*[4] Sahak Part'ew (387), and King Vŕamšapuh (394).

The invention of the alphabet was the beginning of Armenian literature, and proved a powerful factor in uplifting the national spirit. During a single century, Armenian written culture developed greatly, reaching its glory in this century known in literature as The Golden Age. The principal genre of this age was historiography (Agat'angeghos, P'awstos Biwzand, Movsês Khorenats'i, Eghišê, Ghazar P'arpets'i), which up to now is considered to be the original source not only for Armenian history, but also for that of the neighboring nations. Among the developed branches of the literature of the 5th century were philosophy (Davit' Anyaght' [David the Invincible], Eznik Koghbats'i) and translation. The first book that was completely translated into Armenian was The Bible, which was regarded as a masterpiece and was known as the Queen of Translations.

From the 5th century on, the art of translation continued to be developed and became specialized in various schools, fulfilling cultural, cognitive and scientific purposes while transferring the knowledge of the world into Armenian. There began to be translated texts by Greek and Syriac authors such as Athanasius of Alexandria, Basil, Severian of Gabala, Eusebius of Caesarea, Ephraim of Syria, John Chrisostom, Gregory of Nazianzus, Gregory of Nyssa, Proclus, Dionysius Trax, Philo Judaeus, Porphyrus, Aristotle, Plato, and others. The loss of the Greek originals has given some of these versions a special importance; thus, the second part of Eusebius's *Chronicle*, of which only a few fragments exist in the original Greek, has been preserved in its entirety in Armenian.[5] These translations not only contributed to the development of the national culture, they also testify to the richness of Grabar, the Old Armenian language.

The tradition of translation was consolidated throughout the Middle Ages with the addition of Latin treatises by writers from the West such as Albertus Magnus and Thomas of Aquinas. It saw a period of resurgence starting in the early 18th century, thanks to the work of Abbot Mekhitar, who at the beginning of the 1700s founded the Congregation which would later bear his name: the Order of the Mekhitarists.[6] After a temporary stay in the Morea (1703-1715), the Congregation established itself permanently in Venice, giving life and new vitality to a vigorous cultural movement that benefited all Armenian people. It brought Armenian history and literature of the past into prominence; the language was renewed, raising it above the state of vernacular dialect; and finally, classical Greek and Roman literature was disseminated among Armenian speakers. The translations of numerous masterpieces of Greek and Latin antiquity lent authority to the Grabar language. Thanks to this gradual purification, both popular literature and literature in translation found a fertile ground for development, since without a "high" language with a literary value, neither this rich production of cultural publications nor creative works could have existed.

The Mekhitarist Congregation had its home in the Venetian lagoon, on the beautiful island of San Lazzaro, for over three centuries. The community has been wholly involved in initiating and promoting social and cultural activities, dedicating itself to the printing arts, founding and operating schools, and performing spiritual missions. The Congregation is widely recognized for its contribution to the rebirth of Armenian philology, literature, and culture in the early 19th century.

The island of San Lazzaro, or "of the Armenians", as it is called, is known around the world to scholars of Oriental studies as a Cultural Center and the "Armenian Academy of Sciences," the official title given to it by Napoleon.[7] Indeed, one of the main objectives of the Congregation was to create a new bridge between East and West to facilitate intellectual exchange. Wrapped in the strict silence of their cloisters, the Mekhitarist Fathers began their untiring labor of translating the works of the ancient Greeks and Romans and European masterpieces from the time the order was first established. This tradition was kept alive and renewed by the training of countless, excellent translators. Almost all of the immense work of translation was done in the nineteenth century under the combined influence of European Classical and Romantic literatures.

Owing to the guidance or example of the Classicist school, started by such outstanding translators as Fr. Vrt'anês Askêrean and Fr. Eghia Tovmachean, the esthetic taste and artistic awareness of an entire generation was honed and cultivated. The school reached inimitable heights with works by translators like the Hiwrmiwz brothers and, notably, the leader of the movement, Fr. Arsên Bagratuni,[8] the most outstanding representative of Armenian Classicism, author of the epic poem *Hayk Diwts'azn* [Hayk the Giant], which was modelled after Homer's *Iliad*. "The Bagratunian school"[9] is also cited in an article by Emilio Teza, the well-known Italian critic and translator.

Thanks to the work of the Mekhitarist Fathers, Armenians have been given access to and are able to read in their own language—not without a certain amount of pride—not only anthologies but even entire texts by Italian authors (such as Dante, Tasso, Metastasio, Alfieri, Foscolo, Manzoni, Leopardi, Collodi, De Amicis, Giacosa, Vittoria Aganoor, Ada Negri, Papini, and others), from Greek authors (Homer, Sophocles, Demosthenes, Euripedes, Plato), from Latin authors (Virgil, Cicero, Seneca, Marcus Aurelius), and from French authors (Lamartine, Bossuet, Corneille, Racine, Voltaire, Chateaubriand, Fénelon, and so on).

II. References to Dante and his works

Given the background we have just mapped out, it is not surprising that there has been no lack of interest in the ultimate masterpiece of Italian poetry, Dante Alighieri's *Commedia*. Indeed, as a result of the tireless efforts of the Mekhitarist Fathers and their students, Armenians were introduced to Dante's work before many Asian nations and even some European ones, thanks to the great literary mind of Fr. Arsên Bagratuni. He used the traditional ancient Armenian language of Grabar, employing the solemn, sophisticated style that distinguishes the Mekhitarist school.

It can therefore be stated that knowledge of Dante and his writings in Armenian began to be disseminated at the beginning of the 19th century thanks to the Congregation, through their works on world geography, short encyclopedias on the lives of illustrious people, and in studies on Western literature. The name of Dante could be encountered not only in the periodicals of the time, but also in school textbooks, especially those on history and literature. It is known that as early as the first half of the 1800s, the Mekhitarists wrote and published books that were used in the schools of Constantinople, Smyrna and other cities, in addition to the institutions belonging to the Congregation.

In 1802, a book by Fr. Step'anos Agonts', *Geography of the Four Continents,* was published in Venice. Speaking about Florence, Agonts' stressed that the city had given life to various illustrious figures over the course of the centuries. As an example he cites Dante exclusively, describing him as "the famous Italian poet, the father of the Italian language who magnificently embellished a language that was composed of various idiomatic elements proper to different languages, especially Latin, replacing them with forms that truly reflected the nature of Italian."[10] The high consideration with which Dante was introduced into Armenian literature is certainly worth noting.

Opinions were not always positive, however. In 1839, in Venice, Fr. Matt'êos Maghak'-T'êop'ileants' published a two-volume dictionary in Armenian on the *Lives of Illustrious Personages*, presenting to the Armenian world the first detailed information on Dante's life and works. Unfortunately, his negative attitude toward the *Commedia* is evident: Fr. Maghak'-T'êop'ileants' disagreed with Dante's placement of the representatives of the clergy in *Hell*, concluding that nobody had managed to falsify and deride the holy Christian faith to the extent Dante did in his work. At the end of his article, he actually notes with satisfaction that "in the Spanish version certain passages were revised or gone over again and some cantos of *Hell* and *Paradise* were excluded."[11] He is probably referring to the *Index* of 1612, where the *Commedia* appears as banned, "no corrigiendo." The lines to be expurgated were Inf. XI: 8-9, XIX: 106-117, Par. IX: 136-142, a total of 21, which continued to be banned until the *Indice ultimo* of 1790.[12]

Later Mekhitarists and other Armenian intellectuals who made some sort of reference to Dante expressed their admiration for the poet and his immortal work. In 1850, once again in Venice, Fr. Ambrosios Galfayean published a textbook in Armenian entitled *Brief History of the Middle Ages*. In describing the civil wars of Florence, the author says that "the well-known poet Dante, persecuted in his native land, was forced into exile in other cities." He also adds that "The poet Dante composed his immortal masterpiece and called it the *Commedia*."[13] After this appearing in this book, Dante's name was cited with increasing frequency in other literary sources. While Dante was initially introduced to the Armenian reader purely as the creator of the Italian language, later Armenian literature also contains references to his works, especially to the *Divine Comedy*.

As the patriarch of the Armenian and Armenological press, founded in the lagoon city in 1843, *Bazmavêp*[14] (Polyhistory) became the ideal vehicle for publishing and disseminating translations of Dante's *Divine Comedy*. During the years between 1860-70, studies on Dante and his poem were written, and the first Armenian translations began to appear, ushering in a new literary era. When the 600th anniversary of the "Divine" Poet was observed in 1865 and his statue was set up in Florence, the Armenian press covered the event. An image of the statue is actually reproduced on two pages of the *Pazmaveb* review, accompanying an article by Fr. Samuêl Kesarean entitled "Dante's Statue in Florence" and his translation of Canto III of *Hell*. "The translation of *Inferno* Canto III, in which the Poet arrives in front of the Gate of Hell and there reads a dreadful inscription, provides a taste of the Sublime Poem by the immortal Poet, alongside the image of his magnificent bust,"[15] the author writes.

In 1874, once again in Venice, Fr. Garegin Zarbhanalean published a textbook, *History of Medieval and Modern Literature of Europe* which devoted a great deal of space to the history of Italian literature. It includes an entire 40-page chapter dedicated solely to Dante, in addition to the references made to the poet in the sections on Petrarca, Tasso, and others. Fr. Zarbhanalean's study covers the question of the Italian language and literature prior to Dante, followed by a detailed biography based on various sources but primarily taken from the *Vita Nuova*. "The civil wars in his city, the ungratefulness of his fellow Florentines and the exile he suffered for his patriotism kindled sentiments of hatred and vengeance in the affectionate, saddened heart of the Poet. To quench these feelings he took solace in his genius: poetry. Poetry became the shining sword of the Archangel for the Poet, who in a certain sense even appropriated the part of God;" and Zarbhanalean continues metaphorically, "distributing awards and punishments as he best saw fit to those he thought most deserving, and making his voice resonate throughout eternity." [16]

Going on to describe the poem, he writes that the epithet "divine" is fully justified because the *Commedia* is the most wide-ranging and singular work of human genius after the writings of Homer, thanks to its wide variety of poetic genres: the fantastic, the tragic, the historical, the elegiac, and the comic. Zarbhanalean does not agree with the fact that Dante placed pagans in Hell alongside "believers of the holy Christian faith." "Certainly, this is one of the imperfections of his Poem. However, this mixture of the sacred and profane, fiction and truth, was typical of Dante's time. Christianity was so strong that poetic fictions of this sort were harmless to it,"[17] says the critic. He concludes by observing that "Dante is the greatest poet of the Middle Ages, the Homer of modern times. He regenerated the poetry, we might say, that the genius of the *Iliad* had created. While the former drew it out of the abyss, the latter dragged it out of the lethal darkness of barbarism. The distance between the two geniuses, the interval that separates creative power from the power of regeneration, is very short."[18]

It is evident that considerable effort was put into presenting Dante by the *Bazmavêp* review and by the Mekhitarist Fathers in general. The same thing cannot be said of Eastern Armenian literature.[19] It is true that Eastern Armenian readers knew Dante from the *Bazmavêp* review and Russian sources, however, the amount of attention devoted to him was much less, and as we shall see, and the number of translations was very limited.

As early as the 19th century, around the 1850s when Dante started to be known in Armenian literature, M. Nalbandyan, the outstanding writer of this period, a poet and critic, borrowed the poet's name as a banner for his avant-garde ideas, defining the Florentine as "wise and immortal." Nalbandyan spoke about Dante primarily during his early literary activities, in his book *Yaghags haykakan matenagitut'ean* [Armenian Bibliography], believed to have been written in 1855. Nalbandyan presents himself on this occasion as an apologist, an enthusiastic protector of modern Armenian, Aškharhabar. His opponents claimed that to give up the ancient language, Grabar, in order to create literature that was easy for people to understand would lead to its extinction. Nalbandyan responds to this objection by posing another question: "How is one to explain the survival of the European peoples who adopted a language that everyone could understand, building a bridge to the world with the Enlightenment? Not only did they thrive, they continue to do so today."[20] To buttress his ideas, Nalbandyan uses Dante as an example, describing his creation of the Italian language and the opposition the great Florentine encountered from some quarters. On another occasion, Nalbandyan refers to Dante when the Armenian writer Perch P ošyan is criticized for his poem *Sos ew Vardit'er* [Sos and Vardit'er]. "If the author must be criticized for the fact that his work has imperfections," writes Nalbandyan, "we are curious to know which works are perfect. Not even Milton, Shakespeare, Homer or Dante are devoid of imperfections. How is it possible that our eminent philosophers are ignorant of this fact?"[21] But he immediately adds: "We must not forget, however, that the authors I referred to are the greatest poets the world of man has ever produced."

In 1876, Dante's biography was published in the *Dprots' mankavarzhakan* [The Pedagogical School] review in Vagharšapat (now Ejmiatsin):

"In 1298, Dante began to compose the marvelous poem that became his greatest consolation during the bitter years of his exile. Although written in an enigmatic style, it has been translated and commented upon in all the European languages and is so infused with poetic spirit that it continues today to attract readers and capture their attention. It will never age and in no way will it ever lose its uniqueness."[22]

Interest in Dante and his work grew during the twentieth century. Books on the great Florentine and, most importantly, complete translations in modern Armenian, began to surface. Starting in 1919, the translation of Adolfo Padovan's *Figli di Gloria* was published in the *Pazmaveb*. In 1920, a single-volume version saw the light, including the first three chapters by Padovan, the first of which consisted of about fifty pages, dedicated entirely to Dante. Apart from the many merits of the book, which is a celebration of great thinkers and men of action, there was another reason to translate it into Armenian. The book came out after the horrors of the First World War and especially after the Armenian nation—the first Christian state in history—underwent a terrible genocide at the hands of the Young Turks, who conducted savage massacres followed by mass deportations. As the translator's preface makes clear, the book was published as a protest against the monsters and criminals of the twentieth century:

> If we turn our gaze for an instant toward the criminals of our century, the perpetrators of new crimes who are petrified before the sacred cries of innocent children, and if we raise our eyes toward the true geniuses who are the pride of nature, the creators of works which educate the heart and hone the mind, is there any melancholy-filled soul who will not surge with rage at the monsters of our century, whom even Dante would be incapable of finding an appropriate place for in the afterlife?[23]

In 1921, commemorations for the 600th anniversary of Dante's death were held all over the world. At that time, Soviet Armenia was going through difficult times, which were anything but favorable to the celebration of cultural events.[24] Armenians of the Diaspora, however, made their voice heard far and wide. The September 1921 issue of the *Pazmaveb* review was dedicated entirely to Dante. In the introductory article we read that: "For six hundred years Dante has been admired and he will never lose his majesty and beauty. On the contrary, future centuries will continue to admire him because his memory will never fade."[25] It ends with these words:

"*Pazmaveb*, the doyenne of the Armenian press, expresses the sense of its respectful admiration and reverence on the part of a nation that also belongs to the category of peoples of genius, who although still on their knees... are never bereft of hope."[26] In the same issue we find an article by Fr. Ghewond Tayean on "Music in the Comedy" and a translation of Canto I of *Paradise* by Fr. Arsên Ghazikean.

The periodical *Hayastani koch'nak* [Bell of Armenia], out of New York, published the translation of Canto III of *Hell* by Fr. Ghazikean, and M. Ananikean's entire article on "Dante Alighieri."[27] After providing a detailed biography, Ananikean proceeds to tell the story of the great love the "Divine" Poet felt for Beatrice and comments: "The heart that was tormented by this love could not rest in peace until the completion of his great masterpiece, the *Commedia*, one of the magnificent poems that raised Dante to the heights of Parnassus next to the 'summits' of Homer, Virgil, Shakespeare and Goethe."[28]

In 1965, Armenians gave due prominence to the celebrations for the 700th anniversary of the birth of Dante. Both in Armenia and in the Armenian colonies of the Diaspora, ceremonies were organized, articles were published, poems dedicated to the anniversary were composed, and various cantos of the *Commedia* were published. As before, the *Pazmaveb* review dedicated an entire issue (November-December 1965) to the occasion. In the editorial, Fr. Mesrop Chanašean notes:

Thanks to the force of his talent and the undeniable value of his work, Dante provides a literary bridge connecting the ancient and modern worlds. The ancient world, nurtured on Greek and Latin Classicism, had its own separate concepts and arts that find their closure in the *Commedia*; at the same time, it served to open the avenue to new ideas, new tastes, and in a word, a new artistic current. Dante was a great novelty for his time. Indeed, his influence had a strong effect on later generations who took their inspiration from him a few centuries later, successfully preserving his vital freshness and appeal from their times until our own. This is a surprising phenomenon, one that can be explained by the energy generated by the compelling fascination of his work.[29]

Another article in the same issue is on "Dante's Immortality". After giving a sketch of Dante's general characteristics, the author, Fr. Ep'rem Têr-

Ghazarean, briefly recounts the poet's biography, discusses the *Commedia*, and concludes with the minor works. He ends with these words: "Dante is immortal because he gave life to a source of new, infinite light, not only for Italian literature, but for all the literatures of the world."[30] The review also presents an article on "Dante and His Work"[31] by Fr. Hovhannês T'orosean, prepared for a conference to be held in Paris and published posthumously in this issue. Yet another noteworthy piece is that dedicated to the "Centennial of Armenian Translations" by the scholar Fr. Nersês Têr-Nersêsean[32]. The revised translation by Arbun Tayan of the first cantos of *Hell*,[33] *Purgatory*[34] and *Paradise*[35] are also included, as well as poetry dedicated to Dante, notably an excerpt from the *Vision of Death* by Eghiše Ch'arents' entitled "Dante and Ališan."[36]

A solemn ceremony for the 700th anniversary of the birth of Dante was held in the sumptuous Hall of Mirrors in the 18th-century Venetian palace of Ca' Zenobio, the seat of the Moorat-Raphael Armenian College at the time, and was attended by distinguished guests from Armenia, Italy, and elsewhere. On May 29, 1965 in Erevan, a soiree dedicated to Dante was organized with the attendance of the Italian Ambassador.

Armenian interest in the "Sommo Poeta" continues to this day. In 2001, under the auspices of the President of the Italian Republic, the Centro Dantesco of Ravenna honored the 1700th anniversary of the adoption of Christianity as the Armenian state religion organizing an exhibition on the theme of Dante, including sculpture, medals, paintings, graphics, and printed works by Armenian artists. On September 20, 2002, the Ravenna Center for Cultural Relations organized a soiree at the Basilica of San Francesco as part of the cultural initiative "Dante September 2002." The event was entitled "The *Divine Comedy* around the World - 5th Exhibition of International Interpretations," dedicated to Dante in Armenia. During the evening, a reading of *Paradise* Canto XXXIII was given in Italian and Armenian, using the most recent Armenian translation of the *Commedia* by Ruben Ghulyan, who participated in person. This was the first appearance of a new trend in the Armenian literary world, that of translating the *Commedia* entirely into "terza rima".

III. Armenian translations of the *Divine Comedy*

It is rare for a work of genius to receive an equivalent translation or one that adequately expresses its meanings, rhythms, and stylemes. Before reaching a translation that verges on perfection, the same work is often reworked over decades by a number of different experts. Not surprisingly, then, during the second half of the 19th century, following in the wake of Fr. Arsên Bagratuni, various scholars tried their hand at translating the *Commedia* into Grabar. Different interpretations of the same episode appeared, usually in verse, some of which are rhymed but along with others in prose. This phase has been dubbed the "period of Grabar translations" done by Mekhitarist Fathers Arsên Bagratuni[37] (before 1866), Edward Hiwrmiwz[38] (1866), Srapion Hek'imean[39] (1866), Yarut'iwn Esayean[40] (1869) (authorship attributed to him by Fr. Nersês Têr-Nersêsean), Samuêl Gant'arean[41] (1871), Davit' Nazarêt'ean[42] (1871) and Ghewond Ališan[43] (1855[44], 1881[45]).

Fr. Hiwrmiwz's name does not actually appear on his translation. In Fr. Ghewond Tayean's opinion, the text actually belongs to Fr. Samuêl Gant'arean, who later used the pseudonym of Kesarean. As early as 1889, Emilio Teza, in his article *Quali parti della Divina Commedia fossero tradotte in armeno*, confirmed that the translation of the Count Ugolino episode belongs to Hiwrmiwz.[46]

From a chronological point of view, the first person to translate Dante into Armenian was Fr. Ališan. In 1855 he translated the first verse of *Inferno* Canto III to describe the ruins of Ani.[47] While Fr. Arsên Bagratuni undertook the translation with the aim of rendering the *Commedia* into an Armenian poem, he was unfortunately unable to finish it. In the *Pazmaveb* review of 1868, on page 190, there is a note by the editor explaining that Bagratuni had the intention of translating the whole *Commedia*, but that he unfortunately died in 1866. There is reason to believe, therefore, that the translation, which was discovered after his death and published posthumously in 1868, was completed at least one or two years before.

At the beginning of the 20th century, between 1899 and 1930, translations into Aškharhabar were predominant, and it was in this period that the *Commedia* was completely rendered into Armenian by Fr. Garegin Zarbhanalean (1874), Avetik' M. Ezek'ean-Proyeants'[48](1880), Fr. Arsên

Ghazikean[49] (1899), Hrant Alatin[50] (1912), Fr. Aristakês K'asgantilean[51] (1927), Fr. At'anas Tiroyean[52] (1930), Vagharšak Norents'[53] (1930), Arbun Tayan[54] (1938), Hrach' K'ajarents'[55] (before 1966), Soghomon Taronts'i[56] (1966) and Ruben Ghulyan[57] (1985).

The most popular of these first translators was certainly Fr. Davit' Nazarêt'ean (1840-1911), who was able to publish a little book of 200 pages, *Selected Tercets from the Divine Comedy,*[58] which includes 25 long passages, 1754 verses, and annotations. The complete translation of the *Divine Comedy* was finished around the year 1900, but the version in Grabar by Nazarêt'ean remained unpublished. According to Fr. Nersês Têr-Nersêsean, this is because Aškharhabar speakers had already begun to outnumber the people who knew Grabar at that time, and Fr. Arsên Ghazikean had already begun the first attempts in modern Armenian. Emilio Teza gave highly praised this translation and demonstrated how true it was to the original by translating about 15 verses back into Italian, coming to the conclusion that: "It is always faithful and follows the poet almost verse by verse, with a simplicity that in no way detracts from its liveliness…although one could be frightened by the rhyme scheme, there is no reason for courageous translators to be intimidated by it."[59]

All the partial translations, except that by Tiroyean, include cantos from the *Inferno*: to be specific, the inscription on the gate of Hell appears 7 times, while 5 other translations provide the *cantica* in its entirety, resulting in a total of 12 versions of the most popular lines of the *Divine Comedy*. After these come 11 versions of the dramatic episode of Count Ugolino. Undoubtedly, the Mekhitarists displayed extraordinary taste in choosing which passages to translate. But there is another reason why the verses of the *Inferno* are the most popular among Armenian translators: Armenians find the *Inferno* to be a reflection of their personal suffering.

All the translations are from Italian, except that by Vagharšak Norents' done from Russian, a rather common practice during the period of Soviet Armenia. The translators took into consideration the various levels of interpretation[60] of the *Commedia*. Some translated it into rhyming poetry, others into prose, believing that it is impossible to render it into Armenian using "terza rima". The latter, following the philosophy of Saint Jerome - *non verbum de verbo, sed sensum esprimere de sensu*[61]- privileged meaning over form.

At the beginning, Fr. Arsên Ghazikean translated into Grabar. He often used to joke that "[he] even dreamed in Grabar." Later, however, he came to the conclusion that modern Armenian had by then become a language that could be used even for the works of the great classics.[62] During these years, modern Armenian was purified from the influences of the classical language; through his translations, Ghazikean was one of its main promoters. He had a significant role in establishing modern Armenian's status as a literary language, not without provoking reactions from the remaining purists. Ghazikean translated *Hell* and *Paradise* into verse, while *Purgatory* was put into prose. He himself explains why:

> Not only do the results not correspond to the effort put into them, the difficult content will become even more difficult if transposed into poetry. Verse is not essential for poetry, especially in this context where, except for a few episodes, the rest could be written in prose, and even more so as far as the translation is concerned. I therefore trust in my readers' leniency.[63]

His comments and justifications are not convincing. If what he says is true, why did he not translate the entire work into prose? There used to be a widely shared opinion—one that perhaps persists, almost like a stereotype passed on without any proof—that Ghazikean paid more attention to the quantity than to the quality of his translations. It is true that over a period of thirty years, from 1899 to 1927, he published 30 volumes of translated poetry, in all 7,000 pages chosen from the greatest geniuses of world literature. They include Homer, Sophocles, Virgil, Horace, Dante, Tasso, Milton, Foscolo, Leopardi, Manzoni and a few women writers like Vittoria Aganoor and Ada Negri. This comes to a total of about 50 volumes. Nevertheless, the style of Ghazikean's translations is almost always distinguished by its carefulness, faithfulness, harmony, literary value, lexicon, and above all, by the extraordinary intuition that went into the choice of the texts. He had excellent literary taste and considerable linguistic prowess. With his translations of poems by the greatest authors of the world into Armenian, Fr. Arsên Ghazikean was the initiator and artificer of direct communication between Armenian thought and the creative talent of the world's literary geniuses, so much so that some consider him to be the Bagratuni of modern Armenian. The fact is, however, that Fr. Arsên Bagratuni was an inimitable genius, considered without equal in the history of Armenian literary translations. In any case, the famous literary critic Aršak Ch'opanean defined the Ghazikean version as "absolutely faithful to the original, in excellent Armenian and with a rigorous meter,"[64] making it an object of pride in the history of Armenian culture.

In 1930, Dante's *Paradise* appeared in Armenian with a new literary attire, illustrated by Gustave Doré. The translator's name was Fr. At'anas Tiroyean, the author of no less than 30 books on topics of linguistics, philology and grammar, including a 1911 translation of Tasso's *Gerusalemme liberata*. His translation of Dante, although not in rhyme, is distinguished by its innovative meter, defined by the author as "Armenian hendecasyllable",[65] which he himself did not use at all times, or with consistent results. Despite this, Tiroyean's translation has high literary value and is perhaps even better than his predecessor's in some passages, in terms of stylistic consistency and linguistic density.

Arbun Tayan, one of the former students of the Moorat-Raphael College in Venice who then settled in Erevan, managed to produce the complete translation of the *Comedy* after laborious efforts and published it by HayPetHrat[66]. It appeared in three elegant volumes—*Hell* in 1947, *Purgatory* in 1952, *Paradise* in 1959—with illustrations by Gustave Doré and an introduction by Avetik' Isahakyan[67] for *Purgatory,* while he had Alek'sey Jivelegov[68] write the introduction for *Hell* and *Paradise*. The translation is in rhymed verse: the first verse rhymes with the third, while the second is in free verse. The translator's explanation for this choice is:

> Maintaining the complicated system of the "terza rima" of the original in the translation is not as important when there are so many other elements that are more important to preserve, especially because the value of the original Dante does not lie so much in its external beauty as it does in the content. To remain faithful to the content, translators have often given up the meter or the rhymes of the original while others have even given up the verses, translating into prose.

Some years later, in 1969, in Erevan, the Academy of Sciences Press published the *Divine Comedy* in Armenian, using the Tayan translation. This single-volume, luxury edition is illustrated with color reproductions from 15th-century manuscripts of the *Commedia* held in the Vatican Library, the Marciana Library of Venice, and the British Museum. For this revised translation, Tayan consulted the 5th edition by Scartazzini-Vandelli of 1907, the 1870 version by Fraticelli and Camerini, and the 13th reprint of the Scartazzini-Vandelli of 1946, in addition to the 1957 version, edited by the well-known critic and historian of Italian literature Natalino Sapegno. The latter two publications of the *Commedia* in particular became the basis and source for Tayan's revised translation, which came out in its third edition in 1983, published by the Erevan University Press.

Tayan came under Italy's spell as an adolescent. No doubt, he fell in love with Dante and his immortal work while he was a student at the Moorat-Raphael College, inspired by the enthusiasm of Fr. Arsên Ghazikean. Over the years, with his knowledge of the Italian language, Tayan intensified his research, studying voluminous commentaries and widening his specialized studies to other European languages. At the same time he was engaged in his Dante studies and gaining extensive experience as a translator, his knowledge of Armenian was enlarged and enriched, thus making him an able, sophisticated interpreter of Italy's greatest poet.

Although Dante's work is historically bound—it actually consists entirely of events, people, concepts, and languages from a specific historical period—it transcends and traverses all eras, remaining constant in its intellectual and poetic value, emotional impact, and thought-provoking qualities. As such, it takes on the character of a model that continuously attracts new interest from subsequent generations. It is not surprising, then, that a new translation of the *Divina Commedia* into Armenian, by Ruben Ghulyan, thus appeared at the beginning of the 21st century. After doing various translations of Russian poetry, Ghulyan devoted himself to Dante without ever having been in Italy and without ever studying the language at an academic level, a fact which earned him a great deal of criticism. His love for the poem grew out of his reading of Armenian poets like Eghiše Ch'arents' and Hovhannes Širaz,[69] who were influenced by Dante and out of Tayan's translation, prompting him to start learning Italian on his own. His goal was to surpass Tayan and succeed in translating the *Divina Commedia* into "terza rima", a choice which often forced him to stray from the original content and one that distinguished him from his predecessors. Building on the translation experiences of Fr. Ghazikean, Tayan and Losinski, in Russian, Ghulyan managed to realize his dream after about 30 years of work. In 1996 he had already published a first Armenian translation of the *Vita nuova*, which is now ready for its second, completely revised edition. In 2004 he published his version of *Hell*[70], in 2005 that of *Purgatory*[71], and in 2007 *Paradise*[72], although he continues to work on perfecting it.

In conclusion, Dante's translations have enriched Armenian poetic language and have enlarged the confines of its linguistic and stylistic possibilities. Thanks to the translations and the need to transmit the proper message to the reader, in addition to theological vocabulary, many compound words characteristic of Medieval or Western Armenian literature entered into circulation as well as neologisms, idiomatic expressions and some dialectal words. It is worth mentioning that famous Armenian poets (like Ch'arents' and Širaz, for example) have borrowed some poetical forms and styles from Dante's poem, developing them in accordance with their national spirit.

Of course, given the limits of a single article, other topics requiring in-depth study cannot be taken into consideration. We reserve this task for the near future, when we intend to provide an exhaustive discussion of Dante's specific influence on Armenian poets.

Notes

[1] This Feast Day, *T'argmanch'ats' ton*, is observed on October 13, and is dedicated to Mesrop Maštots' and Sahak Part'ew.

[2] A distinctive figure in the Armenian Church, Holy Monk and Doctor of Theology, with special canonical privileges. Mesrop is considered to be the first *vardapet* and the first in a continuous tradition to receive the title, symbolized above all by the *baculum magisterialis* (*gawazan vardapetakan*) which is conferred during a special liturgical rite.

[3] Mesrop Maštots' invented a national alphabet (405) of thirty-six letters; two more (long *O* and *F*) were added in the twelfth century.

[4] His Holiness, the Catholicos of Armenia and of all Armenians is the head archbishop of Armenia's national church, the Armenian Apostolic Church. The first Catholicos of Armenia and of all Armenians was Saint Gregory the Illuminator (302).

[5] In 1818 Mekhitarist Father Mkrtich' Awgerean (1762-1854), a figure of particular prominence in philological studies, published a critical edition with a new Latin translation of the *Chronicon* by Eusebius of Caesarea, which until then was believed lost and which the Armenian translation was able to reproduce in its entirety: *Eusebii Pamphili Chronicon bipartitum, nunc primum ex armeniaco textu in latinum conversum, adnotationibus auctum, graecis fragmentis exornatum, Venetiis, 1818*. See K. Vard. Sarkissian, *A Brief Introduction to Armenian Christian Literature* (London: 1960), 12-30.

[6] On Mekhitar and the Mekhitarians there is a large bibliography. I shall note here only a few key works: on Mekhitar's life and work see M. Nurikhan, *Il servo di Dio Abate Mechitar, sua vita e suoi tempi* (Venice: Mekhitarist Press, 1914); B. L. Zekiyan, *Mechitar rinnovatore e pioniere* (Venice: Mekhitarist Press, 1977). On the order, its history and spirituality, see B. Sargisean, *Erk'hariwrameay grakan gortsunêut'iwn ew nšanawor gortsich'k' Venetkoy Mkhit'arean Miabanut'ean* [Bicentennial Literary Activity and Noted Figures of the Mekhitarist Congregation of Venice] (Venice: Mekhitarist Press, 1905); idem, *Erk'hariwrameay krt'akan gortsunêut'iwn Venetkoy Mkhit'arean Miabanut'ean* [Bicentennial Educational Activity of the Mekhitarist Congregation of Venice], vol. 1 (*1746-1901*) (Venice: Mekhitarist Press, 1936) (the 2nd volume was never published); Leo (Aŕak'el Babakhanian), *Erkeri zhoghowatsu* [Collected Works] in 10 vols, vol. III (Erevan: Armenian Academy of Sciences, 1966-1989), 482-522; K. B. Bardakjian, *The Mekhitarist Contribution to Armenian Culture and Scholarship*, (Cambridge, MA: Middle Eastern Department, Harvard College Library, 1976); R. P. Adalian, *From Humanism to Rationalism: Armenian Scholarship in the Nineteenth Century* (Atlanta: Scholars Press, 1992); B. L. Zekiyan, A. Ferrari (ed. by), *Gli Armeni a Venezia. Dagli Sceriman a Mechitar: il momento culminante di una consuetudine millenaria*, (Venice: L'Istituto Veneto di Scienze, Lettere ed Arti, 2004). Some significant tokens of the general esteem among Armenians for Mekhitar and his work are quoted by B.L. Zekiyan, "Il monachesimo Mechitarista a San Lazzaro e la rinascita armena del Settecento," in *La Chiesa di Venezia nel Settecento*, Contributi alla storia della Chiesa Veneziana 6 (Venice: Studium CattolicoVeneziano, 1993), 221-48.

[7] Alberto Peratoner (ed. by), *From Ararat to San Lazzaro* (Venice: Mekhitarist Press, 2007), 137-38.

[8] Fr. Arsên Bagratuni (1760-1866), Armenian poet, philologist, linguist, grammarian, philosopher, translator. He is the author of Armenian translations of Homer's *Iliad,*

Pindar's *Olympian Odes*, Sophocles's *Electra*, *Antigone*, The *Characters* of Theophrast, *Ars Poetica* of Horace, *Orations* of Cicero, *Oraisons funèbres* of Bossuet, *Britannicus, Mithridate, Iphigénie* of Racine, *Alzire* and *Mérope* of Voltaire, of Foscolo's *Sepolcri*, of Alfieri's *Saul and Paradise Lost* of Milton. For a detailed study see: Gabriella Uluhogian, "Tra documentazione e filologia: le scuole Mechitariste di Venezia e Vienna," in B.L. Zekiyan e A. Ferrari (ed. by), *Gli Armeni a Venezia. Dagli Sceriman a Mechitar: il momento culminante di una consuetudine millenaria,* 223-37; Paola Mildonian, "Autori e traduttori Mechitaristi," ibid., 239-67.

[9] Emilio Teza, "Quali parti della *Divina Commedia* fossero tradotte in armeno," in *Giornale della Società Asiatica italiana,* vol. III (Rome: 1889), 155.

[10] Step'anos Agonts', *Aškharhagrut'iwn ch'orits' masants' aškharhi, Ewropia* [Geography of the Four Continents, Europe] p. 2, vol. III (Venice: Mekhitarist Press, 1802), 20.

[11] Fr. Matt'êos Maghak'-T'êop'ileants', *Kensagrutiwn ereweli arants'* [*Lives of Illustrious Personages*], Vol. II (Venice: Mekhitarist Press, 1839), 636-38.

[12] See "Fortuna di Dante in Spagna", in Enciclopedia dantesca, vol.V (Roma: Istituto della Enciclopedia Italiana, 1976), 360.

[13] Fr. Ambrosios Galfayean, *Hamarôt patmut'iwn mijin daru* [Brief History of the Middle Ages] (Venice: Mekhitarist Press, 1850), 473.

[14] The transcription of the name appeared as *Pazmaveb* until 1970. It has been published without interruption from 1843 up to the present. In the beginning it served for popular education. Later it changed into an Armenological review, and now is the organ of the Mekhitarist Academy of San Lazzaro, Venice.

[15] Fr. Samuêl Kesarean (Gant'arean), "Dantêi andrin i P'lorentia" [Dante's Statue in Florence] *Pazmaveb* 2 (Venice: Mekhitarist Press, 1871), 39-42.

[16] Fr. Garegin Zarbhanalean, *Patmut'iwn matenagrut'ean mijin ew nor daruts' yArewmuts* [History of Medieval and Modern Literature of Europe] (Venice: Mekhitarist Press, 1872), 160. Fr. Zarbhanalean is known in the Armenian world for his texts on the history of Armenian and European literature, used by high-school students. It must be stressed, however, that his publications are not simply textbooks: they are scholarly studies on the literary history of various nations.

[17] Ibid., 173.

[18] Ibid., 185.

[19] Modern Armenian was created in the 18th century, and is divided into two branches: Eastern and Western Armenian. Eastern Armenian is spoken and written in Caucasian Armenia and in the Persian and Indian colonies, while Western Armenian is spoken and written in Anatolian Armenia and in the other colonies. It must be kept in mind, however, that Eastern and Western Armenian are not two separate languages; rather, they are branches of the same language, distinguished by some grammatical, syntactic and phonetic differences.

[20] Nalbandyan M., *Erkeri liakatar zhoghovatsu*, vol. II (Erevan: 1940), 21.

[21] Nalbandyan M., *Erkeri liakatar zhoghovatsu*, vol. III (Erevan: 1947), 326-27.

[22] Dprots' mankavarzhakan [The Pedagogical School] 11, p. II (Vagharšapat: 1876), 433-40.

[23] Padovan Adolfo, *Figli della Gloria,* Tr. by Fr. Sahak Têr-Movsêsean (Venice: Mekhitarist Press, 1920), 5-6.

[24] In 1915 the Young Turk government had murdered one and a half million Armenians and emptied Western Armenia of all its indigenous Armenian population. Of

Armenia there remained only a tiny stretch of arid rock in its eastern sector upon which was founded the first independent Armenian State in some 600 years.

[25] *Pazmaveb* 9 (1921), 273.

[26] Ibid., 274.

[27] *Hayastani Koch'nak* [Bell of Armenia] (New York: 1921) 41, 1228-32; 42, 1262-65; 45, 1358-61.

[28] Ibid., 41, 1232.

[29] *Pazmaveb* 11-12 (1965), 293.

[30] Ibid., 297.

[31] Ibid., 301.

[32] Ibid. 331. Fr. Nersês Arch. Têr-Nersêsean (1920-2006) dedicated years of his work to collecting statistical data on Dante's presence in the Armenian world.

[33] Ibid., 311.

[34] Ibid., 316.

[35] Ibid., 320.

[36] Armenian poet, prose writer and translator, Eghiše Soghomonyan (1897-1937) came of age in an era of mass slaughter, of World War I and the Armenian genocide. He was jailed in 1936 during the Stalinist purges and then died in prison in 1937. Literary or aesthetic consideration of the poetry of Ch'arents' cannot avoid reference to these and related questions of national history and politics. Among the results was *Vision of Death*, his longest poem of 744 lines that deals with Armenian history from the mid-19th century into the beginning of the 20th. It is a journey into the nation's history, a past that appears now as a netherworld of burnt and charred trees populated by the living dead who have suffered the disastrous failure of their national ambitions. At the outset, feeling the need for a companion, Ch'arents' invites Dante from "the grim middle ages." As the poets enter this world of the dead they encounter many characters. Among figures who personify different moments of the Armenian cultural renaissance and political organization, they also meet Mekhitarist Father Ghewond Ališan, a great Armenian scholar.

[37] Fr. Arsên Bagratuni, *Ardzanagir drantsn dzhochots* [The Inscription of the Gate of Hell], *Pazmaveb* (1868), 190.

[38] Fr. Edward Hiwrmiwz (1799-1876), prominent members of the Order, who was promoted to the rank of Archbishop by Pope Pius IX. He translated into Armenian the *Aeneid* and *Georgics* by Virgil, Faedrus' *Fables*, Tacito's *Annali*, *Phèdre* of Racine, *The Adventures of Telemachus* of Fénelon, *Tragedie sacre* of Metastasio, *Paul et Virginie* of Bernardin de Saint Pierre, *Merope* of Alfieri, *Aristodemo* of Monti and *Promessi sposi* of Manzoni.

[39] Fr. Srapion Hek'imean (tr. by), *Hell* XXXII, 124-139, XXXIII 1-90, *Pazmaveb* (1866), 333-35.

[40] Fr. Yarut'iwn Esayean, *Drvag i mah Ukolineay* [Ugolino's death episode], *Pazmaveb* (Venice: Mekhitarist Press, 1869), 90-91.

[41] F. Samuêl Kesarean (Gant'arean) (tr. by), *Ert' Dantêi i Dzhokhs* [Dante's journey towards Hell] *Hell* III, *Pazmaveb* 2 (1871), 43-45.

[42] F. Davit' Nazarêt'ean, *Chašak yAstuatsayin teslaranên Dantêi* [Selected Tercets from the Divine Comedy], *Pazmaveb* (1871), 149-60.

[43] Fr. Ghewond Ališan (1820-1901) was a great Armenian scholar, historian, geographer and poet. He was the leader of the Romantic movement in Armenia as well as its most important exponent. Thanks to his voluminous scientific and literary works, Ališan

is one of the most representative and appreciated authors of the 19th century, also putting out a large collection of poetry (Venice, 5 volumes, 1857-58).

[44] Fr. Ghewond Ališan, *Teghagir Hayots' Metsats'* [Topographic Description of Armenia Major] (Venice: Mekhitarist Press, 1855), 32.

[45] Fr. Ghewond Ališan, *Širak* (Venice: Mekhitarist Press, 1881), 38.

[46] Emilio Teza, ibidem, p.155.

[47] Constructed in the 5th century as a fort, Ani was the capital of the kingdom of the Armenian Bagratid dynasty from 961 to 1045, developing into a vital trading and cultural center. The earthquake of 1319 and the ensuing devastation by the Mongols in 1330 completely destroyed the city. Even today, visible traces of palaces, groups of dwellings, fortifications, bridges, long stretches of the walls and many churches remain, providing evidence that is fundamental for the study of medieval Armenian architecture.

[48] Avetik' M. Ezek'ean-Proyeants', *Thargmanakan erkeri zhoghovatsu* [Collected Translated Works] (Tphghis: 1880), 68.

[49] Fr. Arsên Ghazikean (tr. by), *Chašak Dantêi yAstuatsayin katakerguthenê, Pazmaveb* 1 (1899), 24-27.

[50] Hrant Alatin, *Hosank'* (Cairo: 1912) n. 7, 102 ; n. 8, 122-23, n.10, 155-56.

[51] Fr. Aristakês K'asgantilean, *Geghuni* (Venice: Mekhitarist Press 1927), 52.

[52] Fr. At'anas Tiroyean (tr. by), *Paradise* (Venice: Mekhitarist Press, 1930), 367.

[53] Simon Hakobian, *Evropakan grakanut'ian glkhavor ejerë* [Anthology of selected excerpts of European literature] (Erevan: HayPetHrat, 1936), 49-74.

[54] Arbun Tayan, *Grakan t'ert'* 53 (Erevan: 1938).

[55] Hrach' K'ajarents', the former editor of the magazine *Masis* of Beyrut, supposedly translated several cantos of the *Commedia*, as he himself documents in his letter of May 2, 1966, addressed to Fr. Nersês Têr-Nersêsean. These translations have unfortunately been lost.

[56] Soghomon Taronts'i, *Hazar u mi sirt* [A Thousand and One Hearts.] vol. II (Erevan: 1966), 124-28.

[57] Ruben Ghulyan (tr. by), *Purgatory* XI 1-142, *Sovetakan grakanut'iun* 10 (Erevan: 1985).

[58] F. Davit' Nazarêt'ean, *Hatëntir yAstuatsayin teslaranên Dantêi Aligiereay* [Selected Tercets from the Divine Comedy] (Venice: Mekhitarist Press, 1875), 200. These include: from *Inferno: The Gate and the Vestibule of Hell. Charon* (III, 1-136), *Cerberus* (VI, 7-33), *The Gluttons – Ciacco* (VI, 34-102), *The Wrathful – Filippo Argenti* (VIII, 13-69), *The Angel of God* (IX, 64-105), *The Suicides* (XIII, 22-132), *Geryon* (XVII, 1-27), *The Thieves* (XXV, 46-138), *Count Ugolino* (XXXII, 124-139; XXXIII, 1-78), *Lucifer* (XXXIV, 28-69). From *Purgatorio: Sordello* (VI, 58-151), *The Virgin Mary and the Sacred Ark* (X, 34-72), *To the Proud* (X, 121-139), *Pater Noster* (XI, 1-30), *Climb to the Second Terrace* (XII, 88-136), *Statius* (XX,124-151; XXI, 1-136), *Earthly Paradise* (XXVII 109-142, XXVIII 1-63). From *Paradiso: The Vows* (III, 1-130), *The Roman Eagle* (VI, 1-96), *The Redemption of Man* (VII,1-120), *St. Francis of Assisi* (XI, 43-117), *Invocation to Virgin Mary* (XIII, 1-45), *The Glory of God* (XXXIII, 49-145).

[59] Emilio Teza, *Dante in armeno*, in Bollettino Italiano degli Studi Orientali, I. No. 19, April 10 (Florence: 1877), 362-66.

[60] A key to interpreting the *Divine Comedy* lies in a passage of the *Convivio* (II.1) where Dante claims that the significance of a work can be weighed according to four levels of meaning: literal, allegorical, moral, and anagogical.

[61] Saint Jerome, *Epistula 72*.

[62] *Pazmaveb* 11-12 (1965), 341.

[63] *Pazmaveb* 9-10 (1902), 408.

[64] Aršak Ch'opanean, *Anahit* 1-4 (Paris: 1908), 10-11.

[65] The translator was inspired by Bagratuni, who had studied and defined the meter of the ancient hymns of the Armenian Church. Bagratuni called this "Armenian meter" because he believed it to be the meter of ancient Armenian poetry before the introduction of the syllabic meter in the Cilician era. Tiroyean thus attempted to adapt this meter to modern Armenian.

[66] HayPetHrat – Armenian State Press.

[67] Avetik' Isahakyan (1875-1957) – famous Armenian poet, writer, academician, member of the Armenian Academy of Sciences and a prominent public figure. Born October 19 (31), 1875, in Alek'sandropol (present day Gyumri), Armenia. Isahakyan began his formal education at St. Ejmiatsin Geworgyan seminary (1889-92). In 1893 he attended classes at Leipzig University as a non-matriculated student. He started his literary as well as political careers in his early youth. Upon his return from Leipzig in 1895 he entered the ranks of the newly established Alek'sandropol committee of the Armenian Revolutionary Federation; he supported armed groups and sent financial aid to Western Armenia from Alek'sandropol. He was arrested in 1896 and spent a year in Erevan prison. His first book of poetry, *Erger ew verk'er* [Songs and Wounds], appeared in 1897. He also wrote legends, ballads, fables, and, in 1909, a short philosophical poem called *Abu-Lala-Mahari*. Between 1919 and 1937, he worked on giving a literary form to the medieval epic poem *Sasna Mher*.

[68] Jivelegov Alek'sey (1875-1952) – historian, art critic, literary scholar, theatre expert and enthusiast, Armenian translator. His works are primarily on the art and literature of the Renaissance. Author of a series of books, including among others: *Mijnadarean k'aghak'nerë Arewmtean Ewropayum* [Medieval cities in Western Europe] (1902), *Arewturë Arewmutk'um mijin darerum* [Trade in Medieval Europe] (1904), *Alek'sandr I ew Napoleon* [Alexander I and Napoleon] (1915), *Italakan Veratsnndi aknarkner* [Outline of the Italian Renaissance] (1929), *Dante Alighieri* (1933), *Dramayi tesut'yunë XVI d. Italiayum* [Theory of Drama in the 16th century in Italy] (1953).

[69] Hovhannes Karapetyan (Širaz) (1915-1984) – one of the great Soviet Armenian Poets and writers of Eastern Europe. Born Hovhannes Širaz in Alek'sandrapol on April 27, 1915, only three days after the terrible massacre of Armenian writers and other intellectuals by the Young Turk government. His childhood, spent starving, thirsty and barefoot, took place during the most tragic times in Armenian history. Širaz's poetry is popular in Armenia: Hušardzan mayrikis [Memorial for my Mother] had a printing of 50,000 and sold out in a week. Until his death on March 14, 1984, Širaz published many books, mostly poetry, but also quartets, parables and translations, and he enjoyed the love and recognition of Armenians everywhere as one of the greatest Armenian poets of the last century. He is the author of *Hayots Dant'eakanë* [The Armenian *Danteakan* (Dantesque)], a poem of 4000 verses which the poet likens to 4000 tombstones for the millions of Armenian innocent victims. (See Hovhannes Širaz, *Hayots Dant'eakanë* (Erevan: Nairi, 1991), 343).

[70] Ruben Ghulyan (tr. by), *Dzhokhk'* [Hell] (Erevan: HGM ed., 2004), 240.

[71] Ruben Ghulyan (tr. by), *K'avaran* [Purgatory] (Erevan: HGM ed., 2005), 232.

[72] Ruben Ghulyan (tr. by), Drakht [Paradise] (Erevan: HGM ed., 2007), 226.

Karla Mallette

Dante as Poet of Exile and Resistance

The long tradition of illustrating the *Commedia* underwent a sudden and striking transformation during the last quarter of the eighteenth century. During earlier centuries—starting with the earliest fourteenth century manuscripts—illustrations regularly accompanied the text, depicting the pilgrim, his guide, and the marvels they encountered in the next world. With the modern period, however, artists began to create paintings of prominent characters or scenes from the *Commedia* that were not illustrations of the text but rather stand-alone portraits of Dantean tableaux. Typically these paintings downplayed the narrative impetus central to earlier illustrations of the *Commedia*, which functioned as snapshots of the action described in the text. Rather they isolated a character (or two or three) at a crucial moment in the text. And at their finest they provided revealing psychological exposition of the character. Furthermore, because they had no obligation to cover the whole of the *Commedia*, they tended to exploit first and foremost the dramatic potential of the *Inferno*. Much less frequently did artists choose subject matter from the rather more ethereal *Purgatorio* or *Paradiso*. Joshua Reynolds's 1773 canvas "Ugolino and His Children" serves as a convenient *terminus post quem* for this new tendency. Henry Fuseli— a Swiss artist based in England who also spent time in Rome—created drawings and paintings on infernal themes (see, for example, "Dante and Virgil on the Ice of Cocytus," 1774, and "Head of a Damned Soul from Dante's Inferno," 1770-78). Delacroix would execute his epic canvas "The Barque of Dante" in 1822. Bouguereau weighed in with the strenuous, silly "Dante and Virgil in Hell" in 1850. These paintings illustrate the most striking quality of the new Dantean portrait: they do not shy away from the fantastic qualities of the text. But at the same time they linger over its psychological drama, as if the character depicted were an actor performing a Shakespearean monologue that revealed him in the most raw, honest and (at times) abject light.

The two episodes which most attracted the attention of European artists during this period were Ugolino (signaled by Reynolds's portrait) and Paolo and Francesca. Both its theme and the melodramatic back story made *Inferno* V irresistible to artists, and after John Flaxman's 1793 catalogue of Dante illustrations provided a template for artists the scene was reproduced countless times. Ugolino's appeal, however, is less apparent. His sin (treachery against party) lacks the allure of Paolo and Francesca's. His infernal punishment (frozen in the ice of Cocytus, he gnaws at the shattered skull of his tormentor, Archbishop Ruggieri) makes any portrait depicting his eternal state horrific. The dismal tale of his imprisonment (his persecutors locked him away with his four sons; all would starve to death) would seem to lack dramatic potential. Yet after Reynolds's 1773 portrait, Fuseli (1806) and Delacroix (1849-60) created Ugolinos, and prints of their compositions were produced for the mass market by John British Dixon (of Reynolds's) and Moses Haughton (of Fuseli's). In addition Jean-Baptiste Carpeaux (1860) and Rodin (1881) executed monumental sculptures on the theme. In each case the artist chose to reproduce the pathetic tableau in the prison cell, where Ugolino and his sons await death. In these canvases, Ugolino—in Dante's text a canny manipulator of words and emotions, struggling to make a partisan of the pilgrim, and failing where Francesca so brilliantly succeeded—becomes a tragic hero. He fights to protect those who depend on him, his sons imprisoned with him. He fails not because of any moral flaw on his part but because of the depravity of his persecutors. William Blake (who, of course, himself illustrated the *Commedia*) wrote a letter to the *Monthly Magazine* of London defending Fuseli's Ugolino painting against the horrified criticism lodged against it. "Fuseli's Count Ugolino," he wrote, "is a man of wonder and admiration, of resentment against man and devil, and of humiliation before God; prayer and parental affection fills the figure from head to foot…. [T]he effect of the whole is truly sublime."[1]

The nineteenth century reconfigured some of the key figures from the *Inferno* as tragic heroes (despite the fact that Dante represented them explicitly not as tragic, but rather as sinners facing the harsh justice of their damnation). Paolo and Francesca, Ugolino, Brunetto Latini, Pier della Vigna, and Ulysses came to be seen as characters too big for hell—in some cases too big even for the bulk of humanity, above whom they tower. A particular poignancy colors Ugolino's tale. Political machinations caused his downfall. Thus he came to represent (among other things) the tragic dimension of another of the central heroic figures of the European nineteenth century: the revolutionary elite. Like the leaders of the nationalist movements of the period, Ugolino was imprisoned for his beliefs—despite the truth and justice of those beliefs. Like the revolutionary leaders he stood in a patriarchal position to those who surrounded him. His incapacity to change his sons' fate tormented him, as their incapacity to lead their peoples to liberation tormented the early revolutionary figures. "A lofty soul," mused Foscolo's Jacopo Ortis, "is so far above the multitude that they, affronted by its grandeur, try to chain it or deride it, and give the name of madness to those actions which they, sunk in their mire, can hardly recognize, much less respect." And Blake, lauding Fuseli's portrait, recalled Ugolino's "passionate and innocent grief, his innocent and venerable madness, and insanity, and fury."[2] Ugolino (like the revolutionary elite) could be deemed insane only by a populace so mired in decadence that it cannot see by the true light of virtue.

That this image of Ugolino as a symbol of the nationalizing struggle survived into the twentieth century is demonstrated by the portrait of him produced by Seamus Heaney, Irish poet and Nobel laureate. Heaney, a native of Northern Ireland, moved to the Republic of Ireland in 1972 in order to escape the troubles in his native land. While in residence in the Republic he produced *Field Work*, a collection of poems that grappled with the brutalities of sectarian warfare. *Field Work* concluded with Heaney's translation of Dante's encounter with Ugolino (61-64). Introducing Ugolino—sunk in the frozen lake of Cocytus, gnawing voraciously at the skull of the man who persecuted him in life—Heaney compares him to "a famine victim at a loaf of bread": the introduction of the famine, not present in Dante, suggests one of the most politicized events in Irish history. He softens the manipulative edge of Ugolino's rhetoric.[3] He backs away from the Christological and eucharistic references that Dante used to frame his portrait of Ugolino, above all when he replaces the final image of the episode—a reference to the crucifixion—with a new Biblical measure: "the sins / of Ugolino, who betrayed your forts, / should never have been visited on his sons."[4] In Heaney's version Ugolino is more sinned against than sinning, a distant descendent of those who authored the antique dispute which still, senselessly, claims victims.

In this essay I will explore some of the themes suggested by Heaney's reworking of the figure of Ugolino as a late modern political symbol. I will look at Dante as an emblem of the politically conscious public intellectual in selected twentieth and twenty first century writers. In particular I will consider Dante as a sign of resistance to misgovernment, and as a figure of the sentence of exile which writers who dare to resist oppressive regimes typically endure in punishment for their hubris. My discussion will be divided into three sections: first I will consider two literary scholars and exiles who have meditated on Dantean themes in their works, Erich Auerbach and Edward Said. Next I will look at Assia Djebar and Orhan Pamuk—writers from Islamic states (Algeria and Turkey respectively) who use Dante to symbolize the tension between national language and transnational audience that faces the intellectuals of their nations. Finally I will turn to the nation that, more than any other in the English-speaking world, has generated a need for what Dante may offer the writer of political conscience: Ireland. I will consider Seamus Heaney's manipulations of Dante in greater death, contrasting him to a prominent Irish writer of a younger generation, playwright Martin McDonagh. My survey will be, of necessity, episodic and aphoristic. Dante continues to provide a rich wellspring of inspiration for the modern poet. And the governors of this fallen world continue to furnish stimulation of a darker sort, creating a need for the strident voice of the critic. The present discussion aims to gather some of the most striking examples of modern literature that reads Dante as a poet of resistance, but does not claim to be comprehensive.

I. Said and Auerbach

Edward Said was in the process of forging a career as a scholar of English literature and an acute and productive practitioner of high criticism when the work for which he is (and will be) primarily remembered, *Orientalism*, appeared in 1978. He never pretended to be a professional reader of Dante, and his pages on Dante in *Orientalism*—the only place, to my knowledge, where he directly engages Dante as a writer—are few and unremarkable (68-70). However, Said was much enamored of another scholar's response to Dante. Early in his career he translated an essay by the philologist Erich Auerbach in which Auerbach engaged Dante's work. And again at the end of his career, in a book of essays published posthumously, *Humanism and Democratic Criticism*, Said paused over Auerbach's Dante:

[I]n Auerbach's searingly powerful and strangely intimate characterization of the great Christian Thomist poet Dante—who emerges from the pages of *Mimesis* as *the* seminal figure in Western literatures—the reader is inevitably led to the paradox of a Prussian Jewish scholar in Turkish, Muslim, non-European exile handling (perhaps even juggling) a charged and in many ways irreconcilable set of antinomies that, though he appears to order them more benignly than their mutual antagonism suggests, never lose their opposition to one another. (98)

In Said's reading, Auerbach's portrait of Dante in *Mimesis* represented a way for Auerbach to come to terms with the "irreconcilable antinomies" of exile. This description owes much to the heroic image of Auerbach that has emerged over the last twenty years. Auerbach was a Jew who fled Nazi Germany in 1935. He took a position in Istanbul, arranged for him by another philologist and European refugee, Leo Spitzer. In Istanbul Auerbach would write a sweeping and idiosyncratic literary history of Europe. Subsequent scholars would read *Mimesis* as the record that a philologist managed to salvage from the wreck of Europe, an exile's love letter to the civilization he was forced to leave behind.[5] In the passage just cited, Said points to Dante as the emblematic intellectual in exile, and thus as the hero of Auerbach's epic history of European literature. Dante—according to Said's reading of Auerbach—created both modernity and Europe in the pages of the *Divine Comedy*. But Said seems moved more than anything by the collision of identities in the story he relates, by the paradox that a Prussian Jew writing in Muslim Turkey should elevate a medieval Italian Christian to the role of patriarch of Europe.

Exile is the key to Said's understanding of Auerbach and of Dante, the exigency that defines the work of the modern literary critic. In the stirring closing sentences of the book in which this portrait of Auerbach appears, Said asserts that "the intellectual's provisional home is the domain of an exigent, resistant, intransigent art.... Only in that precarious exilic realm can one first truly grasp the difficulty of what cannot be grasped and then go forth to try anyway" (144). The sentiment of these sentences echoes the spirit of the closing lines of an article written by Auerbach and translated by Maire and Edward Said in 1969. "Philology and *Weltliteratur*"—published in German in 1952, quite late in Auerbach's career—ends with the citation of a famous passage from Hugh of St. Victor. "He is still delicate," Hugh wrote, "to whom his fatherland is sweet; he is strong to whom every land is a fatherland; but he is perfect for whom all the world is an exile." And Auerbach adds: "Hugo intended these lines for one whose aim is to free himself from a love of the world. But it is a good way also for one who wishes to earn a proper love of the world."[6] Inasmuch as we are intellectuals, we are all exiles. Here the two modern critics seem to agree with Dante, on a topic that necessity taught each of them. Exile is less a legal pronouncement or a pragmatic response to adversity than a form of mental discipline: the lens we use to teach ourselves to love a fallen world.

Said's engagement with Dante—suggestive as it is—is not extensive. Dante, for Said, evokes the cultural and linguistic complications that enter the exile's life as he moves from city to city and from state to state. Auerbach's scholarship on Dante, of course, is of a different order. Auerbach wrote about Dante, and wrote ardently about Dante, throughout his career.[7] If Said's Dante reflects his preoccupations with exile, identity, and the voice of the critic, Auerbach's Dante crystallizes his thoughts about exile, identity, and the language of the literary artist. Dante represented the triumphant voice of the secular and *vernacular* literary traditions that emerged in late medieval Europe, began to flower during the Renaissance, and would produce the national cultures of the modern period.

The vernacular revolution of the late Middle Ages shattered the unity of Latin Europe, fragmenting it into linguistic regionalisms. However this same revolution also produced something *properly loveable*, to borrow the intimate and muscular language of Auerbach's "Philology and *Weltliteratur*." Auerbach in exile venerated the fragility of the land from which he had been cast out—which he never saw simply as *Germany*, but always, capaciously, as *Europe*. I use the word 'fragility' here advisedly. Auerbach revered the tenuous complexity of the European literary landscape. He dwelt in voluptuous detail on the linguistic specificities of the texts he analyzed in Latin, Italian, French, Spanish, and English. It seems evident that in his work as philologist Auerbach meant to mount a figural resistance to what he could only have perceived as the *threat* of European unification under the Nazis. Like a European Walt Whitman—that is, without Whitman's tenacious American optimism—Auerbach sang the multitude, the body electric and the body eclectic, of literary Europe.

Auerbach's program, moreover, was avowedly elegiac, and elegiac on many levels. Implicitly he wrote a eulogy for the Europe that perished in World War II. His mourning for the collapse of Latinity as the voice of a *legitimate* European unity is a hair more explicit (see especially his *Literary Language and Its Public in Late Latin Antiquity and in the Middle Ages*). Furthermore, in his essay "Philology and *Weltliteratur*" (8-10), Auerbach openly laments the failure of an academic ideal. Once the scholar might have aspired to a sweeping familiarity with the fragmented multilingual European literary tradition. Now in part because of the success of research—there is so much more to *know*—and in part because students are not trained as they were during the nineteenth century, that ideal is seldom (if ever) achieved.

In Dante, Auerbach sees the triumph of the human intellect in a Europe in which a single man may know everything worth knowing. And in Dante Auerbach situates the emergence of vernacular particularism—somewhat ironically locating the apotheosis of vernacularity in the work of a poet who himself argued fervently for the unification of Europe in a Christian empire. Dante's Italian, so Florentine and Tuscan in formation, transcends the specificities of Florence and of Tuscany to become the voice and the conscience of Christian Europe. So too did T.S. Eliot—his reading of Dante also colored by his experience of the European wars of the first half of the twentieth century—see Dante's language as simultaneously regional and universal:

> Dante's universality is not solely a personal matter. The Italian language, and especially the Italian language in Dante's age, gains much by being the product of universal Latin.... Medieval Latin tended to concentrate on what men of various races and lands could think together. Some of the character of this universal language seems to me to inhere in Dante's Florentine speech, and the localization ('Florentine' speech) seems if anything to emphasize the universality, because it cuts across the modern division of nationality.[8]

Dante, for the scholars who came of age in Europe during the first half of the twentieth century, represents a collectivism of the intellect that combats the political perils of the era—the forced agglutination of Europe under a repressive regime—by means of its delicacy, precision, and (most difficult yet most important) its moral rectitude.

Edward Said, however, was not European. And though he lived on the outskirts of a war it was not the European conflagrations of the first half of the century but rather the ongoing struggle for Palestinian statehood. Said's thundering dismissal of Dante in the pages of *Orientalism*—where he read Dante's damnation of Muhammad as emblematic of the West's transhistorical contempt for the Orient—stands at odds with his much more nuanced reception of *Auerbach's* Dante. What, beyond the autobiographical echoes of a life colored by resistance and exile, did Said see in Auerbach's treatment of Dante: did he admire and aim to emulate the philological precision and sophistication of Auerbach's reading? Did he hunger for the ringing authoritative voice that Auerbach achieved most convincingly when he wrote about Dante? Did he find in Auerbach's Dante a transcendence of the ills of sectarianism, signaled by his attentiveness to the Jewish Auerbach's affection for a medieval Christian writer? Indeed Dante's capacity to affirm a confessional identity while still avoiding the most noxious effects of sectarianism seems today the most poignant touch in Auerbach's portrait of him, more utopian even than the linguistic and philological expertise that Auerbach evokes as a lost ideal.

II. Djebar and Pamuk

If Auerbach and Said approach Dante as scholars—if their interest in him is predominantly philological and historical—Assia Djebar and Orhan Pamuk come at Dante from a different perspective, as artisans who draw on Dante in the service of literary programs that Dante himself could never have imagined. Djebar and Pamuk have used Dante to interrogate a constellation of problems central to their concerns: the language of culture, and the challenge of participating in transnational cultural life from the periphery. Perhaps most interesting for an audience of Dantisti, the two books that I will consider by Djebar and Pamuk focus on Dante's *secondary* works: the *De vulgari eloquentia* in Djebar's case, and the *Vita nuova* in Pamuk's. And in both cases the modern author aggressively reworks the exemplar, producing magnificent and consummately *modern* meditations that use Dante as a touchstone.

Djebar's themes in *Le blanc de l'Algérie* are exile, death, and language; nation, and the damage that sectarian politics can do to the nation.

She writes in the genre of elegy, producing a sort of biographical dictionary in reverse: she uses the deaths of the great writers and intellectuals of modern Algeria (too many of them violent and politically motivated deaths) as a lens to talk about their lives and about the discontents of the nation. The book begins by invoking the medieval author who has become emblematic for modern discussions of such a concatenation of themes: Dante. But unlike other modern writers, Djebar refers in some detail to the *De vulgari eloquentia*, Dante's meditation on the face-off between the vernacular and the language of culture. Like Dante, Djebar grew up speaking a language that has scant literary pedigree—colloquial Arabic. She has never written in formal Arabic, although she has tried. Her decision to write in French has caused her considerable pain: during the 1970s, when she tried to force herself to write in Arabic, she went through an extended period of aphasia; she abandoned writing for a decade and turned to filmmaking. And because of the Algerian regime's Arabization policy she (like other Algerians who choose to write in French) has been anathematized and her "Algerianity" questioned. Certainly as the result of her linguistic *prise de position*, her pages on the language question are among the finest and most prepossessing in *Le blanc de l'Algérie*. She rediscovers the beauty of Arabic on a San Francisco street, listening to two young Americans speak an elegant and American-accented literary Arabic (32/28).[9] She feels nostalgia for "that mother tongue in which I do not write, a language flashing before me like a fugitive in a dress studded with diamonds of poetry" ("une fugitive en robe endiamantée de poésie"; 32/29). When she writes about Camus's "non-langue maternelle" ("maternal non-language" [31/28]), we understand that she refers to his habitually silent mother. But she also draws an implicit and paradoxical parallel between herself and Camus. Both are Algerian by birth; both crossed the Mediterranean to spend much of their lives in France; and (for different reasons) neither has written in Arabic, the mother tongue of their country of birth.

When Dante makes his first appearance in the book, Djebar invokes him as a grammarian (and given the weight that language bears in the book, the designation is no slight) and as an exile (60/52). Djebar seeks the language that her dead might use in order to continue to speak to her: this will be the tongue both of history (the language that allows the past finally to speak) and of the future. Here the central character of the *De vulgari eloquentia* makes its appearance:

> Dante compares this language of the absent dear to us, who in order to appro-
> ach us defy the freezing frontier of our lives behind which we take on weight,
> Dante compares this language—which is like yours, when you come back to
> me intangibly—to the "perfumed panther," the mythical animal of medieval
> bestiaries. (60/52)

In Djebar's reading, the panther that Dante seeks—in the *De vulgari eloquentia* the voice of Italy's literary *future*—becomes the voice of the *past:* the voice of the fallen writers and intellectuals who continue to haunt her.

> The restless movement of Dante's panther—which grants certain passages of
> the *De vulgari eloquentia* the relentless pace of a long tracking shot from a
> horror movie—echoes the nomadic rhythm of Djebar's own exilic life. In an
> essay that Djebar contributed to a selection of texts by writers who write in a
> language other than their native tongue, she talks about the transitory quality
> of her exilic life, about migrations and nomadism. She situates her own au-
> tobiographical movements in a broader cultural context: in Islamic culture,
> woman is *passagère*; "she cannot truly claim a permanent place." Further-
> more vagrancy, Djebar argues, occupies a central and a hallowed place for
> both men and women in Islamic culture. She ends by calling herself "simply
> a *migrant*. The most beautiful label, I think, in Islamic culture."[10]

As *grammarian*, Dante grants Djebar a vocabulary to depict linguistic complexity and, crucially, migrations between tongues. Dante sketched a linguistic map of the world in which no region possessed a single, unify-ing language. So too, in Djebar's telling, Algerians live their lives (cultur-ally, socially, even psychologically) between languages. Djebar relates the story of a man who, though he spoke perfect French, colloquial Arabic, and Berber, refused to speak any language other than classical Arabic. When a doctor prescribed psychotherapy for him it proved almost impossible to find anyone who could treat him in the single language he chose to speak. Once a therapist had finally been found, the doctor sent him out the door with a word of advice, at once rousing and abject: "Soyez simplement algérien!" (32-33/29)[11] The nomadism that Djebar describes in her autobiographical essay reflects the movement between tongues that comes naturally to her as an Algerian (and that this analysand resisted so tenaciously). And in *Le blanc de l'Algérie*, the panther that moves restlessly through the pages of the *De vulgari eloquentia* becomes itself a migrant ("the most beautiful label in Islamic culture"). Pacing between languages, it does not seek a single, uni-fying language but brings its distinctive scent to each. The Algerian tongue that Djebar uses to write what Azade Seyhan calls "an unauthorized biography of the nation"[12] is finally neither Berber, Arabic, nor French, but rather an Arabic-inflected French, a French that remembers its origins *outremer*.

In his novel *The New Life* Orhan Pamuk, like Assia Djebar, engages questions of language and culture in general, and the problem of participating in transnational cultural life from the periphery in particular.[13] As a Turk, however, Pamuk phrases the question differently. Turkey, unlike Algeria, possesses an abundant vernacular literary history, one that Pamuk has written about with intimate passion in *Istanbul: Memories and the City*. Pamuk focuses not on the question of language, but rather on the difficulty of articulating a position between East and West: the importance of distinguishing between modernization and westernization, the possibility of cultural fusion, and the compromises that of necessity attend fusion. The title of the work—*Yeni hayat* (*The New Life*)—suggests the centrality of Dante's work to understanding Pamuk's book. Reading Dante as the key to the work, however, would do it an injustice: any attempt to flatten its breadth would compromise the author's expansive vision. Dante is one ingredient of a cultural stew—evidence of the interpenetration of East and West, like the western clocks that Turks have made their own,[14] or the term *checkmate* which originated in the East but which Westerners have appropriated (280). However, a chorus of characters worries out loud that a Western culture that is essentially irrelevant to Turks and to Turkish history will eclipse Turkish culture.

Pamuk uses Dante as the symbol of a truth concerning Western culture and its meaning for Turks: it can have cultural currency only if it is lived as a Turkish phenomenon, and as part of a Turkish modernity. In the fable that provides the backbone of the narrative, a young man responds to the overwhelming experience of reading a book whose nature is never precisely explained. "I read a book one day," the narrator tells us in the memorable opening line, "and my whole life was changed." Pamuk's narrative (as well as the title of the book) makes Dante into one of the emblems of the book's mysterious contents. Thus (to list briefly the most striking references and parallels), in a pastiche of literary quotations that serves as the intellectual climax of the work Pamuk thrice cites the *Vita nuova* (e.g.: "I had set foot in that part of life beyond which one cannot go with any hope of returning").[15] Pamuk's narrator is angel-haunted (the angel of death, perhaps also an angel of life, makes repeated appearances in the novel). Like the narrator of the *Vita nuova*, he dreams an embodiment of Love, in this case "manifest in a halo of brilliant white, carrying a child in its arms" (36). He plays counting games (echoing the compulsive numerology of the *Vita nuova*) to determine whether he will see his beloved that day (39). His beloved makes herself manifest with a stern and mystical dignity that mirrors Beatrice's: "She was wearing a dress that was pale but not white, it was the lightest of shades to which I could assign no color… the radiance of her face was quite as powerful as the light that the book breathed, but ever so gentle…. She seemed to have been drawn from memory" (19-20).

"Civilizations come," a character observes, "and civilizations go" (95). Culture is a palimpsest; and the permeability of culture is nowhere more palpably evident than in Pamuk's Istanbul. However a contemporary Turkish culture must give primacy to contemporary Turkish experience. Thus the narrator's transformative discovery of the mysterious book is complete only when the narrator strives to *live* the book—first by copying it ("this was how I re-animated everything that the book imparted to me" [37]), and then by entering its pages, joining its heroine on a picaresque journey without destination through the Turkish hinterland. The *new life* becomes a symbol of a transformative experience conveyed to successive generations of readers in the form of a book. Pamuk uses his fantastic, invented book to drive home the central paradox of contemporary Turkish culture: The narrator's point of departure is the boyish premise that only when his life is transformed beyond recognition will he have achieved the promise embedded in the book. The hideous joke at the heart of *The New Life* (at the end of the day, the novel is a shaggy dog tale) is that the narrator's conversion experience returns him to the place where he began: to Turkey, today. The transfiguration that he naively welcomed—imagining that it would relieve him of the burden of inventing a Turkish modernity, by substituting for it an imported Western product—affirms instead the world that he intended to leave behind (and its attendant difficulties). The duty of self-invention, on a personal or a cultural level, cannot be avoided.

The New Life is for Pamuk, as the *Vita nuova* was for Dante, a sophomore effort. This is not to say that the authors' technique or thought lacked refinement, but rather that in both cases the books at once build on previous literary achievements and point to work to come. Both works meditate upon a broken romance in order to study a broader literary problem, paralleling personal and cultural therapeutics. And both authors realized on the page the promises of their early manifestoes. Pamuk would articulate a literary reflection of Turkish modernity—vitally contemporary, ineluctably aware of its past—in his subsequent novels, as Dante would give origin to an Italian literary tradition in the *Commedia*. Both Pamuk and Djebar draw upon the "lesser" works rather than the *Commedia*. One motive for this impulse may, of course, be religious: the turn to the *Commedia* is necessarily less coherent for a Muslim writer than for a Christian. However, the intentions of the *Vita nuova* and the *De vulgari eloquentia* may equally explain Pamuk's and Djebar's instincts. *Le blanc de l'Algérie* and *The New Life* are manifestoes, blueprints for building a literary mansion on uncertain ground. Perhaps the self-consciousness and the very tentativeness of Dante's earlier works speak more effectively to writers who (like Pamuk and Djebar) face the task of forging a literary culture anew among the shards of a previous age.

III. Heaney and McDonagh

I discussed above Heaney's use of Ugolino as a pendulum to his meditations on the troubles in Northern Ireland. "The Strand at Lough Beg," also included in *Field Work*, memorializes a cousin who was killed in sectarian violence. In the poem Heaney describes the moments leading up to his cousin's murder: a dark road at night, a checkpoint, the sudden crack of the gunshots. He imagines his dead cousin appearing before him, like the souls of the dead that Dante meets in the *Commedia*. And in the closing lines of the poem, Heaney borrows an image from Dante's Purgatory:

> I lift you under the arms and lay you flat.
> With rushes that shoot green again, I plait
> Green scapulars to wear over your shroud. (18)

The epigraph to the poem, drawn from *Purgatorio* I (vv. 100-102), clarifies the reference. In the *Purgatorio* Virgil purifies the pilgrim of the residue of hell in order to prepare him for his encounters with the saved; so Heaney washes the filth of a violent death from his cousin's face. In "The Strand at Lough Beg" Heaney works to rescue his cousin from the ignominy of a violent death without idealizing the senseless war in which he died. And in the closing poem of the book, Heaney's translation of Ugolino, Heaney borrows Dante's voice in order to pronounce a damning condemnation of the brutalities of sectarian struggle.

Modern Irish writers have used Dante as a symbol of Irish exceptionalism within the orbit of the English-speaking world: think in particular of James Joyce and Samuel Beckett.[16] Heaney argues Dante's relevance to the poet of political conscience in particular with greater conviction than any other poet of modernity. Given Dante's gravitational pull for Irish writers of conscience—and exilic Irish writers in particular—it seems perhaps remarkable that the most ambitious young Irish writer of the present moment, playwright Martin McDonagh, has *not* used Dante to pace his meditations on violence and reason. McDonagh, born to Irish immigrants in London, has achieved extraordinary success at an extraordinarily young age. In both England and the United States he has garnered critical acclaim and prestigious awards, but has also been faulted for facile violence and intellectual naïveté. The most substantive critical responses to his work argue convincingly that McDonagh's *infant terrible* image serves intentionally to deflect public attention from his craft and his native talent: his fine sense of comedy, surprisingly cogent critique of the absurd logic of terrorism, and stunning linguistic sophistication.[17]

Of McDonagh's output, "The Lieutenant of Inishmore" (first produced in London in 2001) has attracted the most attention on this side of the Atlantic. The play is a giddy interrogation of the rationale of sectarian violence and its affect on those who use it as a political tool. We follow a night and a day in the unraveling of an Irish National Liberation Army (INLA) cell of the most suspect legitimacy. At the outset of the play, the leader's cat is found dead (the death is later revealed to be a political assassination); this event sets in motion an absurdly abrupt escalation of violence, as if the characters (and the audience along with them) were on an express escalator into the depths of the Inferno. The play, viewed in the current perspective, poses a negative question: given the concatenation of problems that McDonagh addresses—identity (both political and sectarian), violence (and in particular politico-sectarian violence)—and given the robust attention bestowed upon Dante by Irish writers before him, why does he *not* use Dante to coordinate his vision?

The question is not quite as idle as it might at first blush appear. "The Lieutenant of Inishmore" begs a Dantean intervention. The assassinated cat is found with its head half gone, like a feline Archbishop Ruggieri. The parallel—had the author intended it—would fit the case admirably. Ugolino was, after all, damned for treachery to party. And in the course of the play we learn that the INLA rank and file have assassinated the cat in order to draw the INLA leader, Padraic, to his native town—to execute him for the crime of treachery. Most keenly, Dante would allow McDonagh to signal the peculiar balance he aims for in all his plays and achieves most effectively here. "The Lieutenant of Inishmore" involves the viewer in a peculiarly Dantean gambit: she or he must choose between the equally uncomfortable options of feeling pity for the damned (in this case, his hapless INLA activists) and haughty superiority to them.[18]

If you strip away the macabre humor that saturates "The Lieutenant of Inishmore," the plot has enough treachery and betrayal to fill the Inferno to bursting. And yet in charting a literary path McDonagh abjures all but the most local references to Irish playwrights (making use of Synge's "Playboy of the Western World" in particular).[19] We might turn to Heaney himself to understand why McDonagh (or any other Irish writer of his generation) might choose to leave the Dante references on the cutting room floor. In his long poem "Station Island," published five years later than *Field Work*, Heaney backpedals from his impulse to use Dante to render his cousin's death in a sublime key in "The Strand at Lough Beg." In "Station Island" Heaney, on a Dantean journey through the uncanny Irish countryside where Saint Patrick discovered the entrance to Purgatory, meets the shade of his assassinated cousin one more time. And the cousin accuses the poet of using Dante to falsify his death:

> 'You confused evasion and artistic tact.
> The Protestant who shot me through the head
> I accuse directly, but indirectly, you
> who now atone perhaps upon this bed
> for the way you whitewashed ugliness and drew
> the lovely blinds of the *Purgatorio*
> and saccharined my death with morning dew.' (83)

It is true that the Dantean setting and the Dantean rhythms of "Station Island," to some extent, second-guess Heaney's strong anti-Dantean stand in these lines. So, too, elsewhere in the poem Heaney seems to rely on the strength of Dante's lines to guide him. See, for instance, the confession that is the emotional heart of the poem and that echoes the felt brevity of Dante's confession in *Purgatorio* 31: "I repent / my unweaned life that kept me competent / to sleepwalk with connivance and mistrust" (85). A few lines later Heaney's pilgrim (as Dante's did) glosses his own confession—and note that Heaney, like Dante, measures out his confession in tercets:

> 'I hate how quick I was to know my place.
> I hate where I was born, hate everything
> That made me biddable and forthcoming.' (85)

In this stereopticon confession Heaney repents his temerity and rejects his birthright; but before the end of the stanza he will recognize and accept the inevitability of character as if it were a fact of nature: "As if the cairnstone could defy the cairn. / As if the eddy could reform the pool" (86). The notion of *place* in these lines summons images both complementary and contradictory: character, constitution, or discipline; a path either chosen or imposed and accepted. Finally, also, place signifies simply *place*. In "Station Island" Heaney returns from the exilic refuge in which he wrote *Field Work*, the Republic of Ireland, to Northern Ireland. He returns to the weight and cadence of Dante's poetry in the same way that he returns to a familiar landscape: it is part of his literary genetic code, the tongue of conscience and, when necessary, of resistance to political brutality.

McDonagh, however, has not lived in Ireland. He was born to immigrant parents, and born therefore to dislocation. And he does not seek the grandeur of Dante's epic style, but rather the edgy transnational vernacular of intransigent youth: hence his literary downward mobility, the Tarantino-esque register of his plays. Thus he has use for neither Dante's regional loyalty nor his literary sublimity. If anything can inspire McDonagh to drink from the well of Dantean reference in future writings, it may well be the difficulty of reconciling tragedy and abjection. At the beginning of this paper I discussed the reconfiguration of Ugolino as a tragic hero by European painters during the nineteenth century. McDonagh's Irish activists, like the revolutionists of the nineteenth century, become collateral damage in the bloody birth pangs of nationalization. However public opinion has by and large downgraded the revolutionists of postmodernity to terrorists. A transnational audience may regard their interventions as ideologically suspect or disingenuously craven (as some critics perceive McDonagh's own plays).

What becomes of the revolutionary activist who seeks recognition of or justice for his nation during a post-national age? His situation is parallel to the orphaned damned of Dante's *Inferno*, read by an audience that does not generally share the author's belief in the nature of the afterlife or the justice of God's judgment. McDonagh, it seems to me, is well positioned to define the next step in political rereadings of Dante, as changing political and cultural trends call into question the exaltation of the heroes of national revolutionary movements. His bumptious revolutionaries spar for absurd reasons, and the violence is preposterously out of proportion to the deeds it purportedly answers. Padraic is clearly a sadist. Mairead, who succeeds him, seems to be inspired by lust and dreams of power. She defeats the murderous Padraic apparently because she is the only character more bloody-minded than he. Her paradoxical innocence—the virginal purity of her violence—seems to promise great things, but in the end she throws it all over; her revolutionary ambitions prove no more than a lark. She walks away from the cause because, as she explains, "I thought shooting fellas would be fun, but it's not. It's dull" (54). The play ends with a bit of business in which two characters abjure senseless violence, but by this point McDonagh's satire has cut too deep for redemption. They're playing it for laughs.

McDonagh's faux-naïve tableau of a modern revolutionary cell begs a question of surprising moment and urgency: whither political heroism in a post-national (and hence post-revolutionary) world? McDonagh uses violence with a particular intimacy, like other serious artists who have won a broad popular audience in recent years—think, in the American ambit, of Quentin Tarantino and Cormac McCarthy. More than they, however, McDonagh seems capable of generating a substantive response to the moral problems posed by the prevalence and banality of violence in contemporary political life. Certainly McDonagh, like Tarantino and McCarthy, seems to have understood that we live in an age when (to paraphrase Henry de Montherlant) peace has the edginess of war.[20] But he, more than his contemporaries, seems also to understand implicitly one of the corollaries of this fact: despite staggering advances in human knowledge over the past centuries, violence still retains a powerful residue of meaning. And although he has not achieved it yet, his plays hold out the promise of squaring a moral circle—reconciling the abject and the sublime—as Dante himself did in the *Inferno*. If he succeeds in finding a way to represent what might be called the Ugolino paradox—that is, to represent both the damnable, grotesque bawdy of sectarianism in Ireland and the persistent, scandalous justice of the cause for which sectarians struggle—McDonagh may yet give the revolutions of the post-national age the face by which they will be remembered.

Notes

[1] *Monthly Magazine* 21 (July 1, 1806), 520-521.

[2] Foscolo 27; Blake *op. cit.*

[3] In his introductory comments, Dante's Ugolino closes on a self-pitying note: "parlar e lagrimar vedrai insieme" (XXXIII, 9). In contrast Heaney's Ugolino gives us the resounding "I would sow my words like curses" (61). Again, in place of the mordant rhetorical question that Dante placed in Ugolino's mouth, "di che pianger suoli?"(XXXIII, 42), Heaney's Ugolino simply calls the reader "hardhearted" (62).

[4] Heaney 63. This reference replaces a Christological reference in the original: Che se 'l conte Ugolino aveva voce / d'aver tradita te de le castella, / non dovei tu i figliuoi porre a tal croce (XXXIII, 85-87)

[5] On Auerbach see Menocal's profile, to my knowledge the earliest biographical tribute to the man and his scholarship (*Shards of Love* 106-15), and Emily Apter's reconsideration of the same narrative ("Global *Translatio*"). Reading Said's career in terms of Auerbach's central influence on it has become particularly irresistible in recent years: see Apter's "Saidian Humanism" and Aamir Mufti's "Auerbach in Istanbul."

[6] Hugh's Latin appears without translation in the Saids' version of Auerbach's article: "Delicatus ille est adhuc cui patria dulcis est, fortis autem cui omne solum patria est, perfectus vero cui mundus totus exilium est" ("Philology and *Weltliteratur*" 17).

[7] Auerbach's major writings on Dante appear in three monographs: *Dante als Dichter der irdischen Welt* (1929; translated by Ralph Manheim as *Dante: Poet of the Secular World*), *Mimesis* (in which Auerbach analyzes the Farinata episode from the *Inferno*; first published in German in 1946, and translated into English by Willard Trask), and *Literatursprache und Publikum in der lateinischen Spätantike und im Mittelalter* (1958; translated by Ralph Manheim as *Literary Language and Its Public in Late Latin Antiquity and in the Middle Ages*).

[8] *Selected Essays* 239. This passage is cited and discussed in Seamus Heaney's essay "Envies and Identifications" (33).

[9] All citations from the text will give the page number in the French edition, then the English translation.

[10] "Writing in the Language of the Other," 27.

[11] Djebar's discussion seems particularly Dantean when she discusses the tripartite complexity of her Algeria—a "linguistic triangle," as she terms it. The "language of rock and soil, the original one let's say," is the Berber tongue (mirroring the vulgar tongue in Dante's discussion). The Algerian elite use a second language—the Mediterranean language of culture—to communicate with the elite of other Mediterranean nations: alternately, during the modern period, Arabic and French (though during antiquity—in Algerian Augustine's day—it was Latin). And governing powers impose a bureaucratic language on the nation (today, Arabic; 272-73/227-28). This "linguistic triangle" was already present in an early speech she gave which predicted the major themes of the book she would write (see "White of Algeria" 143-44).

[12] Speaking, here, not of *Le blanc de l'Algérie* in particular but of the exilic genre of autobiography in general (Seyhan 161).

[13] For another reading of Dante in Pamuk's *New Life*—touching on many of the writers also present in this essay (Said, Auerbach, Hugh of Saint Victor) yet very different from my own reading—see Kathleen Biddick, "Coming Out of Exile."

[14] "Clocks are the only things other than guns that cannot be classified as foreign or domestic" (159).

[15] *The New Life* 258; cp. *Vita nuova* 14.

[16] Joyce's use of Dante, a prominent component of his literary profile, needs no elaboration here. In the case of Beckett I am thinking in particular of the early story "Dante and the Lobster"—one of the most mordant modern responses to Dante, as well as one of the funniest pieces Beckett ever wrote. In another early work, the essay "Dante … Bruno . Vico … Joyce," Beckett writes about the contemporary resonance of Dante's work.

For further evidence of Heaney's extensive engagement with Dante—beyond the works discussed above and later—see also *Seeing Things*. The book begins with an archeology of the Dantean passage to which Heaney refers in "The Strand at Lough Beg": a translation of the passage from the *Aeneid* in which Aeneas plucks the golden bough which "grows … golden again" ("The Golden Bough," 5). In "The Journey Back" (9) the shade of Philip Larkin quotes Dante to Heaney. And the book closes with a translation of *Inferno* III, 82-129 ("The Crossing," 105-7. Heaney also wrote about Dante in "Envies and Identifications" (cited above, note 8).

[17] See, for instance, Lonergan 67-68. Because of the combination of disingenuous anti-intellectualism and violence that characterizes his plays critics regularly compare McDonagh to Quentin Tarantino (see e.g. Lonergan 73 and Pilny 225).

[18] McDonagh's use of language also casts a compelling light on Dante's poetics, and in particular on Dante's exilic recreation of the Tuscan vernacular in the *Commedia*. McDonagh writes his characters' dialogue in an exaggerated version of the western Irish dialect, a travesty of the vaunted eloquence of the Irish. Nicholas Grene writes that "Some critics accuse McDonagh of simply not knowing the dialect well enough to reproduce it correctly, but it may be more deliberate than that: a caricature of the lyricism of Synge-song" (referring to the great Irish playwright J.M. Synge, author of "The Playboy of the Western World"; 307. Grene quotes "The Beauty Queen of Leenane" in demonstration of McDonagh's "uncouth, ungainly and deflationary" manipulation of Hiberno-English: "If it was getting rid of oul lumps I was to be, it wouldn't be with Complan I'd be starting"; *ibid.* And Fintan O'Toole, in a *New Yorker* profile of McDonagh, writes of the language McDonagh puts in the mouths of the benighted inhabitants of his Connemara: "The plays are quite literally mongrels: they are written in an English that uses Gaelic syntax and yields oddly coiled sentences like 'When it's there I am, it's here I wish I was, of course,' and they exhibit an acute self-consciousness about language.") Thus McDonagh–like Dante in, for instance, *Inferno* VI and *Purgatorio* VI–takes his ancestral home to task, creating a dystopian version of it in his plays. And like Dante in the later cantos of the *Inferno* he uses abrasive language in the service of an ideological realism: not (as Dante does) to bring to life a supernatural dystopia, but rather to depict as monstrous the pastoral idyll of western Ireland.

[19] Discussions of McDonagh's knowing references to the work of other playwrights have proved the most effective counter-argument to the accusations of vapidity leveled against him. At the same time critical assertions that McDonagh writes in apparent ignorance of theatrical traditions are used to question the significance of his work. For the former position, see Sierz 224-25; for the latter, although in the context of a generally favorable assessment of McDonagh's work, Pilney 230.

[20] "Il faut faire une paix qui ait la grandeur d'âme de la guerre"; from "Chant funèbre pour les morts de Verdun" (first published in 1924; 221).

Bibliography

Apter, Emily. "Global *Translatio:* The 'Invention' of Comparative Literature, Istanbul, 1933." *Critical Inquiry* 29 (2003): 253-81.

---. "Saidian Humanism." *Boundary* 2 (2004): 35-53.

Auerbach, Erich. "Philology and *Weltliteratur.*" Trans. Maire and Edward Said, *Centennial Review* 13 (1969), 1-17.

Beckett, Samuel. "Dante and the Lobster." In *More Pricks than Kicks* 9-22. New York: Grove Press, 1972.

---. "Dante ... Bruno. Vico .... Joyce." In *Disjecta*, 19-33. London: Calder, 1983.

Biddick, Kathleen. "Coming Out of Exile: Dante on the Orient Express." In *The Postcolonial Middle Ages*, ed. Jeffrey Jerome Cohen, 35-52. New York: St. Martin's Press, 2000.

Djebar, Assia. "Algerian White." Trans. Andrew Benson. *Yale French Studies* 87 (1995): 138-48.

---. *Le blanc de l'Algérie.* Paris: Albin Michel, 1995.

---. "Writing in the Language of the Other." Trans. Isabelle Courtivron and Susan Slyomovics. In *Lives in Translation: Bilingual Writers on Identity and Creativity*, ed. Isabelle de Courtivron, 19-28. New York: Palgrave MacMillan, 2003.

Eliot, T.S. *Selected Essays.* London: Faber, 1951.

Foscolo, Ugo. *The Last Letters of Jacopo Ortis*, trans. J.G. Nichols. London: Hesperus, 2002.

Grene, Nicholas. "Ireland in Two Minds: Martin McDonagh and Conor McPherson." *Yearbook of English Studies* 35 (2005): 298-311.

Heaney, Seamus. "Envies and Identifications: Dante and the Modern Poet." In *Dante Readings*, ed. Eric Haywood, 29-46. Dublin: Irish Academic Press, 1987.

---. *Field Work.* London: Faber, 1979.

---. *Seeing Things.* New York: Noonday Press/Farrar Straus Giroux, 1993.

Lonergan, Patrick. "Too Dangerous to be Done? Martin McDonagh's *Lieutenant of Inishmore.*" *Irish Studies Review* 13 (2005) 65-78.

McDonagh, Martin. *The Lieutenant of Inishmore.* New York: Dramatists Play Service, 2003.

Menocal, María Rosa. *Shards of Love: Exile and the Origins of the Lyric.* Durham: Duke University Press, 1994.

de Montherlant, Henry. *Essais.* Paris: Gallimard, 1963.

Mufti, Aamir R. "Auerbach in Istanbul: Edward Said, Secular Criticism, and the Question of Minority Culture." *Critical Inquiry* 25 (1998): 95-125.

O'Toole, Fintan. "A Mind in Connemara: The Savage World of Martin McDonagh." *New Yorker* 82, Issue 3 (March 6, 2006): 40-47.

Pamuk, Orhan. *The New Life*. Trans. Güneli Gün. New York: Farrar, Straus and Giroux, 1997.

Pilny, Ondrej. "Martin McDonagh: Parody? Satire? Complacency?" *Irish Studies Review* 12 (2004): 225-32.

Said, Edward. *Humanism and Democratic Criticism*. New York: Columbia University Press, 2004.

---. *Orientalism*. London, New York: Penguin, 1995.

Seyhan, Azade. "Enduring Grief: Autobiography as 'Poetry of Witness' in the Work of Assia Djebar and Nazim Hikmet." *Comparative Literature Studies* 40 (2003): 159-72.

Sierz, Aleks. *In-Yer-Face Theatre: British Drama Today*. London: Faber and Faber, 2001.

Carolynn Lund-Mead

For Dante's "New Life"— A Catalogue of Biblical References

> For last year's words belong to last year's language
> And next year's words await another voice.
> T. S. Eliot

Since the beginning of Dante criticism, the poet's relationship to the Bible has been a topic of interest. With every generation it has taken on a new life. The late Amilcare Iannucci was a visionary scholar who recognized the need to revisit and record the history of Dante's relationship to the Bible as it has been noted from the time of the early commentators through to contemporary critics.

Beginnings

When Dante died in 1321 he entered a "new life" as the Dante of the Commentaries, the Dante of ceaseless accretions. In this incarnation he and his *Commedia* were immediately associated with the Bible. Guido da Pisa (1327-28?), one of the early commentators on Dante's *Inferno*, opens his prologue with a dramatic flourish:

Scribitur Danielis, quinto capilulo, quod cum Baltassar rex Babillonie sederet ad mensam, apparuit contra eum manus scribens in pariete: Mane, Thechel, Phares. Ista manus est noster novus poeta Dantes, qui scripsit, idest composuit, istam altissimam et subtilissiman Comediam . . .

(It is written in the fifth chapter of Daniel, that when Balthazar, king of Babylon, was seated at table, there appeared over against him a hand, writing on the wall: "Mane, Thechel, Phares" This hand is our new poet Dante, who has written, that is has set together, this most lofty and subtle Commedia . . .)

Guido alludes to an Old Testament scene: King Belshazzar of Babylon, his lords, wives and concubines, are feasting, drinking from gold and silver vessels looted from the temple in Jerusalem, when suddenly the fingers of a human hand begin writing above the lampstand. The king is terrified; the prophet Daniel, a captive from Israel, is called to interpret the mysterious words. Guido creates a correspondence between the three words written on Belshazzar's wall and the three parts of Dante's *Commedia*, embellishing the comparison with reference to God's arrangement of the world according to the three categories of measure, number and weight as recorded in the Book of Wisdom (11.21).

To a modern reader, of course, the words written on the wall as the prophet Daniel interprets them to King Belshazzar have no basis of comparison with the *Inferno*, *Purgatorio* and *Paradiso* apart from the fact that they are three in number. By means of this extravagent image, however, Guido grants to the *Commedia* origins that are sacred and mystical, to Dante the authority of Biblical texts. Guido clokes the genesis of Dante's poem in Old Testament imagery, invoking a time when Yahweh acted directly on the course of human history, sometimes making use of mysterious verbal messages. Dante's text is analogous to such a message.

It is clear that for Guido and others at this time the Bible represented the pinnacle of authority. By using the Bible as he does, Guido identifies Dante, the new poet, with the Bible. Pietro di Dante also invokes Biblical imagery in his third (and most complete) introduction to the *Inferno* (1359-64). Pietro discloses his plan to "open up" the meaning of the *Commedia*, an act analogous to opening up the Scripture ("Scripture aperitionem perficere", *glossa*, Job 31.35) with the key of David, which in the Apocalypse of St. John the Divine is in the possession of "the holy one and true", "who opens and no one will shut, / who shuts and no one opens" (Apoc. 3.7)[1]. Granting himself mystical powers with this Biblical analogy, Pietro secures his position as an interpreter of the *Commedia*.

Both commentators make Dante's text consubstantial with the Bible, confering upon it an authority that is mysterious, sacred and unassailable. This authority is also exploitable. Guido and Pietro demonstrate a certain creative flair in bringing off these analogies. These commentators, in fact, are following the model of Dante himself, who claims that heaven and earth have set their hand to the creation of his sacred poem ("l'poema sacro / al quale ha posto mano e cielo e terra" *Par.* 25.1-2). In this statement Dante poet asserts his sacred poetic authority as the culmination of the experience he has just described in the Heaven of the Fixed Stars where Dante pilgrim receives the highest accolade from St. Peter after having successfully passed his examination on faith: "tre volte cinse me . . . sì nel dir li piacqui!" ("[he] encircled me three times . . . / I so pleased him by my speech", 24.152-54).

Continuings

Guido and Pietro are among the most significant of the early commentators who begin the process of identifying and commenting upon what they perceived to be references to the Scriptures in the text of Dante's *Commedia*. In their recognition of Scriptural allusions they were followed, with very few exceptions, by every major commentator thereafter throughout every period in which commentaries have been produced, including the present day. All these scholars not only followed but also built upon and added to previous Biblical references noted by their predecessors. Their frequent repetitions suggest the passing on of information from one generation to another, the participating in and maintaining of a process that is open to questioning, criticism, discussion and change.

The generation of scholars following these early commentators was influenced by the way in which humanism changed European intellectual life. In the universities, scholasticism retreated behind the onset of studies that opened up new literary sources in the classics. Philology became the new science, the new value. A handful of fifteenth-century scholars continued the process of noting the Biblical presence in the *Commedia*. While their commentaries closely followed their fourteenth-century predecessors, they also contained new trends. Christoforo Landino (1481), whose commentary became influential into the next century, combined the Christian and the classical in his neoplatonic philosophy which he traced through the "divine" Plato, the Apostle Paul and Dionysius the Areopagite (*Introducution*, 25).

Moreover, changes in the status of the authoritative Latin Bible and in methods of Biblical exegesis had profound effects on the reception of the *Commedia*. Interest in Dante's text began to decline with the destabilization of the official Bible on which its reputation had been founded. The study of languages during the Renaissance opened up the original sources of the Bible for renewed investigation. During this time, three sixteenth-century humanist commentators appeared, though they were doomed to fall into relative obscurity: Alessandro Vellutello, Bernardino Daniello and Lodovico Castelvetro. While continuing the tradition of referencing the Biblical presence in the *Commedia,* they also pursued humanist interest in the classics. Daniello, for example, saw that in *Purg.* 1.71 Dante was using Virgil's classical definition of "libertà" in combination with the Christian.

The exposition of Bernardino Daniello, published posthumously in 1568, was the last complete Renaissance commentary of the *Commedia* until 1732. This lacuna of some one hundred and fifty years coincided with the introduction of Enlightenment scholarship in Europe. Historical-critical challenges made serious inroads into the ontological basis for commentary on what was perceived to be Dante's monolithic theological world, a world that ecclesiastical authority continued to uphold. The commentaries of P. Pompey Venturi and Baldassare Lombardi, (whose work continued to dominate into the next century), stood alone in the eighteenth. Their inquiries reflected new hermeneutic trends. While each was sensitive to the presence of Scripture in the *Commedia,* they were more interested in tracing textual relationships than in commenting on doctrinal matters. Lombardi inquired into textual variants found in various editions of the *Commedia.* He carried this interest over into a critical assessment of Dante's textual incorporation of the Bible. Lombardi noticed, for instance, a discrepancy between the stated hour of Christ's death in the gospels of Matthew and Luke, and in *Inf.* 21.112-14. Later commentators such as Francesco Torraca (1905) and Manfredi Porena (1946-48) took up this matter in more detail.

While emphasis on the Bible as a human document, "written by men for men" at first contributed to the diminishment of Biblical authority, it ultimately opened the way for more secular forms of Biblical criticism in the nineteenth-century.[2] Literary scholars recognized that the new "scientific" forms of Biblical hermeneutics offered a respectable way back into criticism of the *Commedia.* This new science offered tools, never before available, for a reconsideration of the problems presented by Dante's relationship to the Bible. In keeping with the nineteenth-century optimism of pure "scientific" research leading the way to "progress", coupled with a renewed enthusiasm for collecting, cataloguing vand naming, Dantists developed an unprecedented interest in tracking the presence of the Bible in the *Commedia.* With scholars such as Niccolò Tommaseo, G. A. Scartazzini, Celestino Cavedoni and Edward Moore, the search for the Biblical substructure of Dante's *Commedia* was on. Tommaseo (1837) and Scartazzini (1874-82) saw Biblical references everywhere. While contributing an unprecedented number of valuable new insights, their "references" are occasionally far-fetched.

The general tendency, however, was toward more precision. Celestino Cavedoni (1861-62) created a new type of commentary, an annotated canto by canto notation of Biblical references, *Raffronti fra gli autori biblici e sacri e la Divina Commedia*, containing many new insights. Cavedoni's initiative was followed by the English scholar Edward Moore's major work of recognition of both classical and Scriptural references in Dante's works (1896). Moore's groundbreaking study of the role of the Bible in the *Commedia* took the form of an enlightened aesthetic inquiry. Moore was especially interested in Dante's "curious habit (for so it seems at first sight)" of placing Biblical quotations side by side with "so-called profane authors". Moore argued that Dante "considered the people of Rome to be as much God's 'chosen people' as the Jews, the one leading up to the realization of a Universal Empire, the other to that of a Universal Church. Roman and Jewish history were equally 'sacred history' for Dante" (26-27). Moore's discussions of parallel passages was followed by an index of allusions to the Vulgate which to the present day is the most complete in existence (321-334). Beginning with Genesis, this index was organized according to Biblical books, chapters and verses, with parallels not only in the *Commedia* but also in Dante's other works.

Moore was the first critic to reflect on Dante's process of selecting Scriptural references. Where he considered a reference to be "probable but not altogether beyond doubt", he has asked himself the question: "Would Dante's language or thought have been likely to take this precise form, but for the influence exercised on them by the recollections of such and such a passage in Scripture . . .?" (46). Moore's questioning opened up a new era of critical self-consciousness that would flourish in the future. Subsequent scholars have pursued significant in-depth studies of Dante's theory and incorporation of Biblical language. Two scholars of particular note are Giulio Marzot (1956) and Lucia Battalia Ricci (1983), both of whom analyzed vast numbers of Biblical references. Marzot examined Dante's use of Biblical style, themes and modes of expression. Ricci produced a masterful lexical and stylistic study of Dante's Biblical borrowings.

Studying Dante's use of the Bible became important for analysing other aspects of Dante's art. Recognizing that "the influence of the Bible in shaping Dante's ideas on language remains a largely unexplored topic", Zigmund Barański researched the development of Dante's philosophy of language in chapters 1-9 of *De volgari eloquentia.* Barański noted that Dante grounded his discussion in the Genesis tradition, Aware of his dependence upon the authority of Scripture, Dante, nevertheless, "was not only willing to ignore parts of the Genesis tradition, but was also prepared to alter and add to it" in order "to pursue his own ideas on language". Employing his "hallmark syncretism", Dante worked "other intellectual currents" into the Biblical, in order to provide the "coherence and substance" that he found lacking (118).

Barański demonstrated that Dante shaped and manipulated the Biblical text according to his own purposes as an original thinker, philosopher and poet. Other critics have been more conservative. Mario Aversano (1994) insisted that Dante stayed within precise limits: "Dante certo non vuol derogare alla norma di trarre l' 'autorizzazione' dal libro sacro; ma lo consulta e lo interpreta con tanto maggior rigore teologico ed etico, lasciandosi guidare generalmente dai Padri più autorevoli ("Dante certainly does not wish to depart from the precept of drawing on the 'authorization' of the sacred book; but consults and interprets it, generally allowing himself to be guided by the most authoritative of the Fathers, 119).

The divergence of opinion expressed by Barański and Aversano reflects the debate that has bifurcated Dante studies in the twentieth century. In 1921, in keeping with an increasingly secular literary aesthetic, Benedetto Croce presented Dante as a lyric poet struggling to free himself from stifling theological structures. In reaction to this interpretation, Bruno Nardi (1942) claimed that Dante, in continuing the tradition and language of the Old Testament prophets, deserved to be considered a prophet even as they were ("considerato profeta com'essi furono", 319). Much scholarly energy was (and is still being) expended on working out the consequences of this critical split. The Auerbach-Singleton school of thought, focusing on Biblical typology and overarching Biblical-theological themes, was followed by the synthesizing efforts of scholars such as Peter Hawkins, Teodolinda Barolini and Amilcare Iannucci.[3]

The majority of scholars, however, has increasingly treated Dante's incorporation of the Bible as part of the poetic craft that he employs in the creation of his polysemus text. Giorgio Brugnoli, in his philological analysis of Dante cruxes, perceives a creative use of allusions to both classical and Christian sources. He sees, for instance, in Ulysses speech to his company that begins "O frati" (*Inf.* 26.112), not only a reference to the "O socii" of *Aen.*1.198-203, but also an allusion to the Biblical letter of James which addresses an early Christian assembly, "scitis fratres mei dilecti" ("You must understand . . . my beloved brothers", 1.19). Paula Rigo also analyses some of the ways in which classical and Biblical sources co-exist, interacting with and interpreting one another. In addition to creating useful categories of Biblical allusions, Christopher Kleinhenz demonstrates the importance of intertextual readings in context. Whereas previous critics stressed the allegorical level of interpretation, Raffaele Manica recommends an examination of the letter of the Bible and the *Commedia* rather than of the allegorical. Lino Pertile draws on the exegetical tradition in order to add to the scant number of existing allusions to the Song of Psalms, revealing the polyvalence of the symbols that the Church Fathers interpreted in ways that are often mutually contradictory and surprising.

"We shall not cease from all our exploration" (T. S. Eliot)

Amilcare Iannucci took a particular interest in Dante's relationship to the Bible. Iannucci took his stand among those whose Dante embraced the Christian and the classical, the orthodox and original, the roles of both poet and prophet. In a number of studies, he emphasized the interdependence of the classical and the Christian. In his "Teoria e prassi dei generi letterari" Iannucci examined Dante's impulse toward both the classical tradition of the separation of styles and the Christian tradition of a mixture. He argued that in the *Commedia* the Christian tradition of style assimilates the classical without completely destroying it. Part of Dante's originality, he believed, "deriva proprio da questa delicata riconciliazione delle due tradizioni" ("derives precisely from this delicate reconciliation of the two traditions", *Forma ed evento*, 45-46). In several articles on Dante's Limbo, Iannucci explored Dante's recasting of the Christian Limbo in the Virgilian mode. The result was a Limbo "shaped out of theology" while being "appropriated and driven by poetic ends". Rather than playing one off against the other, Dante created in his imagination an "interconnectedness of poetry and theology" ("Dante's Limbo", 73-74). Iannucci was interested in examining the ways in which Dante used the Bible creatively in his polyvalent text.

Iannucci was the sort of imaginative scholar who always had projects in mind. He believed that Dante, if he were alive in our time, would have adapted the means of technology to his own purposes. Iannucci also thought that Moore's nineteenth-century concept of indexing Biblical references was ripe for expression in a twentieth-century technologically-assisted form. Iannucci believed that the creation of a reference tool that provided researchers with shared information of Dante's relationship to the Bible as it had been perceived over the ages would provide a solid foundation for further scholarly exploration. He imagined a catalogue of Dante's Biblical allusions in the *Commedia* as they have been noted by scholars from the time of Dante's death to the end of the twentieth century. Such a compendium, never before available, would make possible a more informed assessment of the role of Dante's most significant intertext.

Iannucci consigned the creation of this catalogue to me. I began by entering Moore's list of some three hundred and sixty identifications into a computer format borrowed from the design created by Robert Hollander for his index of Dante's Virgilian allusions in the *Commedia*. Confirmations of Moore's listings as well as further textual associations came from the Dartmouth Dante Project, which I exploited by beginning with Genesis and ending with the Apocalypse, searching major commentaries to extract Biblical references. These findings I entered into files for careful consideration and rechecking. And finally, I searched through some 150 books and articles, the majority of which were published in the latter half of the twentieth century. These publications contributed newly recognized references, as well as confirmations of and further thoughts on those previously cited.

Each entry in this catalogue presents a passage from the *Commedia* with the relevant Biblical reference(s) below it for comparison. A footnote follows, listing in chronological order the commentators who have noted this relationship. The result looks like the following entry in which Virgil outlines for Dante the future of the glutton Ciacco, who has just fallen back into the filthy slush from which he roused himself to speak to the pilgrim. (Translations have been added):

Inf. 6.94-96*:

> E 'l duca disse a me: "Più non si desta
> di qua dal suon de l'angelica tromba,
> quando verrà la nimica podesta:
> ciascun rivederà la trista tomba,
> ripiglierà sua carne e sua figura,
> udirà quel ch'in etterno rimbomba".

(And my leader said to me, "He wakes no more until the angel's trumpet sounds and the hostile Power comes, when each shall find again his dismal tomb and take again his flesh and form, and hear that which resounds to all eternity)

Mt. 24.30-31:

> et tunc parebit signum Filii Hominis in caelo et tunc plangent omnes tribus terrae et videbunt Filium hominis venientem in nubibus caeli cum virtute multa et maiestate et mittet angelos suos cum tuba et voce magna

(Then the sign of the Son of Man will appear in heaven, and then all the tribes of the earth will mourn, and they will see 'the Son of Man coming on the clouds of heaven' with power and great glory. And he will send out his angels with a loud trumpet call . . .)

1 Cor. 15.51-53:

> Ecce mysterium vobis dico omnes quidem resurgemus sed non omnes inmutabimur in momento in ictu oculi in novissima tuba canet enim et mortui resurgent incorrupti et nos inmutabimur oportet enim corruptibile hoc induere incorruptelam et mortale hoc induere inmortalitatem

(Listen, I will tell you a mystery! We will not all die, but we will all be changed, in a moment, in the twinkling of an eye, at the last trumpet. For the trumpet will sound, and the dead will be raised imperishable, and will be changed. For this imperishable body must put on imperishability, and this mortal body must put on immortality.)

***Mt. 24**: Pietro, Lombardi, Scartazzini, Berthier, Vandelli, Padoan, Singleton; **I Cor. 15**: Guido, Berthier, Vandelli, Fallani, Padoan, Singleton.

The catalogue was planned as both a compendium of Biblical references and a record of the history of the recognition of these references by commentators. In the above example we see that the references were first noted by two of the earliest commentators, Guido da Pisa and Pietro di Dante, and later confirmed by eighteenth (Baldassare Lombardi) and nineteenth (P. Giachino Berthier) as well as twentieth-century scholars (G. Vandelli, Giovanni Fallani, Giorgio Padoan, Charles Singleton) . But the catalogue was designed to be as neutral as possible; it facilitates but does not offer interpretation. By bringing together the above information, this catalogue permits readers to judge for themselves whether these references contribute meaning to the passage. Since we cannot know whether Dante consciously engaged with the subtext or whether the Bible was simply part of his own language, we must judge each reference on its own merits within Dante's text.

The ideal format for this project would, of course, have been a DVD or on-line version with the possibility of translations, ongoing additions and modifications, as well as links to the commentators in the Dartmouth Dante Project and to the full text of the *Commedia*. With the unrelenting progress of Amilcare's illness, however, a book publication seemed the only option. The purpose of this catalogue is to clarify further research. It is hoped that scholars in the future will carry this work into its next technological stages, opening this catalogue up to new additions and modifications, as we have done with those of the past. While Dante's relationship to the Bible is one of the oldest topics in Dante criticism it is also one of the newest, continually generating new life and significance. It is a topic that we need to revisit and rediscover again and again.

Notes

[1] All translations of the Bible are from The New Revised Standard Version of The New Oxford Annotated Bible (NRSV); citations are from the Biblia Sacra Iuxta Vulgatam Versionem. Citations from *La Commedia* are from the edition of Giorgio Petrocchi; translations of the *Commedia* are by Charles Singleton. All other translations are my own. All major commentators mentioned in this essay appear in the Dartmouth Dante Project.

[2] Reventlow, 1045.

[3] For a summary of the course of this process and of scholarly contributions to it, see Iannucci, "Dante, poeta o profeta?".

Bibliography

Commentators Cited, in Chronological Order

Guido da Pisa (1327-28). *Guido da Pisa's Expositiones et Glose super Comediam Dantis, or Commentary on Dante's Inferno*. Edited with Notes and an Introduction by Vincenzo Cioffari. Albany, N.Y.: State University of New York Press, 1974. Ed. of electronic version: Vincenzo Cioffari; text checked by Robert Hollander with assistance from Kyung Han.

Pietro di Dante (1340-41). *Petri Allegherii super Dantis ipsius genitoris Comoediam Commentarium, nunc primum in lucem editum...* [ed. Vincenzo Nannucci]. Florentiae: G. Piatti, 1845. Ed. of electronic version: Robert Hollander.

Cristoforo Landino (1481). *Comento di Christophoro Landino fiorentino sopra la Comedia di Danthe Alighieri Poeta fiorentino*. Firenze: Nicholò di Lorenzo della Magna, 1481. Ed of electronic version: Francesca Ferrario; DDP version prepared by Robert Hollander.

Baldassare Lombardi (1791-92). *La Divina Commedia, novamente corretta, spiegata e difesa da F. B. L . M . C.* [Fra Baldassare Lombardi, minore conventuale]. Roma: A. Fulgoni, 1791[-92]. Ed. of electronic version: Antonia Rossi.

Other Sources:

Alighieri, Dante. *La Commedia secondo l'antica vulgata*. Ed. Giorgio Petrocchi. 2nd ed. 4 vols. Firenze: Le Lettere, 1994.

---. *The Divine Comedy, Translated, with a Commentary, by Charles S. Singleton*. Princeton: Princeton University Press, 1970-75.

Anchor Bible Dictionary. Ed. David Noel Freedman. 6 vols. New York: Doubleday, 1992.

Auerbach, Erich. *Studi su Dante*. Trans. Dante Della Terza. Milano: Feltrinelli, 1963.

Barański, Zygmunt G. "Dante and Medieval Poetics." *Dante: Contemporary Perspectives*. 3-22.

---. "Dante's Biblical Linguistics." *Lectura Dantis* 5 (1989): 105-43.

Barolini, Teodolinda. *The Undivine* Comedy: *Detheologizing Dante*. Princeton: Princeton UP, 1992.

Bible. *Biblia Sacra Iuxta Vulgatam Versionem*. 4th ed. Eds. B. Fischer, et al. Intro. Roger Gryson. Germany: Bibelgesellschaft, 1994.

---. *The New Oxford Annotated Bible: New Revised Standard Version*. 3rd ed. Ed.Michael D. Coogan. Oxford and New York: Oxford UP, 2001.

Brugnoli, Giorgio. *Studi Danteschi I: Per suo richiamo*. Pisa: ETS, 1998.

---. *Studi Danteschi II: I tempi cristiani di Dante e altri Studi Danteschi*. Pisa: ETS, 1998.

---. *Studi Danteschi III: Dante filologo: l'esempio di Ulisse*. Pisa: ETS, 1998.

Cavedoni, Celestino. *Raffronti tra gli autori biblici e sacri e la* Divina Comedia. Città di Castello: Lapi, 1986. First published 1861-62.

Croce, Benedetto. *La poesis di Dante*. 1921. Bari: Laterza, 1966.

Dartmouth Dante Project. Conceived and Edited by Robert Hollander. 1988 <http: //dante.dartmouth.edu/>.

Eliot, T. S. "Little Gidding". *Four Quartets*. 2nd ed. Faber and Faber, 1959.

Evans, G. R. "The Middle Ages to the Reformation." *The Oxford Illustrated History of the Bible*. Oxford: Oxford UP, 2001. 180-191.

Hollander, Robert. "Le Opere di Virgilio nella *Commedia* di Dante." *Dante e la "Bella scola" della poesia*. Ed. Amilcare A. Iannucci. Ravenna: Longo, 1993. 247-343.

Hawkins, Peter S. "Dante and the Bible." *The Cambridge Companion to Dante*. Ed. Rachel Jacoff. Cambridge: UP, 1993. 120-35.

Iannucci, Amilcare A. "Dante, poeta o profeta?" *"Per correr miglior acque . . ." Bilanci e prospettive degli studi danteschi alle soglie del nuovo millenio*. Atti del convegno di Verona-Ravenna (25-29 ottobre 1999). Ed. Enrico Malato. Roma: Salerno, 2000. 93-114.

---. *Dante: Contemporary Perspectives*, ed. Toronto: U of Toronto P, 1997.

---. *Forma ed evento nella Divina Commedia*. Roma: Bulzoni,1984.

---. "Dante's Limbo: At the Margins of Orthodoxy." *Dante and the Unorthodox: The Aesthetics of Transgression*. Ed. James Miller. Waterloo, Ontario: Wilfrid Laurier UP. 63-82.

Jeanrond, Werner G. "History of Biblical Interpretation." Vol. 3 of *Anchor Bible Dictionary*. 433-443.

Kleinhenz, Christopher. "Dante and the Bible: Biblical Citation in the *Divine Comedy*." *Dante: Contemporary Perspectives*. 74-93.

Manica, Raffaele. "Lo spavento del sacro: Presenze bibliche nell'*Inferno*." *Memoria biblica nell'opera di Dante*. Ed. Enzo Esposito, et al. Roma: Bulzoni, 1996. 23-56.

Marzot, Giulio. *Il linguaggio biblico nella* Divina Commedia. Pisa: Nistri-Lischi, 1956.

Moore Edward. *Studies in Dante. First Series: Scripture and Classical Authors in Dante*. Oxford: Clarendon, 1896.

Nardi, Bruno. "Dante Profeta." *Dante e la cultura medievale*. Ed. Paolo Mezzantini. 2nd. ed. Bari: Laterza, 1983. 265-326.

The Oxford Dictionary of the Christian Church. Ed. E. A. Livingstone. 3rd. edition. Oxford: Oxford UP

Pelikan, Jaroslav. *Reformation of Church and Dogma (1300-1700)*. Vol. 4 of *The Christian Tradition: A History of the Development of Doctrine*. 5 vols. Chicago: U of Chicago P, 1984.

Pertile, Lino. *La puttana e il gigante: Dal Cantico dei Cantici al paradiso terrestre di Dante*. Ravenna: Longo, 1998.

Reventlow, Henning Graf. "Biblical Authority (in the Wake of the Enlightenment)." Vol. 5 of *Anchor Bible Dictionary*. 1035-1049.

Ricci, Lucia Battaglia. *Dante e la tradizione letteraria medievale: Una proposta per la* Commedia. Pisa: Giardini, 1983.

Rigo, Paola. *Memoria classica e memoria biblica in Dante*. Firenze: Olschki, 1994.

Rogerson, J. W. "History of Interpretation." Vol. 3 of *Anchor Bible Dictionary*. 425-433.

Singleton, Charles S. *Dante's* Commedia*: Elements of Structure*. Baltimore and London: Johns Hopkins UP, 1977. Rpt. of *"Commedia": Elements of Structure*. Cambridge: Harvard UP, 1954.

Van Engen, John. "Scriptural Authority in the Medieval Church." Vol. 5 of *Anchor Bible Dictionary*. 1028-1032.

James Miller (The University of Western Ontario)

The Straight Way Lost: Jarman and Rauschenberg under the Rain of Fire

Dante makes a surprising cameo appearance twenty-five minutes into Derek Jarman's film of Christopher Marlowe's history play *Edward II*. Marlowe himself would have been surprised by the warm welcome Dante receives at Edward's chilly court, since il Poeta (billed simply as "Poet" in the movie credits) does not figure as a character in the original cast of the play or even as a faint intertextual trace in the allusive weave of Marlowe's verse. What Jarman envisions in the Dante interlude – Sequence 29 in the published screenplay – is the Ur-Moment in the queer reception history of *The Divine Comedy*.[1]

The sequence opens with a close-up of King Edward and his minion Gaveston listening attentively to the Poet. With their elbows positioned on the back of a row of golden chairs, they rest their chins on the backs of their hands and cast their eyes in the direction of the celebrity author. In voiceover the Poet is heard reciting the first tercet of the *Inferno*. Allan Corduner, the gay British actor whom Jarman impishly cast as the Poet, delivers the famous lines about losing the "straight way" with an ominously deadpan earnestness. His Dante sounds like a visiting Ivy League professor whose hyper-correct pronunciation of medieval Tuscan ironically betrays his ignorance of the rules of elision in Italian poetry. In a studious American accent, he punches out every syllable of the *smarrimento*:

> mi ri-tro-vai per un-a sel-va os-cu-ra
> che la di-rit-ta vi-a e-ra smar-rit-ta.

On the middle syllable of "di-rit-ta," Jarman strategically cuts away from the gay intimacy of Edward and Gaveston to reveal the straight face of the modern Americanized Dante. The Poet's moral seriousness, conveyed by Corduner's solemn features and Great Books tone, is visually reinforced by his formal attire (dinner jacket, black tie, red cummerbund). Raising his right palm as if to recite the Pledge of Allegiance, he launches into John Sinclair's plodding prose translation of the opening lines: "In the middle of the journey of our life...."[2]

Cut to a reverse shot of Edward and Gaveston listening behind the first row of chairs in the middle distance, their heads affectionately close together as if they were teenagers on a hot date at the movies. The camera angle places us in the position of the Poet, with the pages of the book open before us on the lower left-hand side of the screen and his right hand poised to punctuate his next lines with dramatic gestures. "I came to myself within a dark wood where the straight way," he gasps, "...was lost!" In the histrionic pause between "straight way" and "was lost," his hand suddenly jerks back and forth, mapping out in the air the crooked way under ground that the hellbent pilgrim is destined to take with his beloved guide.

A reverse shot takes us back to the initial close-up to Edward and Gaveston. On hearing and seeing how the straight way was lost, they immediately turn towards each other and break into cheeky smiles. Gaveston has a wicked glint in his eyes. The private joke they're sharing is not hard to figure out: they've taken "straight" in the modern slang sense of "hetero" and are transgressively projecting their mutual coming-out experience, the morally disruptive start of their queer lives together, onto the allegorical trajectory of Dante's journey. They are clearly taking their cue here not from the straight-acting poet before their eyes but from the queerrousing director behind the scenes – the blasphemous Jarman whose Dantean preference for "byways" rather than "highways" (as his allegorizing note to Sequence 29 suggests[3]) springs from his own mid-life discovery of his "bent" for militant post-gay activism. The Fairy King and his flamboyant Bad Boy are caught in the act of queering the *Comedy*.

Their hermeneutical transgression is over in a moment, for the sequence abruptly ends with soldiers bursting into the hall to remind us that Marlowe's gloomy old show must go on. Gaveston has to be banished as a traitor, alas, and we have to banish flippantly contemporary queer readings with him. After all, shouldn't we be viewing *Edward II* as a Renaissance history play with "tragical" implications? What's the point of turning it into a postmodern Divine Comedy? Yet Dante's intrusion into the play cannot be easily dismissed. The film has comically staged it before our eyes and stamped it on our cinematic memories. It cannot be unimagined now – or critically dismissed hereafter – for Jarman's camera has captured it for contemplation as a kind of breakthrough in the history of Queer.

But what does the queering of Dante's "straight way" amount to? That depends of course on what we understand by the terms "queer" and "queering," which were just coming into vogue in the critical discourse and creative practice of authors and artists during Jarman's final years. In June 1991, two months before the gala opening of *Edward II* at the Edinburgh Film Festival, Jarman appeared at a same-sex wedding ceremony in Trafalgar Square wearing a T-shirt with the defiantly post-gay identity label "Queer as Fuck."[4] (He was to die of AIDS-related complications two-and-a-half years later, on February 19, 1994). Clearly, for him, "queer" was more than a convenient collective noun for all the sexual outcasts living in open defiance of Britain's Heterosexual Dictatorship.[5] To the bitter end he would celebrate hot man-on-man action in the face of AIDS, or as the punning title of one of his AIDS journals put it biblically: "kicking against the pricks."[6] At street level – the literal level of his passionately allegorical response to the epidemic – queering meant fucking with an attitude as well as a condom, and the attitude was, as he himself reflected in his journals, an outrageously romantic rebellion against the forces of taboo epitomized by the British Health Authority. The academic senses of "queering" were intuitively latent for him in the anal pleasures of his engagement with the shadowy figures to be met in the "selva oscura" on Hampstead Heath.

Two rather more polite lines of meaning have evolved for this strategic gerund in recent academic usage. If queering is conceived as a process occurring from the outside in, as an unsettling imposition of queerness on some pre-existing order of straightness, it entails a playful rewriting of a text or a perverse revision of an image that had hitherto been constructed, interpreted, and rendered intelligible only from a strictly heterosexist viewpoint. As a critical strategy this first kind of queering takes off from in-jokes, and as a creative act it gives rise to parodies. On the other hand, if queering is understood as a process occurring from the inside out, as a release of meanings already encoded within texts or images that secretly work against the homophobic culture in which they were constructed, then it would signify a serious exercise of "outing" – a public disclosure of hushed-up queer-

ness – which effectively unsettles the traditional binary of mainstream versus marginal literature and refuses to accept the heterosexist limits of art.
As a critical strategy this second kind of queering results in provocative
illuminations of the hidden sexual significations that have been dismissed,
ignored, or censored in the reception-history of the classics. As a creative act
it prompts redemptive remakes of them.[7]

Which kind of queering does Jarman invite us to observe in the Dante
cameo? To answer this, we must go back to the filmmaker's student days
and trace the bending course of his three-decades-long engagement with the
Inferno. Prompting that engagement was his formative exposure to the Dantean work of another "bent" (and hellbent) artist, Robert Rauschenberg.

1. "To Make Literary Ideas Pictorial": the *Dante Suite*

In 1964, when Rauschenberg was still far from being out as a gay artist in America but was just about to be very in as a pop artist in Europe, the
trendsetting Whitechapel Gallery in East London mounted an exhibition of
his paintings, drawings, and free-standing "combines" or mixed-media as-
semblages of painting, sculpture, photography, and found objects. Included
in this breakthrough show, which ran from February 4 through March 8,
were his thirty-four illustrations to Dante's *Inferno*. Usually classified as
drawings, the *Dante Suite* (as the illustrations are still collectively known in
England) would no doubt have reminded the gallery visitors of the densely
collaged surfaces of the combines exhibited nearby.[8]

Among the enthusiastic visitors to the Rauschenberg retrospective
at the Whitechapel was Derek Jarman, a bumptiously hell-raising but still
discreetly closeted student from the Slade School of Art in Central London.
He had just turned twenty-two. Still burning in his memory of boyhood was
his Dantesque exposure to Catholicism as a student at St. Juliana's convent
school in Oxford. The nuns there, he bitterly recalled, "hacked my paradise
to pieces like the despoilers of the Amazon – carving paths of good and evil
to Heaven, Hell, and Purgatory."[9] Now, at the Whitechapel show, he could
perhaps find a way back to his old paradise by following an artistic path
through Hell with an engagingly ironic, seductively modern Virgil.

Like Rauschenberg, whose subtle gay manipulation of American masculinity codes seems to have struck him at the time with the force of a life-altering revelation, Jarman was secretly struggling with the torments of the closet. He had been raised in a military family with a strict regard for traditional gender roles and sanctified heterosexual monogamy. "I was another young man corrupted and co-opted by heterosexuality," he would bitterly recall about his closeted youth, "my mind still swimming about in the cesspit which is known as family life, subjected to a Christian love whose ugliness would shatter a mirror."[10]

The British version of the closet had hardly expanded its claustrophobic legal dimensions since the dark days of the Oscar Wilde trials. Despite the recommendations for homosexual law reform published by the liberal-leaning Wolfenden Committee in 1957, men publically branded as "homosexuals" in the early 1960s were still subject to tough prosecution and career-destroying imprisonment under the Labouchère amendment. Enacted in 1885, this infamous law criminalizing "any act of gross indecency" between "male persons" in public or in private had led to Wilde's much-publicized conviction in 1895. Though the social as well as legal reasons for striking down the Labouchère Amendment had been clearly spelled out to the British media during Jarman's teenage years, Sir John Wolfenden and his impeccably straight-acting Anglican Committee (along with many thousands of suspenseful male persons behind the scenes) had to wait until 1967 before the British Parliament got around to enacting their controversial recommendations into law.[11]

What would Jarman, growing up under such infernally repressive conditions, have made of Rauschenberg's bold modernist retracing of Dante's medieval journey to the underworld? Did he have a reflexively aesthetic response to the *Dante Suite* in the swoony style of a Wildean acolyte? Apparently not. Stray comments in his student notebook suggest that his immediate response to the Whitechapel show was impetuously creative and sexual: he wanted to use Rauschenberg's collage techniques to push the limits of homoerotic figural art. "Construction...collage...or any form of junk yard art," he rejoiced to discover,

> enables one to bypass the abstraction which seems the inevitable form in which "competent" painting appears in the early 60's – it has characteristics akin to the cinema and has the ability to make literary ideas pictorial.[12]

The *Dante Suite*, with its cinematic sequencing of spectral crowds, vectored footprints, and architectural details, certainly makes "literary ideas pictorial" in a way discernibly opposed to the anti-narrative paragone of Abstract Expressionism.[13] The New York School that Rauschenberg didn't quite belong to, though he drank heavily with its leading lights and danced lightly around its heavy edges, was then at the height of its international influence. Lurking behind Jarman's entirely predictable art-school bitching about the "inevitable" form imposed on "competent" painting by the Abstract Expressionists (via his teachers at the Slade) is a prophetic intuition that his own artistic trajectory would carry him through pop-art collage towards experimental film.

That Rauschenberg's temporally attuned work also marks the beginning of a gay artistic rebellion against the grandiose atemporality of the Abstract Expressionists – and against their critical apologists whose metaphysical dictates promoting "pure" abstraction powerfully resonated with the purging rhetoric of All-American heterosexism – is clear enough now in the cultural aftermath of Gay Liberation.[14] If any of this constrained defiance got through to Jarman in his student days, his political awareness of it was probably no more than nascent. His creative move towards it, however, was already obvious to any authority figure who had eyes to see. By the mid-1960s, his desire to rebel against abstraction by championing the male nude was certainly obvious enough to provoke homophobic reactions not just from his militantly straight father but from his ambivalent teachers. When he produced an overtly homoerotic collage for a school project in the summer of 1966, his father Lance Jarman, a retired RAF officer, ridiculed him for months about his perilously self-incriminating use of male nudes clipped from issues of *Physique Pictorial*.[15] Less callous, though no less controlling, were the critical remarks leveled at his bad-boy exuberance by Sir William Coldstream at the Slade. Coldstream pointed out to him that if he ever wanted to be a successful artist he would have to pay respectful attention to "the acceptable limits of art," which, from the de-haut-en-bas viewpoint of the British cultural elite, were clearly mappable onto the legally enforced boundary between heterosexuality and homosexuality.[16]

If, as these futile protests suggest, Jarman was using Rauschenberg's subversively figural *Dante Suite* to stage his art-school rebellions against British heterosexism, did his enthusiasm for its provocative collaging of the past and the present necessarily mean that he appreciated it as a work of distinctively gay art? Would he have tensely viewed it as a private gay "coding" imposed on the manifestly homophobic allegory of Divine Wrath in the *Inferno* – as it is sometimes, rather casually, viewed today?[17]

Though the *Dante Suite* is not likely to have impressed the trendy Whitechapel crowd as autobiographical in style or content, Rauschenberg had completed it as a private therapeutic project in 1960 following his tempestuous breakup with his partner and more famous collaborator, Jasper Johns, in 1958.[18] No one at the time hailed it as a masterpiece of gay art, and for good reason. Though the once offbeat Greenwich-Village-based artist had depicted the darkest depths of the underworld, his new international work was not at all "underground." On the surface, at least, the subdued and meditative character of the *Dante Suite* set it at a considerable remove from the flamboyant, theatrical, sacrilegious, or naughtily low-brow style coded as "gay" by the taste-policing British media for whom "gay" primarily pointed in the direction of Noel Coward. Where were the signs of homosexual frivolity in these grave American illustrations? Their obvious associations for the British public were with high-class literary culture steeped in venerable religious traditions. Who would have guessed that Rauschenberg's complex erotic-artistic coupling with Johns found a haunting parallel in Dante's complex erotic-poetic coupling with Virgil, the sweet escort destined for a shattering breakup?

Even in New York, where the *Inferno* illustrations now reside on permanent display in the Rauschenberg-Johns Gallery on the fourth floor of the Museum of Modern Art, they are still presented to the public primarily as the fruit of Rauschenberg's intense emotional engagement with a text rather than with a man, or if with a man, then with a long-dead and indubitably straight love poet who had gone through hell for the sake of recovering his long-dead and indubitably straight inamorata. As the product of Rauschenberg's technical virtuosity and originality as a draftsman – he invented a new collage technique called "solvent transfer" just for this project – they overtly reflect Dante's technical virtuosity and originality as a poet.[19] As a musically organized "suite," one illustration per canto, they overtly reflect the textual divisions of the Inferno in the same humble way that its medieval illuminations once did. And as a modernist combination of found media images and spontaneous freehand pencil-drawings, they overtly reflect the elaborate intertextual layering of Dantean allegory with its polysemous references to the past, the present, and the future.

Covertly, however, the *Dante Suite* must have revealed to the artist himself and to a few of his intimates back in New York just how infernal the social and psychological pressures of the closet were becoming for him and for other sexually unorthodox men who had survived the homophobic purges of the 1950s. He placed clues in his drawings for their eyes only; clues to his psychosexual experience under the barrage of fiery religious condemnations of sodomy from the Baptist Church when he was a boy back in Texas; clues to his fearful political reaction after the vicious shower of media attacks against homo-commie-pinkos during the McCarthy era. With poignant self-confession and prudent self-effacement, he had drawn a burning red outline of his own right foot on the sand-coloured paper for his illustration of the desert of the sodomites in *Inferno* 14.[20]

Jarman could not have known whose toes had left an imprint on the damning sand, or what that dire "vestigium" might mean in the context of Rauschenberg's hidden sexual history. He hardly had a sexual history of his own at that point. Though painting would always be his first love as an artist, as a "male person" Jarman was vainly trying to ignore his attraction to athletic lads by focusing his scholarly attention on set and costume design in the Slade's theatre program. His aesthetically momentous exposure to the *Dante Suite* would have its first discernible impact on his innovative model for the set of an imaginary ballet production. "The designs for Stravinsky's *Orpheus*," he noted excitedly in his journal,

> are a direct response to Rauschenberg's '*Dante Suite*', which were shown at the Whitechapel and made a great impression on me.
> The set is black and white, and made up from xeroxes of physique magazines and a variety of fragmented classical motifs. The backdrop contains a haunting portrait of 'A Boy in an Asylum' by [American photographer] Avedon collaged against an Inferno whose gates are the Brooklyn Bridge.[21]

Just how great an impression the *Inferno* drawings had made on him was touchingly obvious in the earnest self-consciousness of his homage to Rauschenberg in this design. Stravinsky was hardly in the picture. For all its "fragmented classical motifs," Orpheus's underworld was not to be a hazily romantic Greek ruin for Hades and Persephone but a harshly updated

Americanized Inferno in the modernist collage-style of the *Dante Suite*. As its gate of abandoned hope, the Brooklyn Bridge would lead the inevitably despairing Modern Poet – Orpheus as Dante as Whitman as Pound? – towards the Manhattan skyline behind which Dis would spread its evil web again through hideous crime-ridden streets. If Dante's damned had "lost the good of intellect[22]," their modern counterparts must be even crazier to live in New York. They must seem more hauntingly trapped than Avedon's straight-jacketed Boy in an Asylum, more brazenly body-obsessed than the posing-strapped models in *Physique Pictorial*. Only in this new pop-art hell could the private objects of closeted gay desire be daringly xeroxed as public spectacle, "collaged" into the backdrop for direly satiric yet deliciously sinful contemplation behind the danced-out mythology of the ideal heterosexual lover's triumph over Death.

Predictably, Jarman went too far. His design was just too queer for comfort. "Sex crept into my work through the theatre, particularly in the underworld scenes in *Orpheus*," he would recall many years later, and a friendly but censorious word of caution came down to him from on high: "One lunchtime Bill Coldstream, the Slade Professor, came into the theatre department, and gave me a bleak lecture, squinting at my designs of naked men in chains. But he didn't attack them directly, he talked of his role as a film censor...."[23]

In the hyper-Rauschenbergian juxtapositions of high and low cultural signifiers with which Jarman constructed his ballet set, post-war American popular culture could be seen as even flatter and phonier than it had appeared before the war in Hollywood's "Dissing" of Manhattan in the 1935 film *Dante's Inferno* (directed by post-impressionist painter Harry Lachman and starring a young Spencer Tracy).[24] The ten-minute Doré-inspired hell sequence in this old talkie, as well as the Manhattan skyline featured in one of its gloriously gaudy posters, may have been in the back of Jarman's mind as he worked on the model for the set. Much later in his career he would splice clips from this film into one of his early efforts at a gay Dantean cinema, a Super-8 infernalization of a punk concert at the archly named London disco Heaven:

23 December 1980: I filmed Throbbing Gristle's Psychic Rally in Heaven with wax earplugs, because for half an hour I had to lean into the speakers to get the best possible angles. I threw the old Nizo Super 8 about in time to the

music, at "stop frame." The band is restrained, almost static on stage...Later I refilmed the result, cutting it together with old black and white footage from the film of Dante's *Inferno*. The result had a persistent strobe which synchronized with the music...It had a powerful effect on audiences.[25]

Through an experimental combination of superimposition and re-filming, Heaven was thus inverted into Hell. It made for a fine punk effect – crude but compelling. The throngs of writhing souls in the far-off glamorized past of Hollywood's morally black-and-white Inferno seemed to howl and gnash their teeth in sync with the throbbing crowds in the tawdry alternative present of London's garish gay underground.

The collage effect of simultaneity that Jarman would achieve through his montage techniques in the Psychic Rally short, and much later and more elaborately, in the Dante sequence for his feature film *Edward II*, was clearly anticipated by Rauschenberg in his solvent transfers for the *Dante Suite*. To create an impression of thronging macho-men on the desert of the Seventh Circle, Rauschenberg had clipped images of American athletes out of magazines and newspapers covering the 1960 Rome Olympics. He had then soaked the clippings in lighter fluid and positioned them on the surface of his paper. By rubbing the damp clippings with a pencil, he had been able to dissolve the printer's ink and reproduce the images as a pattern of striated markings so that a spectral impression of the athletes was directly transferred onto his drawing surface. The present literally "dyed" into the past. Modern sports heroes ironically turned up as medieval sodomites.

Rauschenberg's method of solvent transfer is to collage, then, what Jarman's experimental montage is to cinema. But is there anything corresponding to these visual techniques of simultaneity in the verbal design of Dante's poem that Rauschenberg and Jarman might have emulated in their updating projects?

2. "Wrestling on the Golden Sand": *Aeneid* 6 and *Inferno* 16

Something comparable to solvent transfer and refilming is already at work rhetorically in the calquing of Virgil's Underworld into Dante's Inferno.[26] The desert of the sodomites provides a striking example of the metaphoric solvency of Dante-poet's tropological imagination, the translating medium through which an ancient sequence of consoling Elysian images was lifted from its original pagan context and superimposed with furious Christian zeal onto the sandy surface of the Seventh Circle where it was ironically crosscut with the narrative present of Dantepilgrim's journey. Here is Virgil's invitingly pastoral description of the Elysian Fields as they first appear to Aeneas and the Sybil:

> deuenere locos laetos et amoena uirecta
> fortunatorum nemorum sedesque beatas.
> largior hic campos aether et lumine uestit
> purpureo, solemque suum, sua sidera norunt.
> pars in gramineis exercent membra palaestris,
> contendunt ludo et fulua luctantur harena;
> pars pedibus plaudunt choreas et carmina dicunt.
> nec non Threicius longa cum ueste sacerdos
> obloquitur numeris septem discrimina uocum,
> iamque eadem digitis, iam pectine pulsat eburno.
> (Aeneid VI 638-647)

[...they entered the land of joy, the lovely glades of the fortunate woods and the home of the blest. Here a broader sky clothes the plains in glowing light, and the spirits have their own sun and their own stars. Some take exercise on grassy wrestling-grounds and hold athletic contests and wrestling bouts on the golden sand. Others pound the earth with dancing feet and sing their songs while Orpheus, the priest of Thrace, accompanies their measures on his seven-stringed lyre, plucking the notes sometimes with his fingers, sometimes with his ivory plectrum.][27]

When Dante-pilgrim comes upon the band of athletic sodomites wailing at the start of *Inferno* 16, Dante-poet effectively superimposes apocalypse onto pastoral by subjecting Virgil's Elysium to a series of tropological reversals. Instead of a land of fabulous joy, the pilgrim and his guide enter a site of fierce torment. Instead of fertile plains and lovely glades, they face a prospect of sterile deserts and bleak exposed rocks. Instead of an expansive sky with a glowing sun, a cavernous darkness flashes above them with corrosive flames. Instead of cheerful new stars, the rain of fire strikes them as frighteningly old – at once a throwback to the sulfurous shower at the end of the Sodom story and an outrageous replay of the tongues of flame at the start of Pentecost. Instead of golden sand, they must watch out for burning sand. Instead of blessed spirits who spend their afterlives wrestling and dancing, they encounter damned souls who merely *appear* to wrestle and dance before the pilgrim's easily deluded eyes. Instead of Orpheus ritually joining in the choral ceremonies as their accompanist, Virgil carefully keeps his distance from the combat and Dante suppresses his desire to join the chorus. Ironically, this point-by-point translation of the Virgilian passage into the Seventh Circle does not efface the pastoral allure of the original but rather brings it back nostalgically as a lost world hideously refreshed in the pilgrim's (and the reader's) literary memory so that what has become of Elysium now – now that its mythical immanence has been bombarded *literaliter* by the apocalyptic wrath of a transcendent God – disturbingly co-exists with what it once was in Virgil's epic.

If Jarman had taken a close look at Rauschenberg's striking illustration for *Inferno* 16 in the Whitechapel Gallery show, as he may well have done given his strong personal interest in the treatment of convicted sodomites, he would have seen the visual equivalent of the deeply ironic effect of simultaneity generated by literary calquing in the ghostly modernity of the age-old figures of Virgil, Dante, and the Damned produced by solvent transfers. The sodomitical trio of Guido, Tegghiaio, and Jacopo are represented by the heads of Olympic athletes arranged in a tight circle, grotesquely recalling the rings of baby cherub heads in traditional Catholic depictions of heaven.[28] Dante-pilgrim assumes the modern guise of a slightly paunchy golfer, naked except for a towel, whom Rauschenberg discovered in a 1958 ad for "Pro Fit Golf Shafts" and gleefully transferred into his Inferno as a secular icon of ultra-straight, all-American masculinity. Never a sportsman like his gung-ho hearty of a father, Jarman is unlikely to have picked out the middlesized Pro Fit Man from the original line-up of three contrasting body types in the ad.[29]

Rauschenberg's Virgil, however, would have been easily recognizable from widespread media coverage of the United States Ambassador to the United Nations in the early 1960s. A phantom Adlai Stevenson, his arms calmly crossed, does very well for the diplomatic Virgil of *Inferno* 16. Like the Roman poet, the American statesman looked approvingly towards the future of the human race but sagely foresaw its potential for cataclysmic destruction. Jarman might have noticed that Adlai-Virgil was strategically positioned beneath the white silhouette of an ominously tilting Seattle Space Needle, a futuristic icon of progressive modernity still under construction when lighter fluid dissolved its outline and ghosted it into the American Inferno.[30] Like Dante's Virgil, Stevenson was also renowned for putting his rhetorical skills to use in promoting the imperial mythology of world unity but ended up a surprisingly big loser. Though he had secured the Democratic nomination for president in 1952 and 1956, he had gone down to humiliating defeat in both campaigns.[31]

If Jarman had been looking for the rain of fire in Adlai-Virgil's vicinity, his eye would surely have caught sight of a familiar Cold War nightmare below the horizontal line bisecting the illustration. The firestorm of patriotic rhetoric stirred up against Stevenson in the late 1950s after he had boldly called for an end to aboveground testing of nuclear weapons is ironically suggested in the illustration by a comet-like fireball hurtling towards the bottom of the illustration. Could it be an atom bomb? Kaboom! There was no way a mere Test Ban Treaty could save us from the charring effects of Soviet Wrath. If nuclear war broke out in the hideous present, we would all be in the B-movie position of Dante's sodomites – zapped and zombied beyond recognition, worse off than the Living Dead. Now *there* was a panicky pop-art thought to make the morally selective cataclysms of the medieval underworld seem like happy days.

3. "The Ghost Writer": Dante in Jarman's Journals

"Perhaps the sodomites should be written out of Dante's *Inferno*," Jarman mused in his journal entry for August 1, 1990, "I'll offer myself as the ghost writer."[32] But how could he play "ghost writer" to a poet who had already triumphed in this role, who had become "The Poet" not only by writing about ghosts more vividly than any other author in literary history but also by "ghosting," shadily rewriting, the works of his great classical predecessors?

As a ghost writer of Virgil, his most conspicuous cover, Dante tacitly begins putting new words in the old poet's mouth – a mouth once "faint" in the "wide silence" of death (*Inf.* 1.63) – as soon as they meet in the Dark Wood. Only after their initial exchange of words will a river of eloquence "spread so wide" again through world of the living that its fountainhead, Virgil, will be credited as the immediate source for the current of worldreforming speech flowing out through the Sacred Poem (*Inf.* 1.79-81). And isn't that just how a good ghost writer is supposed to operate? Obscure for now, the transcendent author of the Sacred Poem humbly effaces himself behind his own words, downplays his authorial agency, so that otherwise silent celebrities like the long dead Virgil may tell their "own" stories anew and get fresh credit for it. Eventually word leaks out that the ghost writer (Dante won't have himself named until the top of Purgatory) is the true author behind the text, which of course has already become a classic, and a new literary star is born. Dante's ghostwritten version of the *Aeneid* – the *Inferno* – is validated as a classic at every turn by the miraculous immanence of its "original" author, for Virgil literally retraces his steps through the textual route of the classical underworld-journey as if he (rather than his ghost writer) were engaged in producing a new edition of it by amending its errors and filling in its gaps.

The desert of the sodomites is an egregious gap in the Aeneid underworld, which of course couldn't possibly have contained such a biblical locus; but Dante's ghost-writing quietly "discovers" it for the authorized revision of the journey and fills it with new flocks of spirits whom Virgil is now compelled to recognize. (If Dante had kept a Jarman-style notebook while he was planning the first cantica, he might have jotted down something like this: "Perhaps the sodomites should be written into Virgil's *Aeneid*.") When the macho trio of Florentines dance into view at the cruisy start of Inferno 16, looking like naked and oiled athletes recruited from his own epic, Virgil knowingly bids Dante pause and show them courtesy. "And if it were not for the fire that the nature of this place pours down," he tactfully advises (*Inf.* 16.16-18), suggesting that the fire is a natural phenomenon of the desert rather than a supernatural proof of God's wrath at bad butch tops into branding, flaying, threesomes, and other unnatural practices, "I would say that haste would more become you than them."

You should stop. You should hurry on. As a moral tutor, Virgil usually doesn't give mixed messages. Why does he do so here, of all places, where he clearly senses his disciple's social or perhaps even sexual vulnerability? If Virgil uses his postmortem powers of telepathy to read Dante's secret desires at this point, as he does so often elsewhere, he doesn't let on. Not a word about the unspeakable sin under examination escapes his lips. Is this a courtesy too? Something crucial but perhaps too personal, too delicate, is left unspoken between ghost and ghost writer – something is prudently left unsaid under the censuring and censoring rain of fire – which might explain why Virgil wants Dante to be kind to these sinners, to stop for a polite chat with them, even though the sodomites are known to be violent, and their silent tongues of fire unbearably scorching, and their compromised observers much better off getting the hell out of there.

As a pagan shade in a Christian underworld, Virgil may be forgiven on theological grounds for failing to understand the scriptural significance of the rain of fire. Having died outside the faith, he remains intellectually so – even when he's on the move inside its ever-narrowing prison. But it's precisely because of his broad pagan outlook on human behavior, which extends to man-on-man action of the pastoral as well as epic variety, that he is unforgivably close to erotic collusion with the Boys in the Sand. He had his own boy once. This gossipy revelation is buried as a biographical fact in the Servian commentary on the hot male action (or sultry inaction, really) in his notorious second eclogue. No ardent reader of the eclogues[33] would be tempted to call their author a *violent* lover of men, especially no reader as morally ardent as Dante, but where there's rhetorical smoke, there's fire, and there's certainly a fierce homoerotic glow behind the ancient verse Virgil put in the mouth of his shepherd alter-ego Corydon. "But love burns me," Corydon had wailed, "for who can limit love?" (me tamen urit amor; quis enim modus adsit amori?: *Ecloga* II, 68).[34] The God of the Inferno can limit love, obviously. Love is very limited on this ghastly ground. How ironic, then, that Virgil should find himself traveling now with a younger male companion on the "hard limits" of a raised levee across a locus far from amoenus, looking at charred "flocks" in a hot zone which turns out to be, on close inspection, not only unpastoral but apocalyptically anti-pastoral!

No wonder he is particularly "attentive to their cries" (*Inf.* 16.13): his own lamenting shepherds had anticipated them. His amorous complicity with the flaming wailers who have now become wailing flamers is left unspoken, however, even when they resume their old refrain – literally their "ancient verse" ("antico verso": *Inf.* 16.21). For the rest of this hideously parodic scene, in fact, Virgil becomes a silent witness of their torment. So now Dante brashly undertakes to speak for him, ghost-writing what his favorite author *would have said* to him at the time if only the fire in the scene had been the old pastoral flame of homoerotic desire. Despite his doctrinally induced fear of the even older biblical fire perpetually raining down on the sodomites, the Christian poet acknowledges in his unprecedented confession of empathy for the physical and psychological victims of religious homophobia (Inf. 16.46-51) that his pagan teacher would have "approved" of his own benevolent impulse to hurl himself down among them for a hot embrace.[35]

It was an impulse Jarman not only shared, but acted upon, night after night, in the dark woods and sandy grounds of Hampstead Heath. No silent witness, he. He delighted in playing the unreluctant Dante of the Heath. "I take a deep breath, a double vodka and a taxi to 'The Heath' stop outside Jack Straw's castle," he reminisced in his journal entry for May 26, 1989,

> and walk down through the car park. It's here that danger lurks – on the fringes. The dark woodlands seem by comparison safe and friendly. Do the gangs of queerbashers who haunt the mind lie in wait, thwarted and perverted guardians of propriety – or are they just in the imagination?... I have to admit the Heath has a "reputation." It is considered by many to be off-bounds, for two reasons: as a symbol of the dark into which the gay world has been driven by heterosexual censure, and also as a reinforcement of the critics' respectability, that said nothing goes on on the Heath that doesn't go on behind net curtains, the "respectable" are found in a smoke filled dungeon, such as "Heaven" – a nightclub with an air conditioning system that would please the Prince of Darkness, deep in the bowels of the earth.[36]

With defiant post-coital glee he easily inverts the infernal allegorization of his favorite cruising ground in West London. What the censorious critics of the Heath, both gay and straight, have portrayed as a hell is really a dark woods leading to paradise. And what the respectable gay world might regard as paradise – the famously overrated disco Heaven – is censured as a hot smoky dungeon fit for self-deluded, net-curtain assimilationists unable to smell the sulphur in the unconditioned air. Mixed up with his justifiable fears of being bashed again himself, and with his ever-painful memories of homophobic crimes committed against his friends and former tricks, are literary recollections of the intensely imagined violence of the Seventh Circle.

Thanks to the flippant blasphemies routinely encoded in the names of modern gay hotspots, Jarman could always flip a heaven into hell and make a heaven in hell's despite. But he could not so easily rid his imagination of Dante's sodomites. Their dance in the desert would always haunt his Heath.

Whenever he wandered into its inviting darkness, a pastoral cruiser with vodka on his breath, his erotically directed path through the Here and Now would be twisted into allegory by Dante's apocalyptic vision of what three perfectly respectable Florentine gentlemen – "thwarted and perverted guardians of propriety"– had to endure in the Hereafter. Jarman would always be opposed and attracted to Guido and Tegghiaio and Iacopo under the rain of fire, fiercely resisting their bathetic compliance with Christian respectability yet impulsively drawn to embrace them, as outcasts, despite the physical and spiritual dangers of their blasted cruising ground. By 1990, however, as he had grimly admitting to himself in his journals, it was an impulse he would soon be acting upon only in his feverish dreams – or in his final films. His sight was already blurring from toxo, his skin was burning all over from St. Antony's fire, and his lean body was wasting away to a shade from the unpoetic ghosting of AIDS.

That was the dire medical context in which he mused about writing Dante's sodomites out of the *Inferno*. Hooked up to a sulphadiazine drip, he had just spent two weeks recovering what was left of his eyesight in the Amroth Wright ward for AIDS patients in St. Mary's Hospital, a few tube stops west of the Whitechapel Gallery and his old stomping grounds at the Slade. His stay in the Amroth Wright had been a dark night for his soul as well as his eyes.

"When someone dies here a hush descends," he sighed in his entry for July 23, 1990: "I imagine the same atmosphere in a prison on the day someone's death sentence comes up. I hear a patient say 'Who's next for the cooler?'"[37] If this remark reminded him of the frozen souls in the Ninth Circle ("down there where the sinners keep cool": *Inf.* 32.117), he didn't note it in his journal, but the Inferno had certainly been on his mind as he suffered through the hallucinatory effects of his medication: "Waves of icy sulphadiazine breaking on the farther shores after we have crossed over in a blizzard of pills."[38]

As his vision gradually returned, he was faced with nightmarish visitations from other patients who reminded him of ghosts. He begged his eyes to turn "these will o' the wisps back to human beings,"[39] but they kept appearing dimly in his field of vision. "The kid who has lost his mind wanders through the ward, and comes to stare at me, motionless in the doorway," he struggled to write on the first of August, "I pull down the blind to hide the sun."[40] That day, to strength his vision, he had forced himself for an hour to watch television – a medium he had gleefully scorned for years – but even that mindless escape had brought the Inferno back him in the mediated form of an episode from Peter Greenaway's *TV Dante*. "I switched it off," he snapped, "when the appalling TV Dante appeared in the evening with its silly pundits whose explanations were more obscure than the poem. Trite video wallpaper."[41] What appalled him about it was not just that it main-streamed Dante's profoundly transgressive poem into a shallow vehicle for "expert" (hetero-orthodox) commentary on medieval theology but also that its director had received a lot of funding for the computer wizardry needed to conjure up the damned as mere special effects in a video. "Peter Greenaway gets a fortune to make Dante," he enviously groused, "I think Dante would imprison him in a further circle of hell for the courtesy."[42]

If Jarman were "to make Dante," it would be to remake him. It would be to live his journey anew through the horrors of the epidemic. It would be to rescue his allegory of despair and madness and outrage from the comfortable sanity of silly pundits. Like Rauschenberg's *Dante Suite*, Jarman's counter-Inferno would be a harrowing but triumphant act of modern reinvention rather than a technological exercise in neo-medieval exegesis.

Ironically, it was his hospital-room TV that got him fired up enough again that day to propose the rescue of Dante's sodomites from the *Inferno*. He must also have been watching a popular children's program based on Enid Blyton's toyland fantasy *Noddy*, the cast of which had originally included a villainous Golliwog named Gilbert Golly. In the late 1980s, when the racist implications of this black-faced doll were pointed out to the producers of the show, Gilbert was written out of the series and replaced by a pair of goblins. "*Noddy* has been rewritten, purged of racism and sexism," Jarman harrumphed, "Perhaps the sodomites should be written out of Dante's *Inferno*."[43] Nothing got his rebellious blood boiling more than polite censorship, particularly if it was the quiet internal sort that reflected hypocritical orthodoxies just then coming into the critical spotlight under the term "political correctness." If *Noddy* could be purged of Gollywogs, what classic would be left in tact at the end of the day? Would even the sodomites be purged from the *Inferno*? His proposal to do so as Dante's "ghost writer" was a sarcastic joke at first, its immediate target being the silly pundits and promoters of the respectable bourgeois version of gay political correctness – his particular foes – who would be only too eager to have the censoring authorities wipe away the embarrassing traces of fire and brimstone from the literary record of religious homophobia. But then, if bowdlerized and rendered acceptable to net-curtain gays, the *Inferno* would not be infernal anymore, and it needed to be, especially now in the plague years, when the allegory of the sexually damned was being *lived* out again day by day by the maddened, restless, desperate patients in the Amroth Wright. Queer outsiders, more than anyone, needed to experience the Seventh Circle at full blast in order to perceive the discriminatory foundations of Christian sexual morality in the harshest imaginable apocalyptic glare.

Writing the sodomites out of Dante's *Inferno* was a project Jarman never got around to: he had his own hell to deal with not just as an AIDS patient in the British Public Health System but as Britain's most outspoken apologist for the queer rights group Outrage! (whose "Fuck Me Blind" defiance of the Family Values campaign of the Tory regime spoke to him at an intensely literal level even before his eyes completely gave out).[44] No matter how many times his plagued body went down in the nerve-wracking fight against opportunistic infections, his proud soul remained defiantly up in arms – lobbing words and images with an explosively blasphemous aim against the fire-and-brimstone crusaders who blamed the epidemic on the poofters of Hampstead Heath. What he did manage to accomplish as a Dantean ghost writer before his agonizing death in 1994, ironically, was to write Dante's sodomites into a very queer new work: the screenplay for his filmed attack on Marlowe's *Edward II*.

4. "God Himself is up in arms": *Edward II* Screenplay, Sequence 28

In the hackle-raising second scene of Marlowe's *Edward II*, the haughty Earl of Lancaster whines to his allies, the Elder and Younger Mortimer, about the various noble titles newly heaped on Edward's upstart minion Gaveston after his exultant return from exile in France. The Bishop of Coventry, who had engineered the exile, has just been arrested and disgraced. Lancaster's roiling annoyance at Gaveston's power over the besotted King soon turns to rebellious outrage when the Archbishop of Canterbury stomps in with an attendant and dispatches a furious message to the Pope about the brutal imprisonment of the Bishop of Coventry. The Bishop's sacred garments have been "rent and torn" in the Tower and all his worldly goods "asseiz'd" for immediate possession by Gaveston.[45] Overhearing Canterbury's indignant assessment of the economic consequences of this arrest – not only has vandalism been committed on church property but worse, church property has been confiscated by the Crown – Lancaster boldly inquires whether the Archbishop plans to take arms against the King.

"What need I?" answers the cagey prelate (I.ii.40-41): "God himself is up in arms / When violence is offer'd to the Church." Sacrilege, then, not sodomy, has provoked God's justifiable wrath against Marlowe's justice-flouting Edward.

During the early summer of 1990, when Jarman was shaking the Elizabethan dust off Marlowe's play and crunching its flabby grandiloquence down into the ripped screenplay that would come out a year later under the polemically intensified title *Queer Edward II*, he made several significant changes to the Up-in-Arms episode. Make that "violations" rather than "changes." He was not bent on reverently updating a Renaissance classic, or even reclaiming Marlowe for the Gay Literary Tradition. He was through with "gay." He hated traditional Olivier-style costume dramas. His brusque advice to any film-school twink wondering "How to make a film of a gay love affair and get it commissioned" was worthy of a Droog: "Find a dusty old play and violate it."[46] It was advice harking back to his vigorous punk days in the late 1970s, and he followed it to the letter now despite his rapidly deteriorating health and his Bitter Old Queen status in the eyes of London's more conservative gay circles.

In Sequence 28 of the screenplay, as the Up-in-Arms episode came to be numbered, old Lancaster is replaced by a generic Chorus of Earls who function as a Brechtian bloc of elitist reactionaries. Lancaster may or may not be among them. It doesn't really matter. They're all Lancasters. They have gathered at night around a board-room table to plot the unqueening of the kingdom. (Their resemblance to Tory Party brass planning the downfall of the Iron Lady cannot have been accidental: Jarman no doubt relished the ironic coincidence that Margaret Thatcher had been sent packing from Downing Street by her male underlings only a few weeks before he retired to Prospect Cottage in Kent to work on the screenplay.) The main item of nasty business on the Chorus's agenda is to sign a quasi-official document, drawn up by their leader Mortimer, ordering a second exile for Gaveston. When the Earls repeat the leading question "My Lord will you take arms against the King?" – originally posed by Lancaster to Canterbury – it is Jarman's viciously neo-con Mortimer, a fusion of Elder and Younger, who answers it with the Archbishop's old line: "What need I, God himself is up in arms."[47]

As the heterosexist villain of *Queer Edward II*, Jarman's Mortimer is a mega-butch military man who claws his fascist way to the top by making sexual showdowns at the homo/hetero divide the only name of the game in British politics. In his private life, of course, he prefers randy rentgirls to Royal Family Values and targets the royals for nuclear family meltdown in order to advance his dictatorial career. Notably cut from the original Up-in-Arms speech is the reasonable suggestion that God is angry because of sacrilegious violence done to the Church by the Crown. The rhetorical effect of Mortimer's reply, which leaves out the "when" clause, is to insinuate as a certainty – a very English conclusion befitting the regime Jarman dubbed "Heterosoc"[48] – that God *must* be up in arms because there's a nasty bum-boy on the loose shoving it to the laws of the land and a flaming sod on the throne who deserves a red-hot poker shoved up his arse. Sodomy, then, not sacrilege, has provoked God's sadistic wrath (or at least the politically exploitable backlash of the Earls) against Jarman's masochistic Edward.

To foreground Tory-style sexual politics as the driving force behind Mortimer's rise to power, Jarman also cut the financially fulminating Canterbury from the scene and replaced him with a silently acquiescent "Bishop of York" (sic). Whether the actual Archbishop of York in 1990 – a certain Dr. John Habgood, who was a staunchly conservative opponent of any liberal efforts to assert the moral dignity of gays and lesbians within the Anglican Church – was up in arms at this satiric reflection of himself, Jarman did not record in his journals or in the notes to his screenplay.[49] What this odd substitution clearly reveals, however, is the emergence in Queer *Edward II* of a cruel project of disclosure just coming into Queer Nation-building vogue at the time under the made-for-media term "outing." The Bishop of York is wordlessly outed here in potentia, as a hypocritical guardian of public morals who plays power politics straight-up but must hide a few queer secrets under his vestments. He recalls the smiling Bishop in the film that surely provided Jarman with his infernal model for the cruel satiric design of *Edward II*, namely Pasolini's Dantean-Sadean masterwork *Salò*.[50]

5. "Faggot Pursuits": *Edward II* Screenplay, Sequences 26-29

Though Jarman's textual "violation" of the Up-in-Arms episode seems quite unrelated to his AIDS-haunted meditation on the *Inferno*, the two would come together spectacularly in 1991 when he turned *Edward II* into a film. The shoot began on February 18 and wrapped up on March 28, while the editing process would take up much of his time from the end of May through early August. The imaginative convergence (or collision) of Dante and Marlowe must have come to Jarman much earlier than that, however, for it is critically anticipated and partially realized in the screenplay he wrote the summer before at Prospect Cottage, where, under mounting pressure from his uncertain health and his anxious funders to complete all pre-production tasks for *Edward II* by the end of 1990, he also worked day by day on his feverish AIDS journals and his gale-fanned "Paradise" garden. His maritime pastoral retreat, then, became the unlikely creative locus for a Dantean invasion of allegorical spirits into the Marlovian world of scheming earls and frustrated lovers.

We may never know precisely when Dante came into play as an ally in his ghost-writing attack on Marlowe, but the result of their Jarmanizing fusion would be two remarkable sequences in which the Dark Wood and the Seventh Circle are visited upon Edward's court. As numbered in the published screenplay, the two Dantean sequences – 26 and 29 – seem to have been conceived independently of each other. On the pre-filmed page they also appear to be unconnected with the Up-in-Arms episode.

In Sequence 26, two scenes back from the nocturnal gathering around Mortimer's boardroom, Jarman envisions a mysterious dumb show:

INTERIOR. EMPTY ROOM. DAY.
PRINCE EDWARD. NUDE RUGBY SCRUM.

Prince Edward [young son of *Edward II*] watches the nude rugby scrum from the shadows. Sound of clock ticking away.[51]

Though this dreamlike sequence corresponds to nothing in Marlowe's script, it does correspond to something in Jarman's AIDS journals: his Dantean description of the gay nightclub Heaven. In his director's note for Sequence 26, he recalls the tumble of erotic and artistic associations that gave rise to the eye-popping focus of the show:

> I have a crazy idea of a naked rugby scrum in August [1990] and here it is six months later [February 1991], looking very much like a 15th century drawing or a hot night in Heaven.[52]

The ticking clock reminds him that his time as a sexually hyperactive cruiser at Heaven – like his precious time on the Heath – is running out. It is a surreal memento mori. His queer inner child, embodied in the young Prince Edward, pays no attention to it, of course, for he is imagined here in the pre-adolescent process of discovering his sexual attraction to the ageless aesthetic icon of the Athletic Male Nude (or "Hot Jock" as the iconographers of gay porn have reclassified it).[53] The clock also seems to have reminded Jarman of the hot days in 1975 when he shot scene after scene of nude Roman soldiers "training" on the burning Sardinian sand for his homoerotic revision of the legend of St. Sebastian:

> ...a Roman chariot race, sex and sport. Boxing and rugby, Australian rules football, all faggot pursuits, locker room stuff.[54]

But as the clock ticks away, all these "faggot pursuits" in the arenas of masculinity must end – not in a locker room orgy, as the porn industry would lead poor gay consumers to believe – but in a burial ground teeming with the ghosts of the AIDS dead.

Whether he *consciously* identified his lost gay friends and lovers with the rugby players when he was writing the scrum into the screenplay is not clear, but he certainly becomes conscious of their spectral presence six months later while Sequence 26 is being shot. "The boys emerging from the shadows reminded me of ghosts come to haunt me, all my dead friends," he recalls in his director's notes, reversing Wilde's aesthetic dictate about art and life: "As always life was far more 'advanced' than art."[55] By "life" here, as so often in his AIDS journals, Jarman primarily means the devastating life-experience of gay men during the early years of the epidemic. Prospect Cottage, despite its hopeful name, was where he often glumly looked back at his crowded erotic life and mourned for precious friends hid in death's increasingly dateless night. His agonizing night-thoughts on their symptoms and sufferings – dire signs of what he himself would be enduring when the film was in production – necessarily preceded his wishfulfilling artistic vision of their return-to-life as scrummy boys emerging from the shadow of death.

With the rugby players ghosted into Marlowe like this, can the ghosts of Dante's sodomites be far behind? Surely not. Dante-pilgrims's desire-heated perception of the military sodomites as athletic combatants, naked champions "eying their grip and vantage before exchanging thrusts and blows" ("avvisando lor presa e lor vantaggio / prima che sien tra lor battuti e punti": *Inf.* 16.23-24), may be easily mapped onto the way rugby players look and behave in a scrum. The British sports term "scrum" goes back to medieval military vocabulary derived from the Romance languages: a clipped version of Italian "scaramuccia" via Old French "escarmoche" came down into English as "skirmish." (The same word also turns up as "scrimmage" in the vocabulary of North American football.) What "scrum" means on the modern rugby field is a periodically staged combat, at once defensive and offensive, between two triangular configurations of players representing the opposing teams in a match. The groups bend over in battle-formation and push hard against each other for possession of the ball, which the referee pushes into the tunnel of bodies formed between their lines.[56]

Needless to say, the erotic possibilities of this ball-grabbing, man-handling manoeuvre have not been lost on the perpetually cruising gay male gaze. The hallowed image of boys in a scrum is deeply embedded in the iconography of the all-male-cast studios. In the fiercely erotic vocabulary of Jarman's AIDS journal *At Your Own Risk* (1992), "scrum" is lifted from the quasimilitary idiom of straight men's sports and polemically queered to denote a wild "mating" dance among men with Dionysian sex on their mind. The following reminiscence about a fling he had with a Greek Lieutenant and a sailor-chum in Rhodes when he was twenty-three, only a year after the Whitechapel retrospective, is strategically placed in the journal after a bitter screed against the Thatcherite revival of the Labouchère amendment in Clause 25, a much-protested section of the Tory's Criminal Justice Bill designed to reclassify certain gay activities such as "indecency between men in public" as serious criminal offences:

He and his friend took me to a small flat near the covered market and put ba-zouki music on the gramophone. The sailor brewed strong coffee and brought sweet cakes and served them to us quite formally. Then he disappeared behind a screen and emerged with a piece of silver chiffon spangled with silver stars with which he danced. Men, I learnt, are surprisingly good at striptease. When he had finished he put the screen around us. I fucked the arse off the Lieutenant and afterwards he asked me if all English boys had cocks like mine. The two of them took me to a bar where their mates were dancing with each other and threw me into this scrum.[57]

If the Tories were seeking evidence of gross indecency between men in public, Jarman was determined to let them have it – with a vengeance. Every recollected fuck becomes an occasion for redemptive allegory. The official British opinion that there are "No Queers in the Forces" is given a hilarious Greek twist here in the Lieutenant's drag striptease preceding the scrum. Much as this outrageous memory serves to stick it to the Heterosoc oppressors, it also drives home Jarman's autobiographical project to his queer readers. Like the scrum scene in *Edward II*, his erotic memoir conjures up long-lost ghosts for a pre-emptive canonization. His Greek "mates" are the moral opposites of the self-loathing Boys in the Band, or their Dantean counterparts, the Boys in the Sand. Their free-spirited, unabashedly pagan movements could not be farther from the "dancing of the wretched hands" (la tresca / de la misere mani: *Inf.* 14.40-41) that Dante sees the sodomites perform under divine compulsion as they slap the flakes of fire off their skin. The Lieutenant's "surprisingly good" dance of the starry veil suggests a comic revision either of Salome's tragic striptease or of the ancient Greek dance of the stars, both movements that Dante himself had amusingly re-vived for the lady-like male saints in the Heaven of the Sun (Par. 10.79-80). Heaven is thus flipped into Hell and Hell again becomes Heaven. The sodo-mites return as the chorus of the blessed, and in the thick of their hot scrum dances their drag-redeemed leader, Saint Derek of Dungeness, whose Para-dise, once hacked to pieces by the sisters of perpetual intolerance, is restored through a Dantean act of creative recollection.

If Jarman had consciously projected Dante's sodomites onto the nude rugby scrum while he was writing his "crazy idea" into the screenplay in August 1990 or bringing it to life on the set in February 1991, the director's note on Sequence 26 would surely have reversed his anti-Wildean epigram about life anticipating art. Art, as always in Wilde's aesthetic epigramms, is far more "advanced" than life. If art is ahead of life in the Sacred Poem, then perhaps the "horrible art of justice" ("di giustizia orribil arte": *Inf.* 14.6) meted out to the sodomites might have served to advance Jarman's prophetic understanding of the living hell suffered by positive gay men under the rain of homophobic condemnations descending upon them during the later years of the Thatcher era.

In Dante's vision of the sodomites Jarman might also have perceived a prophecy of his own recurrent dream of the rising of the gay dead through erotic conjuration. This anastatic moment, a ghost-written resurrection intensely imagined by other gay elegists in the late 1980s and 1990s, is always lit in his journals by a revivifying beam of lust: the desiring male subject rushes to embrace his iconic objects of desire or discovers the boys going at it in a shaft of immortal light *despite* the temporal shadows falling around them.[58] Faggot pursuits will never die out. The boys in the scrum will beat the clock ticking in the background. If this idea is "crazy," as Jarman calls it, then it is surely no crazier than the orthodox mystery of the Resurrection or Dante's infernal spin on that doctrine in the Seventh Circle.

Might the idea of a defiant gay resurrection rise to a cinematic revision of the Seventh Circle (or of the whole Inferno) in response to the AIDS Apocalypse? It seems not just artistically possible but culturally predictable – especially for an autobiographical artist like Jarman whose fascination with Dante's apocalyptic self-recovery can be traced back to his art school days in the early 1960s. In the notes for Sequence 26, he associates the naked scrum with "15th century drawing." Crowds of nudes are not thick on the ground in medieval iconography, though they can be tracked down in illustrations of the Seventh Circle in late medieval manuscripts of the *Inferno*.[59] When the boys emerged from the shadows and kicked up the dust on the dirt floor of the set, Jarman may also have been reminded of the flocks of nude figures rising from the ground in fifteenth-century depictions of the General Resurrection.[60] The attainment of eternal life at the General Resurrection is of course typologically inverted, to macabre effect, in the perpetuation of violent death in the Seventh Circle.

In his final journals Jarman was to grow increasingly riled – embittered to the point of serious bible-bashing blasphemy – over the homophobic warnings routinely trumpeted by the British tabloids that AIDS was a sure sign of God's Wrath towards gays.[61] Yet the association of the scrum sequence with the Seventh Circle remains in the shadowy realm of possibility during the shoot. It is just emerging in the director's imagination. It is conceptually latent, thematically nuclear, visually implicit. It does not become explicit, as we shall see, until Jarman (thinking back to Dante via Pasolini) explosively alters the order of sequences in his screenplay during the editing of the film.

6. "We are all exiles here": *Edward II* Screenplay, Sequence 29

While the dumb show in Sequence 26 is Dantean only *in distans*, Dante literally manifests himself *in situ* at the start of Sequence 29. It is not as a faint ghost but as an aggressive authorial presence, an anti-Marlowe conjured up for Jarman's violation project, that the Poet invades the screenplay without warning:

INTERIOR. BEDROOM. MORNING.
EDWARD, GAVESTON, MORTIMER, CHORUS OF EARLS. POET.

Gaveston and Edward seated on golden chairs. A poet reads the opening passages of Dante's "Divine Comedy."[62]

This unnamed poet must be The Poet, of course, for who else would be reciting the first canto of the *Inferno* at a court at this moment in history? No dumb show for him! His vocal performance clearly disrupts the fatalistic flow of the Marlovian script, unexpectedly erupts in the middle of it, effectively corrupts the smooth hard Mannerist purity of Renaissance realpolitik with a medieval allegory of messy personal breakdown and miraculous erotic recovery. Though the textual breakdown in Sequence 29 also marks an intertextual breakthrough – the *Inferno* is now deeply "inside" *Edward II* and must be hermeneutically gestated there along with the mysterious protoporn image of the scrum – the published screenplay offers little help in clarifying the typological or tropological significance of its intrusion. On first reading it seems like just another crazy idea Jarman threw into the mix to see what would come of it. Classic Hollywood-style continuity had never been one of his top concerns as a screenwriter or director.

So why *does* the Poet perplexingly show up here for what seems to be a guest appearance at a command performance? Dante's "folle volo" to

Plantagenet England, a hitherto unrecorded episode in his exile, would probably also have perplexed the real King Edward upon whose unhappy reign the play was based. In preparing the screenplay Jarman must have done his history homework because the chronology of the early fourteenth century makes it *just* possible for the great Poet to have encountered the not-so-great King. *Edward II* was in fact Dante's younger contemporary by nineteen years, and his two embattled decades on the throne (he was crowned in 1307 and deposed in 1327) roughly coincide with the later years of the Poet's exile when the *Comedy* was conceived, written, and first circulated in manuscript.

Though Dante's pop-up in the film turns out to be an even more blatant anachronism than his unheralded presence in the screenplay, Jarman seems to have relished the arcane irony that the Poem might have reached the King's ears one way or another. (No queer filmmaker can rival Jarman as a snapper-up of unconsidered trivia, especially the off-beat hypotheses generated by the rich fantasy life of British literary historians.[63]) The possibility that *Edward II* had even heard of the *Inferno*, let alone heard it dramatically recited in person by its author, is hardly less fantastical than his miraculous exposure to Sinclair's prose. Even if the King had had an opportunity to peruse the original, even if his Florentine bankers had sent him a copy of it hot off the scriptorium, he would probably not have been able to read medieval Tuscan; and even if he'd suddenly received the gift of tongues or found a Sinclair-channeling friar to translate it for him into Middle English, he would certainly not have welcomed Dante's notoriously *de haut en bas* attacks on his royal pedigree or military conduct. His ears would have burned to hear Dante's decidedly faint praise of his father Edward I as the "better issue" of his negligent grandfather Henry III (*Purg.* 7.130-2) or the Celestial Eagle's condemnation of the "thirsty pride" of the Plantagenet monarchs in their maddeningly unjust wars against the Scots (*Par.* 19.121-23). While Jarman's Edward will listen to the Poet with an appreciative smile on his face when Sequence 29 is committed to film, England's King would probably have thrown the calumnious foreigner in the Tower if he had ever ventured across the Channel.

Does the Dante reading function in the screenplay as just another entertainment devised for the King's pleasure by his dilettantish minion? Jarman's Gaveston, like Marlowe's, is a homoerotic event planner with a hidden political agenda. The closeted King must have his revels so that the Faggot within him, inevitably drawn to musicals, will come out for all to see under the queening influence of show biz. "Music and poetry is his delight," Gaveston deviously muses in a voice-over heralding his arrival back in court after his first exile,

> Therefore I'll have Italian masques by night,
> Sweet speeches, comedies and pleasing shows...[64]

Perhaps the expressly Italian character of Gaveston's planned entertainments was Jarman's cue for importing Dante into Sequence 29. After all, Gaveston promises not only "masques" in the Italian style but also "comedies," and Jarman cheerfully delivers the Big One. His Edward will get *The Comedy* recited by The Poet. A Faggot King who truly delights in poetry deserves the very best.

If the Dante reading were just a staged literary "event" on Gaveston's entertainment calendar, it would be hardly more significant than the various other hot gay "acts" – a pair of contemporary male dancers performing a homoerotic pas-de-deux, a hunky stripper with a gold leaf sewn on his jockstrap playing with a long thick snake, Annie Lennox singing a Cole Porter number – gleefully introduced by Jarman into Marlowe's script as evidence of Gaveston's cultural impact on Edward's court. That impact is meant to strike the hidebound Earls as avantgarde, aesthetic, decadent, faggy, and it certainly hits its mark. "What man of noble birth can brook this sight," snorts Mortimer when he and the Earls burst into the royal bedroom and catch the King and his lover at the ultimate "faggot pursuit" – not sodomizing but "poetizing."[65] Edward's imaginative engagement with Dante becomes a symptom of his emergent gay aestheticism, a sure mark of his ignoble feyness and moral depravity. It doesn't matter that the Poet is striving to elevate the concept of nobility to a mystical height unimaginable to most kings at the time, or that his edgy "contemporary" verse will soon be ranked among the noblest of all literary creations in the Western tradition. From the Heterosoc viewpoint of the Earls, engaging with poetry is just not a manly pursuit in medieval (or modern) England.

By introducing the *smarrimento* into the screenplay at this critical point, Jarman effectively deepens the irony of Gaveston's imminent downfall. Here is the devious minion nonchalantly listening to the great poet of exile at the very moment when he is about to be sent into exile (again) himself. So, while the Dante reading doesn't advance the plot, it does provide an explicit typological parallel to Gaviston's subsequent wandering and an implicit tropological gloss on Edward's consequent devastation. If the banished Gaveston plays the role of Dante at the literal level, the distraught Edward, whom the Earls compel to sign the writ of banishment, must suffer Dantean agonies of betrayal and love-loss at the moral level. When the King cries out "Thou from this land I from myself am banished,"[66] the emotional force of his complaint to Gaveston is infernally intensified by its inevitable resonance with Dante's lamentations over his separation from Beatrice in the Dark Wood, which resonate in turn with the later lamentations over his separation from Virgil in the forest of Eden. Whichever separation is ghost-written into the play at this point, Jarman apparently intended to use his allegorical intertext to elevate an unhappy gay breakup in Marlowe to the same mythopoetic status as its hallowed straight (or straightish) counterparts in Dante.

The director's note to Sequence 29 confirms this intention. "I like the opening of the 'Divine Comedy,'" he comments, recollecting the wintry day when the Dante reading was filmed,

> the straight path lost in a dark wood. The byways are the path to the soul, not the highways. A late snow fell, and we were in our shirt sleeves. So much for spring. We are all exiles here.[67]

So Jarman's Edward must lose the "straight path" in a modern sexual sense – as Dante had lost "la diritta via" (*Inf.* 1.3) in a medieval moral sense – if he is to recover his long-repressed soul, his true self, at the end of all the bent "byways" opening down and out to him as an exile from Heterosoc. Ideologically opposed to the pastoral byways that led Jarman to his garden at Prospect Cottage are those updated modernist versions of the old Straight and Narrow, the thronging middle-class "highways" of Thatcherite England.

These allegorical oppositions are clear enough, at least with respect to the sexual politics in the screenplay; but what is the director getting at in his rueful reflection "We are all exiles here"? Where is "here"? Most immediately "here" is the cavernous old horror-film studio at Bray near Windsor where the film was shot. The studio was inefficiently sound-proofed and poorly heated, and on days when the temperature dipped and noise flooded in from a recording session in another part of the building, working conditions must have reminded him of the nocturnal chill of the Dark Wood and the cacophonous hollow of the Inferno. For most days during the five-week shoot, except when he was feeling too ill to direct and assigned his "ghost" director Ken Butler to cover for him, Jarman had to drive over to Bray from the cozy warmth of his cottage in Kent. It would have seemed like a daily exile for him, especially when he was running a temperature and feeling especially sensitive to the cold. Working in shirt sleeves cannot have been pleasant for anyone in the cast or crew under the circumstances. Perhaps that's why he says "we" in his note rather than "I": all the makers of the film are exiles here at Bray, trapped for five weeks together without spring like souls in the perpetual winter at the bottom of Hell.[68]

Beyond the immediate literal level of the studio, however, a more allegorical "here" opens up. Perhaps it simply replays the bleak Dantean prospect of "our life" ("nostra vita": *Inf.* 1.2) in the old Fallen World, where "we" – meaning all suffering mortals – find ourselves wandering as exiles from Heaven. Or maybe, with a more ironic contemporary twist, "here" is the old Fallen World beneath the progressivist illusions of Modern Britain, where "we" – meaning only the bohemian artists opposed to Heterosoc – are defiantly proud exiles from the phony heaven prepared for the prosperous heterosexuals by the Tory Party God. Especially alienated from the godly society promoted by Thatcher's Public Health Authority are the "we" who dare to come out as gay men with AIDS at a time when coming out as either a sodomite or a seropositive was tantamount to self-damnation in the public eye.

In his garden at Prospect Cottage, Jarman fervently imagined himself creating a queer heaven to counter the paradise from which orthodox Christianity had permanently banished him and his fellow sodomites. It would be a theological allegory in sea kale and driftwood, a sacred space for his sacrilegious friends from Outrage! who would riot as extras on the set at Bray in March 1991, and for the Sisters of Perpetual Indulgence who would hilariously "canonize" him as St. Derek of Dungeness on the beach in September of the same year. For his canonization he would wear the golden robe that Edward wears in the film when he welcomes Gaveston back to court. Jarman's political identification with Edward thus presupposes, and intensifies, his artistic identification with Dante.[69]

"But before I finish," vowed the unlikely saint, referring to both his garden and his life, "I intend to celebrate our corner of Paradise, the part of the garden the Lord forgot to mention."[70] Behind all the blasphemies of his later years, then, grows a redemptive project of Dantean proportions, and his AIDS journals provide clear evidence that he himself understood its spiritual implications not only in light of Dante's journey from exile to ecstatic union but also in response to Romantic readings of the Dark Wood as the threshold for self-recovery. "The gardener digs in another time, without past or future, beginning or end," he mystically mused in his rather Coleridgean entry for March 7, 1989:

> A time that does not cleave the day with rush hours, lunch breaks, the last bus home. As you walk in the garden you pass into this time – the moment of entering can never be remembered. Around you the landscape lies transfigured. Here is the Amen beyond the prayer.[71]

Cut to the opening canto of the *Inferno* with Jarman in the foreground as the modern prophet of the Sacred Poem, with Coleridge in the background as Dante's successor among the Romantics:

> Dante, at the beginning of his journey back along the great antique spiral, entered this realm in a dark wood.
>
> *Nel mezzo del cammin di nostra vita*
> *Mi ritovai per una selva oscura*
> *Che la dir itta [sic] via era smarrita*
>
> I'm brought suddenly back to the here and now by the shrill argument voice of the phone. My Person from Porlock is on the line, talking of time with beginning and end, literal time, monotheist time, for which you are unfailingly charged.[72]

Though modern life intrudes on this reverie with its ringing reminders of the literal level, the anagogic impulse to transcend the "straight way" with its linear monotheist reckoning of time grows ever stronger in Jarman the closer he feels to his own death. But could the creative worldreforming project of Dantean allegory persist in a dying man with a big phone bill? Fortunately, despite the outrages of the World, the Flesh, and the Virus, he felt its persistent "impeto" – at least on his better days. From the "great antique spiral" of divinely diversified queer time would spring the loopy creative energy he would need to write the sodomites out of Dante's *Inferno*.

7. "City of Disc": Filming and Post-Production

Thus far we've been considering three key episodes in detail: the Marlovian Sequence 28 (the Up-In-Arms board-room scene, with text adapted from the original play); and the purely Jarmanian Sequences 26 and 29 (the wordless "scrum show" and the celebrity recitation, with text inserted from Dante). Not surprisingly, the translation of these sequences to the screen reveals a complex literal-level expansion of their contents as outlined in the screenplay. Narrative space and time are both drastically affected by their literalization through film.

Thanks to Jarman's wizardly habit of throwing all every "crazy idea" that came to him into the cauldron of his diverse autobiographical writings – longhand notebooks, gardening journals, outlines of imaginary films, annotated drafts of workable screenplays, and director's notes to completed projects – we can retrace the steps in his creative process that led to the production and clarification of certain magically synthesizing effects in his films. One of these effects, his Dantean revision of the nude rugby scrum in *Edward II*, was realized only in the editing process for the film. It is a purely cinematic outcome of his intertextual violations, a revelation of his outrageously saintly project for the redemption of Queer Culture at the anagogic end of his religious outrage.

The vague spaces indicated in the stage directions for each sequence – "Empty Room" for the scrum, "Interior" for the Conspiracy, "Bedroom" for the reading – are strikingly replaced by the gritty concreteness of the palace set conceived by Christopher Hobbs. In close collaboration with Jarman, Hobbs came up with a severely ascetic, quasi-Buddhist design for Edward's court, with rough unadorned grey walls looming over an indeterminate maze of public halls, private chambers, passageways, ramps, and thresholds. For the palace floor the designer wanted to use loose sand, suggesting the raked gardens in Buddhist temples, but dusty dirt had to be substituted at the last minute. This minor material change would lend a dark "primitive" look to the already claustrophobic palace interior. The palace, in fact, is all interior.

There is no outside world for the court to contemplate, not even a window looking out on one. As a result, the action leading up to Gaveston's exile seems to take place in a dim meditation chamber walled up in a Forbidden City, at once eastern and western in character. If it's not a sacred space deep inside the Temple Mount of Borubadur, then it could be a very unholy place akin to a Nazi bunker or a dire block on the far side of the wall in the City of Dis (a Dantean setting Jarman had often toyed with updating as the "City of Disc" in his early short stories and later unfilmed screenplays[73]). As in the Inferno, night prevails in this ambiguously gloomy space. The simple temporal distinctions in the screenplay – "Day" for the scrum, "Night" for the Conspiracy, "Morning" for the reading – vanish into the complexly pervasive shadows. To make an appearance on such a dark set required stagy expressionistic lighting for the actors, whose faces and figures constantly seem to emerge out of the studio shadows into dramatic pools of light from overhead spots or floor-level floods.

During the five tightly scheduled weeks of the shoot, Jarman tended to follow the careful directions he set for himself in the screenplay. This was not his usual practice as a filmmaker, for his films in the 1970s and 1980s had been directed with an improvisational energy that occasionally bewildered his actors and annoyed his crew. Since his rapidly declining health ruled out a leisurely or spontaneous approach to filming, his flair for artistic decision-making in the intuitive heat of the moment seems to have asserted itself during the five months of postproduction work culminating in the world première of *Edward II* at the Edinburgh Film Festival in mid-August 1991.

His most significant artistic decisions in post-production were prompted by the interpretive freeplay of the editing process. He had long ago discovered in his experimental work with super-eight home movies that he could deeply affect the thematic implications of a key moment or a whole scene simply by shifting its position in the original order of sequences planned in his head or jotted down in his notebooks. That profoundly amateur discovery, the semantic alchemy of the editing room, remained a source of aesthetic excitement for him even in the much more professional crafting of his final films.

With the recitation scene in *Edward II*, for instance, he crucially altered the order of scenes leading up to it in a way that not only enhanced

Dante's glossatorial function throughout the film but also clearly infernalized the hitherto mysterious spectacle of the rugby scrum. From the order of sequences worked out in the summer of 1990, as numbered in the published screenplay, we have already concluded that the Poet's unanticipated recitation is only loosely connected to the scenes immediately preceding it. Here is how Jarman originally ordered the sequences leading up to Gaveston's banishment:

Sequence 26: nude rugby scrum
Sequence 27: Isabella and Mortimer complaining
Sequence 28: board-room conspiracy
Sequence 29: Dante reading
Sequence 30: Edward signing the form of exile

And here is how he reordered them for the final cut of the film in the summer of 1991:

Sequence 23: Gaveston flirting with Isabella
Sequence 28: board-room conspiracy
Sequence 26: nude rugby scrum
Sequence 29: Dante reading
Sequence 30: Edward signing the form of exile

A brief scene in which Mortimer and the Queen bitterly air their grievances against the King (Sequence 27) originally separated the scrum from the board-room. In the editing room Jarman pushes their dialogue back eight sequences and replaces it with a discomforting close-up of Gaveston maliciously tempting Isabella to kiss him (Sequence 23). Compared with the rugby scrum, this unexpected flirtation across the Homo/Hetero Divide is a much smarter lead-in to the conspiracy scene (Sequence 28) because it lends credence to the subsequent complaints of the Earls around the board-room by providing glaring evidence of Gaveston's twisted sexual aggression. No wonder the morally outraged Earls think that the King is due for an attack of Divine Wrath: he has permitted his bratty boy to sow discord not only in his realm but in his marriage.

Now, what's to be done with all those naked rugby players? They have to be kept in the action *somehow* – even though their dumb show isn't subtitled with anti-clerical OutRage! slogans as captions for the queering impaired. Ingeniously Jarman pushes the athletes forward two scenes in the film so that they form their scrum in the immediate wake of Mortimer's threatening line "God himself is up in arms."

While the transitional phrase "up in arms" is being uttered like a rallying cry to holy war, the camera pans left along the table to catch the Bishop of York's reaction to Mortimer's theological pronouncement. At first, as if to reflect the inevitable anger in the Countenance Divine and to register the Church's doctrinally reflexive opposition to sodomy, the Bishop turns his sanctimonious face towards Mortimer and obediently smiles. But this official expression of approval swiftly fades, replaced, surprisingly, by an enigmatic frown. (If the real Bishop of York, the morally crusading John Habgood, had paid any attention to his caricatured namesake at the end of this scene, he would no doubt have continued to scowl at the smiling hint that his own perfectly respectable sexuality was being queried here – if not queered – in preparation for a nasty encounter with "the OutRage[!] boys and girls" whom Jarman hailed in his director's notes as "the inheritors of Edward's story.") While his frown is forming, the Bishop casts his eyes to the left towards the shadows and drifts off into what looks like a private reverie. Is he scowling to himself as he contentedly contemplates the hellfire in store for unrepentant sodomites? Or is he nervously grimacing during a closety little flashback to his schooldays when he was first turned on by the sight of strapping lads grabbing each other on the playing field? Or perhaps it's the sacrilegious scene of rough trade in hell – always an intensely imagined religious vision – that's turning him on with a delicious frisson of Sadean cruelty?

Any doubts we may have that the Bishop's fleeting thoughts (whether homophobic or homoerotic) are turning in the direction of the Inferno are dispelled by the sound editing for the transition between Sequence 28 and the repositioned Sequence 26. Before cutting away from the Bishop to the rugby players, Jarman creates a sound-bridge between them with the ominous howling of a wolf in the distance. As the players are "emerging out of the shadows" like "ghosts," the howling grows in intensity. Dubbed into the background mix while the scrum is being formed in the foreground are other hellish sounds – baying hounds, crescendoing winds, screaming shades, growling monsters – which appropriately carry over into the next scene, the recitation from the *Inferno*, at the start of Sequence 29.

Are these infernal sounds extra-diegetic? At first they seem so, for Jarman introduces the wolf-howls from "outside" the foregrounded narrative of Gaveston's impending banishment. However, when the hellhounds begin to bay in the distance and the "bufera infernal" ominously blows through the darkness, the sounds we hear could well be heard by the flock of naked athletes who enter as if obeying an infernal cue. Or so we are led to suppose if we take a theological cue from the Bishop's frown and perceive them as damned souls, the shades of unrepentant sodomites. Though the dubbed mix is still coming from somewhere off-screen, it begins to make sense now as diegetic background noise. Cut to the Dante reading, and the infernal sounds die back and blend in with the extra-diegetic music in the score, a plinking melodic motif played on the upper register of an electronic keyboard. Just before the soundscape of hell fades out completely, its relation to the narrative is ambiguous: it seems diegetic with respect to the experiences described by the Poet (who may be "hearing" it in his mind's ear) but at the same time extra-diegetic in relation to the conspiracy plot about to break in on Edward and Gaveston.

The subtle perceptual effect of this aural bridge is to transform three originally discrete sequences (28, 26, 29) into a super-sequence, a cinematically coherent unit, an allegorical interlude discernible only on the screen. The thematic continuity of the interlude proves to be critically dependant on, and subversively re-readable through, Jarman's psychosexual take on the Dark Wood episode. His romantically queer glosses on the *smarrimento* in *Modern Nature* – the garden notebook and AIDS diary he was editing for publication during his post-production work on *Edward II* – strongly suggest that we should read the Dantean intertext in Sequence 29 *backward* from the Poet's book to the player's bodies to the Bishop's face. Viewing the interlude "straight," which is to say in the usual way we've been taught to read Olivier-style films of Renaissance history plays, we are driven forward by the momentum of the conspiracy plot to read the players' bodies from the Bishop's frowning theological perspective. Their silent scrum must first be interpreted tropologically, then, as a collective embodiment of the unspeakable vice against nature. The dourly heterosexist ecclesiastical interpretation breaks down in the ensuing recitation scene, however, for there we witness not only the Poet reading from his book but also, through a series of rapid cutaway shots, the comically modern (and seriously un-medieval) reaction of Edward and Gaveston to the opening lines of the *Inferno*.

At first glance, to judge from Edward's and Gaveston's smirky reaction to Dante's loss of the straight way, we might jump to the conclusion that they are obviously queering the *Inferno* in the first sense. Even as they share their gay reading of "straight" as an in-joke, they seem to open up the creative possibility of rewriting the entire *Comedy* as a blasphemous anti-Catholic parody (starting with canto one, where Dante would be cruising Virgil in the Dark Wood as if he were Jarman hunting down a hot trick on the Heath). Yet when we look back from their golden seats towards the dark introverted theatre of the rugby scrum, where Jarman not only resurrected Dante's sodomites as the lost boys of Heaven in erotic defiance of the plague but also outed his own queer history as a closeted boy growing up under the hellish repressions of a "normal" Nuclear Family, it is the second kind of queering that seriously emerges in his redemptive project. As his blindness lifted, Jarman came to see very clearly that he did not want the sodomites purged from the *Inferno* because without them there, burnt beyond recognition, the homophobia that Dante was exposing not just in the doctrinal foundations of his faith but in the fearful desires of his own soul would be lost to view.

The on-screen queering of Dante is swiftly disrupted when Edward and Gaveston hear Mortimer and the Earls rush in with their writ of exile. Two quick cutaway shots reveal the Poet's reactions to the Marlovian intrusion. First he whisks off his reading glasses and puts on his long-range specs to see who's arrived. Might Dante himself have two rival readings of his poem – a closeted close-range focus on his own fearful desires and a straight long-range view of his political vulnerability? Clearly worried that the Earls have come to arrest him for leading his listeners astray along the twisted route to hell, he raises a beer bottle to his lips and takes a nervous swig. As he does so, a gold earring on his left ear lobe catches the light. Perhaps he's not as morally or sexually straight as he at first appears, and his "paura" in the Dark Wood is that of an anxious closet case who finds himself on Dark Set too close for comfort to the censorious exercise of heterosexist power. That's the last we see of Dante in the sequence – and in the film. He's cut out at the literal level, relegated to the shadows as abruptly as his sweet leader Virgil is harshly "disappeared" at the coming of Beatrice.

8. "Walls of Tears and Dungeons of Sadness": Queer *Edward II*

Though the Ur-Moment of queering the Comedy is lost along with him, it is not lost on us. The off-screen receivers of the Poem can still carry on where Edward and Gaveston were forced to leave off. If we share Edward's shocked outrage at the disruption of the Dante reading, as Jarman surely encourages us to do, we are at once impelled – critically compelled – to look back at Sequence 26 in a spirit of defiant opposition to the current of religious homophobia that took us there from the "Up-at-Arms" lead-in. A typological re-reading of the scrum is demanded of us if we are to distinguish ourselves from the Bishop and his tropologically vindictive allies.

The filmed contents of Sequence 26 reveal two significant departures from the plans for it in the screenplay. First, as we noticed en passant, the Dark Set turns day into night. Second, in a shot/reverse-shot montage paralleling the crosscutting between poet and audience in Sequence 28, Jarman casts Prince Edward in the role of the lone on-screen spectator of the scrum and cuts back and forth between him and the rugby players for around forty seconds. In a classic L-cut, with the sound transition occurring before the picture transition, the cacophonous cavern of the Inferno is discovered. The little Prince enters first, emerging out of the shadows like an immature version of one of the ghostly boys-to-come. A bright flashlight in his hand, he fearfully casts its intense beam through the gloom and out again – right at us, sitting in the darkened movie theatre – as if he were searching for his off-screen counterparts in the distant future or his hidden accomplices in some nocturnal escapade. Perhaps he is looking for something he's lost in the shadows, or hoping to find some evidence that the lonely gloom is in fact a lusty darkness like the gay-thronged shadows on the Heath.

Reading the Prince typologically, we can hardly avoid comparing him to Dante-pilgrim who wanders through the Inferno with his "lantern" (i.e. Virgil) casting prophetic beams ahead to guide their steps.[74] Just like Dante-pilgrim, who, with the morphing eyes of desire, sees the sodomites in the flesh as naked and oiled champions rather than as charred zombies subject to the flaying corrosion of the rain of fire, the Prince shines his restless beam over the beautiful bodies of the athletes whose combative configuration shows off their ripped thighs and inviting buttocks to best porn-star advantage.

The Prince has no human guide with him, not even a shade, unless of course we count the unseen presence of the director behind him. But if Jarman is working out his own typological identification with Dante here as an extension of the concurrent meditations on the Dark Wood and his sexual coming-of-age in *Modern Nature*, then the Prince must also be psychosexually twinned with Jarman himself. He emerges as a dreamlike double for the pre-adolescent Derek who long ago, in the repressively homophobic England of the1940s and 1950s, went timidly searching for his future objects of desire. Older athletic boys were an agonizing turn-on for him as a schoolchild and even as a college student, he recalls in the retrospective glow of his AIDS journals, and so the spectral rugby players are recruited from his vivid homoerotic memory to stand in both for Dante's athletic sodomites and for the lusty cruisers on the Heath. Since the onscreen spectator is literally an Edward in the making, the queer child of a queer father, he must also prophetically represent the King who will lose the straight way himself – and, thanks to the Poet, will come to *understand* what such an exile entails – in the scene immediately after the scrum. Edward's recollected vision of the athletes may be sexually frightening to him as a child, but as an adult, under the audaciously erotic influence of Gaveston, he can look back on the memory with a smile.

Thus the sexual *smarrimento* of Dante-Edward-Derek does not lead to tragic torments on the deserts of the Seventh Circle. In the queer reading of the *Inferno*, when the straight way of traditional Catholic exegesis is wilfully but unwickedly lost, fear of being scorched by the flames will never prevent the Dantean subject from embracing the forbidden flesh.

Conspicuously absent from Jarman's filmed re-enactment of the dance of the sodomites is the rain of fire. Its descent from on high is threatened by the Bishop's scowling eyes and by all the infernal sound effects, but it never materializes on screen. Even if it had materialized on the set, even if the collective prayers of Jarman's conservative religious foes had been answered by a shower of brimstone, it would still have been strategically edited out of the seeing-is-believing frame of the screen. That the Boys in the Sand must remain miraculously uncharred by God's Wrath is a necessary revelation to sustain hope in the ultimate realization of Saint Derek's redemptive project. What can God's Wrath be but a minatory speech act of the conspirators of Heterosoc? Or what, for that matter, can God be – that Über-Straight Father who's supposedly up in arms against his queer offspring – but a discursive tool of heterosexist powermongers determined to sustain the phantasm of the Nuclear Family?

Jarman was building himself a garden to have an agony in, and agonize he did, especially on queer ceremonial occasions like Pride Day. "Dear Jesus, innocent begetter of an evil and corrupt tradition," he had prayed with blaspheming zeal on Pride Day (June 24), 1989, twinning himself on Christ with the same fervent audacity that had once moved Dante to do the same for the sake of exposing the hypocrisy of the ecclesiastical hierarchy and its political manipulators,

> we know you would join this march, our entry into Jerusalem, would kiss John and consign the born again to the bottomless pit, or rather enlighten them and put them to bed with their brothers and sisters. For we know that the castle of heterosex has its walls of tears and dungeons of sadness. We can laugh at the house of cards called the Family. We demand one right "equality of loving before the law" and the end of our banishment from the daylight.[75]

Built into the dark allegorical set of *Edward II* are these very "walls of tears" and "dungeons of sadness" that Heterosoc perpetually constructs out of legal and religious discourse to trap queers inside "the house of cards called the Family." Though Gaveston fails to escape this ideological dungeon, Edward finally does – though he is literally presented as its prisoner from the opening scene in the film through a series of flash-forwards to the execution in the penultimate sequence.

In an apocalyptic *volte-face* designed to appal the guardians of Family Values as well as the editors of Renaissance Drama, Jarman "rescues" the doomed sodomite by turning the execution scene into a sadistic dream from which Edward awakens to find himself anally unscathed by the red-hot poker heated in the fire of Divine Wrath. His polecate-stroking executioner Lightborn, played by the demonically handsome Kevin Collins with a sexy Geordie accent, turns out not to be a villain, after all, but one of those ever-obliging working-class cuties whom Jarman loved to cruise on the Heath. Having fallen for the King, Lightborn dowses the burning dick of death in the dungeon cesspool and strides seductively towards his new top. (For surely, in this queer rebirth out of the nightmare of heterosexist history, Edward has ceased to be the big bottom Marlowe made him out to be.) As dawn triumphantly streams into the dungeon, they lock lips Hollywood-style, silhouetted against a brightening background. They have evidently decided to end their "banishment from the daylight" in accordance with Jarman's outrageous Dantean insistence on a Happy Ending.

Just as Hell can be flipped into Heaven, so tragedy can be turned into comedy through the visionary will of an exiled poet-prophet. "We are all exiles here," as Jarman reminded not just "the OutRage boys and girls" who inherited Edward's story in the dark days of the 1990s but all future queer children who grow up to be viewers of the film or readers of the published screenplay. To Jarman's typological visualizations of the fearful *smarrimento* that all true believers in the OutRage! apocalypse must endure under Tory rule, one of his screenplay collaborators, Greg Taylor, provided urgent tropological glosses in the form of agit-prop slogans designed to haunt Mrs. Thatcher's worst nightmares of nuclear family meltdown: "nuclear family free ZONE"; "save queer children | from straight parents"; "HETER-*OBNOXIOUS*"; "HETER*OPPRESSIVE*"; "HETEROPHOBIA *liberates*"; "HOMOSEXISM *empowers*."[76]

These harsh squibs fizzle on impact with the hallowing subtlety of Jarman's cinematic vision of the Queer Child's wanderings towards redemptive self-empowerment. Where Dante had doomed his sodomites to wander restlessly across the burning sand forever, Prince Edward ends his *smarrimento* in an enthronement ceremony recalling the canonization of Saint Derek on the cool sand of the beach at Prospect Cottage. Where Rauschenberg had simply identified with Dante's sodomites by leaving the outline of his foot on their damning sand, Jarman effectively leads them out of damnation by writing his own psychosexual history into the very dance that reminded him of a "hot night in Heaven." Anagogy is thus not brusquely discarded but bravely queered in the film's wish-fulfilling final scene. After rescuing the King from the play's scorching denouement, Jarman raises Prince Edward up onto his father's throne as heir to all his faggot pursuits and then raises him up again on top of a cage where his "heterobnoxious" enemies, Isabella and Mortimer, glower beneath him in mute disgrace. As the hope of all queer children still trapped in the Family's dungeons of sadness, Prince Edward also functions as an avatar of the six-year-old Jarman whose Paradise was hacked to pieces long ago by the nuns. When the frightened boy shines his flashlight into the darkness of the movie theatre to seek a way out of the Family, he discovers a homoerotic escape from it in the seemingly infernal but ultimately paradisial vision of the scrum. It isn't "daylight" for him yet, given his tender age; but his Dantean banishment to the "bottomless pit" of homophobia follows an anagogic route towards political as well as sexual freedom thanks to Jarman's counterdiscursive ghostwriting of the *Inferno*.

Notes

[1] A comprehensive account of the queer reception history of *The Divine Comedy* remains to be written. Though I gesture here towards the project of writing a chronologically organized study of the actual (as distinct from Jarman's imaginary) literary and critical traces of Dante's impact on queer authors, artists, and readers through the centuries, my study of Jarman and Rauschenberg primarily reveals the queer desire for such a history – a desire poignantly readable behind the cheeky expressions on the faces of King Edward (Steven Waddington) and Gaveston (Andrew Tiernan) as they listen to the Poet's recitation. Though "queer theory" does receive at least one mention in The Dante Encyclopedia, it is only to point out "the apparent impenetrability of institutional Dante studies" to any critical approach deemed unorthodox by the academic Guardians of the Poet's Fame: see Cestaro (2000), 816. For a brief summary of articles by post- Stonewall gay critics on Dante's treatment of the sodomites in the Inferno and Purgatorio, see Pequiney (1995), 186-7; Woods (1998), 47-8; Miller (2000), 40-3; and Miller (2005), 270-78.

[2] *Inferno* 1.1: Sinclair (1939, rpt. 1961), 23. According to Ahern (2000), Sinclair "abandoned late-nineteenth-century literary English for a neutral tongue that was neither contemporary nor colloquial and that avoided inversion, archaism, and oddity. As with his predecessors, literal accuracy came at the price of diminished intensity. Well received by the general public, Sinclair's translation became the preferred text in college and university courses in the Englishspeaking world." Though displaced by Singleton's prose translation in the 1970s, Sinclair's Dante evidently remained lodged in Jarman's literary memory. Ironically, it was through the "neutral" English of Sinclair (a minister of the Church of Scotland) rather than through the academically preferred English of Singleton (the leading American Dantist of his generation) that Jarman was to Americanize the Poet in *Edward II*.

[3] Jarman (1991), 58.

[4] Peak (2000), 480. In 1992, Jarman produced a series of paintings exploring the relation between his newly proclaimed queer identity and his public history as a Person with AIDS. For reproductions of these polemical works, see Woollen (1996), 126-29, 136. For a discussion of their culminating significance within Jarman's career as an artist and activist, see Parkes (1996), 139. Summaries of the turbulent history of redemptions and contestations of the term "queer" in contemporary critical discourse, can be found in Jagose (1996), 72-126; Epstein (1996), 152-57; and Pigg (2000), 723-24.

[5] I take the phrase "heterosexual dictatorship" from Higgins (1996).

[6] Kicking Against the Pricks was Jarman's working title for a volume of memoirs and director's notes that came out under the title The Last of England in 1987. When the volume was republished posthumously in 1996, the original title was restored: see Preface, 3. Jarman's twist on the phrase "kicking against the pricks" is a miniature example of "queering" in the sense of a blasphemous imposition of homoerotic meaning on a piously straight text. "I am Jesus whom thou persecutest: it is hard for thee to kick against the pricks," the Lord warns Saul in Acts 9:5 (a warning repeated in Acts 26:14). In other words, by defying God, Saul is only hurting himself. The Lord is like a farmer who struggles to move a stubborn ox forward by goading him with a pointed stick or pike. When the ox kicks against the goad, the farmer drives the sharp points of the device deeper into his hide. By taking the biblical archaism "prick" in its obscene sense – the meaning "penis" goes back to the sexual slang of Shakespeare's day – Jarman acts out at a linguistic

level his stubbornly promiscuous defiance of old-time Christian sexual morality. Ironically, as his editor Keith Collins must have realized when the volume was republished, the tropological sense of the phrase lived on to haunt the cheeky blasphemer in so far as it would have grimly cheered his theological opponents. It had a stinging relevance to his agonies in the AIDS ward of St. Mary's Hospital.

[7] My understanding of the semantic history of the term "queering" as a hermeneutical process or reading strategy in literary and film studies owes much to the survey of definitions provided by Goldberg (1994), 1-14, and Doty (2000), 6-7.

[8] For exhibition details, I have relied on Davidson (1997), 98-153, and Kotz (1997), 588. For a reproduction of the entire *Dante Suite* in colour, see Hopps and Davidson (1997), 157-65.

[9] Jarman (1991, rpt. 1992), 22. As if his hyperbolic comparison of these no doubt fairly ordinary nuns to monstrous ecological rapists ("despoilers of the Amazon") weren't polemical enough, he also conjured them up in memory as menacing female robots out of Fritz Lang's Metropolis ("intimidating automata, brides of a celibate God"). On the erotically liberating impact of Rauschenberg's Whitechapel show on Jarman's histrionically nun-repressed soul, see Peake (2000), 116.

[10] Jarman (1992, rpt 1993), 43.

[11] On the legal and socio-political consequences of the Labouchère Amendment and the Wolfenden Report for British gays, see Higgins (1996), 109-22, 155-69.

[12] Unpublished notebook (February 1964): cited in Peake (2000), 92.

[13] For the complex philosophical background of the aesthetic project "to make literary ideas pictorial," and for Dante's prophetic role in the modernist revival of the paragone in painting and film, see Elder (2005), 394-426.

[14] On the cult of heterosexual virility mythologically associated with the New York School, and Rauschenberg's queerly intimate response to it, see Butt (2005), 48-9, 155-6.

[15] Physique Pictorial, the magazine of the Los Angeles-based Athletic Model Guild, was published from 1951 to 1990. For a reprint of the complete run in three volumes, and for background information on its legendary founding editor, Bob Mizer, see Stanley (1997).

[16] Jarman (1993), 67: "I'd bought some muscle mags, and I collaged them into the set for Stravinsky's Orpheus which I was designing that winter. This caused a minor contretemps with the Slade professor Bill Coldstream, who talked about the acceptable limits of art, citing his role at the British Board of Film Censors, while standing with his back to my set." See also Peake (2000), 118.

[17] See Katz (1993), 202: "Where Rauschenberg's allusions to his sexuality are more explicit [than those of Jasper Johns], they require a fairly sophisticated literary background. In one drawing for a series of images illustrating Dante's Inferno (1959-60) he pays particular attention to the canto describing the fate of sodomites. According to Dante, sodomites are sentenced to run forever barefoot over hot sand. And at the top of his drawing, Rauschenberg has outlined his foot in red. The more explicit references to gay culture and his identification with it seems to be the product of a deepening relationship with Johns, for they increase in number and specificity as the relationship develops."

[18] On Rauschenberg's stormy relationship and breakup with Johns, see Butt (2005), 156. Notice of their sexual relationship is discreetly absent from Tomkins (1980).

[19] On Rauschenberg's invention of the technique of solvent transfer, see Blaut (1997), 156.

[20] The outline of Rauschenberg's foot is noted by Katz (1993), 2020, and Auricchio (1997), 138, as an example of the coded imposition of private gay meanings onto the pre-existing "ground" of Dante's homophobic allegory (which is, of course, also an allegory of homophobia, of its psychological operations and social consequences). Their reading overlooks the poignant possibility that Rauschenberg literally "calqued" his own foot onto the infernal sand because he felt akin to the men who burned there in an erotic as well as eschatological sense. While I have no difficulty with Auricchio's main contention (119) "that Rauschenberg's Inferno employs veiled homoerotic imagery intelligible only to a small group of informed viewers," I part company with her on her corollary thesis "that Rauschenberg did not merely update the journey taken by Dante's wayfarer but reimagined it as an excursion through a hidden terrain of same-sex love." My literary contention in this essay is that Dante's journey did not need to be "reimagined" as such an excursion. It already was a transgressive exploration of the theologically exposed (if not over-exposed) terrain of same-sex love.

[21] Jarman (1993), 74. For the photograph of the boy in the asylum, see Avedon (1964).

[22] Inferno 3.18: "c'hanno perduto il ben de l'intelletto." Unless otherwise noted, all quotations from the Commedia in this essay are drawn from the Petrocchi edition as reprinted and slightly revised by Singleton (1970-75). I also draw on Singleton's translation for all English renderings of Dante, unless otherwise noted. Hereafter citations from the Commedia will appear within the body of the essay and will use the following abbreviations: *Inf.* for *Inferno*; *Purg.* for *Purgatorio*; and *Par.* for *Paradiso*.

[23] Jarman (1996), 52, 54.

[24] On Harry Lachman's Dante's Inferno of 1935, see Iannucci (2004), 10: "In this movie, as in Otto's [Dante's Inferno of 1924], Dante's Inferno simply becomes the frame which holds in place the unfolding moral narrative, a narrative of unbridled capitalism eventually subdued and repentant. In this case, the horrors of Hell are staged with state-of-the-art special effects." Surprisingly, Dante's guest appearance in Jarman's *Edward II* is not discussed by any of the contributors to Iannucci's pioneering anthology.

[25] Jarman (1993), 214.

[26] In linguistics, the verb "to calque" (derived from the Latin "calcare": "to press, imprint, copy") specifically denotes the process of copying a phrase or compound word from one language into another by means of word-for-word or root-for-root translation. For instance, the Latin phrase "locus communis" has been calqued into English as "commonplace." A loan translation such as "commonplace" is accordingly referred to as a "calque." In this essay, I use the term "calque" (as both a verb and a noun) to designate a loan translation in a broader rhetorical sense than its original linguistic usage: namely as a kind of extended allusion. Dante's calquing of Aeneid VI in the Inferno entails an elaborate process of retrospective reference and prophetic recontextualization involving the trans-linguistic and cross-cultural transfer of phrases and narrative details from the source text into its "spinoff" – a new work in which the imprint of the old work is still discernible only to be discerned as superseded.

[27] Virgil (1969), 247, for the Latin text; and (1991), 152-3, for the English translation.

[28] See, for example, the triadic arrangement of winged cherub-heads floating around the Virgin in Mantegna's "Sacra Conversazione" (the "Trivulzio Madonna"), dating from 1497, in Milan's Museo del Castello Sforzesco: Martindale and Garavaglia (1967), 119, Plate LV.

[29] The Pro Fit ad is reproduced in Auricchio (1997), 128. The discovery of the obscure commercial sources for Rauschenberg's illustrations to Inferno 15-16 is a breakthrough in modern iconographical research for which Auricchio deserves not merely bibliographical acknowledgment but "grande ammirazion." (Par. 1.98). While I certainly admire her incisive analysis of Rauschenberg's sophisticated exposure of the covert homoeroticism in American sports advertisements and media coverage of the 1960 Rome Olympics, I find her literary commentary on Dante's treatment of the sodomites somewhat less convincing, or at least less probing, than her gender-focused "unveiling" of Rauschenberg's treatment of Dante in relation to the ads for sports equipment and other men's products. While she sees Rauschenberg imposing homoerotic images on Dante's text – in other words, "queering" him from the outside in – I see Rauschenberg (and later Jarman) responding to Dante's already queer fantasy of his relations to the sodomites and therefore also queering his poem from the inside out. Auricchio's reading of the Inferno itself is fairly orthodox. Hence, I am inclined to question her conclusion that Rauschenberg simply used the poem "as a frame that legitimizes an investigation of same-sex affection": Auricchio (1997), 137. Far from legitimizing such an investigation, Dante's allegory of the unstraight way – the "crooked way" ("via torta": Purg. 10.3) of transgression, of unorthodoxy – effectively calls into question any easy assumption of moral legitimacy for Dantepilgrim or his metaphorically wayfaring readers.

[30] For a special issue of Life magazine (December 17, 1965) commemorating the septicentennial of Dante's birth, Rauschenberg created a much less privately coded and more blatantly Americanized series of collages based on the poet's underworld journey. It was appropriately entitled "A Modern Inferno." See Young and Davidson (1997), 567: "The work, a double panoramic image, is reproduced in two foldout sections (six pages in all). The project's recognizable imagery consists primarily of photographs taken from Life and similar magazines, depicting a mushroom cloud caused by an atomic explosion, concentration camps, civil-rights demonstrations, and figures representing "good" (John F. Kennedy) as well as "evil" (Joseph McCarthy and members of the Ku Klux Klan)."

[31] For details about the career of Adlai Stevenson, I have relied on McKeever (1989).

[32] Jarman (1991, rpt 1992), 310.

[33] "Vergilius dicitur in pueros habuisse amorem" ("Virgil is said to have been a lover of boys"): In Vergilii Bucolica II.1, 18. For a discussion of Servius's identification of Virgil with Corydon and of Alexis with Virgil's slave-boy Alexander, and its relevance to Dante's treatment of the sodomites in Inferno 15-16, see Feltham and Miller (2005), 183, 204.

[34] Virgil (1969), 5. The translation is mine.

[35] Dante-pilgrim's empathetic response to the sodomites has provoked predictable expressions of amazement and approval in the commentaries on Inferno 15-16 by gay critics such as Pequigney (1991), Boswell (1994), Holsinger (1996), and Miller (2000).

[36] Jarman (1991, rpt. 1992), 83.

[37] Jarman (1991, rpt. 1992), 305.

[38] Jarman (1991, rpt. 1992), 307.

[39] Jarman (1991, rpt. 1992), 305.

[40] Jarman (1991, rpt. 1992), 309.

[41] Jarman (1991, rpt. 1992), 309.

[42] Jarman (2001), 217.

[43] Jarman (1991, rpt. 1992), 310.

[44] "Fuck Me Blind" is the title of an oil painting by Jarman (dating from June 1993). Combining the saucy frankness of a gay come-on line with the angry rhetoric of the Outrage! demos, the slogan also poignantly refers to the onset of his AIDS-related blindness. The three words were scratched on a swirling black band so emphatically that the pale yellow background of the canvas shines through the lettering. For a reproduction of the painting, see Wollen (1996), 131. On the prominent role of Jarman in the turbulent early years of Outrage!, see Lucas (1998), 58-60.

[45] *Edward II*: I.ii.35-7. This and all subsequent quotations from Marlowe's play are from The Complete Plays, ed. Steane (1969).

[46] Jarman (1991), unnumbered dedication page opposite publication information.

[47] Jarman (1991), 56.

[48] Jarman (1992, rpt. 1993), 4: "Heterosoc, imprisoned by monogamy in the ruins of romantic love, is quite dumbfounded when faced with out plurality." No doubt the satiric neologism "Ingsoc," Newspeak for "English Socialism," was in Jarman's mind here: see Orwell (1949, rpt. 1976), 917. In Jarman's polemical screeds against Anglicanism and its Thatcherite apologists, "Heterosoc" comes to mean not only the heterosexual masses marshalled by Church and State into an army of intolerant conformists but also their institutionalized heterosexism as a discourse of wilful ignorance about sexual diversity.

[49] John Stapylton Habgood, now Baron Habgood, was Archbishop of York from 1983 to 1995. His outspoken support for Christian pressure groups active in Tory-promoted crusades against the "promotion" of homosexuality on the education front made him a lightning-rod for queer activist rage against the Church of England in Jarman's final years. For gay reaction to his moral conservatism, see The Gay Humanist (Spring 1987).

[50] On Jarman's critical admiration for Pasolini, see Peake (2000), 233, and Jarman (1996), 197: "I heard that Pasolini directed Salò in immaculate suits while he put the cast through every imaginable degradation. The film was about degradation. The film was about exploitation and Pasolini had the courage to identify himself with the seedy manipulators. I think it takes some courage or foolhardiness to put yourself on the line in this way."

[51] Jarman (1991), 52.

[52] Jarman (1991), 52.

[53] For a cultural analysis of the homoerotic icon of the Hot Jock, see Pronger (1990), 142-43, 172-73.

[54] Jarman (1991), 52. On the filming of Sebastiane, see Jarman (1993), 144-59.

[55] Jarman (1991), 52. For the epigram "Life imitates Art far more than Art imitates Life," uttered by Vivian in "The Decay of Lying," see Wilde (1994), 985.

[56] The etymologies of "scrimmage" and "scrum" have been drawn from the Oxford English Dictionary vol. 14 (1989), 738, 752.

[57] Jarman (1992, rpt. 1993), 13.

[58] Miller (1993), 266: "In AIDS elegies anastasis comes as a blessed moment of recovery when the dead rise from the mass graves dug for them by the fatalistic discourse of public health and join forces with the living against the World, the Flesh, and the Virus."

[59] See, for example, the crowds of naked sodomites in the medieval illustrations to Inf. 15-16 reproduced in Brieger (1969), vol. 2, 184-94.

[60] On the iconography of the General Resurrection and the Last Judgment in fifteenth-century Italian painting, to which Jarman would no doubt have been exposed as an art student at the Slade and as a gallery-haunting tourist in Italy, see the study of Luca

Signorelli's Orvieto frescoes by McLellan (1998), 40-50. The frescoes were begun in 1499.

[61] For a cultural analysis of the vindictively homophobic spectacularization of the AIDS crisis in the British tabloids, see Watney (1987), 76-84. Watney and Jarman were close friends. Watney's excoriating examination of the tabloids influenced Jarman's 1992 series of "Queer" paintings. See Wollen (1996), 126, 128-129, for reproductions of two paintings – "Letter to the Minister" and "Blood" – which feature collaged front-page headlines ("Vile Book in School," 'AIDS Blood in M & S Pies' Plot') as the heterosexist background for queer superscriptions in the zapping graffiti style of Outrage! agitprop.

[62] Jarman (1991), 58.

[63] The legend that Dante visited England and studied at Oxford University was dear to the heart of Victorian Dantists such as Oxford alumnus William Gladstone. On Gladstone's fervent identification with the Poet as moralist and statesman, see Isba (2006).

[64] Jarman (1991), 12. In Marlowe, the passage reads: "Music and poetry is his delight / Therefore I'll have Italian masques by night, / Sweet speeches, comedies, and pleasing shows" (*Edward II*: I.i.54-6).

[65] Dante refers to "poetizing" (poetando) four times in his journey: *Inf.* 25.99; *Purg.* 21.98; *Purg.* 22.89; and *Par.* 32.30.

[66] Jarman (1991), 62. In Marlowe, the line reads: "Thou from this land, I from myself am banish'd"(*Edward II*: I.iv.119).

[67] Jarman (1991), 58. Above the director's note is the slogan "HETEROBNO-XIOUS."

[68] On the difficult conditions at Bray during the shoot, see Peake (2000), 469-70.

[69] On Jarman's joyful response to the high camp of his canonization ceremony, which took place on the shingle beach beyond his garden on Sunday, September 22, 1991, see Peake (2000), 484-5, and Jarman (2001), 52. Photographic icons of St. Derek of Dungeness, solemnly enthroned and resplendent in King Edward's sparkling gold coronation robes, are reproduced in Jarman (1995, rpt. 1996), 78, and Wollen (1996), 13, 32.

[70] Jarman (1991, rpt. 1992), 23.

[71] Jarman (1991, rpt. 1992), 30.

[72] Jarman (1991, rpt. 1992), 30. According to literary legend, the original "Person from Porlock" was the unwelcome visitor who unwitting interrupted Coleridge during the composition of his visionary lyric "Kublai Khan." Jarman ironically compares his meditative state as a gardener – recoverable whenever he digs into the earth – to Coleridge's irrecoverably lost vision.

[73] On Jarman's City of Disc, which first appeared as an imaginary archeological site in his surrealistic short story "Through the Billboard Promised Land Without Ever Stopping," see Peake (2000), 171: "the archaeology is that of sound and the excavations are directed by poets 'silently sitting with expectant tape recorders and microphones, whilst students of literature quietly brush the earth with sable brushes to release the precious fragments of the past.'" Students of literature need not brush away much earth to recognize this fragment as a phonographic parody of Dante's City of Dis (*Inf.* 9 ff.). For further recollections of this locus in the Modern Inferno, see Jarman (1993), 129: "John and Amethyst walked in the city of Disc, past the great sulphur baths, the pools of saturnalia with their laughing, sighing waters, and the poets with their tape recorders mingling with the ghosts."

[74] Statius's grateful characterization of Virgil as a guiding "lume" (*Purg.* 22.68) ironically recalls Dante's grotesque depiction of Bertran de Born's severed head as a "lanterna" (*Inf.* 28.122).

[75] Jarman (1991, rpt. 1992), 102.

[76] Jarman (1991), 24, 58, 60, 154, 168.

Bibliography

Ahern, John. "Translations in English." *The Dante Encyclopedia.* Ed. Richard Lansing. New York, London: Garland, 2000. 824-30.

Alighieri, Dante. *La Commedia secondo l'antica vulgata.* Ed. G. Petrocchi. 4 vols. Milano: Mondadori, 1966-67.

— *The Divine Comedy.* Ed. and trans. C. S. Singleton. 6 vols. Princeton: Princeton University press, 1970-75.

— *Dante's Inferno.* Ed. and trans. John D. Sinclair. New York: Oxford University Press, 1939, rpt. 1961.

Auricchio, Laura. "'Lifting the Veil: Robert Rauschenberg's *Thirty-Four Drawings for Dante's Inferno* and the Commercial Homoerotic Imagery of 1950s America." *The Gay 90s: Disciplinary and Interdisciplinary Formations in Queer Studies.* Ed. Thomas Foster,

Carol Siegel, and Ellen E. Berry. *Genders* 26. New York: New York University Press, 1997. 119-154.

Avedon, Richard and James Baldwin. *Nothing Personal.* New York: Atheneum: 1964.

Blaut, Julia. "Transfer Drawings, Prints, and Silkscreened Paintings: 1958-1970." *Robert Rauschenberg: A Retrospective.* Ed. Walter Hopps and Susan Davidson. New York: Guggenheim Museum, 1997. 156.

Boswell, John. "Dante and the Sodomites." *Dante Studies* 112 (1994). 63-76.

Brieger, Peter, Millard Meiss, and Charles S. Singleton. *Illuminated Manuscripts of the Divine Comedy.* 2 vols. Bollingen Series 81. Princeton: Princeton University Press, 1969.

Butt, Gavin. *Between You and Me: Queer Disclosures in the New York Art World, 1948-1963.* Durham, London: Duke University Press, 2005.

Cestaro, Gary P. "Theory and Criticism (Contemporary)." *The Dante Encyclopedia.* Ed.

Richard Lansing. New York, London: Garland, 2000. 815-18.

Davidson, Susan. "Combines: 1954-1964." *Robert Rauschenberg: A Retrospective.* Ed. Walter Hopps and Susan Davidson. New York: Guggenheim Museum, 1997. 98-153.

Doty, Alexander. *Flaming Classics: Queering the Film Canon.* New York, London: Routledge, 2000.

Elder, Bruce. "Moving Visual Thinking: Dante, Brakhage, and the Works of *Energeia.*" *Dante & the Unorthodox: The Aesthetics of Transgression.* Ed. James Miller. Waterloo:
Wilfrid Laurier University Press, 2005. 394-449.

Epstein, Steven. "A Queer Encounter: Sociology and the Study of Sexuality." *Queer Theory / Sociology.* Ed Steven Seidman. Cambridge, MA: Blackwell, 1996. 145-67.

Feltham, Mark and James Miller. "Original Skin: Nudity and Obscenity in Dante's *Inferno.*" *Dante & the Unorthodox: The Aesthetics of Transgression.* Waterloo: Wilfrid Laurier University Press, 2005. 182-206.

Goldberg, Jonathan. "Introduction." *Queering the Renaissance.* Durham, London: Duke University Press, 1994.

Higgins, Patrick. *Heterosexual Dictatorship: Male Homosexuality in Postwar Britain.* London: Fourth Estate, 1996.

Holsinger, Bruce W. "Sodomy and Resurrection: the Homoerotic Subject of the *Divine Comedy.*" *Premodern Sexualities.* Ed. Louise Fradenberg and Carla Freccero. New York: Routledge, 1996.

Hopps, Walter and Susan Davidson. Ed. *Robert Rauschenberg: A Retrospective.* New York: Guggenheim Museum, 1997.

Iannucci, Amilcare. "Dante and Hollywood." *Dante, Cinema & Television.* Ed. Amilcare Iannucci. Toronto: University of Toronto Press, 2004. 3-20.

Isba, Anne. *Gladstone and Dante: Victorian Statesman, Medieval Poet.* Royal Historical Society Studies in History: New Series. Woodbridge: Boydell Press, 2006.

Jagose, Annamarie. *Queer Theory: An Introduction.* New York: New York University Press, 1996.

Jarman, Derek. *The Last of England.* London: Constable, 1987.

— *Queer Edward II.* London: British Film Institute, 1991.

— *Modern Nature: The Journals of Derek Jarman.* London: Century, 1991; rpt. Vintage, 1992.

— *At Your Own Risk.* London: Hutchinson, 1992; rpt. Vintage, 1993.

— *Dancing Ledge.* Woodstock, N.Y.: Overlook, 1993.

— *Derek Jarman's Garden with Photographs by Howard Sooley.* London: Thames and Hudson, 1995; rpt. Woodstock, N.Y.: Overlook, 1996.

— *Kicking Against the Pricks.* Rpt. of *The Last of England.* London: Vintage, 1996.

— *Smiling in Slow Motion.* London: Vintage, 2001.

Katz, Jonathan. "The Art of Code: Jasper Johns & Robert Rauschenberg." *Significant Others: Creativity and Intimate Partnership.* Ed. Whitney Chadwick and Isabelle de Courtivron. New York: Thames and Hudson, 1993. 189-207.

Kotz, Mary Lynn. "Exhibition History." *Robert Rauschenberg: A Retrospective*. Ed. Walter Hopps and Susan Davidson. New York: Guggenheim Museum, 1997. 588-613.

Lucas, Ian. *Outrage!: An Oral History*. London, new York: Cassell, 1998.

Marlowe, Christopher. *Edward* II. *The Complete Plays*. Ed. J. B. Steane. Harmondsworth: Penguin, 1969.

Martindale, Andrew and Niny Garavaglia. *The Complete Paintings of Mantegna*. New York: Harry N. Abrams, 1967.

McKeever, Porter. *Adlai Stevenson: His Life and Legacy*. New York: Morrow, 1989.

McLellan, Dugald. *Signorelli's Orvieto Frescoes: A Guide to the Cappella Nuova of Orvieto Cathedral*. Perugia: Quattroemme; Orvieto: Opera del Duomo, 1998.

Miller, James. "Dante on Fire Island: Reinventing Heaven in the AIDS Elegy." *Writing AIDS: Gay Literature, Language, and Analysis*. Ed. Timothy F. Murphy and Suzanne Poirier. New York: Columbia University Press, 1993. 265-305.

— "Alighieri, Dante." *Reader's Guide to Lesbian and Gay Studies*. Ed. Timothy F. Murphy. Chicago, London: Fitzroy Dearborn, 2000.

— "Rainbow Bodies: The Erotics of Diversity in Dante's Catholicism." *Dante & the Unorthodox: The Aesthetics of Transgression*. Ed. James Miller. Waterloo: Wilfrid Laurier University Press, 2005.

Orwell, George. "The Principles of Newspeak." Appendix to *Nineteen Eighty-Four. George Orwell*. London: Secker & Warburg/Octopus, 1976. 917-25.

Peake, Tony. *Derek Jarman: A Biography*. London: Little, Brown, 1999; Woodstock, N.Y.: Overlook, 2000.

Pequigney, Joseph. "Sodomy in Dante's *Inferno* and *Purgatorio*." *Representations* 36 (Fall 1991). 22-42.

— "Dante Alighieri." *The Gay and Lesbian Literary Heritage*. Ed. Claude J. Summers. New York: Henry Holt, 1995.

Pigg, Daniel F. "Queer." *Gay Histories and Cultures: An Encyclopedia*. New York, London: Garland, 2000. 723-24.

Pronger, Brian. *The Arena of Masculinity: Sports, Homosexuality, and the Meaning of Sex*. Toronto: University of Toronto Press, 1990.

Servius Grammaticus. *In Vergilii Bucolica et Georgica commentarii. Servii Grammatici qui feruntur in Vergilii carmina commentarii*. Ed. Georgius Thilo. Hildesheim: Georg Olms, 1961.

Simpson, J.A. and E.S.C. Weiner, eds. *The Oxford English Dictionary*. Oxford: Clarendon Press, 1989.

Stanley, Wayne E. "Introduction." *The Complete Reprint of Physique Pictorial*. 3 vols. Cologne: Taschen, 1997. Vol 1. 6-17.

The Gay Humanist Group. "Positive Images." *The Gay Humanist*. Spring 1987. Online: http://www.galha.org/glh/63/images.html.

Tomkins, Calvin. *Off the Wall: Robert Rauschenberg and the Art World of Our Time*. New York: Doubleday, 1980.

Virgil. *P. Vergili Maronis opera*. Ed. R.A.B. Mynors. Oxford: Clarendon Press, 1969.

— *The Aeneid: A New Prose Translation*. Trans. David West. Harmondsworth: Penguin, 1991.

Watney, Simon. "The Spectacle of AIDS." *AIDS: Cultural Analysis / Cultural Activism*. Ed. Douglas Crimp. *October* 43. Winter 1987. Cambridge, MA: October Magazine and Massachusetts Institute of Technology Press, 1987.

Wilde, Oscar. "The Decay of Lying." *The Complete Works of Oscar Wilde*. New York: Barnes & Noble, 1994. 970-92.

Wollen, Roger. *Derek Jarman: A Portrait*. London: Thames and Hudson, 1996.

Woods, Gregory. *A History of Gay Literature: The Male Tradition*. New Haven, London: Yale University Press, 1998.

Young, Joan and Susan Davidson. "Chronology." *Robert Rauschenberg: A Retrospective*. Ed. Walter Hopps and Susan Davidson. New York: Guggenheim Museum, 1997. 550-87.

Raffaele Pinto (University of Barcelona)

Dante (Inf. V) and Buster Keaton: The Comic Mediation of Desire

The last exhilarating scene of *Sherlock Jr.* (1924) closely resembles the final verses in Canto V of the *Inferno*, not only because it mimics the relationship between Paolo and Lancelot (in the movie, Buster kisses the girl emulating the protagonist of the movie he is watching), but also, and even more subtly, because it mirrors the narrative censoring with which Francesca interrupts her account of the story ("that day we read no more"). In the model-film that reveals the unknown love technique to Buster, this narrative censoring is rendered by the sudden cut between the kissing scene and the shot of the newly wedded couple already blessed with children. This cut and the jump from one situation to another produce an ellipsis that troubles Buster, for he lacks any information or models regarding such a delicate and decisive activity as the procreation of children.

Such a parodic reworking of Dante's verses could be read as simply another chapter in the early cinematic portrayal of two Riminesi lovers' story; a portrayal that, as Amilcare Iannucci has already shown, begins in the United States as early as 1907[1]. It must be noted, however, that this is not a reinterpretation of the tragic story found in Dante. In fact, of the events narrated in Canto V, only the final verses are allusively parodied. Therefore, it is better to speak of an inter-textual relationship, in which the source is quoted and freely re-used in a thematic context that has been completely altered. This increases the quotation's significance from the point of view of cultural reception, for it does not show a director dealing with the interpretation and the trans-codification of a classical text, but rather a classical text that covertly comes back to life, in the form of a creative inspiration within a director's expressive strategy. Such a director does not consider the previous knowledge the viewer might posses of the quoted work. On the contrary, he disguises the quotation, since there is nothing in the plot of the film that resembles Dante's story. The film-maker is interested only in the reading of the book and the kiss, and the relationship between the two lovers and the book – an episode that he recreates as the relationship between Buster and the movie he is projecting[2].

The connection between the two texts – non-existent if one looks at the plot – is very strong on the level of the aesthetic issues that they imply. The final scene of Keaton's film artfully concludes a story that, with the usual melodramatic pretext of a prohibited love, comically explores the existential relationship between the protagonist and cinematic fiction. He even physically enters, although in dream, the story projected on the screen, juxtaposing the rigidity and the weight of his body – a weight by definition unknown to the fictional image – against the airy lightness of the film's characters. Consequently, he suffers all the arbitrary changes in scenery created in the film through editing[3]. Dante faced a similar problem when he imagined (in his quasi-dream experience as well: "I was so full of sleep...", *Inf.* I 11) crossing over to the afterlife with his own body, which was thus exposed to the stimuli of a landscape that, although very concrete in its cosmological order, was only virtual from a living organism's point of view[4]. His body has to suffer the consequences of the afterlife's theological "editing," with all the astonishing changes in scenery it entails. The analogy between the two aesthetic situations is easier to understand if we think that it is equally miraculous and unbelievable for Dante's character to enter the afterlife with his own body, as it is for Buster's character to transport his body onto the screen. Both must cross the threshold that separates reality from fiction. The credibility of Dante's crossing is assured by the theological paradigm in which the poet operates, while Keaton's crossing is assured by the comic register that permeates the film. However, in both cases, it is a matter of entering an area that is fictional by definition with one's body, even though for Dante the fiction of the afterlife is unreal rather than fake, whereas for Keaton the fiction of the film is fake rather than unreal. In order to understand the aesthetic dimension they both share, it must be clear that not only is Dante already talking about cinema but also Keaton is still talking about theology (despite the awareness that either may have had regarding the historical implications of the aesthetic issues addressed by their respective works).

The complexities inherent to Keaton's use of Dante's episode give us the opportunity to reflect on the historical meaning of the inter-textual relationship between the film maker and the poet, considering these issues not only *a parte subiecti* (given the relevance the movie assigns to the verses of the *Divine Comedy*) but also *a parte obiecti* (given the new context in which the poetic text appears in Keaton's film).

An overview of the critical interpretations of *Inferno*'s Canto V will help us better understand Keaton's reading of Dante's verses. In fact – although it makes no sense to expect an explicit interpretation of this episode of the *Divine Comedy* from the actor-director – Keaton's way of reenacting the episode implies a clear choice of those elements he deemed meaningful, and therefore an implicit preference (perhaps *ante litteram*) for one of the many interpretations of the Canto suggested by philology. One of these suggestions proves useful to understanding Dante from Keaton's point of view: that put forth by René Girard, in the context of his theory of the mediation of desire. I am referring to the monograph *Deceit, Desire and the Novel: Self and Other in Literary Structure* (1966) – an exemplary essay in anthropological literary criticism – in which the theory of triangular desire is expressed for the first time. A theory the scholar later developed in articles and volumes that have progressively broadened its original field of application. However here we will focus exclusively (and freely) on its main principles.

Having postulated the necessity of a mediator in any given relationship of desire, the development of modernity (and in particular the secularization of culture), can be interpreted as the process through which the desiring subject draws closer to the mediator, a model to imitate or a rival to defeat. Such an act of approximation reduces and almost nullifies the transcendence of the model, which from external – that is mimetically inaccessible – becomes internal: "The closer the mediator approaches the desiring subject, the more transcendence dissipates... It is precisely in the *internal* mediation that the deep truth of *modernity* resides."[5]. In the archetypical novel *Don Quixote* the two pairs "Don Quixote – Amadis" and "Anslemo – Lotario" (the latter characters of *El curioso impertinente*, a short story within the novel) show respectively the maximum and the minimum distance between subject and mediator (external mediator – internal mediator). The "novelistic truth" would thus consist of rendering the otherness that resides in every desire explicit, while the "romantic lie" covers such otherness with the illusion of a desiring subject that is absolute and authentic[6].

Girard uses Canto V of the *Inferno* as the object of analysis in a monograph dedicated to this topic [1978], along with other classical texts that depict the desiring subject as it chooses an object following the directions of a model, which thus functions as a mediator. In an interview, the scholar summarizes this issue as follows:

> As we already know, Francesca is the one who recounts the story of their love affair. Francesca is the wife of Paolo's brother, and initially they did not seem to be in love with each other at all. They passed the time reading the chivalric romance "Lancelot of the Lake," in which Queen Guinevere, encouraged by the traitor, Galehaut, falls in love with Lancelot. At the same moment in which Lancelot kisses the queen, Paolo and Francesca kiss. Thus their love affair begins... One of Dante's explanations lies in the line "Galeotto fu il libro e chi lo scrisse." This means to say that books are not innocent, behind every book there is an author trying to seduce you, who pushes you to imitate him. In my terminology, the book performs the function of *mediator*, as a *model* for Paolo and Francesca: their love therefore is, in a certain sense, *a copied love*.

This series of texts, which spans from Dante to Keaton (including, according to Girard, *The Red and the Black's* Julien Sorel, *Madame Bovary*, *The Eternal Husband*, and Marcel of Proust's *Recherche*), allows us to isolate the most historically productive element of *The Inferno*'s Canto V. Without a doubt, this Canto is the most in-tune with modern aesthetics, in which, as Dante anticipated, literature (understood as fiction) plays the role of the ideal model, replacing myth and religion (each "true" by definition[7]). Here desire acquires an imitative character in the context of a culture in which the subject (reader or viewer) internalizes the other, adopting it as a model for behavior. The hero and the saint, because they are supernatural, are "inimitable," and therefore cannot be internalized as practical models of behavior. Their exemplary nature is fundamental to defining ideological values and ethical contents, but it excludes a complete mimesis of identity, like that allowed by the literary examples (as well as the cinematic ones) mentioned above. Both, the mythical hero and the saint, are placed in a transcendental dimension, beyond the reader's reach. Their mediation is, therefore, completely external. Instead, the modern novel, by drawing closer to the mediator, allows for its mimesis, and even for an identification with it. By emphasizing the mechanisms of identification and imitation Dante describes, we will be able to appreciate Girard's contribution to a deeper understanding of the text.

Let us briefly reread the episode in light of its relationship to the novel's otherness that the adulterous couple tests within their own experience of desire. After the first brief tale of the sentimental events that tie her to her brother-in-law and provoked her husband's revenge, Francesca is asked by Dante to recount the two lovers' intentions and the way in which they came to discover their desire for one another (vv. 118-120):

> "Ma dimmi: al tempo d'i dolci sospiri,
> a che e come concedette amore
> che conosceste i dubbiosi disiri?"

> ["But tell me, in the time of gentle sighs,
> with what and in what way did Love allow you
> to recognize your still uncertain longings?"]

His question concerns one of the ethical aspects of desire particularly dear to the poet: the expressivity of desire, which, beyond pure sexuality, represents the primary objective of love tension, and is cultivated by poetry precisely because it acts as an engine of expression[8]. This is how Dante understands desire in the *Vita Nuova*, where he states that the words written in Beatrice's praise are the ultimate purpose of his love for her ("in words which prose my lady", cap. XVIII). The question posited to Francesca implies that their mistake was not desiring each other – desire being a prerogative of *gentili* hearts – but rather misinterpreting the purpose and the expressive modality of desire. It was not desire that condemned the two lovers, but the purpose for which it had been cultivated, and the way in which it had been communicated. If it had remained hidden, or expressed in a different manner, there would not have been any sin. Therefore, it becomes essential, in order to understand her mistake, that Francesca narrate (for the poet and the reader of the *Divine Comedy*) the situation in which the two lovers discovered each other's desires. In other words, how that which should have remained buried in the depths of the heart came to surface and expressed itself.

This question poses an anthropological issue in which we can easily recognize a trait of our culture and mentality: the expressive dialectics between internal experience and its verbal external manifestation. Francesca is invited to speak precisely about this dialectic. Within the dichotomy articulated by desire – between the latent dimension of subjectivity and an actualized dimension – and in the poetic aspiration to reconcile it with an integrated perception of personality – as Dante explains in Canto XXIV of *Purgatory*, where he defines his own poetics – the values of the subject's autonomy and the ethical preponderance of desire – which is the bases for such an autonomy – are here displayed in a literary fashion[9].

Francesca's response, which involves the reading of a novel that narrates the loves of Lancelot and Queen Guinevere, situates such a reading experience at the same point in which the "word of the heart" (the *verbum cordis* of St. Augustine) should be transformed into the "spoken word" (the *verbum oris*), thus occupying the expressive space in which personality is recovered, and synchronizing the internal with the external. This vicarious function, which mediates or substitutes the verbal expression of the internal experience, and therefore orients the subject's tension of desire within the world, constitutes the authentic meaning of the modern novel. Thanks to the novel the original experience of the subject discovered by lyrical poets acquires a wider and more popular social irradiation within the minds and the behavior of those who read novels[10]. Of course Dante coveys not only the modern novel's historical originality, but also the perverse potential for materialistic degradation, that is the amputation suffered by the personality when sexuality is experienced as an end in itself, and not as energy for the spiritual strengthening of the subject. By mimetically identifying with the characters who act on the literary stage, the reader's desire – instead of being poetically exalted by the word that renders it spiritual and redeems it ("words which praise my lady") – is degraded in a novelistic way through the sexual consumption of the object ("While all his body trembled, kissed my mouth"). However, the poet does not refuse the mediating function of literature – which poetry (at least his) performs according to a very noble project of humanity's cultural redemption. Rather, he refuses its novelistic degradation, in other words the perverse use (let's call it a-critical) the novel makes of such a mediation, directing the reader's desire toward the low and not the high, toward matter and not the spirit.

By denouncing the novelistic genre as the one responsible for the sin committed by the two courtly lovers, Dante inaugurates literature's great reflection on the exemplary function of *fictio* (according to *De Vulgari* II ev.2, poetry "nichil aliud est quam *fictio* rethorica musicaque poita"), and on the duty assigned to it (previously unimaginable): that of elaborating the mental and behavioral models that were culturally prestigious and socially effective.

That which surprises and scandalizes is the new prerogative of sanctioning values shared by all, a duty previously performed by myth and religion, and which would later be passed down to literature, cinema, and television: the new twentieth century means of producing *fictio*. Dante's realism must be understood within the framework of such a historical development, and therefore, in a deeply pragmatic way, disconnected from the ancient theory of realism in art (derived from Aristotle). It is not a matter of mirroring the world – and suggesting verisimilar, and therefore believable, interpretations of it – but rather it is a matter of reconstructing the world fictitiously, in such a persuasive way that the work of art may suggest and authorize values and behavioral models, and consequently mediate the readers' desires. The reader discovers his or her life goals by identifying with the characters, presented as worthy of admiration and therefore as models to imitate. In the end, it is a matter of parodying the hagiographies, as Dante in fact does in his *Vita Nuova*, turning its content (clearly perverse, from a Christian standpoint) and its goals (not edifying but corruptive) up-side-down.

The idea of the book or its author as *galeotti* (that is, models for deviance, persuasively offered to the readers' mimetic desire) can be found in two other classics of proto-modern literature: Boccaccio's *Decameron* – whose title explicitly quotes *Inferno V*, for the book is "cognominato *Principe galeotto*" (and therefore reclaims, in a positive way, that refusal of transcendence that Dante denounces as negative in the novel) – and *Tirant lo Blanc*, a Catalan novel by Joanot Martorell (1490), on which Cervantes writes:

> In honor of the truth it behooves me to say, my dear sir, that this book surpasses all others in the world in matters of style. Furthermore, here knights eat, sleep, die in their beds; they dictate their last will before dying, and one can find many other things of which there is no mention in other similar books. This notwithstanding he who wrote it (for, unnecessarily, he wrote so many absurdities) would merit to be held captive for the rest of his life[11].

What matters here is that Cervantes' attitude toward Francesca's episode, which he mentions when condemning Martorell "a galeras," because of his realism[12]. Drawing from Boccaccio's quotation (*galeras* = *galeotto*), the author of the *Quijote* shows a certain familiarity with Dante's text, and suggests that, in his opinion, the episode constitutes a modern archetype for the structuring a novel, according to an understanding of novel that identifies realism – that is, the mundane light in which the chivalric characters are presented – with literature's perverse modeling function. From Cervantes' point of view such a mundane light increases the power of persuasion possessed by those fictional characters, and therefore increases the deviant appeal to readers as gullible as Don Quixote. It is not surprising that in the initial phases of the modern novel, literature's ability to influence people's behavior is felt as perverse, especially when its moralizing character is not explicit, and therefore every novel is deemed as *galeotto* in the end. On the contrary, the perception writers had of such a phenomenon reflects the unprecedented – and therefore radically modern – character of the literary culture expressed in the novel, of which Paolo and Francesca's characters serve as the first examples[13].

Thus we understand why Francesca is the first in along series of typically modern characters, who at every aesthetic turn of the West's cultural evolution pose the same issue regarding the exemplary validity of literary *fictio*. At the very moment in which she accuses (V.137) the novel and its author of acting as ruffians Francesca reveals the true essence of her sin; by speaking on behalf of the lovers, they uncover that which should have remained hidden. Such a sin is but the general law of modernity, which consists of substituting the mythical and religious truth as ethical models, with the poetic *fictio*. The same is true, obviously, for the myths of classical antiquity because Francesca's passion cannot be reconciled with that of Jesus nor with that of Dido (whose love for Aeneas is impossible to imagine as an attempt to imitate a fictional heroine[14]).

As previously mentioned, Girard's theoretical suggestion also includes – within the triangular structure of desire – a historical function of progressive approximation between the mediator and the subject. This coincides with the process of secularization of European culture, which can be easily recognized in the appropriation, by celebrities and film stars, of the exemplary function previously performed by literary and novelistic characters, and even earlier by saints and heroes[15]. The aesthetic content of cinema must be analyzed within this process. The technology of cinema serves a project of civilization in which the mediator of desire is powerfully pushed toward the viewer. Thus, he or she is able to identify with the fictional model in a way that is much more intense than any other previous aesthetics. This causes the line between fiction and reality to fade, a phenomenon that is typical of twentieth century aesthetics. The great literature of the past century has routinely underscored the painful estrangement caused by such a confusion, which seems to preclude the traditional existential bearings of the subject. Cinema (understood as an aesthetic device) is responsible for such a process, and illustrates its positive aspects, which consist of an improved capacity to control the subject's identification mechanisms. The phenomenon, along with the radical approximation of the fictional model, is explained by the W. Benjamin in the previously mentioned essay. It consists of the critical attitude that cinema provokes in its audience, no matter how ignorant it is of cinematic techniques[16]. It is precisely through such a spontaneous critical attitude – deprived of an ideological prospective – that the spectator acquires, thanks to cinema, a control over the object of his or her desire, and therefore over the construction of his or her individual identity. In this way, cinema implements – on a level of greater amplitude and depth – the project of civilization implied by the modern novel, handing the celebrity over to the famished desiring praxis of the spectators, who, in the movie theater (or in front of the television), search for and find models to emulate, and through which they can justify their life choices. Furthermore, the pervasiveness of image technology has such a monopoly over aesthetic perception that it is capable of neutralizing any form of justification (ethical and political), expect that of the audio-visual *fictio* it produces.

All this suggests that literature and cinema have a relationship of historical development (with the same aesthetic paradigm), as well as a relationship based on reciprocity and thematic influences (between different aesthetic languages). By strengthening the audio-visual perception of reality through technology, cinema increases (within the real world) the power of attraction that literature exercises on the values of transcendence in modern times, rendering them completely secular, perhaps irreversibly. Within the cinematic expression, comedy is that which advances the processes of myth deconstruction, presenting reality as the extension of images and even as their degraded copy[17]. This is not only true for the origins of cinema, as we saw in Keaton[18], but also for its later developments, as one can see in Woody Allen's films. The screenplay of his *Play it again Sam* (1972) is clearly inspired by the movie we started with. In Allen, the perception of the exemplary role played by cinema's fiction is explicit, and the comic register serves to denounce its aesthetic and (anti)ideological radicalism.

In Keaton's cinema, desire's mimetic logic is at its peak when it literally pierces the screen and invades the pseudo-sacred space of the hero, who descends from his literary pedestal and becomes an accomplice, or even a double, of the subject-spectator. The clear separation between cinema's fiction and the spectator's reality is abolished, and the two different spaces intermingle. In the case of *S. H. J.*, the crossing of the screen is literal, as we already mentioned. But in the case of the *Cameraman* (1928), the protagonist's re-doubled movie image, in the final scenes of the film, convinces the girl that he, and not the vain rival-antagonist, deserves the prize of her love; as if to say that it is only through cinema's mediation, which transforms the body into image, that the subject can hope to participate in the erotic exchange, becoming in turn an object of desire, and therefore making his expectations of the world come true. However, this is the same process of crossing the screen, for the final result, in both cases, is the complete and therefore comic abolition of the distance and the threshold that separate the imaginary models sacrality from the desiring subject's experience. Woody Allen draws from Keaton's pioneering intuitions in his *The Purple Rose of Cairo* (1985), when his two protagonists cross the threshold that separates reality from fiction: the male exiting out of the screen and the female entering it. It is precisely this crossing that I define as "the comic mediation of desire," for through it, modernity completes the project of total and uncompromised identification of the subject with its mediator, who is finally deprived of any pretense of distance and authority.

Now I would like to point out that such an identification can, on the one hand, only be cinematic, due to the realism implicit in the cinematographic effect: at the movies we see things, we do not imagine them, as we do when reading[19]. On the other hand, such an identification can only be a comic one, and therefore pre-rational, for the profanation of the transcendental space to which every image refers[20] implies a free Dionysian desire that, if completely rationalized (that is, recognized as pure impulse), would immediately contradict the official ideology through which power tries to preserve some form of separation and therefore an appearance of transcendence. The deconstructive function of laughter is intrinsically hostile to ideologies and, even more so, when ideologies are used to justify power. The cinematic comedy is therefore the most "galeotto" of expressive registers, for the approximation of the model, and the crossing of the threshold that separates reality and fiction, are experienced just below the spectator's level of awareness. Yet such an approximation and crossing are socially and culturally necessary in order for the subject to freely construct its individual identity on the ruins of the exemplary models emptied by technology. The ridiculous characters of Buster Keaton, Frank Capra and Woody Allen are paradoxically those that best expose (more than any other epic, tragic or melodramatic character of the movies) modernity's fundamental utopia: the individual is heroically the master of his own destiny[21].

Finally, such comic mediation points to the postmodern surpassing of modernity's aesthetics: a surpassing that is clearly aimed at a complete virtualization of the subject with the help of new technologies. It is obtained by merging reality and fiction, that is turning *fictio* into the environment in which the subject constructs his own identity, and by projecting himself onto reality, according to a life project devised in complete autonomy, which involves not only personal identity (through the construction of roles in the new spaces of socialization offered by the internet), but also the body's biological matter (through genetic engineering and plastic surgery). The results of such a virtualization of the subject are often abhorrent, for they are not supported by an educational system capable of directing the citizen in the implementation of such new possibilities and responsibilities. This, however, should not diminish the value of the objective progress they signify in matters of personal autonomy. Such progress is far from being assimilated on the level of analysis and planning by political culture (especially the Italian one). From this perspective, the concept of "fiction" (understood in its technological form) and that of "freedom" (politically understood as the complete democratization of social life) are mixed with one another, for one serves as the prerequisite for the other[22]. In fact through cinema, comic mediation celebrates its triumph and presents itself as the utopian nucleus of modernity, an unshakable project of aesthetic emancipation that sacrifices all ideologies for the individual's happiness (for all individuals), and finally demonstrates that the starting point of the historical process that renders transcendence human, by nullifying distance, is Dante's *Divine Comedy*: a fundamental work of modern *fictio*, whose title alludes to – at least according to one of its meanings – the abolition of any threshold of separation from transcendence, that is the poetic deconstruction of divinity and the authority connected to it[23].

Notes

[1] Such history begins with the brief ("about ten minutes") film by William W. Ranous, *The Two Brothers / Francesca da Rimini*.

[2] I do not exclude the possibility that the allusion to the *Divine Comedy* might be indirect, filtered by one of the cinematic versions of Francesca's tale. In that case, it would not be a matter of the reception of the poet's work, but rather of its influence. For the purpose of my argument, the difference between the two scenarios is irrelevant.

[3] In these dream sequences, Keaton's refined critical approach focuses on the loss of weight of the actor's body – that is its conversion into an image. Here he comically expands upon an observation Pirandello formulated in his 1915 novel entitled *Si gira* (later renamed *I quaderni di Serafino Gubbio operatore*). Pirandello's observations were elaborated by Walter Benjamin in his essay *The work of Art in the Mechanical Age of Reproduction* (who read them in Léon Pierre-Quint's *Significacion du Cinéma, L'art cinèmatographique*, II, Paris 1927, pp.14-15). Below is a quotation from the passage that sheds light on the artificial and fragmentary nature of film images, which is caused by an amputation of the body: "For the film, what matters primarily is that the actor represents himself to the public before the camera, rather than representing someone else. One of the first to sense the actor's metamorphosis by this form of testing was Pirandello. Though his remarks on the subject in his novel *Si Gira [Ö]*were limited to the negative aspects of the question and to the silent film only, this hardly impairs their validity. For in this respect, the sound film did not change anything essential. What matters is that the part is acted not for an audience but for a mechanical contrivance – in the case of the sound film, for two of them. "The film actor," wrote Pirandello, "feels as if in exile – exiled not only from the stage but also from himself. With a vague sense of discomfort he feels inexplicable emptiness: his body loses its corporeality, it evaporates, it is deprived of reality, life, voice, and the noises caused by his moving about, in order to be changed into a mute image, flickering an instant on the screen, then vanishing into silence ...The projector will play with his shadow before the public, and he himself must be content to play before the camera." [...] The feeling of strangeness that overcomes the actor before the camera, as Pirandello describes it, is basically of the same kind as the estrangement felt before one's own image in the mirror. But now the reflected image has become separable, transportable," *Illuminations*, ed. H. Arendt, (New York: Schocken Books, 2007).

[4] Regarding the issue of Dante's physicality in crossing to the afterlife, see my *Fingo ergo sum. Elementi di teoria poetica della modernità. Lettura del canto XXVI del 'Purgatorio'*, in "Tenzone. Revista de la Asociación Complutense de Dantologia", 2005, n° 5, pp. 171-211.

[5] Girard., p. 80.

[6] An example of such an illusion, which clarifies *e contrario* Girards triangular model, can be found in this passage taken from one of Balzac's short novels, entitled *Massimilla Doni*, that, I believe, best represents the way in which desire romantically escapes all attempts at literary mediations: "Reclining on a sofa, after returning from a drive about eleven in the morning, beside a table on which lay the remnants of a dainty breakfast, the Duchess Cataneo let her lover toy with that muslin gown without saying 'Fie!' at his every movement. Emilio sat on a low chair at her feet, holding one of her hands between both of his, and gazed at her in complete self-abandonment. Do not ask if they loved each other; they loved too well. They were not at the point of reading in the book, like

Paul and Francoise; they were so far from it that Emilio dared not say, 'Let us read.'" In this passage, note the contrast between the two lovers' behavior and that of Paolo and Francesca in Dante's episode, thus implicitly defined as an example of a desire that is not authentic but mediated.

[7] In the same way in which, in the *Poema*, the historical truth possessed by Aeneas and St. Paul (*Inf.*II), is replaced by Dante's own poetically fictitious experience.

[8] The Italian lyrical tradition, from its origins, moves the dialectic of desire from the realm of sexuality to that of expression, in other words from the body of the loved one to the word that expresses the passion. I retraced this lyrical motif to Giacomo da Lentini's poetry (*La parola del cuore*, in AA. VV., *La poesia di Giacomo da Lentini. Scienza e filosofia nel XIII secolo in Sicilia e nel Mediterraneo*, Centro di Studi filologici e linguistici, Palermo, 2000, pp. 168-191).

[9] On this issue see my *Gentucca e il paradigma poetico del 'dolce stil novo'*, in "Tenzone. Revista de la Asociación Complutense de Dantologia", 2002, n° 3, pp. 191-216.

[10] These novelistic triangles Lancelot – Guinevere – Arthur and Tristan – Isolde – Mark reflect the lyrical triangle *trobador – midons – gilos* (the husband). The first Italian cinematic portrayal of Paola and Francesca's story (*Francesca di Rimini*, 1910) helps to shed light on the abstract model of triangular desire implied both by lyrical poetry and the novel, and finally by cinema. This version – where Francesca's role is played Francesca Bertini – introduces a "tristian" element in the screenplay: Gianciotto sends Paolo to ask for his future wife's hand, and then the two youths return by sea. On the ship, the two "learn to love one another" and, while reading a novel, they kiss.

[11] "Aquí comen los caballeros, y duermen y mueren en sus camas, y hacen testamento antes de su muerte, con estas cosas de que todos los demás libros deste género carecen. Con todo eso, os digo que merecía el que le compuso, pues hizo tantas necedades de industria, que le echaran a galeras por todos los días de su vida" (I 6). Quoted from Miguel de Cervantes, *Don Quijote de la Mancha*, Edición del Instituto Cervantes 1605-2005, Dirigida por Francisco Rico, Círculo de lectores, Barcelona, 2004, I p. 91 e II p. 709.

[12] Cervantes read the word *galeotto* in *Inf.*V as a metaphor for the conditions in which the damned are kept in hell. In chapter XXII of the first part of the *Quijote*, the protagonist of the novel encounters a group of convicts (galeotti), and the episode functions as a parady of Dante's *Inferno*: "Los galeotes son las almas de los pecadores del infierno, don Quijote, en sus preguntas a ellos, es Dante" (Avery, 1974-75, p. 10). Martorell's sentence "a galeras" is therefore analogous to Francesca's condemnation of the perverse realism typical of the chivalric novel.

[13] High culture's diffidence toward the novel (ignored from Aristotle on) is a constant in the history of literature. Its canonization as a literary genre can be traced back to 18th century England, but only after it had renounced its historical denomination (*romance*) in favor of a term (*novel*) less compromised on the level of fiction. This condemnation is usually motivated by the fictional nature of its inventions. See, for instance, Petrarca, *Triumphus Cupidinis*, 66: "sogno d'infermi e fola di romanzi"; Boccaccio, *Elegia di Madonna Fiammetta*, 8,7: "li franceschi romanzi, alli quali se fede alcuna si puote attribuire"; or a 15th century Latin text quoted by E. R Curtius: "ex lectione quorundam romanticorum, id est librorum compositorum in gallico sermone poeticorum de gestis militaribus, quorum maxima pars fabulosa est" (I, 2-5).

[14] In verbalizing her passion for Aeneas to her sister Anna, Dido reflects the ancient paradigm according to which desire is seen as the worship of the identical; in other words she projects the same feeling she felt for the husband Sychaeus on the Trojan hero (IV,

20-23: "Anna, fatebor enim, miseri post fata Sychaei / Coniugis et sparsos fraterna cae-de penates / Solus hic inflexit sensus animumque labantem / Impulit. Adgnosco veteris vestigia flammae" [I shall say it: since that time / Sychaeus, my poor husband, met his fate, / and blood my brother shed stained our hearth gods, / this man alone as wrought upon me / and move my soul to yield. I recognize / the signs of the old flame, of old de-sire. (trans. Robert Fitzgerald, The Harvill Press, London, 1981)]. By translating literally this last verse in *Purg.* XXX 48 (*conosco i segni dell'antica fiamma*), speaking about the emotions provoked by Beatrice in the earthly paradise, Dante brings together that which, in Virgil, is apparently divided between the two objects of Dido's desire. In reality, this reflects a tension of desire which remain constant, which does not imply any "otherness" that divides the desiring subject between the self and its model. The otherness of Dante's desire for Beatrice is shown, on the level of mimetic mediation, through the celestial collocation of the loved one, which distinguishes the character since her first novelistic appearance (in *Vita Nuova* II 1: "the woman who my mind beholds in glory"). This is made explicit in *Ladies who by insight* 29: "My lady is desired in highest heaven." "One imperfection only Heaven has: / the lack of her; so now for her it pleads / and every saint with clamor intercedes" (19-21). The other with whom the poet competes in desiring Beatrice – and who, therefore, is drawn into the subject's field of experience – is he tran-scendent community of the blessed: "One imperfection only Heaven has: / the lack of her; so now for her it pleads / and every saint with clamor intercedes" (19-21).

[15] See Walter Benjamin op. cit: "the film responds to the shriveling of the aura with an artificial build-up of the "personality" outside the studio. The cult of the movie star, fostered by the money of the film industry, preserves not the unique aura of the person but the "spell of the personality, the phony spell of a commodity".

[16] Ibid., "Mechanical reproduction of art changes the reaction of the masses toward art. The reactionary attitude toward a Picasso painting changes into the progressive re-action toward a Chaplin movie. The progressive reaction is characterized by the direct, intimate fusion of visual and emotional enjoyment with the orientation of the expert [die Lust am Schauen und am Erleben in ihm eine unmittelbare und innige Verbindung mit der Haltung des fachmännischen Beurteilers eingeht]. Such fusion is of great social si-gnificance. The greater the decrease in the social significance of an art form, the sharper the distinction between criticism and enjoyment by the public. The conventional is uncri-tically enjoyed, and the truly new is criticized with aversion. With regard to the screen, the critical and the receptive attitudes of the public coincide." Please note the removal of an ideological prospective from the aesthetic judgment that, according to Benjamin, cinema causes in its audience when the spectator experiences "the direct, intimate fusion of visual and emotional enjoyment with the orientation of the expert."

[17] In this respect, Cesare Segre's diagnosis of the status of twentieth century literary fiction and the radically new dialectic between cinema, reality and invention, is particu-larly illuminating. Although focused on literature, Segre's analysis carefully identifies the abolition of the separation between reality and fiction (an abolition that image technology generates and which is reflected by the literary discourse): "Sino al Novecento, si può dire che gli scrittori partono da concezioni empiriche ma abbastanza stabili di realtà, rivolgendosi, per trovarne gli elementi antinomici, alle sfere del religioso, del mitico, del magico, della leggenda. Col Novecento si verifica un capovolgimento: la sicurezza della realtà entra in crisi, mentre si disseccano le fonti dell'assurdo 'istituzionale' (religione, mito, etc.). La dialettica realtà / irrealtà viene dunque impiantata ex novo, e solo sul ter-reno della incrinata e sfuggente realtà. È per questo che nella narrativa contemporanea

non è stabilita una zona precisa di pertinenza dell'irreale e del meraviglioso: divenute sfuggenti le proprietà del reale, è anche compromessa l'identificazione del suo opposto. Il meraviglioso (sempre in senso negativo: l'assurdo, l'incubo) si annida nella quotidianità, la rende ancor più impervia, nemica, incomprensibile. Se il meraviglioso tradizionale metteva in forse le leggi fisiche del nostro mondo, il meraviglioso moderno smentisce gli schemi d'interpretazione che l'uomo nella sua lunga parabola ha messo a punto per la propria esistenza. Il nuovo meraviglioso è una mimesi stralunata dall'orrore delle scoperte." ["Until the twentieth century, one could say that writers began with an empirical concept of reality that is rather stable, turning – in order to find its antonymic elements – to the religious, mythical, magical or legendary sphere. During the twentieth century, one can detect a sudden inversion: the assurance of reality collapses, while the sources of the "institutional" absurd (religion, myth, etc.) are exhausted. The dialectic reality versus non-reality is articulated in a new way, based on a faulty and fleeting reality. This is why, in contemporary narrative, one cannot find a specific zone assigned to non-reality and imagination: once reality's characteristics have become fleeting, its opposite becomes equally compromised. The imagination (understood in a negative sense: the absurd, the nightmare) can be found in the everyday life, making it even more impenetrable, hostile and incomprehensible. If the traditional imagination contradicted the physical laws of our world, the modern imagination invalidates the interpretative categories devised by man throughout his long existence. The new imagination is a mimesis deranged by the horror of new discoveries], from the entry *Finzione* [Fiction] *Enciclopedia*, Einaudi, Torino, 1979, vol. 6, pp. 215-216).

[18] In addition to Keaton, one could mention Frank Capra, who since his debut as a director (under the supervision of Harry Langdon, for whom he directed and/or wrote the screenplay for three films: *The Strong Man*, 1926; *Tramp, Tramp, Tramp*, 1926; *Long Pants*, 1927) focuses his research on the modern status of fiction and the mediation it performs between the desire of the subject-reader-viewer. In *Long Pants*, the mind of the protagonist is deranged by reading novels that prompt him to undertake a series of comical adventures, with the goal of obtaining the love of a woman.

[19] "It is impossible to 'see and feel' reality as it unfolds *outside of a specific visual angle*: and this visual angle always belongs to a subject who sees and feels. This subject is a subject in flesh and blood, for even if, in a fictional movie, we choose an ideal point of view – and therefore a point of view that is somewhat abstract and non-naturalistic – it becomes realistic and eventually naturalistic when we place the camera and the sound recorder in that specific point of view: it will appear as something seen and heard by a subject in flesh and blood (that is a subject with eyes and ears)." From: "Observations on the Sequence Shot," in *Heretical Empiricism*, ed. Barnett (Bloomington: Indiana University Press, 1988), pp. 233-37.

[20] The transcendence of images is inscribed in human culture and serves as its original foundation. See: *Exodus 20, 3-6*, which comments on the first commandment, "Thou shalt have no other Gods before me. Thou shalt not make unto the any graven image, or any likeness of anything that is in heaven above, or that is in the earth beneath, or that is on the water under the earth. Thou shalt not bow down thyself to them, nor serve them: for I the lord thy God am jealous God, visiting the iniquity of the fathers upon the children unto the third and fourth generation of them that hate me; and shewing mercy unto thousands of them that love me, and keep my commandments." This threat alludes to the ancient magical power of images, a power capable of tying together the hostile forces of nature by means of iconic control. Such power continues to influence the modern

imaginative strategies of desire, which enormously augmented by technology, causes the subject to appropriate the image, thus exercising the transcendence hidden amid the otherness of any given image.

[21] Two great Italian examples of screen crossing and comic mediation of desire, both played by Alberto Sordi, are *Lo sciecco bianco* (1952) by Federico Fellini, in which the innocent protagonist experiences a tragic-comic love story with the hero of a *fotoromanzo*, and *Un americano a Roma* (1954) by Steno, whose protagonist identifies with the characters of American movies so much that he plays them within the context of proletarian Rome where he lives. Compare the opening scene of *Un americano a Roma* (a close-up of Sordi at a movie theater while he watches a movie) with the opening scene of *Play it again, Sam*, and the final scene of *The Purple Rose of Cairo*.

[22] Jean Baudrillard's analysis is particularly insightful for it captures the new and generalized nature of simulacrum that reality has acquired in the context of a modular economy that is purely reproductive, and because it sheds light on the new interactive relationship between subject and the meaning of the world. However, Baudrillard's analysis does not go as far as Benjamin's (from which it stems) because the scholar does not recognize the potential for emancipation that the technological revolution affords to the individual subject, who for the first time in human history has the opportunity to build himself (even biologically speaking) as an autonomous vessel of meaning. See *Symbolic Exchange and Death*, (London: Sage Publication, 1993, pp. 50-86). Also see the passage in which the "strong symbolism" of "sure signs" (sure because they are perfectly balanced between an original reality and a fiction subservient to it) is accurately denounced as typical of ancient civilizations: "If we take to dreaming once more – particularly today – of a world were signs are certain, of a strong 'symbolic order', let's be under no illusions. For this order has existed, and it was a brutal hierarchy, since the sign's transparency is indissociably also its cruelty. In feudal or archaic caste society, in *cruel* societies, signs are limited in number and their circulation is restricted. Each retains its full value as a prohibition, and each carries with it a reciprocal obligation between castes, clans or persons, so signs are not arbitrary. The arbitrariness of the sign begins when instead of bonding two persons in an inescapable reciprocity, the signifier starts to refer to an disenchanted universe of the signified, the common denominator of the real world, towards which no-one any longer has the least obligation" (p. 50).

[23] It seems that the criticism on Dante's *Divine Comedy* has failed to acknowledge that the title *Poema* appears for the first time in a context that focuses on the responsibility of poetry in regard to content, which, although true, appear to be lies (*Inf.* XVI 124-128: "Faced with that truth which seems a lie, a man / should always close his lips as long as he can -- / to tell it shams him, even though he is blameless; / but here I can't be still; and by the lines / of this my comedy, reader, I swear -- / and may my verse find favor for long years…", followed by the monster Geryone's description, "that filthy effigy of fraud"). The poetic language appears to be a degraded allegory, an otherness of meaning that appeals to the most perverse techniques of sensual seduction in order to capture the reader's intellectual consent to a truth that is completely hidden. *Comedy*, therefore, also means a discourse in which truth and lies are inextricably intertwined, because the reality is filtered through many, and sometimes despicable, fictional disguises. The oath on the "lines/ of this my comedy," – blasphemous because it substitutes a poetic text for the bible as a source (pseudo) religious legitimacy – reveals, in a very explicit manner, the *Comedy*'s intention to profane the truth principle symbolized by religious authority.

Bibliography

William Avery, *Elementos dantescos del Quijote*, "Anales cervantinos", T. 13-14, 1974-1975 , pags. 3-36.

Jean Baudrillard, *Lo scambio simbolico e la morte*, Feltrinelli, 1979.

Walter Benjamin, *L'opera d'arte nell'epoca della sua riproducibilità tecnica*, Einaudi, Torino 1971.

René Girard, *Menzogna romantica e verità romanzesca. Le mediazioni del desiderio nella letteratura e nella vita*, Bompiani, Milano 1965.

René Girard, *The mimetic desire of Paolo and Francesca*, in *To double business bound* (1978) , pp. 1-8.

Amilcare A. Iannucci, *Francesca da Rimini: the movie*, in "Dante", I – 2004, pp. 67-79.

Amilcare A. Iannucci, *Forbidden Love: Metaphor and History (Inferno V)*, in *Dante: Contemporary Perspectives* (a cura di A. A. Iannucci), University of Toronto Press, Toronto 1997, pp. 94-112.

Pier Paolo Pasolini, *Osservazioni sul piano sequenza* [1967] in *Empirismo eretico*, Garzanti, Milano 1977.

Raffaele Pinto, *La parola del cuore*, in AA. VV., *La poesia di Giacomo da Lentini. Scienza e filosofia nel XIII secolo in Sicilia e nel Mediterraneo*, Centro di Studi filologici e linguistici, Palermo, 2000, pp. 168-191.

Raffaele Pinto, *Gentucca e il paradigma poetico del 'dolce stil novo'*, in "Tenzone. Revista de la Asociación Complutense de Dantologia", 2002, nº 3, pp. 191-216.

Raffaele Pinto, *Fingo ergo sum. Elementi di teoria poetica della modernità. Lettura del canto XXVI del 'Purgatorio'*, in "Tenzone. Revista de la Asociación Complutense de Dantologia", 2005, nº 5, pp. 171-211.

Cesare Segre, voce *Finzione, Enciclopedia*, Einaudi, Torino, 1979, vol. 6, pp. 208-222.

Piotr Salwa (University of Warsaw)

Dante in Poland: a Disturbing Monument[1]

In order to understand what Dante has represented for the Poles over the past few decades, it is necessary to go back to the 1800's and Romanticism.[2] A real dialogue between the Polish culture and Alighieri began at that time and therefore it must not be forgotten when attempting to evaluate subsequent events. The dialogue with Dante often appears to be — even now — an internal debate within Polish culture, and its point of reference is not Alighieri himself, but the specific interpretation that has been given in Poland to his personality and his work. This particular condition is not exclusive to Dante — the destiny of Petrarch or Ariosto seems quite similar — but in this case it appears particularly significant.

Romanticism is a milestone in Polish reception of Dante. In the imagination of the Poles, the Poet has been forever marked by romantic connotations. Prior to that period, the reception of Dante had not been particularly brilliant. In Poland, for centuries, his works had been met with little interest and even less admiration. There is no denying that his name was known and quoted: the authors referred mainly to his political and Latin texts, yet nevertheless we find that his works "in volgare" were mentioned, as well.[3] This is not surprising, considering the large number of Polish youths that studied in Italian universities. Nor was it surprising that Mikolaj Rej, the most representative Polish poet, was named *Dantes noster* (although we cannot be sure if this label had a positive meaning).[4] The XVI and XVII centuries were periods of important cultural exchanges between Poland and Italy: not only did the Poles travel to Italy for educational or political reasons, but there was also significant traffic in the opposite direction — particularly by intellectuals that sought a position in aristocratic courts, by merchants competing for business in Eastern Europe, by diplomats and officials of the Italian queen of Poland — Bona Sforza. Italian was — after Latin — the most widely known foreign language.[5] In this context the "fortuna" of Dante seems rather marginal, when compared to that of Ariosto or Petrarch. This was most likely due to the hostility of the ecclesiastical hierarchy —devoted to the Papacy and opposed to the Empire — toward Dante's political ideas.

Romanticism changed this situation drastically — as it did in many other areas of Europe — although for motivations different from the aesthetic and literary ones. Those years were of great importance to all subsequent periods of Polish culture and intellectual life. The most discussed moral and ideological problems of the time – namely devotion to and sacrifice for the homeland, exile, destiny of the Poet-Prophet, faith, pure and spiritual love – were tribulations found also in Dante's works. The new interest in his Poem assumed various forms: a direct influence on the most appreciated Polish authors, various translations, literary studies, journalistic texts.[6] The effects of that time are still felt today. Dante was and continues to be perceived from a specific Polish perspective, which determined the choices and sometimes the manipulation of his texts and ideas. For a long time Dante existed for the Poles as the author of two works alone — *Vita Nuova* and *Commedia*. These were considered exclusively sublime poetry, in an idealistic sense, and an expression of his moral engagement and religiosity. Dante as a philosopher, literary critic, local politician and adversary of the Pope, seemed less captivating. Another poignant characteristic of those times was the fact that the interest in Dante's work grew outside academic institutions (which in XIX century Poland were ruled by foreigners and could not develop freely) taking on a more ideological and less scientific character.[7]

These are the conditions Polish followers of Dante had to deal with in the past and even recently, in the academic world, in the official art, or in the intellectual milieu. In my opinion the role of the academic and erudite research has been modest, at best. Although both significant figures and works have existed, the academic dantology has remained somewhat marginal, unequipped to create its own school or even guarantee a continuity of research and teaching.[8] A new found interest in Dante has recently emerged as a reflection of contemporary anglophone cultures' interest in Dante's legacy.[9] However, the reasons for Dante's reliable and enduring reputation in contemporary Polish culture must be sought elsewhere. On more than one occasion the *Commedia* has been the inspiration — although challenging — for successful stage representations (not only domestic, but also international) that became artistic events of primary importance.[10] The theatrical representations of Dante's work were able to rouse a strong emotional response because of their particular perspective on a new analysis of the human condition — which continued to be seen as eternal, universal, but at the same time rife with new connotations, especially after World War II and the Holocaust. During the Communist period the press and the so-called "social-cultural" reviews (aimed at the general, though educated public) played an important role. They often talked about themes concerning Dante, his life, his works and his popularity, providing their readers with notions going far beyond the curricula of school programs. Dante underwent a process of radical "modernization": he simply had to become "progressist", since according to the official propaganda such a characteristic was essential to true genius. Sometimes this manipulation was extremely biased, thereby producing quite artificial effects.[11] On the other hand, one cannot help but ask if this does not prove that the *Commedia* was far from being relegated to the function of an archival document.

If during the Sixties the interpretation of the Poem could still spark an animated discussion among Catholics and "progressists" (the former emphasizing the Poem's scholastic, Christian and moral tradition, the latter emphasizing the Poem's attention to pity, comprehension, toleration, and its humane perspectives in opposition to the rigid and severe official ideology), in more recent years the interest in Dante can be seen mainly in periodicals that can be categorized as liberal catholic, intellectual and universalistic. In particular some prestigious journals (such as "Tygo d nik Pow szechny," "Znak") pay constant attention to this field, while some renowned intellectuals, critics and translators return regularly to dantological issues (Tomasz Łubieński, Paweł Lisicki, Jarosław Mikołajewski). Remarkably, newer periodicals found a place for Dante in their initial publications — perhaps using him as a "trade-mark" of serious engagement. Recently, new evidence of the lasting — yet in some ways modified — interest in Alighieri has come to light. Dante continues to be the subject of academic criticism, and to be discretely brought to the attention of the educated public. One example is the recent exhibition of Józef Panek's engravings — one of the key players of contemporary Polish art (who died in 2001) — inspired by the *Commedia*.[12] Dante's spirit is a frequent source of inspiration for numerous Polish artists, as their regular participation in Ravenna exhibitions demonstrates.[13] The Polish public is informed about the most important events connected to Dante abroad (and it is curious to note the growing role of the Anglophone mediation for Dante's "fortuna" in Poland). From time to time cultural institutions host some *lecturae Dantis* and public television finds time for films like Peter Greenaway's famous vision of the *Commedia.*

An interesting proof of the lasting — though not always conspicuous — presence of Dante is found in the discussion organized by the renowned periodical "Literatura na świecie" on the translations of the *Commedia* an the issues connected to it.[14] The discussion was truly exceptional, not only because of the subject (the journal is interested mostly in contemporary literature), but also because of its animated and controversial character. Critics and translators discussed their points of view, stressing problems and difficulties, and presented very idiosyncratic proposals (such as translating Dante from the English prose versions), along with erudite comments, and finally a version of the original Italian text reduced to a "sound and rhythmical basis". The debate revealed on the one hand a strong desire for rebellion and innovation, which questioned the old *idées recues*, while on the other hand it shed light on other enduring characteristics regarding Dante's presence in Poland, namely that Dante's fame is associated almost exclusively with the *Commedia*, that the Poem is very much alive in the Polish tradition due to the "imported" modern translations in languages other than Polish,[15] that there is little tolerance for pragmatism in translation, which must be absolutely intelligible and flawless from intellectual and artistic standpoints. The discussion was accompanied by seven different versions of Canto II of Inferno, and by an essay by Jorge Luis Borges (instead of one by an academic authority).

Translations obviously represent an important chapter of Dante's life in XX century Poland. It should be noted that the Polish tradition in this field seems surprisingly poor, especially if we look for complete versions of his major works. One should keep in mind, however, that also in this respect the Poet's "fortuna" in Poland has been shaped by specific cultural factors, as well as by the profound social and political changes that took place throughout last century. In fact, everything that happened in the XX century had been determined by the previous period. In Poland, Dante has always been an author whose works were (and still are) read mostly, if not exclusively, by the cultured public. Also, his works were (and still are) included in some high school curricula as mandatory readings (despite the risk of causing boredom and rejection among young people, instead of the desired intellectual and emotional response). Consequently, our considerations should refer to these "uses of literacy" and to these particular readers. A survey of the editions containing Dante's texts in Polish leads to the same conclusion: they are generally aimed at a public with a good education and cultural aspirations, but which cannot be qualified as an intellectual *élite*. [16]

The first important wave of Polish translations of Dante's works appeared rather late, as an effect of the enhanced interest in the Poet awakened by Romanticism, in the second half of the XIX century. They were mostly selections from the *Vita Nuova* or the *Commedia*. However, this doesn't mean that Dante's legacy was previously unknown to Polish readers. One of the consequences of Poland's loss of political independence at the end of XVIII century was the implementation of foreign education systems and a diffused and sound knowledge of foreign languages. Although Italian was no longer widely spoken (as it was in XVI-century Poland and Lithuania), French still remained the language of elegance and salons, while a good knowledge of German and Russian was not only useful, but almost compulsory in everyday life. Undoubtedly, it was compulsory in numerous kinds of professional careers and many people — clerks, teachers, merchants — practically lived in a bilingual *milieu* (although it could be considered a forced one). Moreover, if the first contact with Dante was to take place at school, it was often in an Austrian, Prussian or Russian institution. Latin was a mandatory subject in schools of general education with the exception of the strictly professional ones. As a consequence, any motivated reader did not really need a Polish translations to get acquainted with or enjoy Dante's work, for he had ready access to German, French, or Latin editions. [17] The evidence given by Igor Bełza, a distinguished Soviet critic, born and raised in a well-known Warsaw family, seems to be typical: when remembering his first contact with Dante's *Commedia*, before World War I, he talks about promenades with his mother in the most beautiful park of Warsaw, reading the Poem in its original version while improvising translations *ad hoc*. [18]

However, this was not the case for a more general and less intellectual middle-class audience, who was not as familiar with international books and press, and tended to choose less demanding readings and easily accessible publications — but nevertheless interested in literature, culture and European tradition. This middle class must have been the real target of the first fragmentary (and less ambitious) Polish translations. The lack of pretensions in such initiatives can be seen in the number of "private" translations unintended for publication, and in those published by periodicals only in short excerpts. But if dissemination and availability were the primary goals, they do not seem to be the only ones. One must also consider the individual motivations, such as the challenges posed by the complexity of Dante's texts, which allowed for a display of the translator's skills and "bravura".[19] However, it is easy to detect in the translations a clear echo of that national romantic ideology that, as we have seen, looked to Dante for a perfect expression of its own values and problems: deep emotions, political passions, suffering, despair of exile, moral commitment, prophecy of liberation.[20] The motivations behind these difficult texts had to be particularly intimate (if not their true *raison d'être*), for they were meant for *connaisseurs*. Therefore in the complete versions of *Commedia* or *Vita Nuova* (as well as the *Rime*), the educational aspect did not play a significant role. Consequently, the function of these translations was to provide the reader with a version of a Dante's text that — although not unique nor original — could be the closest to him emotionally and become the most familiar, the most appreciated, and the most enjoyable. The question was that of presenting a text that was better than the others in producing emotional effects, in emphasizing images of a strong lyrical and emotional nature. But all this should be considered from a wider perspective: according to the mentality of the time such an endeavor was a kind of patriotic activity, aimed at giving more dignity to the Polish national literature by enriching it with works by one of the greatest European authors. The patriotic commitment, which was impossible in other fields, was supposed to be reflected in literature, thus contributing to the emancipation of the nation.

For this reason translators selected those passages from Dante's work that best suited such aims. It is not surprising, then, that the *De Monarchia*, the *Convivio* and the *De vulgari eloquentia* were rarely quoted, while the *Commedia* boasted, in a relatively short period, three complete Polish translations and — which seems even more significant — the publication of a great number of short fragments in numerous popular periodicals. They were seldom extracted from *Paradiso* or *Purgatorio*. The absolute record belonged to *Canti* III e V of *Inferno*. It is not surprising either, that the *Vita Nuova* followed closely the destiny of the *Commedia*, appearing first in translations of short isolated pieces and then in three integral versions. In all these selections it is easy to notice the preference for themes such as love, virtue or exile, and for forms such as the sonnet, frequently practiced by

Polish romantic poetry. The same logic was behind the Polish versions of the *Rime*, published as an independent volume after World War I. [21]

This *corpus* has little changed over the XX century, even if its social and cultural context underwent deep and significant changes. In the newly independent Poland the Polish language — and consequently translations into Polish — received the seal of approval from the official, state culture. A new readership was born, educated in Polish schools and somewhat less familiar with foreign languages. In the communist era, all literary texts were inserted in the framework of the regime's cultural policy. But new translations remained rather marginal until recently, when new trends emerged. On the one hand, Polish readers could finally read in their own tongue all the Latin treatises of Dante, published in annotated academic editions.[22] On the other hand, they could observe several attempts to give a new and modern life to Dante's poetry through the reinterpretations attemped during cultural manifestations destined for a wider audience. However, the most significant initiative has been the publication of a new translation of the *Commedia* in a modern style, in a seemingly quotidian language.[23] The new text must have come as a surprise to the Polish audience — attached to old habits — for it emphasizes colourful, ordinary and material details, it uses everyday colloquial expressions, it stresses humour, irritation and anger, and thus it reduces pathos and eases tensions. The translator's ambition — as she explains in her exhaustive introductions to all three parts of the Poem — was that of reviving the *Commedia* and making it attractive for common readers, as it was at the time when it first circulated. But it is easy to note a conscious and complacent sense of rebellion, as well: her attitude towards respectful, precise and pedantic traditions is more than ironic. Her imitation of the Poet – by forging neologisms, resorting to regional terms, and indulging in anachronisms, etc. – is not only liberating, but also provocative.

Polish culture tried to domesticate Dante in a pretty specific way — emphasizing idiosyncratic and subjective attitudes towards his work — and for this reason the actual presence of Dante in contemporary Polish intellectual and artistic life can be, in my opinion, exemplified in a significant way by three famous writers: Witold Gombrowicz, Stanisław Vincenz and Czesław Miłosz. Their writings are not very recent, but they can be considered symbolic — this authors chose to emigrate after World War II for political reasons, just as the first Polish admirers of Dante had done a century earlier.

The first of them — Gombrowicz — dedicated several pages of his *Diaries* to Dante, which were later collected in a small bilingual Polish-French edition, then translated into Italian, as well.[24] The publication had little resonance, but provoked some indignant criticism. Gombrowicz is an unconventional author, explicitly provocative, irreverent, defiant, critical of the most sacred opinions. In his derisive, scornful texts he purposefully attacks those artists who are placed on a pedestal and are perceived as official historical monuments, venerated and beloved even by people completely incapable of understanding them, but ready to subscribe to the convention without a second thought, because of their conformism or mental laziness. The greatness of Dante must have posed a challenge to him; however, it would be rather surprising if Gombrowicz had the same opinion as all the other critics. His attacks on Dante demonstrate a sound knowledge of the *Commedia* (even if the writer consciously rescinds the wisdom of "danto-logues") and, above all, a strong emotive participation, which proves that his rebellion is a reaction to the expressive force of the Poem.[25] Alighieri emerges from these attacks as a powerful and influential artist. Gombrowicz's attitude does not stem from misunderstanding, but rather from the clash of two different personalities and sensibilities. Wouldn't this clash be in fact understood by Dante himself?

In his effort to engage Dante — both, the man and the artist — in his text, but with his own sensibility, Gombrowicz finds the *Commedia* not only primitive, boring, repetitive, limited, simple, of dubious quality and affected by peasant imagery, but also monstrous, evil, cowardly, cruel and full of empty words. His attacks seem typical of his usual style: they seem sensational, but in fact he utilizes hyperboles, grotesque imagery and non-sense:

> When I put down my essay on Dante, I included some remarks that shocked many people. Why have I written certain things? Simply because they are part of my reality. I am at my place and I have the right to say it. If Dante bores me, if I consider myself superior to him, I say it without fear: it is my right to do it.[26]

One has the impression that Gombrowicz tries to attack Dante in order to find desperately a way to defend his own liberty as an artist and intellectual in front of an exceptional authority. He also wants to shock his readers in order to awaken their sensibility:

O Divine Comedy, what are you? A clumsy work of the little man Dante? An immense work of the great Dante? A monstrous work of a perfidious Dante? A rhetoric recitation of Dante, the liar? An artificial firework? A true fire?[27]

One can find indications of perplexity in facing Alighieri's work also in the writings of Stanisław Vincenz, otherwise a great admirer of the Poet.[28] What Vincenz seeks and finds in Dante is the mythical unity of human civilization, capable of destroying spatial and chronological boundaries, forcing us to participate in the same spiritual world. The writer – born and raised in a frontier region where different nations, peoples and cultures (such as those of Slavonic, Hebrew, Hungarian, Romanian and Valach origins) intermingled for centuries, and were educated in accordance with Western European classical standards — finds in Dante echoes and references to eternal folk myths, and detects traces of cultures that are seemingly distant, but in fact close to one another in their universal aspects. In order to read Dante it is necessary to make a real effort, but in exchange the reader receives access to a poetic world that contemporary art is no longer able to create: this is a universal type of poetry, in which the individual is able to perceive the spiritual cosmos. It is inhabited by voices and spirits of different times, different myths, different religious forms, where the figure of Dante appears similar to that of Noah, as the creator of a new world.

For Vincenz, the past and the future are joined in Dante's world in a unique reality that enables us to better realize our own insignificance. One of the most important aspects of Dante's art consists of making us feel closely linked to archetypes, our ancestors and our childhood. Following the Romantic poets (and examining the profound analogies between their inspiration and that of Alighieri, rather than superficial influences), he believes in the absolute value of poetry, and he affirms the greatness of Dante just as strongly as Gombrowicz tries to deny it. Nevertheless he seems to struggle with boredom and fatigue, as the Poet descends from the peaks of human intellect and makes his discourse more concrete. He accepts Dante as a source of hope, but his veneration fades as Alighieri becomes more vindictive and severe, promoting an idea of justice which does not correspond to the progressive humanism of the XX century. At this point Dante ceases to be effective and loses his ability to bring moral satisfaction.

The third of these authors, Czesław Miłosz, seems less expansive. He adopts a different point of view. The problem he is interested in is neither Dante himself, nor the *Commedia*, but rather the vision of Hell — *Inferno*.[29] In his opinion — and he speaks only about his personal experiences as a reader of Dante — the representation the Poet provides does not convince the modern reader, and the text as a whole remains obscure when it is deprived of the tiresome references to the commentaries and the notes. One should wonder why Hell doesn't seem interesting nowadays. Among the different levels of meaning, the most attractive one today is the allegorical, while everything concerning political treatise, the author's personal history and that of his family, along with possible esoteric meanings, remain unimpressive. What's more, the account of the wanderings through the afterlife forces the reader to feel a hostile bewilderment, due to this world's strange topography, its confusing classical mythology and Christian elements, its parallel treatment of historical truth and literary fiction, and its incomprehensible moral judgments.

For Milosz, understanding *Inferno* requires a tremendous effort. We become aware of the fact that we are not at all prepared to comprehend an art based on allegory and to interpret a text that is situated somewhere between poetry and theological treatise. In fact, it is the expressive power of the Poem that provokes dissatisfaction — above all in the readers who seriously consider the questions of salvation and damnation. How was it possible that Divine Love could create a place for such cruel tortures? The answer — says Milosz — is to be found in the doctrine of St. Thomas Aquinas. Nevertheless we blame Dante for having praised a God that could have created a better world, but refused to do so. We don't believe in either absolute individual liberty, nor in the absolute individual responsibility of man conditioned by genetics, his times, and his social *milieu* ... But this is not all. If on the one hand it is difficult to feel a true pity for the damned souls — we are not sufficiently familiar with the crimes they committed — on the other hand Milosz fears that *Inferno* can appeal to some secret inclination of our souls that takes pleasure in seeing other people suffering — for some theologians Hell's punishments was the exclusion from celestial joys.

Milosz, Vincenz and Gombrowicz represent an extremely idiosyncratic way of considering Dante and his work. This seems to constitute strong evidence of the fact that Alighieri in contemporary Polish literature is not reduced to a conventional, historical and academic being. If on the didactic level some old stereotypes still prevail, they do not remain fruitless. Dante continues to be a universal symbol of greatness, solitude, civil and moral engagement, for he deals with those fundamental problems that continue to haunt us despite the passing of time.

Notes

[1] In this study I resume the issues discussed in my article *Dante in Polonia: una presenza viva?*, "Dante Studies", CXIX, 2001, pp. 187-202.

[2] On this subject see the essential bibliography of W. Presiner, *Dante i jego dzieła w Polsce. Bibliografia krytyczna z historycznym wstępem*, Toruń: Towarzystwo Naukowe w Toruniu, 1957; and the recent study of A. Litwornia, *"Dantego któż odważy się tłumaczyć?". Studia o recepcji Dantego w Polsce*, Warszawa: IBL (Studia Staropolskie, Series Nova), 2005.

[3] On the cultural exchanges between Poland and Italy in the Middle Ages and the Renaissance see T. Ulewicz, *Iter romano-italicum Polonorum*, Kraków: Universitas, 1999.

[4] See J. Ślaski, *Noster hic est Dante (Dalla fortuna di Dante nella Polonia cinquecentesca)*, in F. Cale (ed.), *Dante e il mondo slavo*, Zagreb: Jugoslavenska Akademija Znanosti i Umjetnosti, 1984, vol. II, pp. 613-18.

[5] See the recently published work by W. Tygielski, *Włosi w Polsce w XVI-XVII wieku*, Warszawa: Biblioteka "Więzi", 2005.

[6] Dante's influence on Polish Romantic poets and their attitude toward the Florentine genius is widely discussed in various studies; see for instance the classical studies by Z. Szmydtowa, *Dante a romantyzm polski* and *Norwid wobec włoskiego odrodzenia*, now in Id., *W kręgu renesansu i romantyzmu*, Poznań: PWN, 1979; and I. Bełza, *Romantyzm polski a Dante*, now in Id., *Portrety romantykow*, Warszawa: Pax, 1974.

[7] See in particular the contributions by J. Klaczko, *Les causeries florentines*, Paris: Plon, 1880, and J. I. Kraszewski, *Dante. Vorlesungen über die „Göttliche Komödie" gehalten in Krakau und Lemberg 1867*, Dresed 1870.

[8] However, at least two names of Polish critics of Dante deserve to be mentioned: K. Michalski, author of *La gnoséologie de Dante* (Kraków: PAU, 1950), and K. Morawski, author of numerous articles and a monographic study *Dante* (Warszawa: Pax, 1965).

[9] See T. Pióro, *Dante nasz współczesny*, "Literatura na świecie", 1995, nr 4, pp. 327-28; J. Olejniczak (ed.), *Po Dantem. Wybór materiałów z VIII konferencji pracowników naukowych i studentów Instytutu Nauk o Literaturze Polskiej Uniwersytetu Śląskiego*, Katowice: Górnośląskie Centrum Kultury, 1996.

[10] See J. Szajna, *Dante żywy*, in F. Cale (ed.), *Dante e il mondo slavo*, cit., vol. II, pp. 639-642; S. Widłak, *La "Divina Commedia" nel Teatro Rapsodico di Cracovia*, ibid., pp. 721-26.

[11] See my article *Dante e la critica polacca degli ultimi anni*, in F. Cale (ed.), *Dante e il mondo slavo*, cit, vol. II, pp. 589-96.

[12] See J. Fejkiel (ed.), *Jerzy Panek's Dante*, Kraków: Jan Fejkiel Gallery, 2002.

[13] See Dante in Polonia. *Ottantaquattro scultori polacchi contemporanei interpretano Dante Alighieri* (exhibition catalogue), Ravenna: Centro Dantesco dei Frati Minori Conventuali, 1997.

[14] See "Literatura na świecie", 1985, nr 4, pp. 2-46.

[15] On this subject new evidence comes from a Polish translation based on a German version by K. Vossler, see Dante Alighieri, *Boska Komedia*, Polish translation by B. Antochewicz, Wrocław: Gajt, 1993.

[16] Short translations are published by a wide range of popular periodicals of different nature: "Tygodnik peterburski", "Gazeta Warszawska", "Czas", "Kronika rodzinna", "Poziarnie", "Rodzina", "Tygodnik Ilustrowany", "Przeglad polski", "Chimera" and others.

[17] Proof of this specific condition is to be found in some Polish libraries where a large number of foreign, mainly German, editions of Dante's works is still preserved.

[18] I. Belza, *Dante i Slowianie*, "Kierunki", nr 14/1976, p.8.

[19] See for instance the French translation, now in Krystyn Ostrowski, *Oeuvres choisis*, Paris 1875.

[20] See n. 5.

[21] The most popular sonnets from the *Vita Nuova* were: *Tanto gentile e tanto onesta pare, Vede perfettamente ogni salute, Spesse fiate vengonmi al cuore*; and from the *Rime*: *Di donne vidi una gentile schiera, Guido, i' vorrei che tu e Lapo ed io, Lo Re che merta i suoi servi a ristori, O che parlando andate.*

[22] Dante, *O języku pospolitym*, przeł. i oprac. W. Olszaniec, Kęty: Antyk, 2002; Dante, *Monarchia*, przeł. i oprac. W. Seńko, Kęty: Antyk, 2002; Dante, *Biesiada*, przeł. i oprac. M. Bartkowiak-Lerch, Kęty: Antyk, 2004.

[23] Dante Alighieri, *Piekło. "Boskiej Komedii" część pierwsza*, przeł. A. Kuciak, Poznań: Klub Książki Katolickiej & Biblioteka Telgte, 2002; Id., *Czyściec, "Boskiej Komedii", część druga* — 2003, *Raj. "Boskiej komedii" część trzecia* — 2004.

[24] W. Gombrowicz, *Sur Dante*, trad. A. Kosko, L'Herne, Paris, 1968; Italian version *Su Dante*, trad. R. Landau, Milano: Sugar, 1969.

[25] According to M. Głowiński, *Gombrowicz poprawia Dantego*, "Te ksty Drugie", 5 (2000), pp. 58-67, the aggressive attitude toward the *Commedia* (more precisely toward the *Inferno*) — absurd and without foundation — is only a facade that serves to the writer as a device to express in an oblique way his reflections on pain and suffering.

[26] W. Gombrowicz, *Su Dante*, trad. R. Landau, cit., p. 60: "Quando ho scritto il mio saggio su Dante ho incluso delle osservazioni che hanno urtato molte persone. Ora perché ho scritte certe cose? Semplicemente perché appartengono alla mia realtà. Sono a casa mia e ho il diritto di dirlo. Se Dante mi annoia, se mi considero superiore a lui, lo affermo senza paura: è un mio diritto."

[27] W. Gombrowicz, *Su Dante*, trad. R. Landau, cit., p. 40: "O *Divina Commedia* co sa sei dunque? Opera maldestra del piccolo Dante? Immensa opera del grande Dante? Opera mostruosa del perfido Dante? Recitazione retorica del bugiardo Dante? ... Fuoco d'artifico? Fuoco vero?"

[28] Stanisław Vincenz, *Czym może być dziś dla nas Dante, Dantyzm w Pol sce, Ar cy dzie ło a mit ludowy*, in Id., *Eseje i szkice zebrane*, tom I, Wrocław: Wirydarz, 1997, pp. 197-328. See also Id., *Węże u Dantego*, in Id., *Z per spektywy po dró ży*, Kraków: Znak, 1980, pp. 234-39.

[29] See Czesław Miłosz, *O piekle*, in Id., *Ogród nauk*, Paryż: Instytut Lite racki, 1979, pp. 83-101.

Grzegorz Bednarski: *Inferno* IX, 118-123 (pastel, 25 × 35.5 cm)

Grzegorz Bednarski: *Inferno* XXIV, 100-105 (pastel, 31.8 × 48 cm)

Grzegorz Bednarski: *Inferno* XVIII, 127-133 (pastel, 50 × 35 cm)

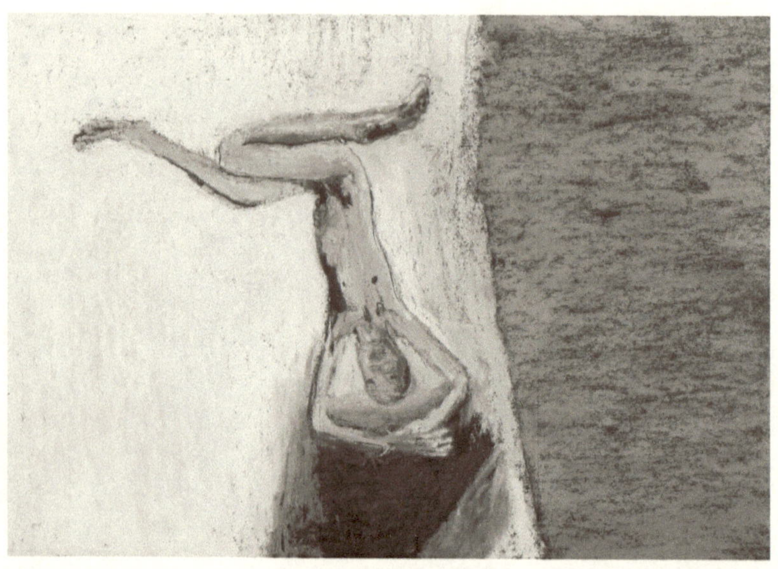

Grzegorz Bednarski: *Studies for Dante: Falling (Studia D)* (pastel, 37.5 × 50 cm)

Grzegorz Bednarski: *Studies for Dante: A Figure* (pastel, 37 × 48 cm)

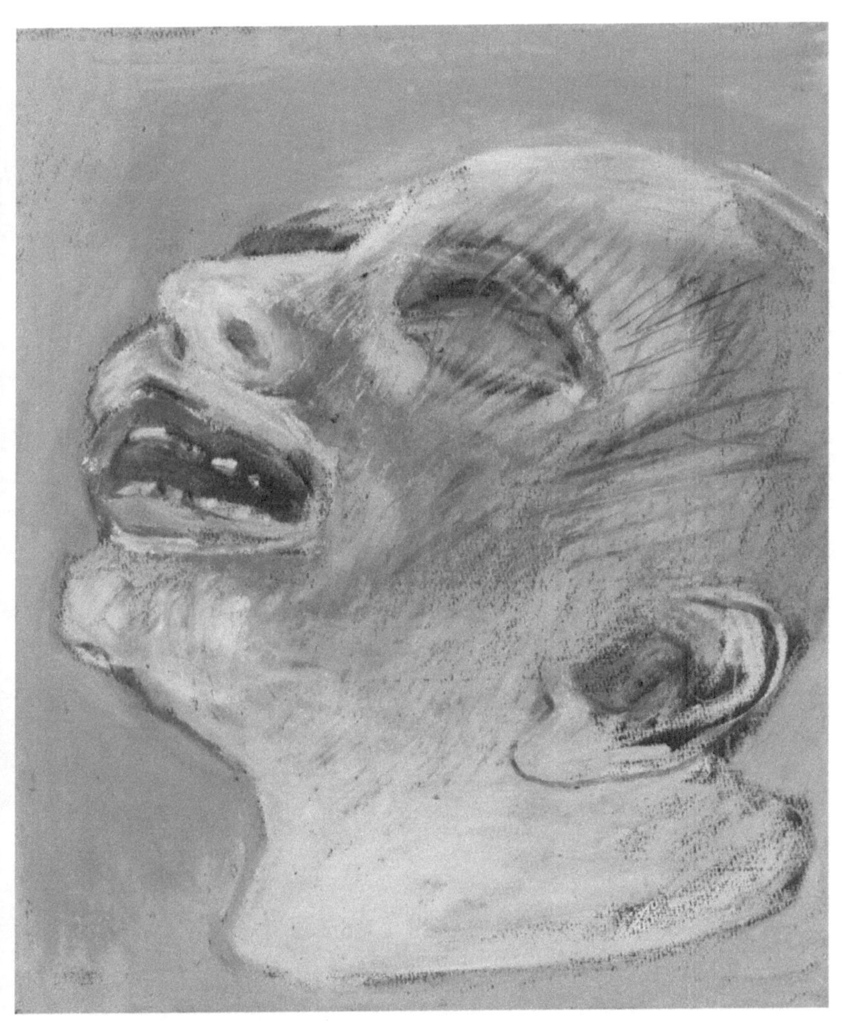

Grzegorz Bednarski: *Studies for Dante: A Head* (pastel on black paper, 27.5 × 24.5 cm)

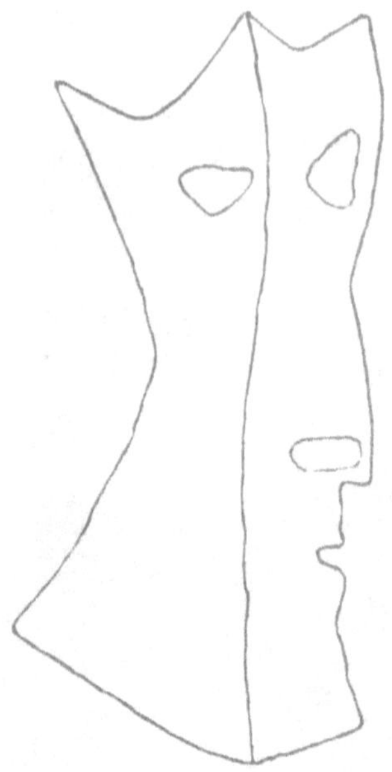

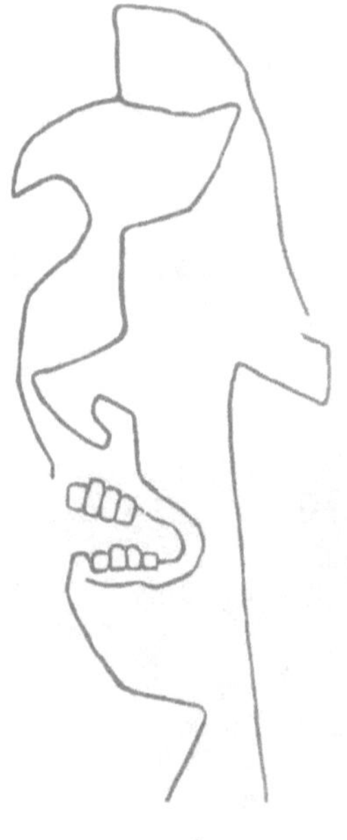

Jerzy Panek, *Dante (Profile III)*, 1965/91 (woodcut, 32 × 16 cm)

Jerzy Panek, *Old Harlot*, 1965/91 (woodcut, 36 × 45 cm)

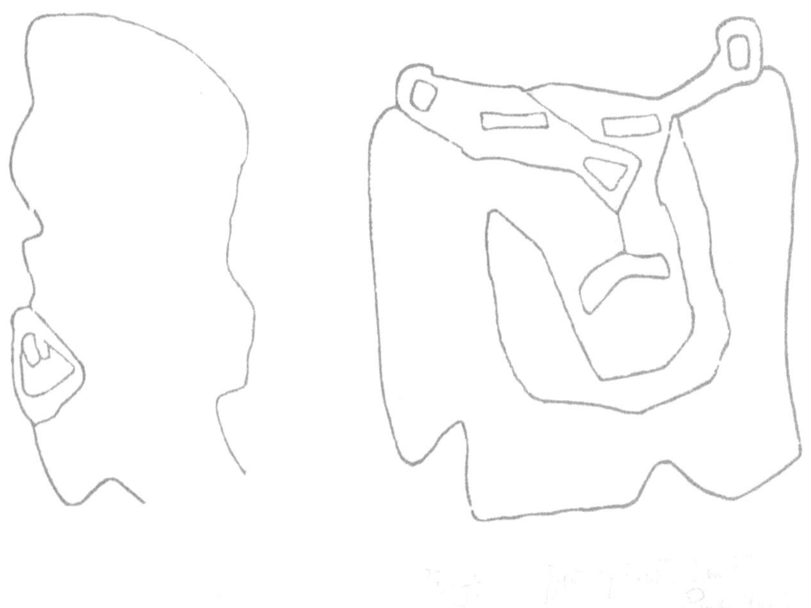

Jerzy Panek, *Harlot*, 1966/91 (woodcut, 33.5 × 17 cm)

Jerzy Panek, *Lion II*, 1966/92 (woodcut, 36 × 32 cm)

Natascia Tonelli (Università di Siena)

La morte di Madonna: Dantean Motifs in 20th-Century Italian Metrical Poetry

"Di necessitade convene che la gentilissima Beatrice alcuna volta si muoia": in chapter twenty-three of the *Vita Nuova*, the path that leads toward Beatrice's death is about to end. A series of deaths anticipate her own (Beatrice's friend, then Beatrice's father), and the dream/vision the Poet has at the beginning of the book is about to reveal its inherent meaning. At this very moment, Dante experiences a pathological episode of frenetic melancholy, which affords him the capacity to presage the imminent and inevitable catastrophe. Even Beatrice will die – as everyone who shares the miserable condition of being human – but Dante places great emphasis on this event, stressing unequivocally the necessity of her death. "Certainly it must some time come to pass that the very gentle Beatrice will die," as Rossetti beautifully translates.

The novelty of love exalted in the book – the *poetica della lode* and its implications – lies in Dante's identification of an inexhaustible subject matter. The words that praise his woman are not only a means to achieve earthly happiness, but also earthly happiness itself. He is no longer concerned with the attainment of a result. He is not interested in communicating his love and pain (to an audience, or better yet, to the loved one), nor does he seek a reward for his love. The poetic word of love stands on its own, regardless of the presence or existence of its object. The attainment of a truly disinterested praise can be reached only when the object of love is absent. Beatrice's death affects both Dante's love for her and the poetry he will dedicate to her. Dante demonstrates that his renewal is concrete, that love transcends death – or rather that love is actually indifferent to death – and that his particular outlook on love serves as perpetual inspiration for poetry. Beatrice's death enables Dante to experience the authenticity of his motives and statements. These premises, first found in the very texts of the *Vita Nuova*, are later developed in his major work, throughout the following decades.

Her death is in part caused by these poetic necessities, for the disappearance of the object of love gives rise to the possibility of inventing the book of memory and the poems that accompany it: the function "*morte della protagonista*" constitutes the main structural element for the invention of the first real *canzoniere*. This is another of Dante's inventions.

Another reason for her death – less frequently noted, but relevant nonetheless – is the perpetuation of desire caused by the definitive absence of its object: the death of the beloved, the object of desire, marks the impossibility of fulfillment; and the inexhaustibility of desire implies an never-ending search, in which writing seeks to fill the void left by the object.

These are the basic premises that, albeit somewhat schematic, will help us understand the immediate and lasting success of Dante's invention; an invention that has contributed much to poetry (at the cost of a long list of young women unjustly stripped of their lives), and that extends uninterrupted from Fiammetta and Laura to the present time.

Laura shares the same destiny as Beatrice, representing the only inspirational muse for her poet. In reconstructing the history of the literary motif "*morte di madonna*," it is difficult but not impossible to distinguish instances that follow Dante's model from those that follow Petrarch's. However, it is worth noting that this motif, together with a series of accessory elements – which we will discuss later – continues to evoke, even in contemporary Italian poetry, Beatrice's archetype. In fact, this motif is often accompanied by the metrical forms typical of traditional poetry: the sonnet's structure and rhymed verses.

The motif I call "*la morte di madonna*" is, in my opinion, a diegetic-lyric function – if such an oxymoron is acceptable – always present in the history of literature. Naturally, it works not only in a literal sense – as an explicit reference to the death of the lover – but also, and more importantly, as a source of reflection on the complex relationship between poetic practice, muse and death. Today, this motif is typically found in traditional poetic forms[1] and rhymed verses that often display clear inter-textual Dantean or Petrarchean references. One example, which may seem *a latere* in respect to our topic, comes from a little known text by Tommaso Landolfi, which represents an extreme remaking of the *Vita Nuova*, and testifies to the success of the Dantean *libello*, in particular from a formal point of view. In fact, *Breve Canzoniere* (1971) is, like the *Vita Nuova*, a real and perhaps anachronistic *prosimetro*. But it is also more than that. The poetry it contains – "14 sonnets in an old style," as the author says, "with a *contentino*, bringing the collection to 15"[2] – is analyzed and, we might say, "divided" (to use a scholastic technical expression employed by Dante in regard to his own poetic texts) according to the prose that accompanies, coordinates, and connects it from a narrative point of view. No woman dies in *Breve canzoniere*, but the structural problem of the woman as a source of poetic inspiration is addressed head on. In a paradoxical reversal of perspective, it is the woman who discusses, divides and explains the sonnets, disrupting the traditional stance of faithful poet-lover. In the *Vita Nuova*, Beatrice is not allowed to speak, and will do so only at the top of mount Purgatory. In the *Vita Nuova*, her only form of expression is the *saluto*, which she immediately withdraws. Her silence, like her later absence, is the premise of Dante's successful poetic operation. Landolfi's rewriting, on the other hand, is a dialogue with the loved woman, whose merciless speech reveals the artificiality – to the point of destroying the poetic value – of the "*canzoniere*" dedicated to her. Since she is the one reading and commenting the poems, the poet places himself in a position of weakness from which he cannot escape. In fact, he should draw inspiration from her, along with literary judgment and the disclosure of the dynamic of desire. From the very beginning the poet as subject in search of a voice, declares that his creative impotence derives from her presence. Such impotence is intrinsic to the satisfaction of desire, and is connected to her availability and the love she offers (in fact, "impotence" is the term he uses, and which she jokes about: "Excuse me, but I wouldn't call it impotence"). Here is an excerpt of the dialogue:

> [him]
> – […] do you see this notebook?
> [her]
> – It is the notebook of your creation.
> – No, the notebook of beginnings
> – What does that mean?
> – How long have we been together?
> – For nearly one year
> – Well, for nearly a year this notebook records nothing but beginnings: heads, little chicken heads, without tails.[3]

In this novel that speaks, in a postmodern way, about the impossibility of writing love poetry, the ineptitude of the "poetic I" prevents the necessary homicide of the woman, who at once generates desire and provides satisfaction. In his conscious dialectical and conflictual treatment of the tradition here recalled (there is another trace of the *Vita Nuova* in the idea of an open notebook, containing only beginnings, or as Dante might have called them "rubriche") Landolfi explicitly declares, at the outset of the book, that the woman must be killed in order to realize his poetic ambitions. But he tells her, asking for her advice, and thereby thwarting any literary success:

> *I decided to kill her; I have to kill her and I cannot do otherwise; I cannot conceive of anything else. She drains all my vital energy and prevents my existence...*[4]

Despite his plan, the incapacity – or, better, the impossibility – to sacrifice the woman and to turn her into his muse in perpetuity, condemns her to life, and forces the poet to achieve satisfaction, and thus "non-existence." In other words, poetic impotence. The themes addressed in Dante's distant *libello* continue to constitute an issue Landolfi experiences in the same terms and, strikingly, in the same forms. I will provide here other examples of how this issue is addressed, and I will try to illustrate what the *Vita Nuova* – along with the enrichment made by Petrarca with *Rerum vulgarium fragmenta* – has to offer this genre.

The first element pertains to the main event: the death of Beatrice is preceded by a premonitory dream/vision in chapter 23 of the *Vita Nuova*[5]. This is a motif that, thanks to its specific reiteration and amplification in Petrarca's *canzoniere*, becomes canonical in the genre of "love songbooks in death."

In the 1980s, Italy witnessed a steady revival of traditional meters, producing texts of unquestionable value, aside from any ideological considerations. Among these works, Giovanni Giudici's 1986 collection (Torino, Einaudi) entitled *Salutz* holds a place of prominence, and is a de facto *canzoniere*. We must mention here the "formal" nature of this book, for we will later compare it to similar cases. In fact, this text represents contemporary poetry's closest, most conscious and rigorous reflection on the relationship with the great tradition of love lyric, given its themes, language, and forms. It is poetry about poetry. The first difficulty Giudici must overcome is the legitimacy of returning to these themes[6]: the solution he provides is disguise. The *canzoniere* is about love, but the real name of the woman does not appear; she is called Midons. The name Minne means, purely and simply, Madonna, Love with a capital L, the personification of Love. A woman who, at once, is and is not, both true and invented, a project and object of poetic practice, whose existence is the goal of the "canto" and whose absence is its very condition:

> But are thou – thou that are not even
> Thou who at the same time are true
> and not true
>
> …
> If you did not exist there would be no poetry.[7]

The role of the poet as the subject of poetry and as the solipsistic protagonist is reaffirmed and artificially recreated in a masked language, so the condition of unappeasable desire may instigate poetry ("E siete squadernata, siete aperta / Voi che m'imprigionate prirgioniera / Voi che su me restate / Bocca, fonte e riviera / Alla mia sete invanamente offerta – / Così perdura più che non s'estingua"). Nowhere does it state that the love is not real, nor that the love is not incarnated by an actual human being. We can eventually infer its real existence just as we can about characters whose reality is entirely dependant on their literary re-elaboration. The condition is the same as in the poetry about Beatrice or Laura. But there is the additional revelation of the artifice, which is quite clear to the author and is manifested to the reader by the distance produced through the evocation – by employing the fictional name Midons – of the function of the woman's absence. One can address Midons only using the antiquated form of address – the "Voi," here translated as "thou" – thus forming a sort of agreement with the reader concerning the reconstruction of another world in which such a discourse is legitimate. A world that is recreated through these linguistic elements, which are small but strong signals, capable of magically evoking the amorous *salutz* and the genre it implies. Returning to the formal aspects, it will suffice to quote the author's note: 7 parts "all comprised of 10 poems, each 14 verses long [...] Coincidentally, the poem *"Lais"* [...], with its 20 verses," brings the total number of verses in the book to a thousand. It is, thus, a book of fixed structure comprised of precisely 1000 verses. According to the Italian canonical tradition, they alternate between hendecasyllables and heptasyllables, and are organized in groups of fourteen, like sonnets. They share the morphological immanence of the sonnet. Their various rhythmic features are undoubtedly allusions to the sonnet. It is thus a *canzoniere* of sonnets "written in a graceful unknown language" ("Scritto in leggiadra non saputa lingua") in which the reflection on the relationship between death, poetry and desire plays a prominent role. Here we find a description of the poet's own death caused by love, along with the posthumous remorse and suffering of the loved woman, a motif that is more specifically related to Propertius, Cavalcanti and Petrarca, but is realized in terms drawn from Dante's *Rime Petrose*, where not even the *rêverie* of the posthumous tears of the repentant woman is allowed. Thus the woman becomes an anti-Beatrice, made of stone.

But above all, Giudici reveals that, in order to reach the goal of inspiration, the death of the woman-muse is inextricably connected to poetic production.

> Laser of my words –
> Incinerate thee thus
> For fire, for love.[8]

She is both the "mother" and "daughter" of these words. On the one hand she is their direct source of inspiration, and on the other, their creation. These words, in order to function, require the object of love to die. "Thus thou shall be the rostrum / that punctures my brain / Thou shall be my gold drool and line and net [...] For thou are mother to me / as thou were daughter" ("Però voi siate il rostro / Che mi fora il cervello / Siatemi bava d'oro e filo e rete [...] Onde madre a mesiete / Per ciò che foste figlia"). The woman's role is crucial to the poet's survival, for his life coincides with his poetic word: "Since my word is my body / Word by transubstantial virtue / Secluded in thine breast / I parchment and ink" ("Essendo la mia lettera il mio corpo / Parola per virtù transustanziale: / In seno a voi riposto / Io pergamena e inchiostro"). The traditional motif of the dream of death, which precedes the actual event, is also present, and is linked to the necessity of the woman's death, as stated in the piece (IV, 3), which concludes:

> I live on thee, dreamt in dreams dead
> As he who faithfully believes
> In the most false of faiths.[9]

Let's move from the dream to the actual death of the woman. Giorgio Caproni followed this theme in much of his work and dedicated at least two collections to it. These works date to the 1940s and 1950s, a time when the choice of the *forma chiusa* (metrical poetry) – and the sonnet in particular – had a greater significance than it did forty years later, among the neometric poets. A significance that Caproni would campaign in a famous section of *Passaggio d'Enea*. The "meek // fiancée so completely / dead" ("mite / fidanzata così completamente / morta") of the opening verse of *Sonetti dell'anniversario* is the main object of that collection. Caproni celebrates the anniversary of her death, as Dante does with Beatrice's ("quasi per annovale…") in chapter 34 of the *Vita Nuova*. She also serves as the central theme of an unfinished novel, and will continue to nourish Caproni's poetry, in a conscious and explicit way, until the sonnet *In memoria*, written in 1951. It is not by chance that the poet asks the woman's forgiveness for having resorted to her death, in order to receive the gift or "fruit" of poetry:

> Perdonami se torno alla tua morte,
> a ricordarti sui tenui stradali
> dove ti vidi irrompere, o sul ponte
> la cui neve ti spense….
>   […] e quali spari,
> quali spari il mio cuore ha se tu tocchi
> col tuo fuoco più fatuo ancora i rari
> istanti delle lacrime? Nel lutto
> tu mi perdonerai se in me perdura
> il falò del tuo alito – se a frutto
> torna un istante di tenebra, e dura
> nelle mie dita…

(Forgive me if I go back to your death,… In mourning you will forgive me if the bonfire of your breath endures in me – if a moment of darkness becomes fruitful and lasts in my fingers)

Even more significant is the collection *Versi livornesi*, which follows the death of his mother, Anna. In representing the mother as a youthful and certainly unconventional figure, he expresses a loving desire that is sanctioned by death, which transformed her in an argument-instrument of poetry.

The most explicit indication is found in the last piece of the series: a version of the Calvalcantian *ballatetta* (and thus an explicit revival and reworking of the *stilnovo*), in which the radical alternative to Dante's "culpability" in killing Beatrice is found in the poet's own death. While rewriting Cavalcanti, Caproni does not send his soul – by means of the *canzone* – to the woman in order to tell her of his own death. Rather – in a version of the text reminiscent of Dante – he seeks the dead woman for one last posthumous encounter. He, her child and boyfriend, sends his soul to look for her among the girls of Livorno – she is the finest and earliest to rise – in order to tell her something that is unspeakable. Here I will cite from the beginning, middle and end of the beautiful *Congedo*:

> Anima mia, fa' in fretta.
> Ti presto la bicicletta,
> ma corri. E con la gente
> (ti prego, sii prudente)
> non ti fermare a parlare
> smettendo di pedalare
>
> …
>
> Mia anima, non aspettare,
> no, il loro apparire.
> Faresti così fallire
> con dolore il mio piano,
> e io un'altra volta Annina,
> di tutte la più mattutina,
> vedrei anche a te sfuggita,
> ahimè, come già alla vita.
>
> …
>
> Dille chi ti ha mandato:
> suo figlio, il suo fidanzato.
> D'altro non ti richiedo.
> Poi, va' pure in congedo.

Caproni's Annina embodies both mother and the dead girlfriend, the dual inspirational function of the feminine muse. She is sought in the early morning, when dreams and apparitions are thought to be the most authentic.

The final point I would like to make pertains to the postmortem apparition of the woman, which is realized in many different ways, and holds many interpretative possibilities. Caproni, for example, has imagined an encounter with Annina at the café in the station where she takes her final leave at dawn, and mourns the loss of her own life (*Ad portam inferi*). The multiple possibilities offered by this *topos* lie between the two models of Beatrice and Laura. Beatrice plays an active role in the realization of Dante's destiny, and takes responsibility for it. In the *Divina Commedia*, she is instrumental to Dante's salvation and becomes its powerful instrument. She is a motherly figure, an example of severity and rigor, and she condemns the living lover's desire. A desire in the strictly erotic sense, and as a source of poetry: one need only think of Beatrice's embittered words in Purgatorio that inveigh against the *pargoletta* subject of Dante's rhymes, which are characterized by a more sensual love. Laura, undergoes a maternal transformation and becomes indulgent and comforting. Postmortem, she reconstructs the relationship lover-muse, based on the reciprocity of affection she confesses, and speaks to the poet about his desire. She discusses the theme of desire insofar as it is connected to poetic production.

In this regard, Gozzano's reworking of this theme is brilliant. There are two texts I wish to consider – *Una risorta* and *Un'altra risorta* – dealing with two women who are loved (or, better yet, could be loved) and return to visit their friend, thus pointing to his death.

Una risorta is a series of quatrains in heptasyllables that closes with an explicit Dantean citation, thus placing it under his aegis: "one who while dreaming / is wishing to dream" (*If.* XXX 137). Here Gozzano's life is incomplete, he has reached the end of passion (a sort of sexual apathy), his dreams have ended and so has his will to write. However, the dead woman continues to dream and above all to desire. The positions of life and death are inverted. Here is how the living poet describes his life:

> È come un sonno blando,
> un ben senza tripudio;
> leggo lavoro studio
> ozio filosofando..
>
> La mia vita è soave
> oggi, senza perché;
> levata s'è da me
> non so qual cosa grave…»

(*my life is like a slumber, and I do not know what heavy thing she has unburdened from herself*).

She intervenes responding:

«Il Desiderio! Amico,
il Desiderio ucciso
vi dà questo sorriso
calmo di saggio antico…

(*you have killed desire and it is this that makes you seem an ancient wise man*)

Ah! Voi beato! Io
Nel mio sogno errabondo
Soffro di tutto il mondo
Vasto che non è mio!

Ancor sogno un'aurora
che gli occhi miei non videro;
desidero, desidero
terribilmente ancora!...»

(*I desire, desire…, I still terribly desire*)

The dead woman desires terribly and dreams: she has delegated the primary psycho-affective functions of life, while he is left with a sort of ataraxy. The ironic antiphrasis of tradition is even more explicit in the following text, where, after having quoted Petrarca, Laura herself is mentioned: "I'm thinking of Petrarca who was joined / on the street by Laura, as I am joined by you." ("Penso al Petrarca che raggiunto fu / per via, da Laura, com'io son da Lei…"). But what a "Laura in the bloom of youth" ("Che Laura in fior di gioventù") he encounters! Gozzano depicts himself rejecting life, in a "voluntary renunciation."

ritrovo i sogni e le mie fedi spente,
solo in disparte l'anima s'oblia…
Vivo in campagna, con una prozia,
la madre inferma ed uno zio demente.
Sono felice.

(*My dreams are by now extinguished; I live in the countryside with my great-aunt, my sick mother and an insane uncle. I am happy*)

The only possible form of "happiness" resides in exile from the world and in forgetting: in other words a non-life. This new Laura, who appears as he strolls down the street in *Un'altra risorta*, certainly displays the opposite characteristics of Petrarca's Laura, who was even more beautiful and "in her freshest and most flowering age" ("nell'età sua più verde e più fiorita") when dead. In Gozzano, the first look immediately reveals her old-age:

"Mi volsi e vidi i suoi capelli: bianchi."

(*I turned and saw her hair: white*)

But like Laura, she becomes maternal ("a good / sister, with a gentle maternal eye"), despite the fact that she is already in her forties. But this is precisely what makes her beautiful, "differently beautiful." In a final expression of vanity, and with some irony, she says:

"Che Laura in fior di gioventù!...
Irriverente!... Pensi invece ai miei
capelli grigi… Non mi tingo più" :

(*What a Laura in the bloom of youth!...
Irreverent! … Think instead of my
grey hairs… I'm not dying them anymore*)

It is a ironic, to be sure, but if one thinks about it, the process of aging is reserved to the living, not the dead. In the *Canzoniere*, Petrarca ages and his hair changes color, and so does the quality of his desire for Laura, who is dead and thus frozen in her youthful beauty for all eternity. In this complete reversal of life and death, where the dead continue to age, live, dream and desire, the only space left to the poetry of the living – to Gozzano's poetry – is that of meta-poetry, irony, the shadows of twilight.

But what is the position of women, if any, along this journey that seems to condemn them at best to a postmortem life without a hairdresser? I would like to conclude with the voice of a female poet, who is still living (thank God!) and still writing, one of the first voices to revive metrical poetry in *forma chiusa* at the beginning of the 1980s. In her volume *Donna di dolori* (Milano, Mondadori 1991), Patrizia Valduga presents a monologue, with rhymed couplets of hendecasyllable, about a woman "dead and buried in a state of decomposition." Here, the implicit dialogue with tradition appears in a dramatic way. It seems a woman who writes poetry in the forms of the "founding fathers" cannot express herself in any other way than by playing the role tradition has constructed for her. The dead woman reflects upon the poets she admires the most (chiefly among them, Dante), by using their very words.

However, she condemns herself to silence for she invokes a new Orpheus to save her ("I die even more, serene night… / is there really no Orpheus for me?"), and she renounces an autonomous voice and poetry.

Tu che vivo ti mescoli a me morta,
resta perché è per te che qui si muore
Se quel che vedi non ti lascia più
È perché vivi in me soltanto tu

(*You who live, you mingle with me as I'm dead, because only you live in me*)

Valduga's *topos* appears to be a dead end. She says it herself – and very well indeed – when speaking of the dream of death, concluding the poem with another Dantean citation ("as if the dream were a real thing"):

come se il sogno fosse cosa vera,
e come se l'aurora fosse sera,
e come se una nera notte. Nera.

There is no alternative if poetry remains attached entirely to the masculine poetic logic, unless something goes awry. But not, as in Carducci, where the loved Melisenda welcomes the last words of her dying poet Jaufrè Rudel, for poetry is a masculine prerogative and will die with the death of the poet. On the contrary, there could be a complete reversal of perspective if the male muse of a poetess were to die. Although this happens in some *canzonieri* written by female poets, this is not desirable. I will close this article, which is nothing more than a brief introduction to a larger project I am working on, with a simple note. A few years ago, a book was published by a good Florentine poet, Rosaria Lo Russo, entitled *Musa a me stessa* – a title that seems very promising, at least in regard to female poetry. But this is another story, in which Dante plays no role, and remains largely, if not entirely, to be written.

Notes

[1] It's possible to find non traditional forms in Montale's *Xenia*.

[2] T. Landolfi, *Breve canzoniere*, Firenze, Vallecchi, 1971, p.42.

[3] "[lui] – […] vedi questo quaderno? [lei] – È il quaderno della tua creazione. – No, il quaderno dei princìpi. – Che vuol dire? – Da quanto tempo stiamo insieme? – Da circa un anno. – Ebbene, da circa un anno questo quaderno non registra che princìpi: capi, minuscoli capi di gallina, senza coda."

[4] In italic in the text: *"Ho deciso di ucciderla: devo ucciderla, non posso farne a meno, non so immaginare nient'altro. Ella risucchia ogni mia forza vitale e m'impedisce di esistere… "*, T. Landolfi, *Breve canzoniere,* cit., p.14.

[5] See in *Breve canzoniere* the extra sonnet, the fifthteenth (Landolfi, *Breve canzoniere,* cit., p.40). It describes a dream provoked by fever, whose content is not revealed, but hinted to as *'inverecondo'*, pertaining love and death.

[6] And here lies the reason for the failure of *Breve canzoniere*: the woman ridicules the behaviour and the verbal solutions adopted by the poet, deeming them 'antique' and out-of-date.

[7] "Ma siete voi - voi pure che non siete / Voi che in un tempo al vero / e al non vero equalmente / rispondete…/…/ Se voi non foste non sarebbe il canto."

[8] "Laser di mie parole - / Così vi incenerisca / Per fuoco, per amore."

[9] "Vivo di voi sognata in sogno morta: / Come colui che fedelmente crede / Nella più falsa fede."

Mary Alexandra Watt (University of Florida)

The Commedia's New Life in Columbus's "Other World":
A Dantean Foundation for the New World Project

By the time Giovanni Domenico Tiepolo painted his 1791 masterpiece *Mondo Novo*, the New World, (Appendix B) it seemed indeed that the entire colonial project had passed Italy by, relegating Italians to the role of watchers, gawking at a representation of the New World while the rest of Europe experienced it first hand. Consigned by the intricate politics of Renaissance Europe to a position of national impotence, Italy lacked the unity found in Spain, France, England and the Low Countries that facilitated expansion into the newly discovered lands on the other side of the Atlantic.

The Tiepolo fresco, therefore, reflects one of the direct consequences of Italy's lack of national cohesion and its occupation by foreign powers as the people of Venice, a city once a giant in commerce and exploration, turn their backs to the actual seas, cover their heads and stare into a contraption common in the 18$^\text{th}$ century, a three dimensional diorama of a world that most Italians could only imagine.

The fresco thus reflects in visual form the duality inherent in the Italian response to the New World project. The actual or what might be termed the literal level of the fresco depicts a people left behind, excluded from the commercial exploitation and colonization of the New World. The hawker's device and its evident popularity illustrate the extent to which Italians, eager to see this New World, had to content themselves with an artist's impression. By not depicting what the hawker's spectacle shows, Tiepolo not only forces the viewer to engage in a mental exercise, but at the same time speaks to the role played by imaginative construction, that is, artistic and literary construction, in the Italian perception of the New World. Like the ideal city of the Renaissance artists, this New World was a construction that took into account the actuality of its existence and then recreated and reinterpreted it, transforming its discovery into an act on the stage of world history, a page in God's book of the world, or in the case of Tiepolo's fresco, an allegorical painting in the gallery of the cosmos. In fine, if Italy could not be there physically, it could nonetheless be there in the imagination. And by imagining it, poetically, artistically, culturally, it sought to shape this new place, this new world in ways that those actually there might not.

If indeed, as Giuseppe Mazzotta has suggested, the most emblematic feature of Renaissance culture is its compulsive *cosmopiesis*, or "worldmaking"[1], never has this been truer than in the case of the Italian literary and cultural response to the Mondo nuovo and to the figure of Christopher Columbus, in particular.[2] In the decades and centuries following his historic journeys, Italian poets and writers almost invariably elevated Columbus from Genoese navigator sailing for Spain to apostolic warrior fighting on the side of Christendom. In such literature, the discovery of the western landmass constitutes a reconquest of Paradise and signals the coming of the apocalypse and the eventual triumph of the church militant.

Though the expediency of such an interpretation in the context of the Counter-Reformation is undeniable, its emergence precedes that crisis and its genesis cannot, therefore, be linked solely thereto. Columbus's letter on his first voyage had barely been translated into Latin[3] and disseminated in Italy when in 1493 Giuliano Dati wrote a poetic version of it in Italian. And while it may be tempting to view the emergence of the Columbus myth merely as a consequence of the *cosmopoietic* urge noted by Mazzotta, a closer look at the figure of Columbus himself, as well as his writings, suggests that the Italian literary and cultural treatment of the New World owes as much to the medieval imagining that facilitated Columbus's journey in the first place as it does to fifteenth and sixteenth century humanism. Indeed, a closer look at both the earliest Columbus poems and Columbus's own writings suggest that the Italian Renaissance interpretation of Columbus relied significantly on the exegetical model presented in Dante's *Divina Commedia* in its understanding and presentation of Columbus as a new Paul and thus heir to an apostolic tradition that transcended nationalism.[4] Accordingly, it can be argued that the interpretation of Columbus that emerges in the sixteenth and seventeenth centuries was greatly facilitated by the existence of the Dantean exegetical model and by the auto-exegetical project undertaken by Columbus himself, both of which allowed Italian writers to perceive Columbus's journeys as a fulfillment of the prophecies promulgated throughout the Middle Ages and by Dante Alighieri in particular. I would argue then that while the burgeoning arts of the Italian Renaissance facilitated the cosmopoietic treatment of Columbus and the New World, it is the recognizable affinities between the figure of Columbus and Dante, together with the link to the medieval apostolic tradition that such affinities forge that made the figure of Columbus so well suited for cultural exploitation.

The most obvious and most crucial of these affinities is found in Columbus's reliance on the Dantean cosmos that permits or even compels Columbus to set forth on his journey and sail beyond the Pillars of Hercules in the first place. Although Columbus puts great store in Franciscan apocalypticism, as well as a great number of medieval prophecies, it is Dante's literary imagining of the *aldila'* that lies at the heart of Christopher Columbus's unique cosmology. And it is Dante's eschatology that urged Columbus to journey towards what he called an "otra mondo," an "other world" (Keller 43) and to perceive his discovery as destiny, preordained and as another page in the medieval book of the world.

We know from Columbus's own writing that his view of world geography came not only from his familiarity with many of the medieval maps and representations of the physical world extant in the fifteenth century but also from his familiarity with the great body of millennial literature circulating during the same period. We have a very good sense of Columbus's inspiration for his theories on what lay beyond the Mediterranean from his astonishing book, the *Libro de las Profecias* which recounts all of the prophesies he believed he was fulfilling in sailing west to reach the East. We know for example, that Columbus was highly attached to the theories of Roger Bacon and Pierre D'Ailly. Both Bacon, in his *Opus Maius* (1268)[5] and D'Ailly in his *Imago Mundi* (1410)[6] endorsed the hypothesis of a vast ocean filled with countless islands and possibly a large undiscovered continent symmetrically equivalent to Europe, Asia and Africa. Columbus, in fact, had his own copy of the *Imago mundi* and had made over 800 notes in it. (Columbus 10)

At the same time, as a sailor, Columbus would have been familiar with the many travelers' tales that circulated in the ports of 15th century Europe. The English and the Scandinavians told tales of having sailed the northern Atlantic, and it is possible though unproven, that he had also heard the Brendan tales. (Flint 91) Columbus was clearly interested in travel literature for he quotes Marco Polo and Mandeville's Travels. (Columbus 23).

The *Libro de las Profecias* makes it clear as well that Columbus put great store in references to unknown lands found in scriptural passages and apocryphal gospels. But Columbus's time in Spain had also made him aware of the widely circulating prophecies of a coming apocalypse. In addition to D'Ailly's *Imago mundi* that intertwined legends of Eden with the eleventh century prophecies of Joachim da Fiore, Columbus was an ardent believer in the prophecies of Peter of Aragon.[7] Peter had prophesied the coming of a Last World Emperor, (West and King 33) that is, a King of Aragon who would conquer all of Spain, attack and capture Moslem lands and enter Jerusalem victorious. In the late fifteenth century the popular John Alamany reprised an earlier prophecy propagated by Ramon Lull in the late 1200's that predicted that a "new David" would rise up against the Moors, evil powerful men and bad clerics. Alamany, like Peter of Aragon also prophesied that this new David would be the Spanish Monarch.

In all likelihood Columbus's familiarity with these prophecies arose out of his close associations with a number of religious orders that also propagated them. Columbus had spent extended periods of time in Franciscan convents and there is some evidence that he was actually a member of the Third Order of St. Francis. Certainly he was in contact with the apocalypticism associated with the Observantine Order that also took its inspiration from the Franciscan Spirituals.[8] Irrespective of how he gained such knowledge, however, there is no doubt, although little is known of Columbus's formal education,[9] that he was aware of these prophesies as he cites them in his own *Libro de las Profecias*. Moreover, Columbus cited a number of them when making his case to Isabella and Ferdinand. (Columbus 29) (It is not insignificant that ultimately it was Columbus's appeal to prophecy and scripture that convinced the Catholic monarchs to endorse his enterprise).

Of all the authors cited by Columbus, however, be they medieval, ancient or scriptural sources, Columbus's own journals point to an even larger reliance on the writings of Dante Alighieri in his interpretation and reconciliation of the various prophetic traditions mentioned above. Although in his numerous marginalia Columbus underlines and annotates the Joachite prophecies, and concludes that the world will come to an end around 1650, his view of the apocalypse owes more to Dante than to Joachite thought. Unlike Joachim, Columbus believed the new heaven and the new earth had already been created and that it was really only a matter of discovering them. Like Dante who saw the other world as physically existent, Columbus saw its discovery as the hallmark of the apocalypse.

Similarly, like Dante, Columbus is no enemy of imperialism,[10] and in this respect his apocalypticism can be said only to have been informed by the Joachite prophecies, not guided by them. Indeed Columbus's view of the end times is significantly in tune with Dante's own vision of a world monarch as espoused in his *Monarchia* and found throughout the political cantos of the *Commedia*.

Perhaps even more striking is Columbus's undeniable reliance on the cosmology posited in the *Divine Comedy*. More than any medieval geographer, Dante seems to have provided the greatest support for both Columbus's perception of the world and his conviction that his journey is pre-ordained. Indeed, Columbus's perception of the earth as pear-shaped is almost identical to that proposed in the *Commedia*. Columbus's earth (Appendix A, figure i), like Dante's earth (Appendix A, figure ii) is pear-shaped rather than perfectly spherical. Columbus's departure from a spherical configuration is created by the existence of a mountainous landmass, located in the western hemisphere antipodal to Jerusalem.

More than this, however, what most suggests a debt to the Dantean cosmology is the fact that Columbus, like Dante locates Earthly Paradise atop this antipodal landmass. Surprisingly few writers have commented on these similarities, but the obvious did not escape Edward Everett Hale who notes:

> Any reader who is interested in this curious speculation of Columbus should refer to the "Divina Comedia" (sic) of Dante, where Dante himself held a somewhat similar view, and describes his entrance into the terrestrial paradise under the guidance of Beatrice. (207)

In both Dante's case and Columbus's this marks a substantial departure from the cartographic conventions of the time. Medieval *mappae mundi* typically placed Asia and the East to the top of the map with Terrestrial Paradise somewhere east of Eden, that is, somewhere above or beyond the unknown world (Columbus 18) and did not posit an antipodal location. In his journals and letters though, Columbus, having reached what he believes to be the antipodes, earnestly contends that what he has "discovered" is Earthly Paradise. And while Columbus relies on the Bible as proof of the physical existence of Earthly Paradise it is the *Commedia* that not only provides Columbus with its physical locator but also the eschatological key to its whereabouts or perhaps more accurately its "whenabouts."

For Columbus, as for Dante, Paradise could be found because it was perceived as a real location, and Columbus, like Dante locates it directly antipodal to Jerusalem atop a mountainous landmass. Eschatologically, however, for Dante and for Columbus, Paradise could not be reached until the end of time; just as heaven and hell were real locations that could not be visited until the end of one's own time except by divine appointment. When Columbus, during his third voyage, reached the mouth of the Orinoco River in South America, he saw its tributaries as consistent with the four rivers that flowed from Eden. Believing he was near the top of the earth where the Garden of Eden would be located, Columbus became acutely conscious of the implications such discovery had in the context of the apocalyptic prophecies. In his letter describing the 1498 journey he announced that the land he has found is the lost Eden. (Cohen 216-224) Columbus's apocalypse then is understood in terms of its etymological root, that is, an unveiling.

Having made the discovery, Columbus then set about recording his cosmology and reconciling the physical in terms of the allegorical implications. He infers from his observations that the earth

> is like a half of a very round pear which had a long stem, as I have said, or like a woman's teat [*una teta de mujer*] on a round ball. (Morison 286)[11]

A few miles inland he expected to arrive at the bulge of this "pear-shaped" earth on top of which was to be a promontory, on top of which he expected was located the legendary site. (Columbus 18) In a 1502 letter to Pope Alexander VI (Rodrigo Borgia), Columbus later wrote,

> I believed and still believe that there in that region is the Terrestrial Paradise. (Columbus 18)

Significantly, however, having located Earthly Paradise Columbus did not go any farther inland. He explains that the reason he has left the mouth of the river, is that he has fear of entering Paradise without a directive from God.

> Not that I believe it is possible to sail to the extreme summit or that it is covered by water, or that it is even possible to go there. For I believe that the Earthly Paradise lies here, which no one can enter except by God's leave. (Cohen 224)

Like Dante's Ulysses[12] Columbus feared the destruction that befalls the navigator who goes beyond what has been providentially destined. Indeed, notwithstanding all of the prophecies on which Columbus relied to predict the discovery of new lands he had found nothing in them that would point to himself as the appointed revelator.

Similarly, while Columbus sees this new world as ripe for conversion, he does not necessarily see himself as God's appointed reformer. There is no doubt that Columbus believed that the people should be converted to Christianity, as he says in the same *diario*, and Fray Bartolomé makes clear that here he has written the admiral's actual words,

> Because I believed they were people who would be better freed [from error] and converted to our Holy Faith by love than by force ... and I believe that they would become Christians very easily for it seemed to me that they had no religion.[13]

There is little in these diaries though that would indicate that Columbus saw it as his charge to effect such conversion. Yet eventually Columbus did come to see himself as so appointed. After the discovery, he says that the idea of crossing this western ocean (West 12) was planted in his head by God much earlier, around the time he was living in Santo Porto[14] with his wife. Columbus also writes that his discovery of the New World was a reward for the Spanish *Reconquista* and would provide the means of financing the eventual recapture of Jerusalem, the next step in the apocalypse. More significantly, Columbus also asserts that he was the appointed agent of this apocalypse.[15] In a letter written in 1500, he explains,

> Of the New Heaven and Earth which our Lord made, as St John writes in the Apocalypse, after He had spoken it by the mouth of Isaiah, He made me

the messenger thereof and showed me where to go. (letter to Torres cited in Keller 51)

Moreover, Columbus begins exploiting the meaning of his own name and adopts the signature "Christo ferens" ("Christ bearer.") How then did Columbus come to this belief that he was in fact divinely appointed agent of the apocalypse? How, precisely, was this poor expatriate sailor able to justify his belief in such a charge?

I would suggest that if it was Dante who provided the road map to Paradise in the first place, then it was equally Dante who provided the paradigm that permitted Columbus to legitimize his voyage and discovery as divinely willed. For it is in the *Commedia* that Columbus would have encountered another soul seemingly unworthy yet nonetheless called to make such a journey, and be permitted as well to see Paradise, notwithstanding his seemingly unworthy estate. Dante's question, "Why me? I am not Aeneas; I am not Paul?"[16] was the same one that Columbus asked and reflected the same self-doubt that had kept him at the mouth of the Orinoco, fearful of sailing inland to penetrate Paradise. At the same time though Columbus would have found numerous affinities in Dante's life and his own that would eventually allow him to adopt the figure of Dante as a paradigm for preordination.

Columbus, like Dante, was a stateless person living in exile. Like Dante, Columbus was "anxiety ridden about his social status." (Cachey 22) But Dante's thinking also aligned with Columbus's. Both men explicitly perceived the world both literally and allegorically. Columbus, for example, states in his *Libro de las Profecias* that he always follows the standard medieval exegetical tool, the *Quadriga* of Thomas Aquinas (Columbus 17) when studying scripture, that is, the fourfold methodology used by Dante and expounded in his famous letter to his Patron Can Grande della Scala. Columbus also notes that in addition to this fourfold methodology, he also employs a system used by Nicolas of Lystra (Columbus 17) (*Glossa ordinaria*) in order to expand his hermeneutics to a two-fold literal meaning, similar to that known to Dante scholars as *figura* and fulfillment. Like Dante, Columbus also harbored a great desire to write a long poem. (Columbus told his confessor, that the genre in which he wished to issue the final product of his handbook was a long apocalyptic poem. (Columbus 35))

Just as for Dante, the Reconquest of Earthly Paradise in the *Commedia* was a staging for reentry into the Holy City, into that Rome where Christ is a Roman,[17] for Columbus, it was a staging point from which Christianity could finally spread and conquer the entire unknown world.

Moreover, Columbus' desire that the people of this new land should be converted recalls the cleansing mission of Paul, and in turn of Dante whose literary journey was aimed at bringing about a New Jerusalem.[18] Through his absorption of the Dantean model, Columbus thus finds himself indeed a Christ bearer, legitimately appointed. But Columbus does not go so far as to pronounce himself as a new Paul. Just as Dante did not explicitly call himself a new Paul, Columbus allows others to infer this through his new signature, his journals, his letters and most notably his *Libro de las Profecias*.

But more importantly, the more Columbus's world began geographically to resemble that suggested by Dante, the more Columbus came to see himself as a divinely appointed agent of the apocalypse, like Dante, deposited at the foot of the mountain atop of which lay Terrestrial Paradise. Like Dante, Columbus began to see himself as being at the center of salvation history.

Similarly, the more that Columbus's exegetical processes came to resemble those used by Dante, the more Columbus came to see himself less and less as an infernal Ulysses, a sailor destined to crash on the shores of Mt. Purgatory and more and more, like Dante, Paul and Aeneas before him, as a legitimately appointed agent of God, permitted by privilege to enter the "other world."

Notwithstanding, however, the seemingly undeniable reliance on Dante in Columbus's writings, nowhere in the extant documents does Columbus acknowledge a debt to Dante. To a Dante scholar this is at first somewhat troubling. It is impossible to imagine that a voracious reader, an Italian reader no less, such as Columbus who has a proven familiarity with Thomas Aquinas, St. Augustine, Joachim of Fiore and a host of other medieval authorities would not have been familiar with Dante. In fact Dante's *Commedia* was well known in the Renaissance, and was fodder for the emerging mass of cartographers of the 15th century who indulged in "mapping mania,' including the mapping of Dante's afterworld. One is, therefore, tempted to go off in search of a lost Columbus letter, to find a document where Columbus explicitly states that he could not possibly have sailed but for the guiding presence of the Florentine poet. However, I would suggest that this lack of citation does not detract from the proposition that Columbus had Dante's world in mind as he set sail. Rather I would posit that it merely indicates that the cosmology of Dante was as much a part of Columbus's consciousness as our modern day perception of universe based on Galileo's heliocentric model. Just as Galileo's universe has now become the prevailing norm and to cite it would be redundant, so too might Columbus have found it unnecessary to cite Dante.

But even if Columbus was not relying consciously on the Dantean model, his discoveries were consistent not only with the prophecies that foretold Christianity's triumphant return to Jerusalem, but they also confirmed the validity of Dante's own prophetic vision, as the poet's allegorical journey had now materialized in the physical or literal world. For Columbus's contemporaries with a professed knowledge of Dante, Columbus's discovery would have confirmed the accuracy of Dante's cosmology and underlined the legitimacy of the poet's prophetic stance. But most importantly it would have legitimized Dante's paradigm as the typological model for this new apostle, Columbus. Columbus thus becomes a "type" of Dante just as Dante was a "type" of Paul and of Aeneas before him.

As a result, the Columbus figure that many of the great minds of the Italian Renaissance and Counter-Reformation inherited was already established as a legitimate heir to an apostolic tradition that starts with Aeneas and continues through Paul.

Moreover, at the time that Columbus made his journeys Galileo's thinking was still more than a hundred years in the future and the hermeneutic approach to the world espoused by Dante and the theologians had not been abandoned. Thus this literalization of the "otra mondo" in no way deprived it of allegorical significance. It is not surprising then that the first chronicles of Columbus's voyages equally embraced the multiple layers of history and remained free to attach allegorical significance to the literal events they reported.

At the same time then that contemporary cartographers confirmed Columbus's New World as the world imagined by Dante, so too did the Italian Renaissance writers confirm Columbus as the inheritor of the Dantean journey, informed in turn by the journeys of St. Paul and before him Virgil. Columbus was thus revealed as another exile, a new Apostle traveling westward on the road to the New Jerusalem.

Accordingly, in the wake of the New World discovery, the Italian literary treatment of the figure of Columbus endorsed the notion of Columbus's discovery as providential and confirmed the Italian and, consequently, the Pan-European impression of Columbus as an inheritor of a long standing tradition of apostolic voyagers eschatalogically linked to the establishment of Rome as the New Jerusalem.

Not surprisingly, Italian Renaissance writers were quick to imagine the Columbus episode as an historical event with ontological significance and significantly, to exploit the Dantean model in interpreting such significance. Torquato Tasso, for example, looks to Dante to confirm Columbus's legitimacy. In Canto 15 of *Gerusalemme Liberata* Tasso not only includes a reference to the eventual discovery of a hidden land by "un uomo de la Liguria"[19] but he also explicitly contrasts Columbus's success in reaching the New World with Ulysses's failure.[20] But it is not the Homer's Ulysses to which Tasso makes reference, rather his paraphrasing of Ulysses's journey and Ulysses's eventual destruction are a clear reiteration of *Inferno* 26. Tasso thus invokes a Dantesque reading in which Columbus, like Dante, was able to complete a journey that the pagan voyager was not. Though not expressly, but still rather obviously, it is clear that Tasso had the *Commedia* in mind when presenting Columbus as the inheritor of the apostolic tradition embodied in Dante's great poem.

Situated thus in the center of universal history, Columbus can not possibly be confined by nationalism and thus he emerges in the Italian literary tradition as more than a sailor on the Spanish payroll, but rather as a harbinger of a greater Empire to come. Tasso's work is, therefore, by no means unique in its use of a Dantesque model in its treatment of the Columbus figure as the sixteenth and seventeenth century saw a genuine flowering of Columbus epics. In most of these works, as Irene Marchegiani Jones points out (410), the authors invariably transform an act of discovery into an act of conquest and the most prevalent features of these stories are the warrior and adventurer elements. These Columbus poems tend to focus on the spiritual imperialism of Roman Catholic thinking, presenting Columbus not only as an apostle, however, but also as a crusader, a warrior of God, claiming the New World not for the Spanish Empire but for Christendom.

Significantly, the Spanish political context is rarely acknowledged except to the extent that Columbus's journey is situated in the context of the Reconquista which in turn is characterized as the Christian defeat of Muslims rather than as a Spanish victory over Granada. The Italians in downplaying Columbus's Spanish connections, disseminated a perception of Columbus as Italian and thus as an heir to the Roman Empire. Columbus thus becomes an epic figure, situated alongside Aeneas in the Roman tradition and Paul in the Christian tradition, as the Italian Columbus epic adopts the same literary laying on of hands epitomized in the *Commedia*.

In particular, Tommaso Stigliani's *Il Mondo Nuovo* is representative of this trend. Stigliani (1573-1651) heartily embraces the Dantesque Columbus, embellishing the story of Columbus's "discovery" with countless details that were not part of the actual voyage but which create paradigmatic affinities between Columbus's journey and that of St. Paul and of Aeneas as absorbed by Dante's own journey in the *Commedia*.

Poetically, Stigliani, like Dante in *Purgatorio I*,[21] invokes the spirit of poetic genius by using the image of the boat.

> Gonfia ancor' hoggi col tuo santo fiato,
> la debil vela del mio basso ingegno. (I:3. 5,6)

The cosmology on which Stigliani relies is also the same on which Columbus relies, and which was propagated by Dante:

> Già navigando col suo stuolo armato
> Nel mare occidental, ch'Africa serra:
> Il buon Colombo dal Rè Hispan mandato
> A ritrovar gli Antipodi sotterra (I:6:1-4)

Just as for Aeneas, and Paul, and even for Dante[22] the road to the New Jerusalem is interrupted by shipwreck, so too for Stigliani's Columbus, is the road to Paradise interrupted by shipwreck.

And just as Aeneas, Paul and Dante[23] receive a divine message urging them on despite the setback, so too is Stigliani's Columbus visited by a messenger of God. While Stigliani's Columbus wanders about in the strange land in which he has been stranded he is visited by an angel who dispels his fears and urges him on, telling him it is God's will that he sail on, discover a new world and convert all of its inhabitants.[24] The shipwreck, the western voyage and the visitation create an unmistakable figural relationship between Aeneas the founder of the pagan Rome, Paul the founder of Christian Rome and Columbus the discoverer of an even greater Christian empire, one that fulfills the Virgilian prophecy of an empire without end in time or space.[25] The Stigliani work thus responds to Columbus's or perhaps more to the protestations of those who would ask "Why Colombus, he is not Aeneas, he is not Paul?" by answering firmly, "Ah but he is .. he is a new Aeneas and a new Paul for a new world!"

Thus Stigliani depicts Columbus as an even newer Aeneas, expanding Roman dominion beyond the known world and an even newer Paul than Dante was, bringing Christianity to an even broader "otra mondo." Thus while Stigliani also absorbs a medieval cartographical convention that attributed spiritual dominion over the unknown world to St. Paul, his epic also continues the literary laying on of hands referred to above that facilitates and legitimizes Italian spiritual imperialism. When Dante is mitered and crowned on the brink of his entry into Terrestrial Paradise in *Purgatorio 27*, he becomes the culmination of the figures of Aeneas and Paul in his fusion of temporal and spiritual authority in one person. Stigliani (and to a certain extent the other authors of Renaissance Columbus epics) builds on the Dantean paradigm and effects in it a further evolution. In proposing Columbus as the natural successor to Aeneas, Paul and Dante, Stigliani thus continues and surpasses the literary projects of Virgil, the author of Acts, and Dante in asserting Roman (i.e. Roman Catholic) dominion over the known world and the newly discovered New World.

But more importantly, in adopting Dante's fusion, Stigliani is able to take Columbus's dual role as Imperial agent and Apostle to the New World and in turn, produce a third persona, the Warrior of God. Paying little heed to the historical record, Stigliani has 5000 soldiers accompany Columbus on his journey! (2:15) This departure from actual events was not lost on some critics who disturbed by such fictionalization. The poet Alessandro Tassoni, for example, in a letter dated sometime between 1625 and 1630 criticized Stigliani's epic for its lack of realism and pointed out that Columbus sailed with a fleet of three ships and considerably fewer than 5000 men. Tassoni's criticism extends, however, beyond the stretching of historical fact to the literary transformation of the figure of Columbus himself. He points out that Columbus was "piuttosto gran prudente che gran guerriero."(280) Tassoni's criticisms though, could not stem the tide of the proliferation of Columbus epics that appropriated and reformed the figure of Columbus, as the Italians continued to propagate the idea of the Genovese sailor as an Italian Holy Warrior fighting on the side of Christendom.

In the Pan-European imaginings of the Italian Renaissance writer, the New World thus became the extension of an Empire that could not be defined by time or space, the fulfillment of prophecies ranging from the Virgilian to the Dantean. But most notably it is Dante's establishment of a literary heredity flowing directly from Aeneas, to Paul to Dante that enabled Renaissance writers to add Columbus to its patrimony. Through the *cosmopoietic* project of the Italian Renaissance the discovery of the New World, Columbus's "otra mondo" became the incarnation of Dante's word, the fulfillment of Dante's *figura* and the promise of paradise his *Commedia* offered. As the terminus of a new pilgrimage to a new Jerusalem, this Earthly paradise was thus poised to become that Rome where Christ was a Roman. Concomitantly, in the literary imagining of the Italian Renaissance, Columbus as Christ bearer and Holy Warrior became the appointed agent of the apocalypse, in his reconquest of Paradise, his conversion of the other, and in his establishment of an Empire that was both temporal and spiritual.

In the New World then, Dante's literary imagining was given new life and in turn, gave new life, producing a New Man who inherits and continues his charge, making the allegorical literal and giving the literal an allegorical meaning that continues to beg interpretation. Given its allegorical nature, this New World, this "otra mondo," or other world, indeed knows no bounds in space or time, though it may, like Tiepolo's diorama, remain accessible only through the arts and the cosmopoietic power of literary imagination.

Notes

[1] As Professor Mazzotta has observed, the Renaissance was obsessed with the creation of new worlds from literary utopias to architectural ideals. While the Renaissance artist used his paints, and the architect his pen, for the writer, his "world is his word or his poetic language." (*xi*)

[2] Pietro Bembo's *Historia Venezia* (1551) discusses Columbus and the impact of the discovery. Torquato Tasso's *Gerusalemme Liberata* (1575) in canto 15 "foretells" the advent of Columbus. Other notable versions of the Columbus or New World epics are Tommaso Stigliani's *Il mondo nuovo* published in twenty cantos in 1617 and in 1628 in 34 cantos, Alessandro Tassoni's *L'Oceano* (1630) and Guidobaldo Benamati's *Delle due trombe i primi fiati cioè tre libri della Vittoria navale e tre libri del Mondo Nuovo* (1622). Irene Marchegiani Jones provides a detailed list of a number of other new world poems that remained unfinished. (410)

[3] Translated into Latin by Leandro Cosco. (Marchegiano Jones 410, f.1)

[4] In his marvelous article, "Columbus and the Invention of America," Theodore Cachey observes that Italy played a central role in the European invention of America but itself remained "on the other side of the threshold of early modernity as defined by the emerging European colonial nation state." (19) Professor Cachey, in exploring the Italian cultural response to the discovery and colonization of the Americas, notes the irony in the fact that while Italy as a nation does not participate in the age of exploration and colonization to any meaningful extent, the entire movement seems to be led by Italians. Cachey considers this irony in the context of the Italian Renaissance noting that while Italy lacked a sense of nationhood, its absence was compensated for by the creation of a farther reaching persona, that is, that of the Italian as a Pan-European, a type of super European, providing leadership in the fine arts, the literary arts and the arts of courtly behavior and political strategy.

[5] Bacon based his findings on the stories of travelers and ancient geographers and insisted that the southern hemisphere was inhabitable.

[6] Cardinal Pierre D'Ailly (1350-1420) was a renowned theologian and chancellor of the University of Paris. His *Imago mundi* suggested the possibility of reaching the Indies by sailing west.

[7] After the death of his wife in 1358 Peter, the son of James II of Aragon, joined the Franciscan order and in 1377 published his *Exposicio' de la Visio' Damunt Vita*.

[8] For a thorough discussion of Columbus's Franciscan connections see Flint, 191-195. See also the entirety of J.L. Phelan, *The Millennial Kingdom of the Franciscans in the New World* and Delno C. West, "Medieval Ideas of Apocalyptic Mission and the Early Franciscans in Mexico."

[9] We do know that it is safe to conclude that he was predominantly self-taught and became a serious student after settling in Lisbon in 1476.

[10] Valerie Flint in referring to the political leanings of Pope Pius II, cites K.M. Setton (215) in remarking that Pius "had been for some years as much an imperialist as Dante, who could preserve his illusions because he had never had to discharge the political responsibilities of high office." Flint adds that the "same words might well characterize the early Columbus." (56 f. 38)

[11] Keller 49, footnote 26, Sale, *Conquest of Paradise*, 176. See also Morison, *Journals*, 286: "But as for this other hemisphere I maintain that it is like a half of a very round pear which had a long stem, as I have said, or like a woman's teat on a round ball."

[12] Dante recounts the story of Ulysses in *Inferno* 26:85-142.

[13] "Por cognosci q era gente q mejor se libraria y conVrteria a nrā Sācta fe con amor q no per fuerça:" (Dunn 64).

[14] Columbus lived in Portugal from 1476-1488. In 1479 he married Felipa Perestrello e Moniz of a well connected but impoverished family of Italian and Portuguese origin.

[15] Columbus frequently insisted that his "enterprise of the Indies" was the fulfillment of prophecy rather than the result of the mere reason and study." Indeed in his first of two books, *Las Privilegias*, he propounds that the Lord chose him as an instrument for the fulfillment of the ancient prophecies. He would be the one to rescue Christianity by before the coming apocalypse which he believed would come around 1650 by spreading Christianity around the world and by providing gold to finance the crusade to reconquer Jerusalem and the Holy Sepulcher. (Columbus 63)

[16] "Ma io perché venirvi? O chi 'l concede? Io non Enea, io non Paulo sono:" Inf. 2:31-2.

[17] "Di quella Roma onde Cristo è romano" *Purg.* 32:102.

[18] For a more detailed examination of Dante's reforming mission, see Diana Glenn, *Dante's Reforming Mission and Women in the Comedy*.

[19] "Un uom de la Liguria avrà ardimento / A l'incognito corso esporsi in prima:" 15:32:1-2; "Tu spiegherai, Colombo, a un novo polo / Lontane sí le fortunate atenne / Ch'a pena seguirà con gli occhi il volo / La fama c'ha mille occhi e mille penne." 15:32:1-3.

[20] "Ma quei segni sprezzò ch'egli prescrisse / Di veder vago e di sapere, Ulisse. / Ei passòle Colonne e per l'aperto / Mare spiegò de' remi il volo audace: / Ma non giovògli esser ne l'onde esperto, / Perché inghiottíllo l'ocëàn vorace; / E giacque co 'l suo corpo ancor coperto / Il suo gran caso, ch' or tra voi si tace. / S'altri vi fu da' venti a forza spinto / O non tornovvi, o vi rimase estinto." 15:25:7 – 26:8.

[21] "Per correr miglior acque alza le vele / omai la navicella del mio ingegno," *Purg.* 1:1-2.

[22] In *Inferno 1* Dante uses language that evokes the image of a shipwreck survivor. "E come quei che non con lena affannata / uscito fuor del pelago a la riva / si volse a l'acqua perigliosa e guata, / cosí l'animo mio, ch'ancor fuggiva, / si volse a retro a rimarar lo passo / che non lasciò già mai persona viva." (*Inf.* 1:22-7)

[23] In *Aeneid* 4:265-76 Juno, through Mercury sends a message to the languishing Aeneas, exhorting him to leave Carthage and go to Rome to fulfill his destiny. In *Acts* 27:22-5, Paul's ship is tossed on stormy seas and eventually the Apostle is stranded on Malta. During the storm, however, an angel appears to him advising him not be afraid, that he will make it Rome.

[24] "L'angelo gli ripose, il Rè celeste / Haver lui solo à tanta impresa eletto / e che che non paventasse à le tempeste, / Ne prezzasse del mar l'irato aspetto. / Seguendo pur per l' umide foreste / La cominciata via con forte petto. / Perche di là da l'Ocean profondo / Troveria fermemente un novo Mondo." *Mondo nuovo* 1:17.

[25] "His ego nec metas rerum nec tempora pono imperium sine fine dedi." *Aen.* 1:275-80.

Figures

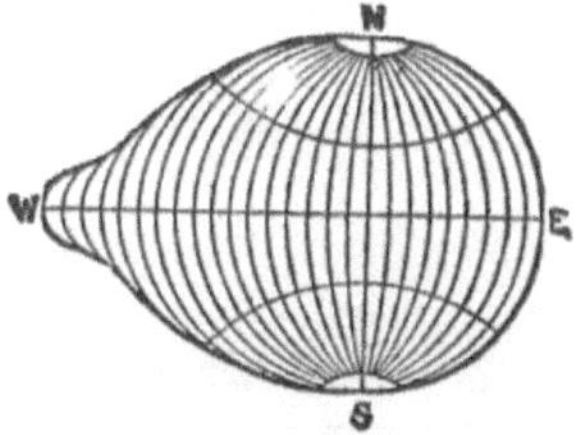

Figure i – The PearShaped Earth of Columbus
(From *Paradise Found*; William Fairfield Warren, 1885. p. 307)

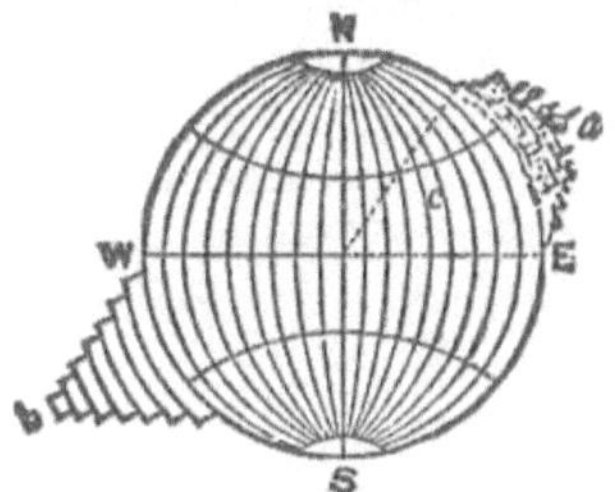

Figure ii – The Earth of Dante (From *Paradise Found*;
William Fairfield Warren, 1885. p. 307)

Images

Tiepolo, Giovanni Domenico, Italian painter, Venetian school (b. 1727, Venezia, d. 1804, Venezia). Mondo Novo (detail) 1791, Detached fresco, Museo del Settecento Veneziano, Ca' Rezzonico, Venice.

Bibliography

Alighieri, Dante. *La Divina Commedia. 3 vols.* Ed. Natalino Sapegno. Florence: La Nuova Italia, 1985.

Cachey, Theodore J. "Italy and the Invention of America" *The New Centennial Review* 2.1 (2002), 17-31.

Cohen, J.M. Ed. Trans. *The Four Voyages of Christopher Columbus: being his own log-book, letters and dispatches with connecting narrative drawn from the Life of the Admiral by his son Hernando Colon and other contemporary historians.* Harmondsworth: Penguin, 1969.

Colon, Cristobal. *Libro de las profecías.* Ed. D. D. Francisco Morales Padron. Madrid: Testimonio, 1984.

Columbus, Christopher. *The Libro de las profecías of Christopher Columbus.* Trans. Delno C. West and August Kling. Gainesville: University of Florida Press, 1991.

Dunn, Oliver and James E. Kelley, Jr. Eds. Trans. *The Diario of Christopher Columbus's First Voyage to America. 1492-1493. Abstracted by Fray Bartolomé de las Casas.* Norman: University of Oklahoma Press, 1989.

Flint, Valerie J. *The Imaginative Landscape of Christopher Columbus.* Princeton: Princeton U.P., 1992.

Glenn, Diana. *Dante's Reforming Mission and Women in the Comedy.* Leicester: Troubadour, 2008.

Hale, Edward Everett. *The Life of Christopher Columbus from his own Letters and Journals and Other Documents of his Time.* Chicago: Howe, 1891.

Havely, Nick. *Dante and the Franciscans. Poverty and the Papacy in the Commedia.* Cambridge: Cambridge U.P. 2004.

Keller, Catherine. "The Breast, the Apocalypse, and the Colonial Journey." *The Year 2000: Essays on the End.* Eds. Charles B. Strozier and Michael Flynn. New York: NYU Press, 1997. 42-58.

Marchegiano Jones, Irene. "Alessandro Tassoni e Guidobaldo Benamati: poeti dell'impresa di Colombo." *Italica,* 69:3 (Fall 1992) 410-420.

Mazzotta, Giuseppe. *Cosmopoiesis. The Renaissance Experiment.* Toronto: University of Toronto Press, 2001.

Morison, Samuel Eliot, Trans. *Journals and Other Documents on the Life and Voyages of Christopher Columbus.* New York: Heritage Press, 1963.

Phelan, J.L. *The Millennial Kingdom of the Franciscans in the New World.* Berkeley: University of California Press, 1970.

Setton, Kenneth Meyer. *The Papacy and the Levant (1204-1571) Vol. 2.* Philadelphia: Diane, 1976.

Stigliani, Tommaso. *Il mondo nvovo Del Caualier frà Tomaso Stigliani. Diuiso in trentaquattro canti. Co gli argomentoi dell'istesso avtore.* 2d ed. Rome: Giacomo Mascardi, 1628.

Sale, Kirkpatrick. The Conquest of Paradise: Christopher Columbus and the Columbian Legacy. New York: Plume / Penguin, 1991.

Tasso, Torquato. *Gerusalemme Liberata, vol III.* Ed. Angelo Solerti, Florence: Barbèra, 1896.

Tassoni, Alessandro. *Le lettere di Alessandro Tassoni. Tratte da autografi e da copie pubblicate per la prima volta nella loro interezza da Giorgio Rossi. Vol. 2.* Bologna: Romagnoli, 1901.

Virgil. *Aeneid.* Ed. Charles E. Bennett. Boston: Allyn & Bacon, 1904.

Warren, William Fairfield. *Paradise Found. The Cradle of the Human Race at the North Pole.* Boston: Houghton Mifflin, 1898.

West, Delno C. "Medieval Ideas of Apocalyptic Mission and the Early Franciscans in Mexico." *The Americas* 45:3 (Jan. 1989) 293-313.

Finito di stampare
nel settembre 2012
da Stampa Editoriale - Manocalzati (AV)

9 781946 328618